Hello again, magicians!

Once more, Jason June welcomes us into his teen magicians' world, and this time the stakes are so high I'm shaking. In this sequel to *The Spells We Cast*'s dazzling story of magic, humor, romance, and friendship filled with Texas-size swagger, Jason June brings his duology to an epic and unforgettable finale.

The book you're about to read is packed with unpredictable twists and so much heart. I hope you too will root for sweet, sensitive Nigel and snarky, sexy Ori as they battle the dreaded Knife and unravel the mysteries of the Guild's origins.

The best stories are the ones that are filled with magic but remind us of our humanity. Jason June is a bright light in this dark world, showing us that the magic we make is within ourselves.

Congratulations on surviving the Culling! Now defeat the Knife!

xoxo
Mel

Melissa de la Cruz

 MELISSA de la CRUZ STUDIO

THE
MAGIC
YOU
MAKE

JASON JUNE

HYPERION
Los Angeles   New York

First Edition, October 2024
1 3 5 7 9 10 8 6 4 2
FAC-004510-24199
Printed in the United States of America

This book is set in Garamond Mt Pro
Designed by Marci Senders

Library of Congress Cataloging-in-Publication Data
Names: Jason June, author. • Jason June. Spells we cast.
Title: The magic you make / Jason June.
Description: First edition. • Los Angeles : Hyperion, 2024. • Audience:
Ages 12–18. • Audience: Grades 7–9. • Summary: "Sunshine/grump soulmates
Nigel and Ori must overcome magical corruption and an evil force inside
Nigel"— Provided by publisher.
Identifiers: LCCN 2023058687 • ISBN 9781368089241 (hardcover) •
ISBN 9781368089982 (ebk)
Subjects: CYAC: Magic—Fiction. • Gay men—Fiction. • Love—Fiction. •
Fantasy. • LCGFT: Fantasy fiction. • Novels.
Classification: LCC PZ7.1.J8754 Mag 2024 • DDC [Fic]—dc23
LC record available at https://lccn.loc.gov/2023058687

Reinforced binding

Visit www.HyperionTeens.com

SUSTAINABLE FORESTRY INITIATIVE
Certified Sourcing
www.forests.org
SFI-01681

Logo Applies to Text Stock Only

To Andie—If there's one person I know whose heart can create magic, it's you.

PROLOGUE
1994

Jameson watches as the last drop of magic is sucked from his best friend, a golden flash that pours out of Reggie's open mouth before blinking once and vanishing. Jameson has always found it hard to believe that magic just disappears once it's taken from magicians who fail the Culling. How could something so pivotal to their identity just . . . stop, die, one second here and the next gone, like the countless magicians murdered by monsters while serving the Guild?

If only that power went somewhere, stored away to prevent the magical saturation the Guild warns would destroy them all. If that were the case, Jameson would go to the ends of the earth to find his friend's power, magical balance be damned. *One* extra magician couldn't tip the scales to destruction, right? Because if anyone deserves to keep their power, it's Reggie Barrett. Reggie believes in the Guild more than anyone, almost more than his own mother, who watches on, red nail polish glistening from the hand hanging limply over her mouth in shock, as her son becomes the only Barrett ever to fail the Culling and be stripped of their powers.

Reginald Sr. has his arms firmly crossed over his chest, pulling the bolo tie around his neck taut and looking anything *but* shocked. He looks disgusted. As soon as that golden power is extinguished, he turns his back on his son, transforms into a falcon, and dives from the fifth floor's marble railing to the entry platform below. A short, piercing scream from his beak triggers a portal, and he's gone without a single backward glance. Not one.

Jameson witnesses it all from over the shoulder of his own father, Anthony Adebisi, and his heart clenches each time his dad pats his back in their embrace. His mom, Carole, can't stop laughing.

"You did it, Jay," she keeps repeating with glee, tiny, excited flames dancing around her fingertips. "You did it! I always knew you would."

"Tell that to my fingers," Anthony says. "Those bones you nearly broke as we were watching in Dispatch would beg to differ."

Carole swats at Jameson's father as he releases his son. "You better stop now before I singe your eyebrows, Tony," she says.

But Jameson only half hears them. Just like he half celebrates finally making it into the Guild, finally killing a Depraved all on his own, saving two lives. The Depraved had been stalking a group of swimmers in Barton Creek when Jameson, inspired by the rushing water, cast a spell and filled the monster's stomach with magic piranha that ate it from the inside out.

For a moment, Jameson is lost in his imagination—real life always inspires his fantasy manuscripts. He'll have to put a scene like that in his next story. Then he remembers: No matter what he writes from now on, the words he stamps from his old-school typewriter to the page will be soaked with sadness. Because he can't imagine a world where his best friend isn't by his side.

"I'll be right back," Jameson says. He tries to catch Reggie's eye, but the failed elf apprentice's gaze is fixed on the cold marble floor as he nods along listlessly while Adela says something to him.

"Reggie . . ." Jameson says, but from there, he doesn't know where to go. Words normally flow so easily for him, but now he's all dried up.

"It's good you're here," Adela says, the quietest Jameson has ever heard her. Normally, Adela Barrett is boisterous, exuberant, her confident laugh echoing through the twenty-five floors of the Guild. Now, Jameson has to lean forward to hear her.

Adela motions toward Jameson, her down-turned eyes trying to capture her son's. "See, Reggie? This might change your plans from here on out, but it doesn't have to change everything. You still have a friend. Life isn't over."

Reggie finally speaks up. "Ma, just—" But he stops, shrugging. Instead, he reaches forward and grabs Jameson's hand. Reggie doesn't get caught up in that macho crap that so many boys back home seem to. He is open, honest, vulnerable, even with another guy, not worrying if someone calls him a sissy, a pansy, gay. He just calls it being a friend, and that is the only label that matters.

"Let's get out of here, huh?" Reggie whips around, suddenly all business. Jameson feels a weight lift from his chest to see his friend show that typical Barrett energy, but something holds him back from following. It's not hard to figure out what: Once they walk out of the Guild together, Reggie will never be back.

But Jameson doesn't have long to sulk. Because his best friend is flinging them both over the banister.

They've *always* left the Guild with a running jump over

balconies, casting spells to stop their fall long before hitting the ground. Jameson would use a sensible levitation spell, while Reggie would stick his fingers in his lips and summon a golden falcon—an homage to his two families: the Barretts' way with animals and his dad's favorite form to shift to.

"REGGIE!" Adela shrieks, and Jameson sees the moment Reggie remembers he doesn't have magic to break his fall. But at least he has Jameson.

Jameson's dark hands glow gold with magic as he calmly thinks, *Float*.

Does he imagine a spark of longing in his friend's eyes as their fall slows to a pace that barely rustles Reggie's hair or Jameson's neon-blue windbreaker? When their shoes finally touch the entry platform, Reggie's sullen again, motioning toward Jameson's glowing fingers. "Guess you'll have to call the portal."

Jameson nods. "Guess so." He traces a golden door in the air, filling it with the intention to leave. But the fae spells the Guild put in place for members to come and go as they please require sound to trigger the portal. Jameson can't think of a single stupid rhyme. The only thing that registers is how the next time he sees these gold-streaked walls, he will be alone.

He opens his mouth and all that comes out is a strangled sob. But somehow it's enough to activate the portal, a slight purple tinge coating his golden doorway.

"This is it," Reggie says, looking around one last time, his eyes raking over every floor. Then, without another word, Reggie steps through the door, pulling Jameson behind him. Jameson barely feels the healing, refreshing power of portal travel—it will take more than a simple spell for them to get over this.

But when they step into Zilker Park, with the lights of downtown Austin reflecting in Lady Bird Lake, Jameson realizes all is not lost. This has always been their favorite place in the whole world, magical and human alike, and it still is.

"It's *not* it. You know that, right?" Jameson says. He motions toward the park. "This still exists." He punches his friend in the shoulder. "*We* still exist. I know our plans are going to look different, but the Guild is one far-off dimension. We have the whole rest of the world to see each other in. Things don't have to change."

Reggie finally lets go of Jameson's hand. "But it changes everything, Jay." Nobody but his parents and Reggie call him that, nobody but the people closest to him. "You know that."

Jameson shakes his head. "It just changes where we hang out. Not whether you're my best friend. I'm still coming here with you." He nods across the lake, toward the bustling town. "I'm still going to those bars with you when we turn twenty-one. Hell, I still plan on being your roommate, telling you when you're making an ass of yourself in front of girls. Are you changing all those plans on me, too?"

"Wait a minute, you're all of a sudden into bars now?" Reggie's smile only half reaches his lips. "That's not the Jay I know."

Sure, Jameson would rather stay at home and read a good book, but if he can't fight monsters with Reggie anymore, he'll do whatever he can so their friendship together doesn't end.

"Okay, maybe I'll stay home and some of your *ranch dudes* can go to the bar. But you know what I mean."

"That's what I thought." Reggie doesn't sound convinced. But Jameson's on a roll, his heart picking up the pace. Normally, he's the quiet one, but he needs Reggie to know that their futures aren't over. That they can make something good of this moment.

"I'm going to devote every last day to figuring out some way you can be in the Guild," Jameson says. "Maybe you can't have your magic anymore, but it's not right for you to be cast out like that.

Everyone knows you're one of the best in our year. *Everyone.* A single mistake doesn't make you a bad magician."

"Stop calling me that," Reggie barks. "I'm not a magician anymore, Jameson."

"But don't you get it?" Jameson squeezes his friend's shoulder, more certain of this than anything he's ever said in his entire life. "You *are* a magician. All of them are, every last person who's had their magic taken from them. You were born a magician, and you'll always be one, whether or not you can use your powers. I swear it, Reggie, I'm not letting this go on anymore. You'll be back in the Guild again. Everyone who's been cast out will. *I swear it.*"

"How?" Reggie asks.

Jameson opens his mouth to speak, but no words are there. No plan. "I'll come up with something, Reggie. I may not have all the answers now, but I will. We'll still have our whole lives together."

Reggie sighs, his shoulders slumped deeper than Jameson would like. "I wish I could feel as sure as you, Jay." He stares at his fingers, the ones that used to light up just as gold as Jameson's but are now only dull and pale. Jameson hates thinking that about his best friend, but it's true. Reggie's hands will never again look the way they did when they were casting spells together.

Jameson scoops Reggie into a hug, swinging an arm over Reggie's shoulders and pulling him into his chest. "We may not know all the answers, but there's one thing we do know for certain."

Reggie just barely glances up, the moon reflecting in his sad, hazel eyes. "Hmm?"

"I'd do anything for you."

Reggie meets his friend's gaze then, his small smile just a tad bigger than before.

"Me too, Jay. Me too."

CHAPTER
ONE

"People don't know what the hell they're talking about when they make sayings. *Like finding a needle in a haystack?*" Ori scoffs. "Please. Finding a needle in a haystack would be so much easier than this. They should say, *Like finding a freaking tree in the middle of the Appalachians.* They all look alike!"

Of course Ori would find something to complain about. It hasn't even been twenty-four hours since we escaped being killed by one of the worst Depraved the world's ever seen, and in all that time we've avoided being tracked down by a group of power-hungry magicians who most likely want us dead. Not to mention I even magicked a roll of double-ply toilet paper so we could at least *wipe* during our night spent in the woods. These are reasons to *celebrate*, but Ori's got to Ori and snark about something.

"If three eighteen-year-olds could just spell our way to the entrance, you bet your ass the entirety of the Guild could figure it out, too," Bex says. "Besides, the fact that there's thousands of trees here means there's almost no people—so almost no demons or Depraved. The last thing we need is the Guild seeing us in Dispatch because they were alerted by some demon's presence."

In a silver flash, Bex uses her goblin powers to transform into a unicorn. Her black hide glistens and her silver horn flashes in the light splintering through the treetops. "Gimme a minute. I know we're close." She takes in a huge breath, sniffing. She gives me a weird look before glancing away, and I fight the urge to smell my pits. It's not like I've had the chance to shower, and fighting an army of monsters then trekking through the woods for hours on end tends to work up a sweat. I can't smell great.

"We don't have time for you to play horsey!" Ori stamps, and with an aching heart I'm reminded of Frosty plunking their hooves in indignation. I miss them, I miss the ranch, miss simpler days when I was practicing spells with Meema instead of reliving her blank stare just after she was murdered. Instead of running from the Guild, a fugitive even after defeating the Knife.

A sharp pang hits me in the chest, and I swear the claw in my pocket throbs. Maybe *defeat* the Knife isn't exactly what we did, thanks to Ori bringing me back to life after I sacrificed myself to kill the monster. He created an effigy of me with his sprite power by fusing the claw tied to my bloodline with a piece of the heartstone that once kept the Knife alive. A weird feeling in my gut makes me think *I'm* now tied to the monster, so that's great.

"I'm not *playing horsey!*" Bex huffs. "Little known fact to those ignorant to shape-shifting"—she gives Ori a very pointed glare—"unicorns can smell magic. *You* can see magic's different colors, but unicorns smell the unique scent of each person's power. So this *horsey* can lead us directly to the portal, if you give me a second to catch the scent. Or would you prefer to go it alone?"

Ori opens his mouth to no doubt come back with some serious snark, but I don't need Bex to gore him through with her horn right now, even though Ori probably deserves it.

"We couldn't do this without you, Bex," I say, stepping between them. "So, uh . . . sniff away."

"Thank you!" Bex turns her big unicorn ass toward us, flicking Ori with her tail as she takes in a few more breaths, whinnying when she's caught something. "Found it!"

In another silver flash she transforms into a squirrel and scampers up the trunk of the nearest birch tree.

Ori's narrowed eyes follow her. "If I catch you taking another nut break, so help me!" he hollers. "I'll curse you so that tail never goes away. Don't think I won't do it."

"Hey," I say, wiping a bead of sweat from my forehead with the sleeve of my flannel. It is *hot* in these mountains, just days away from July. "Come here."

I pull him toward me, and he presses his lips to mine. His breathing slows, I feel his shoulders drop, and he places his thin fingers on my chest. When we finally pull apart, Ori looks deep into my eyes and whispers, "You're starting to smell."

I knew it.

Ori plucks at his own shirt, sparkling clean despite his near-fatal stab wound yesterday. "I cleaned *this* so you wouldn't pass out on me," Ori says, all smirks, per usual. "The least you could do is return the favor."

He's right. As soon as the adrenaline from the battle wore off, it hit me that Ori's outfit was literally covered in his own blood—all thanks to Laurel, a magician hellbent on being the best in her generation, who decided that sabotage by way of claw-stabbing was the right move. When I broke out in a cold sweat just looking at the shirt, Ori caught on and cleaned up immediately. Even still, I push him back, maybe a little harder than just playfully. "Excuse me. I'm sorry not all of us have the ability to never break a sweat."

"I was born this way. But there's a spell for that, you know?"

Yes, of course there is, but growing up on a farm in the middle of Texas you learn that some things can't stand up to the very real power of humidity. Keeping the spell intact so that it never affected me would require all my strength, but with the charge Ori's kiss just gave me, it can't hurt to craft one magic hankie to humor my boyfriend.

If that's what we're calling each other. I mean, it's only been five days since we ran into each other for the first time in thirteen years. But those were a really intense five days.

I take a breath, centering myself in that way my elf ancestors discovered all those years ago, and pull my golden magic into my fingers. I trace the outline of a small square, filling it with cooling intention, and the hankie blinks into existence. As I wipe it against my forehead the sweat evaporates, the cool sensation after a welcome relief.

"Everything's going to be fine," I say. "We're going to find the Resistance. Bex at least knows it's a maple tree that holds the portal. "

Ori doesn't look convinced. "In a forest full of millions of maple trees! And don't even get me started on Bex."

On cue, Bex rockets down a tree trunk so quickly it's like she fell. She lands on her little paws and transforms back to herself: light brown skin, dark shoulder-length hair, rocking a Joan Jett shirt and studded black jeans from her dad's clothing line.

"Okay, so the thing is, all these other squirrels have marked this territory since the last time I was here—"

"Meaning they *peed* on everything," Ori interjects.

"And one in particular has really asserted dominance."

"So *that one* peed all over everything," Ori says. "Remind me not to touch anything."

"Well, now that we know Ori understands squirrel biology." Bex catches my eye before rolling hers. "The good news is I keep getting faint whiffs of magic, so I know we're close to the portal. We're lucky this particular entrance hasn't changed location recently, or else we'd *really* be lost. The first time I was here? Took me eight days to find it. My entire spring break gone, just like that. You're lucky it's only been a day." Bex's eyes go wide and her nostrils flare. "Wait." She flashes into a unicorn again—her majestic head bobbing as she sniffs repeatedly—then back. "We're practically on top of it."

Bex jogs a few yards, jumps over a small stream, then slaps her hand on the trunk of a tree. "I found it."

"Thank god," Ori and I say together, and when he looks my way, I grin.

"I don't know how much more of your bellyaching I could take," I say.

"Oh Jesus, *bellyaching?* Sometimes you're so Southern it's embarrassing." Ori turns his back and walks a few steps before glancing over his shoulder. "Come on, cowboy."

I can't stop the thrill that cascades from my heart to my toes when he calls me that.

I'm so glad he brought me back to life.

A flare of gut-wrenching guilt follows. There were dozens, maybe hundreds, of other magicians who weren't so lucky. Taken out by the Horde—the Knife's Depraved minions—after Ori's and my magic went haywire and revived them. Because our connection—which is supposed to be founded on love but has caused so much pain and heartache—got out of control.

How can I live with myself knowing I did that? *We* did that?

And if we hadn't, Meema would still be alive.

Ori has stopped just before the stream. "You coming?"

He seems so unbothered by it all. Carefree, almost. A sudden burst of anger pushes my guilt aside. It's so strong I almost see red.

How can he act like the world isn't crumbling without Meema in it? His mom made it out alive, so everything's all hunky-dory?

I shake my head to clear the thoughts grating against my skull. I know they aren't fair. What happened to Meema wasn't because of him.

At least not fully.

"Coming." I hustle to his side. "Sorry."

"Hey." Ori reaches out and grabs my hand, and any anger I had left evaporates with the sparks between us. "Let's do this."

Together, we walk to the maple, nothing about its bark indicating it's any different from the rest of the trees in the Great Smoky Mountains.

Bex leans against it coolly and looks at Ori when she says, "Told you I'd find it."

"This tree is the portal?" I ask.

Bex nods.

"And we've got to activate it like the usual ones?"

"You bet," Bex says.

I turn to Ori. "You know what this means."

Ori crosses his arms. "Seriously?"

I try, but I can't hide how much I love what's about to happen. I'm sure Meema would describe my expression as a shit-eating grin.

Oof. Just like that, my smile falters. I can't believe she's gone, that I can't turn to her for advice or reassurance. What would she think of me now? We did kill the Knife—or thwarted its plans, for now—but I'm not sure anyone could say we were victorious. Not after learning that the Culling is entirely unnecessary, that a small faction of the

Guild's founders created the lie that others had to lose their power so they could hoard magic for personal gain, draining magicians they deem unworthy just to keep themselves on top.

I want to say that, in my heart of hearts, I know Meema wouldn't have willingly gone along with letting the Culling continue when it's not needed. But . . . I can't. She was always about getting to the top. Sure, I never actively saw her try to bring anyone down in order for her to succeed, but my entire childhood was structured around her lessons, lessons she designed to show Barretts were some of the most powerful magicians out there. What would it say about me if I was raised by a woman who could watch her own son get his power taken from him for no good reason? I've got to get to the bottom of how the Guild became the corrupt organization it is today, and whether or not Meema was in on it. The first step to that is finding out what the Resistance knows.

Ori gently places his long, thin fingers on my shoulder. "Where'd you go?"

I shake my head. "Nowhere. Just wondering what song you're going to choose, Swiftie."

Ori pulls back with a scowl while Bex laughs. "Yeah, we're ready for our concert," she says.

"You people are the worst," Ori grunts, but he knows we've got a job to do. He doesn't even pause to search for words, lyrics waiting on the tip of his tongue.

"It's us, hi, you're the portal we need.
We three, inside, everybody agr—"
Grrrrrrrrrr.

The hairs on my arms stand on end.

Ori didn't get stuck on the word.

Something's growling.

Ori catches my eye, his fingers lighting up with pink sprite magic.

Bex sighs. "I guess no one said this would be easy, huh?"

The three of us turn together to face the monster behind us.

Correction: monsters.

We're staring into the frenzied yellow glares of a pack of wolf demons.

CHAPTER
TWO

Hooooooooow, ow, ow, ow!

The demons' muscular bodies are twice as big as normal wolves'. They're covered in matted gray-green fur; their rotted fangs drip with saliva. And immediately after their synchronized demonic barking, silence descends. I hear nothing: not a bird chirping in the trees, not wind ruffling the leaves, not a squirrel in the distance as he pees.

My hands blaze gold and my right arm flies out so I can lock my fingers with Ori's. On contact, our magics swirl together, creating that abalone color of us, supercharged by our feelings for each other.

I let out a short, sharp whistle that I can't hear, and thankfully my magic lasso instantly appears coiled around my arm. It's really true, what Meema said all along: The more you practice magic, the easier it becomes. Gone are the days when I had to pull and stretch my magic to become a rope, then roll it elbow to thumbs and tie the end into a knot myself. My familiarity with the spell makes it easy to visualize, and the charge from this soulmate connection fills me with conviction and love. Emotion really can strengthen your power. And having a soulmate doesn't hurt.

These demons don't stand a chance.

Everyone moves at once. Bex morphs into a tiny sparrow, zipping through the air like a missile, piercing in one eye and out the other of the nearest wolf demon as it leaps toward Ori, ready to sink its teeth into him.

"Oh shit," I breathe, even though my words don't register. "That was badass."

The monster's corpse collides with Ori, hundreds of pounds of demonic bulk pinning him to the dirt as they crash to the forest floor.

I loop my lasso over the thing's head, nudging Ori with my boot. And just like that, my whole body lights up with our magic. My muscles bulge with it, and in one fluid movement I whip the beast up and over my shoulder, slamming it onto the ground behind me. Dirt and moss and fallen branches fly everywhere with the force of it.

A second later, I'm flipped onto my back. Massive paws push me into the ground, jaws snap barely an inch from my face. I pour all my strength into keeping this wolf from literally biting my head off—but it's draining quickly. Thick strands of drool soak into my flannel, and my skin goes numb everywhere the saliva touches. If I'm not fast, I won't be able to feel my arms to cast magic or my legs to run. As in, I'll become a real nice meal for this critter in no time.

Ori digs around in his bag of tricks and pulls out a Bluey plushie. Its little legs go from blue to pink as Ori creates an effigy of it and twists its front arm. The wolf demon's right paw, pressed into my chest, snaps to the side. As the demon's weight droops, I use its imbalance to push it off me, scrambling to my feet.

The injured wolf tries to come at me anyway, but with a silver shift, Bex becomes an elephant and wraps her trunk around the monster to lob it into the trees. But her victory is short-lived when the remaining wolves all pounce onto her thick gray hide, sinking their long fangs into her skin. The ground vibrates as she pounds her massive legs in an attempt to shake them off.

Ori nudges my shoulder. It's time to combine our spellwork, to use our connection to end our enemies once and for all. He starts slapping the toy's limbs to its side repeatedly.

"Huh?" I have no idea where he's going with this.

Ori rolls his eyes. Then he snaps his own hand to his side and stands ramrod straight.

Oooooooh. He wants me to glue the demons' limbs to their hides. We tried the same thing during our second Culling task—but of course it went haywire, nearly taking out Pallavit in the process. We're better now, more in sync. We destroyed the freaking Horde, for crying out loud.

But you also woke it up.

Meema's face flashes through my mind again, and I slap a hand to the side of my head. Now is not the time to get wrapped up in guilt, or else Bex and Ori might get added to the list of casualties.

With Ori's effigy aglow, I let my magic pool into my fingers, thinking all the sticky thoughts I can muster. *Elmer's glue, the aftermath of barbecue sauce coating your fingers, toddlers in general.* Power oozes off my fingers, thick and syrupy, and I glue the effigy's legs to its body. With three ground-shaking thuds, the demons fall off Bex's back, jaws snapping as they roll helplessly in the dirt. It looks like they're still howling their silencing curse, but with my fingers coated in sticky magic, I can fix that. I smear my power over the doll's lips, and the demons' jaws slam shut. Sound steadily returns to my ears.

Bex shifts back, her chest heaving, but she's smiling. "Damn, we make a good team."

I jut my thumb in Ori's direction. "But this one makes a terrible mime." I mimic how ridiculous he looked sticking his arm to his side and standing up straight.

"I got the message across, didn't I," Ori says, unbothered.

"I'm just saying." I pull him in for a one-armed hug and kiss the top of his head. The numbness in my chest from the wolf drool vanishes. "Don't quit your day job."

A rustle out of the corner of my eye, just behind Bex, grabs my attention.

"Bex! Watch—"

"OUT!"

It's a scream, but it's musical.

It's also a spell. A fae spell. The wolf demon that was prowling closer to Bex flashes purple and slams backward into a tree, falling to the ground unconscious.

Then from behind that tree steps an uncomfortably familiar magician.

Jaleesa.

The Guild's found us.

I fling my lasso at Jaleesa, and Ori tosses Bluey and blinks his hand into his bag to grab a new doll, while Bex shifts into her own version of a supersized wolf—just as ferocious, but without the rotting fur or dripping fangs. Jaleesa doesn't move as my rope finds its mark and I tighten it around her middle. But why would she? It's really her voice we should worry about.

"God, cowboy, not everything can be fixed with a rope," Ori says, wiping a pink thumb over the doll's mouth to seal Jaleesa's shut.

I shrug. "Once a ranch hand, always a ranch hand."

A silver flash and Bex is human again, walking right up to Jaleesa. "Guys. Something's different about her." She takes her in from head to toe. "I don't think she's trying to mess with us."

"Oh please," Ori snaps. "I'm not falling for that. She and her girlfriend tried to kill me. Almost did!"

It's true. The last time we saw Jaleesa, Laurel had just stabbed Ori with the claw my great-times-a-ton-grandpa created to defeat the Knife. Ori's teeth were splattered with blood, the claw protruding from his chest, and in my heart I knew that if I didn't act, I'd lose the one person I felt connected to with my whole body and soul.

But then, Jaleesa *did* step in. She prevented her psychotic nymph girlfriend from finishing the job and teleported the two of them out of there in time for me to heal Ori.

"I think you're right," I say to Bex. "We can at least hear what she has to say."

Ori scoffs. "What is it with you and your obsession to let everyone *in*? Hasn't the last week taught you the only safe thing is to keep people *out*?"

I close the distance between us and pull him into me with my hand not holding the lasso. "You let me in and look what happened."

"We unleashed the Horde," he says in a quiet growl.

"But we also defeated the Knife."

Ori can't meet my eyes. "Maybe," he mutters under his breath, with a pointed glance at my pocket where the claw throbs, keeping me alive. Potentially keeping the Knife alive, too.

"Look," Bex says. "I say we let her talk. And if she tries any fae magic, I just slap one of these over her mouth." Her arm flashes into a slimy tentacle. "All in favor?"

Bex looks at me with hope. She's always been the one to prefer building bonds over brute force. Ori, on the other hand, shoots me a look and loudly says, "No. Nay. Whatever."

I can't bear to see Ori's look of betrayal, so I take in Bex's beaming smile while I eke out, "I'm in."

I feel a fresh stab in my back, right behind my heart—our connection letting me feel Ori's hurt. Even still, he gives in with a sigh. "Fine." He swipes his spell from the doll effigy, and Jaleesa's mouth unseals.

"Jesus, I thought you were going to take all day. I'm just trying to tell you to run away."

Ori rolls his eyes. "One more rhyme and I'm sealing your mouth shut again."

"The Guild knows you're here."

I snap my fingers and my lasso disappears. "What do you mean?"

Jaleesa rubs feeling back into her arms. "Alister is gathering his allies. He wants to come in strong, completely overwhelm you. He's not going to let you get away this time. They inducted us overnight and assigned us duties. You're lucky I was given Dispatch watch and was the first to see you. I was able to slip away to warn you."

Of course Alister wouldn't rest until we were caught. The power-hungry nymph and biggest gasbag of the Guild knows all about the Culling being fake, having told me as much when he thought I would die. I know in my bones he won't stop hunting us until we're gone for good, his secret going to my grave.

"Why would you help us?" Ori asks. "Why not just let us get caught?"

Jaleesa locks eyes with me. "Because you said Laurel and I have it. What you two have." She motions between Ori and me. "And if you get caught, we have no hope of figuring out how to harness it."

Ori blows a huge raspberry. "Dream on!" he says. "We're not helping you become as powerful as we are."

"Maybe it's not about that," Bex says. "Maybe it's about leaning in to love." She looks at me. "This is what I've been saying all along."

Jaleesa looks over her shoulder, anxious. "They're going to be here any second."

"Then we'd better go," Ori barks.

Jaleesa nods. She doesn't try to stop us. "Just think about what I said. I mean it that I never wanted you dead."

"Jaleesa," Ori warns. "What did I say?"

He turns his back on her and stomps over to the tree that's supposedly the portal to the Resistance. "We're going to have to change portal locations now that she's seen it," Ori says.

"Yeah," Bex says, joining him. "We are."

Ori clears his throat and sings.

"It's us, hi, you're the portal we need.

We three, inside, everybody agrees.

Don't look too closely at our past or what we did to get here.

It must be exhausting always rooting for the antihero."

Well, if *that's* not a depressing reminder of everything we royally fucked up, I don't know what is. But he's not wrong. When we mess with the Guild, people die.

The maple tree glows purple, fae magic activated by Ori's sad song. Or his triumphant one. I guess it all depends on the choices we make from here on out. Can we fix this? We can't bring anyone back. Not the ones who died trying to clean up our mess.

I take a step toward the portal, and the claw shifts in my pocket. The claw that Ori used to make an effigy of me, fusing it with the Knife's heartstone to get the blood pumping again in my chest, to get me to take a breath after who knows how long. It seems unfair that I got to come back and nobody else ever will.

Bex walks through the portal, and Ori beckons. "Let's go, cowboy." He steps through and is gone in an instant.

But before I can follow, Jaleesa grabs my fingers. On instinct, my skin glows with magic, ready to protect myself, but the desperate look in Jaleesa's eyes stops me. "Take this," she says, shoving something into my hand.

I open my fingers to see a tiny purple bell sitting in my palm. "What is it?"

"It's a fae spell. Ring it and we'll be able to talk, no matter where you are. You need allies inside the Guild, Nigel. Trust me."

Trust. People have been saying that my whole life, like it's so easy. Trust that the magicians who came before you have it all figured out. Trust that the Guild's methods are time-tested and necessary. And look where that's gotten me. Look where that's gotten those dead magicians—all needlessly killed because we were forced to participate in a Culling that was a hoax in the first place.

"The Culling isn't necessary, you know," I say, quick and sharp. "It's all a lie." I don't know why I say it. Maybe it's about taking a shot at real trust, not built on deceit. Maybe I just want her to feel a fraction of what I do.

Jaleesa looks like she's been slapped. "What? But what about—"

"There's no such thing as magical imbalance. The whole thing is a power grab orchestrated by your girlfriend's dad and his ancestors before him."

"Just Alister? Are there others?"

I shrug, and that's when I really feel the weight of going up against the Guild. I don't know how many people are involved. Who was behind thousands of magicians having their powers stripped away for no good reason? One, two, the whole group? *Meema?* I can hardly stomach the thought.

But one thing sure feels certain: "Laurel must know," I say.

"She couldn't," Jaleesa breathes. "She would never go along with that."

"Is that so?"

Jaleesa doesn't move. She knows it's a possibility, just as much as I do.

Movement catches our attention. One of the remaining two

wolf demons has freed its front two legs from the curse Ori and I cast. *How are they doing that?* We were able to thwart Horde soldiers and the Depraved just yesterday. We freaking awakened the Horde just before that! How is this pack of wolves resisting our power?

The demon hobbles toward us, and Jaleesa launches into song.

"Monsters crawling,
it's time to go back.
Not sticking around
to become demon snacks."

She pops away just before the demon can bite her. I take advantage of its bewildered pause to leap through the portal, out of the woods, and into the Resistance.

CHAPTER
THREE

THERE'S SOMETHING COMFORTING ABOUT FLYING THROUGH THE whirl of purple magic into wherever the Resistance headquarters is. Feeling magic performing exactly how it's supposed to, the fae power seeking out any nicks or bruises to heal.

But the moment of peace is over practically as soon as it began. You'd expect the Resistance to be headquartered somewhere grand, someplace that rivals the gold-streaked marble halls of the Guild. But I've landed in the foyer of a house. The paneled portion of the wainscoted walls is teal, the length above it covered in misty-blue wallpaper with interlocking branches perched on by finches and small, intricately drawn flowers dotted here and there. Stairs directly in front of me climb to a second floor ringed by a worn, deep-brown railing, closed doors along the walls marking unknown rooms. A hall next to the staircase leads to an open door, beyond which I can see a farmhouse sink. On either side of me are antique sliding doors, the same teal as the wall panel, topped with stained glass and half pushed into pockets. Beyond the doors on the left is a dining room with a long table set for twelve. The wood floors creak as I take a step to look through the open doors on the right into an old-timey drawing room. A framed needlepoint of the Guild symbol hangs on the wall with cursive words underneath that say: *The Culling is a lie.—Book 2005-3.*

Ori's in this room, standing next to Bex, who hovers near her dads sitting on a couch. Ori catches my eye with his trademark smirk. I know he's ready to take on the Guild as soon as possible, to start making a plan right this second. But a very welcome voice rings out first.

"You made it," Jameson says.

He looks nothing like he did when we last saw him: on the brink of death, blood pouring from a gash in his shoulder. His dark skin isn't clammy, his eyes aren't unfocused.

I'm unprepared for the huge wave of relief that washes over me. There's one person, at least, we can subtract from the death count.

"You're alive," I say, and surprising even myself, I practically run to Jameson so I can hug him, hard. He's taller than me, and my head fits into his shoulder. By the way he warmly embraces me back, I think I might finally know what it feels like to be hugged by a fatherly figure, for the first time in my life. Not something I'd ever learn from my own dad, but here we are. Tears spring to my eyes, and I jolt back before I completely break down.

"You've had to deal with so much." Bex's dad, Yamato, rises from the overstuffed couch, Kenneth following just after. "More than any other apprentices."

"What?" Bex quips. "You're saying not every apprentice has the honor of being hunted down by magicians who want to take their magic, or better yet, just kill them entirely?"

"Enough of that," Kenneth says, shooting her a serious look. "Nobody's joking about my daughter getting murdered."

Bex shrugs. "*I'm* the one they want dead!"

"Hey now," Yamato says. "Don't sass your father." The rings on his fingers clink together when he beckons her to him. "But come here. Nobody's laying a finger on you as long as I'm around."

Bex steps close to her dad, who wraps her up in a hug. Kenneth folds himself over them. You don't have to ask to know these three people mean more to one another than anything else in the world, and I know Bex makes every decision with her family in mind. She's worked hard to hone her magical talent so she can change the world for the better. Her dads are gay, Kenneth is trans, and they're a Japanese American family. Some folks in the human world want to belittle them for being all three. Add in the pressures of the Guild that pit magicians against one another, and Bex has had way too much to try and take on.

I wonder what they talked about, in that time between when Bex quit the Culling and when she helped us defeat the Knife on Mount Rainier. I can't picture a family coming together after such a dramatic event, seemingly even closer than before. The one family member who ever boosted me up is dead, and I could never imagine Dad hugging me like this. Like he wants me. Like he loves me.

Which means it's just me now.

Ori sidles up and laces his fingers with mine. "You're not alone," he whispers. I meet his eyes, my mouth open in bewilderment. I'm still getting used to having a *soulmate*. At least, that's what Jameson called Ori and me, what Kenneth and Yamato are, too. It's a heck of a word for people who've known each other for less than a week, but I know the devastation I felt when I almost lost him was real. The comfort I feel when he whispers those words to me now is real, too.

I can feel his annoyance that I humored Jaleesa like ants crawling over my skin, but I also feel a tenderness in my heart that tells me he wants to be there for me no matter what. I want so badly to lean in to this connection, to see what else we can do with the spells we cast. But we need guidance. We can't kill again. Even if the blood isn't technically on our hands, it was our magic that set this fatal ball rolling when we released the Horde.

Jameson looks at our clasped hands and smiles. "It's good to see you both here." He meets my gaze. "I was afraid we were going to lose you. The use of the claw. When your grandfather used it all those years ago, it resulted in his death. Yet you stand here now, without even a scratch."

"About the claw. Ori—"

He clenches my hand. Hard enough that it actually makes me yelp like a coyote zapped by one of Meema's spells protecting the chicken coop.

Ori shakes his head the tiniest bit before saying, "Sorry. Still jumpy. You know. From saving the world."

Yamato laughs, the studs in his ears catching the light as his shoulders shake. "I guess it would have that effect, wouldn't it?"

But Jameson's like a dog with a bone. "You were saying, Nigel? About the claw and Ori?"

My eyes dart to Ori's for just the briefest moment. He clearly doesn't want me to share the whole story, but I don't know why. I'll wait until I can ask him about it later. For now, I say, "Ori. H-he saved me. Somehow . . ." I scramble for an explanation. Jesus, why am I such a terrible liar? "Um, it's got to be the soulmate connection." My eyes drop to the floor. "Could be worth looking into."

"Indeed," Jameson says. His gaze lingers on me, not suspicious or wary but just taking me in, and that almost makes it worse. I can't tell what he's thinking, but the claw sits heavy in my pocket.

Ori is quick to change the subject, looking around at the old drawing room. "So this is the Resistance, huh? The group working to bring down the nation's leading organization of corrupt magicians, holed up in what's essentially a British grandmother's house? Bold choice."

Yamato crosses his arms. "That's what I said." I snort. It's not hard to imagine that punk fashion designer Yamato wasn't pleased with the aesthetic.

"But *where* are we?" I ask.

"Inside a transitory locale spell," Jameson says, like it's the most obvious thing in the world. "More commonly known as a heart home."

"Um, sounds sweet, but I need a little more than that," I say. While Meema had me studying magic ever since my powers manifested, our focus was mostly on what was in the physical world.

"It's a spell that creates a sort of in-between space, similar to the one used to create the Guild," Jameson explains. "We're in a location that is both somewhere and nowhere. You wouldn't find it on a map or be able to give directions to this specific location. But it's created by what is inside my heart. My ideal home."

"Your ideal home smells like mothballs," Ori says.

Yamato laughs and Kenneth nudges his husband with a hip. "I like it. The Guild is all cold, imposing. This says warmth. All are welcome."

Bex kisses her dad on the cheek. "Agreed. But we really need to work on the *all* part. There's . . ." She counts heads. "Six of us here, and what? A couple dozen other members? A measly group of rogue magicians aren't going to be able to bring down the entire Guild. We need numbers."

"*A couple dozen others?* That's, like, thirty people against an army of thousands." Ori looks like he was just told he'd have to wrangle a rampaging bull with licorice rope. "We're screwed."

"Wait," I say. "You said when we left Mount Rainier there was someone important we had to meet. Someone who could explain everything. Who's that?"

Bex motions to her dads with an expression that clearly says *Uh, duh.* "They're right here."

"Oh."

"What?" Bex says with a grin. "You didn't think it was going to be some huge reveal centered around you, right? Why can't my dads and I be the big heroes?"

"Well, I'm . . ." I'm completely stumped, that's what I am. "I guess I . . ."

"Don't worry," Bex says. "I know your instinct is to be all cowboy, guns blazing, thinking it's up to you to save the world. But just remember, it's going to take all of us to do that."

I nod. "Right." Heat rises in my cheeks.

"So where is this *all of us* if we're the only ones here?" Ori asks.

"In other heart homes," Jameson says. "We choose to scatter ourselves, so if one of our locations is ever discovered, the rest can carry on. The Resistance can still thrive."

"Are you going to tell us who they are, or . . ." Ori lets the question linger.

"Keeping their identities a secret protects them *and* you," Jameson clarifies. "Should any of us be caught by the Guild."

"We're all spelled so we can't rat anybody out," Yamato says. "We can show you other members, but their names are sealed by magic."

Kenneth nods. "Can't be too careful."

"And you're trying to stop the Culling, right?" I ask. "That seems to be the most immediate way to change the Guild. Imagine how many more demons and Depraved could be stopped if we let *every* magician keep their power. How could the Culling have gone on for so long when it was never necessary to begin with?"

The room goes completely silent. Ori looks expectantly to the adults while Bex smiles pleasantly, but Kenneth, Yamato, and Jameson look like they've just been hit over the heads with a muck rake.

"The Culling isn't necessary?" Yamato asks.

Kenneth turns to his husband. "This could change everything."

"What evidence do you have to support this?" Jameson asks. "With magical balance on the line, ending the Culling without being absolutely sure could doom us all."

"Are you kidding me? It's literally written on your wall." I turn to Bex. "And you said—"

"I know, I know." Bex nods. "This happens every time. I know the Culling's not necessary, and I've told these guys . . ." She looks up to the ceiling as she counts under her breath. "At least thirty-eight times."

"You've never told us this before," Yamato snaps. "I'd remember something this huge, Bex, come on."

"I know you think that, Dad; you say those exact words every time. It was annoying at first, but now it's kind of funny." She gestures to the needlepoint behind them, and all three senior magicians turn to look. "Why do you think we have reminders like that all over the house? Go grab *Book 2005-3* for all the details."

Ori sighs. "This is just typical. The first actual lead we have to make change is that the Culling is pointless, and the Resistance *literally* can't remember it?"

"Wait . . ." Kenneth turns his wide-eyed bewilderment to Ori. "The Culling isn't needed?"

Bex motions to her dad. "See what I mean? It's like this every time. I think the most I've ever seen it sink in is five minutes. We keep reminders in every room in each Resistance heart home, but it inevitably leaves the squishy folds of their brains."

"How do *you* know all this?" I ask. "Why does it stick for you but not for them?"

"I have a theory, but we'll get to that." Bex leaves the drawing room to enter the adjoining library. Teal shelves line all available wall space, stacked with books. Over a faded blue Persian rug perch two plush, light blue, overstuffed couches, one with a cross-stitched pillow with *The Culling is a lie.—Book 2005-3* on it. I can easily picture best-selling novelist Jameson reading in here with a smile on his face, but right now he just looks perplexed.

Bex goes directly to a shelf in the corner and picks out a book that's indistinguishable from the rest: black bindings with gold accents. "It's all in here," she says, the numbers *2005-3* becoming clear as she gets closer. "Jameson spelled the history into this record." She turns to the elf magician. "A fail-safe, so you'd know it wasn't made up."

"I wouldn't put anything in these books that wasn't thoroughly researched and confirmed," Jameson says softly. "So that must mean the Culling is really all a hoax."

Bex nods, holding up the book. "Every last detail is in these pages. The Resistance first learned about the Culling nearly two decades ago. Imagine all the magicians that would exist if we could stop it!" She talks faster as she gets more amped up. "With higher numbers we'd be so much more successful against the Depraved. Generations from now there could even be enough magicians that we'd be safe to share the existence of magic—one of the founding goals of the Resistance—and then humans could learn ways to stop making Depraved in the first place. It would be beautiful!" Her face falls suddenly. "What a cruel irony that the magicians who could actually end the Culling can't remember, right? We're the first three Resistance members to retain this knowledge in almost eighteen years."

"Whoa, slow down," Ori says. "Nobody said anything about becoming Resistance members. We're not just jumping into something without knowing all the facts. Besides Bex, if no members could remember the truth, who even told you about the Culling to begin with?"

Bex chews her bottom lip before turning to me. "Your mom. Well, she didn't tell me exactly, but she was the one who first got the truth to the Resistance, where it was written down. It's all in this book."

A flare of anger gallops through my chest, making my breath short. The woman who abandoned me the night of my birth discovered the truth about the Culling? Am I supposed to be *thankful* she somehow discovered the Guild's secret?

"Horse shit," I say, throwing my hands up. "What a freaking fantasy cliché! My mom *left me*. You're telling me someone that heartless discovered the Guild's corruption? Next you'll tell me she's the one who'll stop it. Where is she, anyway? She *still* can't face me."

Jameson clears his throat. "She's gone," he says. "Missing. For over seventeen years now. That much I know."

"But she was able to remember all this about the Culling, and I am, too, and now you guys," Bex says. "It must be that someone's casting a spell over official Guild members, making them forget whenever they learn the truth. I mean, it makes sense, right? Why else could we remember, and Nigel's mom, but none of the magicians inducted into the Guild?"

So many thoughts stampede through my mind. It's too much. Too unbelievable. "This can't be right," I say. "It can't be that we finally know this terrible secret about the Guild, and we still can't do a thing about it."

Not even an hour ago I thought we were going to change everything. I even told Jaleesa, hoping to gain an ally on the inside.

Jaleesa!

I tap my hand over the fae bell in my pocket, nestled next to the claw. I contemplate pulling it out right then and there, but something tells me I should keep this a secret. Yet another artifact for me to keep to myself, I guess.

"I need a minute."

Ori reaches for my fingers. "Sure, we can go somewhere. Just decompress."

"Alone."

The hurt that flashes through our connection does nothing to make me catch myself. I can't have him hovering over me, too, telling me I'm wrong for contacting Jaleesa again.

"We have a room for you," Jameson says, pointing upstairs.

I jump up the steps before he even finishes his sentence. I have no idea where I'm going, but I'm anxious to get some space.

I fling the first door open at the top of the landing. The room is simple: same old floorboards, same wainscoted walls, this time with a bed and a solitary window letting in sunlight even though there's no sun outside in this in-between realm. The bed is unmade, and a record player sits on a chair in the corner, various vinyls scattered around it. A dresser is on the far-left wall, one of the drawers open with a T-shirt hanging out of it. Bex's room.

I open the next door to a room that's clearly occupied by two people. Kenneth and Yamato. The next is impeccably neat, with a typewriter on a desk under the window. Jameson.

When I slam his door shut, I hear him call from below. "Take the staircase on the other side of the landing." I look across the balcony and sure enough, a skinny staircase leads to the floor above. "There's a room in the attic we've been saving for you."

Locked away for everyone's protection. As you should be.

I trudge up the stairs, my boots landing heavily on each step. When I fling the creaky attic door open, I'm surprised by how welcoming it is. The exposed wood is immaculately clean. A large bed with a brass frame sits on top of a woven rug, end tables on either side holding glass lamps.

I don't deserve this.

Why should you live somewhere clean and safe when you're the reason so many people aren't alive at all?

Visions of Meema swirl through my head: riding triumphantly on her golden bull, blowing cursed kisses that disintegrated the Depraved, throwing her head back and laughing with glee every time I master a new spell.

Then she was killed in the middle of the most gruesome magical battle of this century. Betrayed by Alister while trying to save my life by sacrificing her own. I begged her not to—and it was my distraction that allowed Alister to murder her.

"I'm so sorry, Meema." Now that I'm alone, my tears flow freely, the dam unleashed. "I'm so sorry."

I fall onto the mattress, realizing how sore every part of my body is the second I'm off my feet. This shouldn't be the case. Ori's touch heals my wounds, and mine his, but maybe this soreness isn't physical. Maybe every atom of my body is racked by grief.

Meema didn't deserve this. Even if she did know about the Culling. I can't believe I'm even considering it, but as one of the most powerful members of the Guild, there's a chance she knew. What does that say about me if she did? Am I destined to make other magicians suffer so that I can be the strongest of my generation?

Is that why I woke the Horde?

"GOD DAMMIT!" A flare of power bursts from my fist, crashing through the lone attic window.

Guilt squeezes my chest. I'm given a warm place to stay and the first thing I do is damage it. Meema would be so disappointed in me. I'm disappointed in myself for even doubting her intentions.

She was the greatest magician in my family. She was the greatest magician in the Guild. She was the greatest woman I knew.

And she's dead because of me.

Ringing Jaleesa's fae bell will have to wait. At least for a couple more minutes.

Because this sadness won't let me do anything else but cry.

CHAPTER
FOUR

THE GUILD IS IN AN UPROAR. BURSTS OF EVERY COLOR OF MAGIC reflect off the white walls as all members—or their phantom doubles—swirl through the gold-streaked tower, headed for one floor: Dispatch. Everyone wants to be the magician to spot Nigel or Ori again. Jaleesa sighs. Magicians are just so *dramatic*. And confusing.

But right now, she's grateful for the chaos. It's exactly the distraction she needs to get her girlfriend alone, to ask Laurel if she's keeping the biggest, most consequential secret of their magical lives from her. Jaleesa reaches into her pocket to pull out a tiny acorn with a drop of Laurel's magic inside, allowing her to find Laurel at all times. The nymph always said she had nothing to hide from her girlfriend. Apparently, that isn't true.

> *"Girlfriend to question.*
> *Unsure of her morals.*
> *Show me the place*
> *Where I can find Laurel."*

Jaleesa cringes. Ori was freaking right. Fae rhyming can seem so juvenile, but it really did make controlling her power easier, voicing her intention like that. Even still, she's quickly getting sick of sounding like a terribly written children's book. She makes a mental note to conquer casting spells with just a sound ASAP.

The acorn in her hand glows purple, and a vision swims before her eyes: Laurel swinging gently in a vine-woven hammock in the nymph wing of the Guild. A deep scowl etches Laurel's forehead, matching the one Jaleesa knows is marring hers.

She marches to the nymph archway, her heart picking up the pace with every footstep. How could Laurel keep this from her? But maybe she's getting ahead of herself. It could very well be that Laurel doesn't know. Maybe Alister hasn't told her yet.

Neither the gently babbling brook leading into the pond on the first floor nor the breeze blowing through the trees sprouting from the nymph dorm's walls calm her. The only thing she connects with are the flames that glow from the mouth of a cave leading to the basement, where fire nymphs play with embers.

Jaleesa is *pissed*.

The acorn tugs her hand upward, but Jaleesa doesn't need it to find Laurel; they've cozied up together in that exact hammock so many times. With a quick song she's levitating up, up, up until she pushes through the boughs of a weeping willow to find her girlfriend waiting in silence.

"I was wondering when you'd show up," Laurel says, her curt tone stoking the fire of Jaleesa's anger. "You weren't helping *them* again, were you?"

"Of course not! You heard me yourself." The lie jumps quickly to Jaleesa's tongue. She knows that, like so many others, Laurel watched her confront Bex and the boys from Dispatch. But Jaleesa had spelled her own voice so that all onlookers would hear were overly dramatic statements like "What have you done?" or "You have to stop!" Everything the rogue trio said back would have sounded like a soap opera: "We'll never work together!" and "I'll never trust you!"

"I didn't help them, Laurel, now *or* yesterday," Jaleesa continues. "All I did was stop you from becoming someone you're not. You're not a murderer."

"It's not murder, Jaleesa!" Laurel spits her name out, then catches herself. "It *wouldn't* have been. It would have been self-defense. Of the Guild! Of us! I can't believe you don't see that!"

Jaleesa takes a fortifying breath. "What *I* can't believe is that you never told me about—" She stops mid-sentence, her conviction deflating like a leaky balloon. "Y-you never told me . . ."

What was it that she wanted to say? There was something Laurel was keeping from her, or might be keeping from her—she was sure of it. Something Nigel had said, but what?

"I tell you *everything*, Jaleesa!" Laurel's voice is fever-pitched, verging on panic. She's never spoken to Jaleesa like this before. It only adds to the fae's disorientation. What is going on? Why did she come here?

"I just— I have to go."

Jaleesa leaves as quickly as she came, shaking with nerves as she flies to the entry hall. She practically sprints to the platform and triggers a portal to take her home, and only when her feet hit the rooftop of her family's SoHo townhouse does she catch her breath. Nothing makes her feel at ease like the noise of New York City—nothing except being in Laurel's arms. Well, *before* everything that's happened this past week. Now the city seems a surer bet: Cars honking; delivery drivers yelling; tourists laughing, pointing, getting in the way on the sidewalk—Jaleesa loves the symphony it all creates.

It's hot and muggy the last week of June, but Jaleesa doesn't care.

She takes a deep breath under the beating sun and soaks up all the sounds, letting them wash away the echoes of Laurel's angry, panicked voice. The even more disturbing feeling that her brain is letting her down, that she's forgetting something massive, slowly starts to subside.

That is, until a sweet tinkling melody joins the sounds of the city. Her fae bell. *Nigel!* Nigel is the one who told her the secret, the one Laurel may have been—is?—keeping from her. What it is, she still can't remember, but at least she knows she didn't make it up.

Jaleesa hums a matching tune to the bell and her voice travels to Nigel's ear, wherever he is, and vice versa.

"Nigel," she says. "I didn't expect you to ring so soon. But I'm glad you did. I—"

"Can you remember what I told you about the Culling?" His voice is rushed and a bit hoarse, his words coming out thicker. Almost like he's been crying.

"The Culling?" She racks her brain—but she knows exactly what every magician knows, nothing more. Something tickles the back of her mind, like it might come to her, but it never does. After a too-long silence, Jaleesa says, "No. Nothing."

"Well, hell," Nigel mutters. "Then it's true."

"*What's* true?"

"The Culling isn't necessary. I've told you once before. Somehow, someone has made it so you can't remember."

Jaleesa sucks in a breath.

"But that's illegal. No Guild members can cast spells against another, except in self-defense."

"Exactly," Nigel says. "And it's not just you. Any Guild member who's told the Culling is unnecessary forgets. Well, except for those who are keeping this fucked-up truth hidden."

Jaleesa sways on her feet. "Who would do this? Why?"

"Alister's in on it, I know that for sure. But we're wasting time. You're going to forget everything I've told you, and soon."

Jaleesa's stomach turns. She has no control. Someone can just pluck her memories from her brain whenever they see fit.

"I need you to remember this," Nigel continues. "Look for evidence that someone is casting spells against the majority of Guild members. That's all I need you to remember. Start with Alister. I know this is confusing, but we'll figure this out. And if—" He stops himself suddenly. "Never mind."

"What is it?"

"It's just—if you *do* find something—I need . . . I need to know if Meema knew anything about it. If you find anything that links Meema up with Laurel's dad, any indication she was in on this spell, too, I need you to tell me."

"Oh god, my mom," Jaleesa blurts. "Does she know about the Culling?"

Jaleesa's head swims with the thought. Her mom appreciates magic more than anybody, believing magic is a gift that should be allowed to flourish. It's why Jaleesa couldn't let Laurel kill the boys. If she's learned anything from her mom, it's that.

"I don't know. But tell me you'll at least remember this part. Promise me you'll look for evidence of someone spelling Guild members. Got it?"

"Yes."

Jaleesa can almost feel his sigh of relief through the connection.

"That's all for now," Nigel says. "Don't worry about the specifics of the Culling."

Jaleesa's brow furrows in confusion. "What specifics?"

She feels like she should know, but she can't quite pin it down.

"Nothing." Nigel huffs. "Do you remember what I need you to do?"

"Look for evidence of a spell cast against the Guild."

"Good," Nigel says. "That's exactly it. Reach out to me when you find something."

"Yeah. Will do."

Their connection cuts off instantly. This time, the city sounds rushing back in do nothing to calm her swirling thoughts. *A spell against the entire Guild?* Who could do that? *Why* would they do that?

Jaleesa dashes to the rooftop door and races down the stairs in search of her mother. Like most other Guild members, Pallavit Devi's phantom presence is in the Guild, hovering around Dispatch, but her physical body will be at home, recuperating from the battle on Mount Rainier. And when Pallavit needs to recuperate, she always sings.

Sure enough, her mother's operatic scales echo up from the first floor. When Jaleesa's boots hit the hardwood of the living room, her mother's singing stops immediately.

"Beta!" Pallavit trills. "The triumphant hero, returned!"

Heat rushes to Jaleesa's cheeks. "I don't know about triumphant."

Pallavit waves her off. "Bullshit. Who else rushed in to apprehend the Guild's greatest enemies while the rest of us were taking naps? *Resting.*" She blows a raspberry. "We're ridiculous."

The Guild's greatest enemies. There goes ever telling Pallavit about being in contact with Nigel, if that's how she sees him. Jaleesa's never kept secrets from her mother, but that's just one more line to add to the list of things she didn't see coming this past week.

"I just wish . . ." How to bring this up? "I wish there was a Guild-wide spell we could cast to *forget* all this," Jaleesa says. "The Culling being such a disaster, I mean."

"We wouldn't do that even if we could. Learning from the toughest parts of our life is what makes us stronger."

Jaleesa relaxes at that *if*. So at least memory wiping is off the table.

Pallavit opens her arms and beckons her daughter close. "I know this was a traumatic week. But Guild life isn't always like this. Will you find yourself in life-threatening situations? Always. But that's why we train hard to give you the skills needed to defeat your enemies. That's why you were accepted into the organization to begin with." Pallavit holds her daughter at arm's length to look her in the eyes. "Because you proved you are strong enough for this life. We won't be fighting monstrous hordes every week. I promise."

Jaleesa lets out a sad laugh. "Right." Now that she has this moment, just the two of them, she may as well ask the other question that's been bothering her since her mission with the boys. "Do you know anything about a love magic?"

To Pallavit's credit, she doesn't look at her daughter like she's stupid. She pulls her bottom lip between her teeth while she mulls it over. "You mean like a love spell? Or a love potion?"

Jaleesa shakes her head. "More like a person's magic made more powerful by love."

Pallavit's face softens. "Oh, sweetheart. I've been meaning to talk to you about that. I think it's time for you to consider spending less time with Laurel."

Jaleesa lurches back like she's been hit. "Excuse me?"

"Please don't mistake my meaning," Pallavit says, genuine concern tinging her words. "I'm fully supportive of you, no matter who you love. You know I don't agree with Alister's views. I threatened to cast so many curses on him if he ever said a single word to you. But I do worry you're putting too much into a relationship right now. Develop your own skills, in magical *and* human society, before you decide who to invest in. You need time to understand what it is you need in a partner; Laurel may not be that. I mean, look at your dad and me. We didn't start dating until I was thirty-two. You've got plenty of time."

Jaleesa's throat clogs with unexpected emotion. She had never really considered a future without Laurel, at least not until yesterday. Hearing her mom suggest Laurel might not be the best girlfriend for her—so casually, like suggesting she put on a different jacket—is a level of disinterest Jaleesa wasn't prepared for.

"Right. Thanks, Mom." Jaleesa turns on her heel, wishing there was someone she could turn to. Her mom doesn't get it—not yet, anyway—and her girlfriend is quickly becoming someone she doesn't recognize.

Maybe if Jaleesa can find out the truth about what's going on— whatever spell Nigel wants her to investigate—it will offer some clues about how to help Laurel become the girl she once knew. Or maybe Nigel and Ori can help them reignite their connection, so she won't feel quite so alone.

But in the meantime, she'll have to do this shit herself.

CHAPTER
FIVE

JAMESON'S FEET CRUNCH AGAINST THE GRAVEL DRIVEWAY WINDING up to the Barrett home. Bex's boots bite into the rock, too, as she materializes beside him. The elf is so anxious it makes him want to crawl out of his skin. Not because he thinks they'll be caught; he volunteered to take over watch of the property for the Guild under the guise that he'd keep a lookout should Nigel return. It was the perfect cover to be able to talk to his old friend without arousing suspicion.

What's set Jameson's nerves on edge is uncertainty. Uncertainty that's all thanks to the note in his hand: *Tell Reggie about Adela. Restore his memories. He can help you reveal the truth about the Culling.*

He can read the words clearly in the moonlight, but would be able to recite them even if he couldn't see. The first two sentences are easy enough to understand, and he remembers writing them just minutes ago, before he left his heart home. But the last?

"We're going to have to go over this again, aren't we?" Bex asks.

"Go over what, exactly?"

Bex sighs. "The Culling's unnecessary. Power-hungry magicians have been using it to limit the number of magicians so they can hoard power for themselves." She hefts one of Jameson's books, which she had held against her side. "You wrote it all down in here, in case you think I'm lying."

Jameson knows Bex is trustworthy. He knows he wrote this note. But how is it that Reggie can help? His former best friend hasn't been the same since they took his memories away. None of them could have anticipated the monster Reggie would become after. But maybe it's not too late. Maybe he can bring back the man he knew eighteen years ago.

"Come on," Bex says, moving toward the front door. "Let's get this show on the road."

She's already knocking on the front door when Jameson catches up to her. "Bex, we need to tread lightly. Reggie isn't the friendliest of men."

"We're going to have to talk to him, one way or another." Bex knocks again and calls, "Mr. Barrett? Mr. Barrett, are you in there?"

She pounds on the door, with no answer.

"He may be somewhere else on the property," Jameson says. *Or perhaps passed out drunk*, he thinks, but loyalty prevents him from saying it. Besides, he had a part to play in Reggie turning out the way he did.

Bex wraps her fingers around the doorknob and turns. "It's unlocked," she says, but the smile falls from her face when she swings the door open and is met with the telltale sound of a shotgun being cocked. Their hands fly into the air as they stare down the barrel, then up to the unshaven, rage-filled face of Reginald Barrett Jr.

"Hiya, Reg," Jameson says.

"What're you doing here?" Reggie growls, the gun not wavering an inch.

"Um." Bex swallows. "This feels a little too *on the nose* for Texas. Mind showing us some of that Southern hospitality everyone goes on about?" Her fingers twitch ever so slightly, motioning for him to put the gun down.

"Don't move a muscle!" he says. "Not one, ya hear me? I know how you magicians are, and I'm not afraid to blast trespassers on the spot."

"Noted," Jameson says. "Reggie, I promise we come in peace. I have news you need to know."

"It's about Ma, isn't it?" he growls. "I can feel it. The spells she cast ain't working anymore." He glares at Bex. "You shouldn't even have been able to open that door." He locks eyes with Jameson and states the facts: "She's dead."

"Yes, Reggie," Jameson whispers.

His oldest friend stands stock-still, the gun pointed at Bex's chest, and everyone holds their breath. Then, finally, Reggie's rushes out in a deep shudder and the gun swings down to his side before he drops it to the floor. Bex and Jameson exhale together, and the elf steps forward to comfort his former friend.

"She's gone," Reggie says, stunned. "She's gone."

Jameson nods. "She is."

"I'm an orphan." Reggie glances to the portrait above the mantel of the legendary magical cowgirl and her son. It was taken two years after he failed the Culling, but the bright smiles on both of their faces show their new normal was still full of love. Adela never moved it, even after everything went to shit.

After Jameson *helped* everything go to shit. It's his biggest regret.

Jameson puts a hand on Reggie's shoulder. "But you're not alone."

The energy goes taut. "Yeah, right." Reggie shrugs him off, backing up a few steps. "You haven't set foot on this property in almost twenty years. And you have the balls to tell me I'm not alone? Where were you this whole time, Jay? Huh? Far as I can tell, I've been nothing *but* alone. My own mother abandoned me to spend every waking second with her grandson, making sure she wouldn't have yet another failure on her hands." His face reddens the longer he talks. "This changes nothing. I've been alone my whole life."

"Nobody forced you to become the man you've been, Reggie," Jameson says, his heart picking up pace in a way it hasn't in decades. He doesn't get anxious, he doesn't get angry, he's always measured, even. Mystery is what has kept him safe among magicians and monsters. But being face-to-face with his friend is forcing free feelings he's locked away. And what is a friend if not a person who tells their loved ones the truth, even if they don't want to hear it?

"Fuck you," Reggie snarls.

"I think you just proved his point," Bex says.

Reggie wheels on her. "What are you doing here, anyway? I don't even know you, and you barge in here like you own the place. *I* own the place now, and I want you out." To Jameson, he adds, "Both of you. I've made it this long on my own. I don't need anyone else."

"And what about your son?" Jameson asks.

"What about him?" Reggie spits.

"He lost arguably the only adult who ever loved him. You're going to abandon him now? Make him as much of an orphan as you are?"

Reggie huffs. "Wonder Boy doesn't need me."

"He didn't make it into the Guild," Jameson says flatly—and, bastard that he is, Reggie actually has the gall to smile.

"Like father, like son. Not so wonderful after all, is he?"

"Jesus, you really *are* as awful as Nigel made you out to be," Bex says. "For your information, he's on the run, because he's *so* strong the Guild feels threatened by him. He killed the Knife when even your own however-many-greats grandpa couldn't all those years ago. Suck on that, you asshole."

Reggie laughs. "We got a live one here, don't we?" He saunters into the massive great room, heading toward the kitchen and grabbing a beer from the fridge. With a *crack*, the can is open. He takes a few swigs before wiping his mouth with his forearm. "Naw, sounds like Nigel doesn't need his old man. Not if he's taking down those monsters. Why would he want another one 'round him?" Then his eyes pop wide, taking in the home around them. "What? Does he want the place? Let me guess, he thinks it's his *birthright* because his dear old dad is such a piss-poor human. Typical magician superiority complex. Well, he can have it. I'll pack my shit and leave."

Jameson's chest swells with pity as he watches his friend go down a rabbit hole of hate. He misses the man he formerly knew. But hopefully there's a way to bring him back.

"It seems we have more in common than you think, Reggie," Jameson says. "We both have things we don't remember."

Reggie cocks a wary eyebrow. "What're you talking about?"

"That's why I'm here. To tell you everything that has transpired since your son was born. Because while there does not as yet appear to be a way to cure my memory lapses, I have the key to fix yours."

Jameson pulls a golden key from around his neck, a small spell he's worn tucked beneath his shirt since Nigel's birth. He takes a step forward. "If you let me use this, that is. When everything is clear again, Bex has a bit more history you need to learn, written inside that book she holds. I think you'll find the truth elucidating. There's still time to fix some of the wrongs of the past. Together."

"Please," Bex adds. "If only because you'll be one of the few people who actually remembers what I have to tell you. I'm starting to feel like a broken record."

Reggie smashes his can against the kitchen counter, beer foam flying. "I fucking knew it. *I knew it.* Goddamn magicians, always up to tricks." He eyes Jameson suspiciously. "You honestly think I'm going to let you cast against me after all these years? I don't trust you. You're one of them now." He points to the golden key. "I'm not letting you anywhere near me with that."

A bead of fire swirls around Jameson's heart. Reggie always was stubborn. He never could be told what to do, not even when they were kids.

A memory pops into Jameson's mind, a welcome turn of events after starting to feel like his own brain can't be trusted. "You remember what I told you?" Jameson asks. "After our Culling, by the lake?"

Jameson knows in time he'll have to confess that he altered Reggie's own memories, but for now, it's a relief to have this shared past. Even when the elf had to completely alter his friend's understanding of reality, he wouldn't have erased this particular moment for the world. Because he meant what he said, and he's stuck to it. He's devoted every day since he made that promise to creating change.

There's only the steady *drip, drip, drip* of beer pouring off the island as Reggie stews. Finally, he nods. "I remember."

"I promised you, Reggie," Jameson says, lifting the key. "I'm trying to keep that promise. This is the way."

Reggie grunts but nods his head, permission for Jameson to move forward. "Get on with it."

Jameson doesn't hesitate. He's by Reggie's side in two quick strides, inserting the magicked key into the side of his friend's skull. It slips in easily, half the gold light no longer visible as it enters the folds of his friend's brain. One quick, painless twist and Reggie's eyes close; he's swaying on his feet. As the seconds tick by, Reggie's fingers twitch, his toes tap, he mutters under his breath. When his eyelids flutter open, the look of anger that's been etched on his face for eighteen years is replaced with a deep frown of worry.

Or maybe it's regret.

Reggie looks deep into his friend's eyes, and Jameson sees a spark there that he hasn't seen in years.

Reggie pushes Jameson aside, ducking his head into the sink to vomit.

"It's all right," Jameson says, patting Reggie's back. "It's all right."

"The hell it is!" Reggie's voice is warbled in the steel basin. He wipes his mouth before lifting his chest and taking deep, heaving breaths.

"Jameson," Reggie says, his eyes swimming with tears. "What have I done?"

CHAPTER
SIX

My eyelids slowly flutter open; they've never felt heavier in my life. Meema's face rushes into my memory immediately, hard reality slamming into my heart. But I have no more tears. Just emptiness.

Fwip, fwip, fwip.

I turn my head toward the noise. Ori's sitting on the other side of the mattress, clutching something in his right hand while his left moves back and forth methodically. His shadow is long on the wall, the only light coming from the bedside lamp by Ori's side, casting a warm amber glow. I glance out the window and see that it's dark, the otherness outside this house black and dotted with tiny pinpricks of light. Stars, but not. Everything's fake in a *transitory locale spell*.

"What are you doing?" My voice is hoarse.

Ori stops, turns around, then sets a chunk of silver wood and a small switchblade on the bed.

"Carving," Ori says.

"I didn't think you did that." This whole time, I've only ever seen Ori use existing objects as effigies: a clump of Play-Doh, a bent paper clip, a bundle of twigs twisted into a figurine. It's a power no other sprite descendant has ever had; all the others carve effigies out of sprite wood, enchanted blocks of timber.

Ori shrugs. "Sure, I was born great, but my extra abilities didn't manifest until Cassie." He sighs. I know we're both remembering what Jameson told us before we blinked away to battle the Knife: that Cassie's final thoughts of love for her brother likely boosted Ori's power, much like our connection does. "Mom trained me with carving long before that. It's the sprite way. It settles me when I'm anxious."

"You? Getting anxious?" I prop my pillows on the brass bars of the headboard and lean against them. "I didn't think you'd ever admit to that."

Ori smirks, playful, cocky, just for me. He knows I'm teasing. "I guess we still have things to learn about each other after *five whole days* together."

"Yeah, like, why can't you just use the same toy over and over as one effigy?" I ask.

"That's the first thing you want to know about me?"

I nod with a shrug. I don't know where the question came from, or if it was waiting somewhere back in my mind. But I guess with Ori mentioning there's still so much we don't know, I want to get started on knowing him. Now.

"I'm not exactly sure why," Ori says. "Since I'm the only one who can do it. But I've always thought of them like paper towels."

I bark out a laugh.

"What?" Ori says. "It's accurate. There reaches a point where a paper towel can't sop up anything else without tearing apart. There's just a point where my effigies can't take up any more magic. A spell or two and they're done." He points to his trusty backpack resting against the wall. "There's a twin backpack to that one back at my dad's house. Dad keeps a steady stream of toys delivered to his place that he just plops into the bag when he has a minute, and it shows up in mine. He was extra on top of it during the Culling, knowing I'd have so many challenges to face. When the toys are all used up, I put back as many as I can and he donates them. I was pretty proud of that spell, being able to turn each bag into an effigy of the other. Another thing Cassie helped me out with." He looks up to the ceiling. "Somehow."

"Your dad?" I've never heard him mention his father before. Ori knows plenty about *my* dad—our connection has even shown him scenes from my childhood.

"He's a good guy," Ori says. "Human. Just wants to bond with me however he can. He recognized that the more Mom hounded me to give up my magic, the further I pushed her away. Dad knows I need to live life my own way, especially after Cassie. He tried to tell Mom to cool it, but—" Ori sighs. "My parents divorced a couple years ago, and when I had to move in with Mom to have access to all her sprite texts, Dad and I started sending notes to each other through our bags. I wrote to him a couple hours ago to let him know I'm safe, even if he won't see me for a while. I hope you'll get to meet him someday. Once we've figured"—Ori gestures between us—"all of *this* out."

He scoots next to me, and his long, pale fingers rest on my chest as he leans down and kisses me. It's everything all at once: slow, fast, hard, soft, hungry, aching. Relieved that we both made it out alive. That his idea worked. That our connection was strong enough for him to bring me back from wherever I went when I died.

I feel all those things, too. When my hands stroke his back, when my tongue brushes gently against his, when he slightly nips my bottom lip. I can feel the magic of us swirling between our bodies. Feel my power igniting. But just as quickly, the reality of all that's happened in the past few days crashes back down on me.

Ori pulls back, his forehead creased with worry. I know he can feel my racing thoughts.

"What do you want to do?" he asks. "Next, I mean?"

I shrug. "I don't know that I trust myself to make the right decisions. I thought I'd got past it, doubting our power. But now that Meema's dead? Now that *all those people* are dead?" My body sags, weighed down by guilt. "What about you? You're as much a part of this as I am."

The words sound snappier than I intended. I don't mean for there to be blame in my tone, but somehow, it's there.

You're just trying to shirk the responsibility for so much heartache. If you'd focused instead of getting caught up in a crush, everyone would still be alive.

"I'm trying to be less . . . closed off," Ori says. "At least when it comes to you. I tried denying what was going on between us through the Culling, and it was a waste of energy."

"Don't you think that's the whole problem?" I ask. "We needed to deny it. We *should have* denied it."

My throat clogs with emotion. I grunt, frustrated. I shouldn't be the one crying. *I'm* the one who did the damage. It's possible Meema did, too. Yet I'm lying here feeling sorry for myself instead of finding answers.

"It's going to be okay, Nigel," Ori says, lying down on my chest. He fits there perfectly, his gangly frame a few inches shorter than mine, slotting into the crook of my arm like my body was made for him.

With him lying next to me, I now get a solid view of the wood carving on the bed. It's about six inches tall, of a man who's got a broad nose, wearing a cowboy hat with moppy hair poking underneath. It's me. Even though, personally, I've only ever worn a cowboy hat when Meema forced me to for family pictures.

I pick up the figure. "You're pretty good."

"Admiring yourself, cowboy?" He nudges my boot with his socked foot.

"Honestly . . . I'm the *last* person I want to be with right now," I say. Joke's on me though. There's no escaping myself, no matter how much I want to.

"I don't think we should stay here," Ori says, quickly, bluntly. He's motionless against my chest, but he sounds hurried. Like he'd blink away right now if he could.

"Where else would we go?" I ask.

"That's the problem. The Guild will hunt us no matter where we end up. But I don't want to be stuck here either."

I hesitate. Only when he says he *doesn't* want to be stuck here do I realize that I maybe *do*. Not stuck, but a member.

"The Resistance is our best way to end the Culling," I say. "Bex said that all the magicians here have that same goal. Why go it alone?"

"But agreeing to join another magical organization when we just escaped one seems pretty stupid. They say they have all these good intentions, and I don't think they're lying, but can we really trust them? We don't *know* them. We can't just sign up for them to use us as tools. How is that any different from the Guild?"

He makes a good point. While the Resistance's goals seem noble, the Guild's did, too. Is there something the Resistance isn't telling us?

Then again—was there something *Meema* wasn't telling me about the *Guild*? I can't leave before I know for sure whether she was in on the Culling plot or not. She was among the most powerful magicians in the group, included in so many major decisions. How could she *not* have known?

Your dad's a monster, your mother abandoned her own

son, you allowed so many to die. There's no way Meema wasn't terrible, too.

"What is it?" Ori asks.

"Do you think Meema could have known about the Guild?" I feel a stab of guilt that I've voiced my doubt, but there's no taking the words back.

Ori stops the slow trail of his fingers along the lines of my shirt. "I think it's a possibility. If the Guild has kept up this tradition for centuries, then at least a small faction of its members must be fueling it. It would make sense if they were powerful members."

"Like Adela Barrett," I say, gruffly, my throat constricting around her name.

Ori nods into my chest. "Like Adela Barrett." He tilts his head up now so he can look me in the eye. "But I know that what's in here"—he taps over my heart—"is pure and good. So it's a possibility that your grandma was, too. I *know* my sister was good, and I've always *thought* my mom was, but maybe I shouldn't assume. Maybe she didn't want me in the Culling so badly because she knew how unnecessary it was, and it took her daughter dying to see what a shit show she's caused. I'm going to ask her about it. About everything. When the time is right."

"But how will we know when that time is?" I ask.

"We can't know it. We'll just have to go with our gut. Emphasis on *our*. We don't need the Resistance. Let's go it alone, Nigel. Create our own heart home, live there until the Guild just forgets about us and moves on to some other monsters to chase—" I suck in a breath. "*Not* that we're the monsters," Ori adds. "You know what I mean. Besides, it's not just the Guild we have to worry about."

"It's not?"

His fingers trail down to my pocket, his pointer finger pressing on the lump of the claw buried within. "The Resistance can't find out about this. We don't know how they'll react. What if they think you're as dangerous as the Knife? What if they try to pry the heart-stone from the claw?" His voice catches in his throat before he finally whispers, "What if it kills you?"

My chest tightens. I hadn't thought of that.

"Okay, so we don't tell them," I say. "That doesn't mean we can't work with them to end the Culling. I'm joining the Resistance." I hope the *And that's final* is implied.

Ori goes still. "Nigel . . ."

"Just hear me out," I start, heat rising in my cheeks.

"*You* hear *me* out," Ori interjects. "No one can be trusted. As long as there's power involved, power to be held over others, you have to assume everyone is in it for themselves. I don't want others to get so accustomed to using us as tools that they don't think about what's best for us. That they completely forget about our safety. I'm worried about I—" His voice catches, and he takes a wobbly breath. "I'm worried about losing you."

A solitary tear slides down his cheek, and I instantly deflate.

You're such a fucking monster that you made your soul-mate cry.

No. I can't let this mentality get to me, or it's going to affect my power. Magic is fueled by intent, and if I'm constantly doubting myself, I'm only ever going to screw up at a time when I need my power most. I'm not the monster here. The Depraved are monsters. The Knife was a monster.

Was *a monster? The Knife lives on.*

My heart stops cold. I know with a bone-deep certainty that the voice in my head—the one that sounds so much like me, but harsher, meaner, more vile—is what I fear most:

The Knife. Inside me.

"Nigel?" Ori squeezes my hand, concerned. "What is it?"

I can't tell him what I know. It will only make him more sure we have to leave.

I stare back at him, my eyes following the path of that solitary tear. The Ori I know doesn't cry, he doesn't show weakness. I guess I never considered what it was like for him when he saw me die. I don't know the pain he went through before he brought me back.

"I'm sorry," I say. "I don't want to lose you either."

"Could've fooled me when you went all diva on us and stormed out."

"Hey." I poke a finger in his rib, and Ori pokes right back.

"You were a diva, cowboy. Ha! Diva cowboy."

"Oh great." I roll my eyes. "A new nickname."

Ori burrows his head deeper into my chest. We're silent for a moment, until Ori says, "Are you sure you don't just want to do this from here on out?"

"Lying in bed for the rest of eternity *does* sound like a pretty great option."

Ori laughs softly. "Yeah, it wouldn't be so bad. Although you can't fall asleep with boots on in the bed again. I know where those things have been."

I kick them off by the heels. "Never again." Then I kiss him on top of the head.

"We don't need anyone else, Guild or Resistance member," Ori insists. "Let's build our own lives, just the two of us. We can figure out our powers; we were starting to get control on our own. Nothing went wrong after we awakened the Horde. We focused. We can stay in control, of our power and our lives."

I think back to the last day of the Culling, to how we stopped those Depraved in Vegas, how we used our skills together, creating our shining abalone power to take down the Knife. We were getting the hang of it.

You got to learn how to trot before you get to the gallop, darlin'.

A different voice this time, not the grating intrusions of the Knife, but welcome advice remembered from Meema's lessons.

"I'm staying, Ori," I say, and his frustration crawls through my skin like an angry spider. "I can't let what we did happen again. It'd be stupid to go before Kenneth and Yamato teach us anything. And to be able to do that while getting rid of the Culling? It's two birds, one stone. You've got to see that."

Ori's silent for what feels like an eternity. But he finally shakes his head and says, "Fine. We can stay."

I can't stop the grin that breaks across my face.

"Not so fast," Ori snaps. "I'm saying we can join, but we're not taking orders from anyone. We make a heart home where we can train with Bex's dads. We see if we can tell the Guild the truth about the Culling. But this isn't permanent. I want the option to leave whenever we want."

As soon as he says it, I feel a weight lift off my shoulders. Ori says he might bail, but I know if I pull on our connection enough, he'll stick around. We're not meant to be without each other.

"Thank you." I wrap Ori in my arms and push my mouth against his. Ori presses back, letting his weight fall on me as I pull him closer. He drapes a leg over me, moving to straddle my hips.

But then he sits back, and the pressure of his leg against my pocket makes the claw dig into my skin, a searing heat blaring from my thigh to my heart.

"Wait!" I lift him with my left leg, just enough to grab the claw from my right pocket. As soon as it's in my palm, the heat subsides, pulsing warmly against my skin. It's almost comforting. I hold it out toward the light, taking a good look at it for the first time. Still the same chipped keratin, gray with age. But embedded straight through the center is a chunk of the heartstone, bright red. In this shape, it almost looks like an eye. And the longer I look, the more familiar its color seems. Maybe it's a trick of the lamplight, but the shade of red reminds me of Meema's Fiery Soul lipstick.

They say magic is all about intent. What if this isn't any different? Maybe my new reality can be shaped by my perception. This doesn't have to be the Knife taking me over. This could feel right—that this jewel is fused with our family's claw. That together, they brought me back to life. Meema will watch me through the heartstone now, checking that I make the right decisions instead of letting the Knife's voice get the better of me.

"Do you feel different?" Ori asks, staring at the claw.

I do, but now that I know the Knife is somewhere inside of me, I can control it. I think back to the hate I felt for the Guild magicians who chased us after we defeated the Knife. I think back to the guilt and shame I've been feeling, so strong I almost don't recognize my own thoughts. Because they're not entirely my own anymore, are they? The Knife is in there, bringing my darkest thoughts to the surface, letting them fester.

Ori doesn't need to know that. He would only doubt what I can do. He would reconsider our mission to change the Guild. But I can control this. What he doesn't know won't hurt him.

So I lie. For good reason.

"Just ready to take on the world with you," I say. "Together."

Joining the Resistance, training, taking on the Guild—all that can begin in the morning. In the meantime, I let our connection, built on so much goodness, drive the Knife from my thoughts. All I need right now is to take full advantage of a safe, private moment with my soulmate.

So I meet Ori's lips with my own, and I do just that.

CHAPTER
SEVEN

LAUREL CAN'T GET HER HANDS TO STOP SHAKING, HASN'T BEEN ABLE to since the Culling. Too much anxiety, too much desperation. But she needs to keep her body in check now as she follows behind her father. Alister stands tall, his shoulders pushed back proudly, as he makes his way to the center platform of the tribunal floor. He's one of the few magicians with the authority to call the entire Guild to order, and its thousands of members arrive in droves—in their physical and phantom forms—to fill up the stands that face her dad.

A man suddenly steps between Laurel and Alister, causing Laurel to crash into the newcomer's side.

"Watch it!" she snaps on instinct, but the man doesn't register her words. Laurel recognizes him now: Benjamin Dewbery, a water nymph. The white skin around his eyes is red and inflamed, his eyes just as irritated, from the tears that flow freely down his splotched cheeks. "She's gone," he says, his voice thick with emotion. His hands clench into fists, pulverizing the soaked tissue that sits between his fingers. "I'll kill every last Depraved for what they did to Adrienne. My only sister." He wails again, deep grief splitting Laurel's heart in two.

She's been hearing sounds like this ever since she and Jaleesa returned to the Guild. Anguished cries mixing with the thumps of bodies as magicians fall to their knees, overwhelmed by grief. Mourning friends and family members pierced through by the skeletons of Horde soldiers; or skewered by the quills, talons, and teeth of demons; or zapped into charred husks by twisted Depraved magic. She may not have seen the battle with her own eyes, but she sees each corpse as if she had been there.

"I'll kill those boys, too," Benjamin goes on. "They did this! THEY DID THIS!"

Laurel's stomach squirms. She doesn't know what to say. She doesn't know how to fix any of this. And she can't stop thinking of all the things she could have done to prevent this from happening.

Alister, however, knows just what to do. The ever-practiced politician stays cool, calm, and collected, even in times of intense emotion. He turns on the heel of his polished monk-strap shoes and places a comforting hand on the wrecked man's shoulder.

"I know, Benjamin," he croons. "I know." He pulls the nymph into a hug and lets him cry on his shoulder. "There, there." From anyone else, the repetitive phrase could sound insincere, but Laurel can feel that her dad means it. She knows he'll stand there with Benjamin for as long as he needs to compose himself.

Laurel's heart swells with pride—then, just as quickly, an icy pang deflates it. This man, whom they hardly even know, can cry on Alister's shoulder, but she's never been able to. Alister's constantly on her case to fight better, cast better, *be* better. She remembers once, when she was thirteen years old, she broke down in front of him.

She was so tired of hearing again and again how she'd failed, and not once how proud he was of her, how much he loved her. He'd knelt in front of Laurel, right there in the backyard of their Wyoming estate, where she'd been trying her hand at growing poisonous plants. She'd passed out after pricking herself on her own sleep-inducing thorn, and he'd just revived her.

"I'm hard on you *because* I love you," he said. "I need you to be the best, because if you're not, you'll die." He nodded to the plants. "By your own hand, if you're not careful." Then he looked out into the woods, lost in memories Laurel can't yet comprehend. "There are enough monsters out there that want you dead. You need to be the best so that nothing and no one can ever harm you. You need to be the best so you can *lead*, Laurel. You can't give anyone a reason to doubt you. If you do, you'll lose your power. Someone else will determine the course of your life, when you should have been able to shape not only your own future but the entire country's."

He gave her such a tender look, the first Laurel could remember. It filled her with so much pride and hope and passion. She knew then she would do whatever it took to become what her father envisioned of her.

Now, as he walks Benjamin and Laurel to their seats, she sees the power her dad wields in action. Every eye in the room follows him. No one makes a sound as Alister slowly makes his way back to the middle of the floor, where he stands on the central platform like it's his stage.

"Loss," Alister says, and though he hardly raises his voice, the room pays such rapt attention that it's as though he bellows. "We've all experienced a catastrophic loss. One hundred seventeen members, gone—just like that. A blow to our hearts, to the life force of this organization. Their spirits—so dedicated to good, to protecting the magical and human worlds alike—lost to the universe, rejoining the stars that give us our strength. But too soon. Much too soon." Alister locks eyes with his daughter. "All these deaths could have been avoided."

Laurel's stomach squirms. Is he about to tell everyone what she did?

But her father smiles at her instead, his eyes loving, showing the crowd how grateful he is that his daughter was not among the souls lost. She feels it, too, the display of adoration practically lifting her off her seat.

"Nigel Barrett and Orion Olson are a threat," Alister continues. "To magic and humankind. Not in generations has one of our own unleashed monsters of such magnitude. Not in generations have a few magicians stood to topple the world as we know it—not just through the unconstrained chaos of their magic, but through the incalculable weight of their powers. Powers that should have been stripped. Powers that threaten the delicate magical balance the Culling is meant to keep."

Laurel feels her feet ground beneath her, feels the most solid she has since hearing those cries of despair from her Guildmates. She had to do what she did because the boys were a threat. *Are* a threat, which must be stopped.

"We've been searching for them the past day and a half, to no avail," Alister continues. "And throughout this time, I cannot stop thinking how we let them go from this tribunal once before. Too many among our ranks voted to let them saunter out of the Guild. Look where that got us. One hundred seventeen members, friends, family, who we'll never see again. Two fugitives evading capture, casting who knows what spells and endangering us all. What's next? Human casualties? An increase in the Depraved? Magic coating the air, destroying each and every living thing we've sworn to protect?"

Alister gazes on his fellow magicians. It's impossible, but to

Laurel it feels as if he's able to look at every single member in the eyes, connecting with each of them, calling them to his cause.

"But a vow is just words. *Action* is what counts. *Action* that proves our loyalty to the Guild, that backs up the vow we've made to protect human- and magickind. I stand before you today not as a leader calling for another vote. I stand before you as a worried magician, a citizen of this earth who is scared for its future—and above all, a *father*, worried for his child. I ask each and every one of you to submit to questioning."

The assembled magicians swirl with confusion and doubt. A Guild-wide questioning is unheard of, an offense to many who've lived their lives by the letter of magical law. Their hurried whispers gather into a frenzied wind, Alister letting it build before delivering the words that calm the coming storm.

"It stands to reason that someone—maybe more than one—in our ranks is aiding the boys. How else could they go undetected when we have dedicated all our strength to finding them, using every magical tool at our disposal? Someone *must* be helping them escape. Helping them avoid the trial and inevitable punishment they deserve for what they've done.

"I'm asking you now: Return here in person, all of you. Eschew your phantom double and present yourselves, in the flesh, to your brothers- and sisters-in-arms. Let us each take residence in this hall, in our most sacred of spaces, so that we know without a shadow of a doubt that none of our own are plotting against us."

Alister walks slowly toward the stands, his steps echoing against the marble walls, until he's barely a foot away from the first row. Right in front of Lyra Olson. Ori's mom. He gives her a sympathetic look, not the one of disdain that he so often gives his political opponents. "I believe we should start the questioning with you." His eyes search the stands until he finds Yamato and Kenneth Sasaki. "And the two of you. All of us know what lengths we would go to, to protect our own children. No one could blame you for wanting to help them. But we need answers. We *must* stop the threats to our planet's very existence."

The three accused don't say a word. Lyra crosses her arms without breaking eye contact. Yamato looks like he's debating shifting right then and there to take out Laurel's father. Kenneth nods softly to himself. But every other magician looks at them with conviction. It's clear whose side they're on.

"So," Alister calls to the assembly. "Who will submit themselves to questioning?"

In a burst of movement, thousands of hands shoot into the air, Lyra's fastest of all, Kenneth's and Yamato's just after. Not a single magician stands in defiance.

"Then come home, friends. Let us grieve together, move forward together, knowing we have done everything we can to stop the forces working against us—even if those forces come from within our own ranks."

A burst of admiration powers Laurel's legs, making her stand practically as tall as her dad.

"Please proceed to your Ancestral wings," Alister commands. "Questioning will begin shortly."

Thousands of phantom bodies fade from the stands as their physical counterparts barge through the entry hall portal. Goblins shift into flying forms and sprites blink to Alister's side to thank him for boosting the spirits of their members when no one else could. There are hungry smiles, determination etched on faces, everyone eager to see justice served.

But there's only one face Laurel wants to see. One person she *must* have by her side as the Guild enters this new chapter. She just has to make sure they're on the same page.

As if feeling her desire, Jaleesa materializes by her side.

"Can we talk?" Jaleesa asks, and Laurel's relieved the fae wants as much assurance they're together on this as she does.

"Of course." Laurel's breathy with delight. Jaleesa is the only person who can make her like this, make her feel like a kid with a crush, even when the world is crumbling around her.

"Come on," Jaleesa says. "Let's go to our spot."

Laurel knows exactly where she means: the hollowed-out tree trunk nestled deep in the forest of her family's Wyoming property. But she shakes her head, hard. "We can't," Laurel whispers. "Didn't you hear Dad? Anyone who leaves the Guild right now is going to look suspicious. Follow me."

She walks Jaleesa over to the rematerialized balcony railing and pulls her girlfriend to her side, breathing in the smell of Jaleesa's perfume mixed with the faint, musky smell of her favorite leather jacket. The familiarity strengthens Laurel's resolve. They have to get back to *them*, have to stop letting those insufferable boys fuck up their relationship.

Laurel blasts a vine from her hands and uses it to swing with Jaleesa down to the second floor training grounds. She hustles over to the forested area of the level, knowing that if anyone sees them, they can claim to be training for the battles that are sure to come. She lets magic pool in her palms and conjures two bamboo shoots. Jaleesa would always call them Laurel's all-natural light-sabers, then laugh in gorgeous, melodic tones. Yet as her spears burst from the ground, Laurel accidentally smacks one out of the way but catches the other, only for it to slip out of her sweaty grip. It clatters against the trunk of the nearest pine, then falls to the mushroom-dotted soil with a muffled *thump*.

Jaleesa is silent.

"God dammit!" Laurel looks around guiltily, trained her whole life by her dad's PR team never to let her composure slip. If she were caught losing control on camera, it could ruin the entire family's image. But no one's around to hear; they're all swarming the floor below, awaiting questioning. Which is what Laurel should be focusing on, too.

"Why are you so jumpy?" Jaleesa asks.

Laurel scoffs. "Are you serious?" She motions to the balcony, toward the sound of all the commotion.

"The Laurel I know doesn't get worked up when there's a mission at hand," Jaleesa says, her tone more distant than Laurel's ever heard it. "That Laurel gets focused. Determined. The way you're acting now is almost . . . guilty."

Rage builds so strongly in Laurel that the conjured bamboo curls in on itself. "Guilty?! I'm not the one who *helped Nigel and Ori*." She whispers those last few words. Even if she's pissed, she doesn't want her girlfriend to get caught. "I don't blame you for what you did. Back in the cave, when we tried to retrieve the claw."

Jaleesa recoils, incredulous. "You don't blame *me*?"

"We had the chance to stop them," Laurel says. "We wouldn't be here—interviewing the entire Guild—if you had let me go through with it."

"I couldn't let you do that," Jaleesa says. "You're not a murd—"

Laurel puts her hand up to stop Jaleesa. "No one can know what went down in that cave. You'll be questioned, and if they learn you stopped me, they'll believe you're in league with the boys. But we both know they'll go easy on you; my dad won't let you look bad, since it makes me look bad. We're around each other all the time."

Well, they *were*, but Laurel can feel Jaleesa already becoming distant.

"We need to get your story straight. It has to be just honest enough, vague enough, that there's no lie. So tell them this: You were confused. Because you were. You know of the Guild rule forbidding any magician to kill another except in dire circumstances of self-defense, and you were uncertain if the moment called for that. That's not much of a stretch, is it?"

Jaleesa only shakes her head, uncharacteristically quiet.

"You were just trying to protect me." Laurel knows that no one will question *her* devotion to the Guild. They'll see her attempt to stop Nigel and Ori from escaping as an act of loyalty. When she really thinks about it, they're not wrong. "But you see now that I *had* to do it."

She *did* have to do it, all of it. She had to be the best, and she had to prove to her father that she'd heard him that day in their forest. *She* was going to be the one to control her destiny, and that of the country. No one could take that away from her. Those boys were already stronger than everyone else when she did what she did. She couldn't let *them* choose the direction magickind would take. Maybe they'd get so powerful that they'd unleash even more monsters. She had to stop them, and if her choices had casualties, it was worth it in the long run. It was for the greater good.

Even still, Laurel can't escape the echoes of her fellow Guild members' mournful cries. She can't help the nagging thought that she could have chosen differently and still bested the boys.

She shakes her head as though she could dislodge those thoughts from her mind. She needs to stay committed. She needs to protect Jaleesa.

But Jaleesa takes a step back, the simple move a stab in Laurel's gut.

"I'm not sure of much anymore," Jaleesa says flatly.

"Jaleesa, please. We're on the same page, aren't we?" Laurel allows a tinge of desperation to creep into her voice. She needs Jaleesa to hear how much she cares about her.

"Do you know of any spells cast against the Guild?"

Jaleesa's change of subject is so sudden it gives Laurel whiplash. Her breath comes in short bursts, her heart pounds against her chest.

"The Depraved cast against Guild members all the time," Laurel says softly.

"That's not what I mean. What if a magician cast some kind of curse against the rest of the Guild?"

"One magician couldn't do that. It'd take too much power."

"So a group of magicians then," Jaleesa snaps.

Laurel's nostrils flare, a smell of fear seeping into them. But it's not from Jaleesa.

"No," Laurel says, trying to sound as emotionless as possible. "Haven't heard of it."

Jaleesa tilts her head to the side. She doesn't blink, she just stares, Laurel feeling smaller and smaller the longer her girlfriend lets time pass.

Jaleesa finally changes the subject, and it takes all of Laurel's willpower not to sigh in relief. "What if they could teach us something? Nigel and Ori? Give us tips about our connection? What if they weren't lying when they said we could be as powerful as them?"

"WHY WOULD YOU WANT THAT?" Laurel shouts, but Jaleesa doesn't budge. The fae plants her feet firmly in the grass, looking at Laurel as if she's never seen her so clearly before. Laurel closes the distance between them, grabbing Jaleesa's hands. The fae's throat glows purple, an instinct readying herself to cast defensive spells, and Laurel's heart breaks to think that Jaleesa could ever see her as a threat.

"We *can't* be as powerful as them," Laurel whispers urgently. "You see that, right? If we become as powerful as them, *our* magic will get out of hand. *We'll* be considered the enemy. We can't give them"—she swallows—"can't give my *dad* another reason to hate us.

Let's just stick to the plan. We're the strongest in our generation as it is. We can't be anything else. You get that, don't you?"

Silence stretches between them, and it makes Laurel want to crawl out of her skin.

"Look at how they're suspecting Lyra and Yamato and Kenneth," Laurel insists. "If you keep going down this path, they'll go after your mom next. Is that what you want?"

Without missing a beat, Jaleesa says, earnestly, "No."

"Good. So you know what to say when you're questioned, right?"

Jaleesa chews her cheek before nodding.

"And once the boys are caught, we'll go back to doing things our way, right?"

Jaleesa sighs. "Yes."

Laurel squeezes Jaleesa's fingers as tight as she possibly can, desperate to make her girlfriend feel her love. She *needs* Jaleesa to know that she's only doing this to protect her. "Promise me."

"I promise," Jaleesa says, with enough conviction that it eases Laurel's pounding heartbeat.

The nymph believes it. She's gotten through to her girlfriend.

At least, that's what she tells herself.

CHAPTER
EIGHT

JALEESA CAN TELL BY THE DESPERATE LOOK IN LAUREL'S EYES THAT the nymph just wants things to go back to normal. But what even is normal anymore? When your girlfriend can so casually talk about murder, when so much of the Guild sees two awkward boys as monsters rather than the twitterpated dorks they are, Jaleesa feels like she's living a different reality than everyone around her. She has to do something to ground herself, and she knows just the place to go.

"*Secrets to learn,*
 I just have to look.
  Time to soar
   Through the pages of a book."

Jaleesa's sneakers lift off the ground, and she zooms out of the training level faster than she anticipated. Her whole being needs answers *now*, and she might as well start with learning whatever she can about mass spells or curses. It's what Nigel told her to do. A nagging at the back of her brain like an itch she can't scratch tells her she should know more, but she can't remember what. Every time her mind latches onto something, it's whisked away like a whisper in a roaring wind.

When her feet hit the marble floor of the library, she looks back over the railing. Thousands of magicians are gathered on the bottom level, making their way to their respective Ancestral wings, per Alister's orders. Awaiting questioning. She should go down there soon, but for now, she'll take advantage of their fervor to get some time alone.

Her ponytail swings behind her as she practically sprints to the section of tone tomes. Rather than writing spells down, fae imbue the sounds of their spells within the pages of their books. Explanations, recitations, histories, all transferred to the listener's mind with a simple sung note or melody. The process is quick and efficient, and typically allows fae to progress in their magic faster than their Guild counterparts, and Jaleesa is thankful for that now.

Ten minutes in and she's already listened to four dozen tomes regarding mass spells. They all have one thing in common: multiple magicians. It's too difficult for one magician to cast against so many people; it'd drain power too quickly. A single fae could cast on a group, but they'd need another magical object to boost them, typically one that was cursed.

That's the other fact that weighs Jaleesa down with each tome she listens to: Most spells intended to be cast on multiple people are curses. Why do so few people want to do mass good, but so many are willing to spread darkness without a second thought? It seems that's one thing magicians have in common with humans: Negativity comes too easily. The tones describing it make Jaleesa squirm, make her stomach swim with nausea. They're deep, grating, vibrating through her bones in a way that makes her want to plug her ears or leave. But she promised Nigel she'd find out as much as she could.

"Where have you been?"

"Ah!" Jaleesa yelps as she snaps the tone tome in her hands shut. The resounding clap does nothing to drown out her heartbeat pounding in her ears.

Pallavit marches over to her daughter, snatching the book from Jaleesa's hands. "I've been looking everywhere for you. And you've been up here listening to—" Pallavit cracks the book open with an elegant flourish as the ominous notes of a mass spell to induce paralysis billow down the hall.

Pallavit shuts the book slowly, deep lines etching into her forehead. She doesn't say a word, just sings three short notes as her throat glows purple. Her faecraft instantly cuts off all sound rising up from the floors below. Jaleesa knows this spell. It's the same one her mom used whenever her parents argued and didn't want their daughter to hear. Whatever is said next will be for her ears only.

"Why are you doing this?" Pallavit barks, hoisting up the tone tome before slamming it back onto its shelf.

"I'm studying," Jaleesa says, the lie coming so easily she even shocks herself. "Who knows when we'll have to battle another swarm of enemies like the Horde? What if the Depraved learned something from the attack? Like that there's strength in numbers. We should embrace that, too."

Pallavit crosses her arms. "Try again. The Depraved are so singularly focused on their own hunger that they'll never work together. They flocked to the Knife because they knew it would feed them, not because they were building an army." Pallavit takes a step closer to her daughter, looking over her shoulder even though her spell prevents anybody from listening in. "Jaleesa, is there something you need to tell me?"

Maybe you should *just tell her*, she thinks. Jaleesa's never distrusted her mother before. She's been able to rely on Pallavit for as long as she can remember. From sitting on her lap while they listened to records to mimicking sounds her mother sang in an attempt to master new spellwork, Jaleesa has always known without a shadow of a doubt that her mom would help her through anything.

"Did those boys say something to you?" Pallavit asks, before her eyes pop wide. "*Do* something to you?"

Pallavit acts in a rush, her hands grabbing Jaleesa's shoulders, tugging her every which way as she looks for any signs of harm. Jaleesa's been through this before, many times, when she came home bruised from training sessions with other fae. Sometimes there'd be lingering effects of curses, like the time one of her classmates covered Jaleesa in pimples. Other times, the curses would be less obvious, like that time she'd been spelled to always write her *qs* as *ps*. After every motherly inspection, Pallavit would always bemoan the fact that no magic could reveal what had been cast against another magician. You always had to go by what you could observe with your own senses.

"Mom, stop." Jaleesa gently removes her mother's hand and sets it by her side. "I'm fine."

She wants to tell her mom everything, tell her about Nigel's suspicions of a Guild-wide spell, and that she might have been able to build a connection with Laurel as strong as Nigel and Ori's. At least before Laurel became this unrecognizable, bloodthirsty, alternate-reality girlfriend that she is now. It'd be so good to get these worries off her chest.

Jaleesa opens her mouth to spill it all, but Pallavit speaks first.

"I'm sorry." Pallavit sighs. "This whole thing has me on edge. Even though I know you're fine, I can't shake the fear that I'd lost you. When you didn't come to the mountain, I thought you were dead." Tears well in Pallavit's eyes. Jaleesa's caught off guard. Her mother never cries. But seeing teardrops leave tracks on her cheeks reminds Jaleesa how much Pallavit cares for her. She should tell her the truth. Tell her everything.

"Alister is waiting to question you," Pallavit says. "But don't worry. I'll be there, too."

Her mother's statement stops Jaleesa's words in her throat. Alister was Nigel's prime suspect of casting against the Guild. All sorts of alarm bells ring inside Jaleesa's mind, knowing that her mom is cozying up to him.

Pallavit cups Jaleesa's cheek, seemingly unaware of the suspicion sweeping through her daughter. "The questions won't be deep. You and Laurel are too close." Laurel said as much. "If he suspects you of treason, others would suspect Laurel as well. He'd never let his daughter embarrass him."

Even with so many questions still unanswered, Jaleesa experiences the most clarity she's ever felt in her life. The Guild is all pomp and circumstance. If Alister can question his own daughter—clearly a conflict of interest—then this whole "investigation" is a sham. People will claim that magic can make everyone tell the truth, but no one can guarantee those spells are actually cast. And there are so many ways to counteract them if they are. Magicians have the same weakness as humans, having to take everyone at their word. And just like humans, magicians lie.

Lie, like Jaleesa does as she's being questioned in the nymph dorm, seated on a toadstool next to a babbling brook. It's all lying by omission, but still. It isn't the whole truth, despite the fae song Pallavit sings that prevents any false statements from leaving Jaleesa's lips. Jaleesa says everything Laurel told her to in the ways Pallavit's spell will allow. She claims she didn't want Laurel to kill the boys, recites how killing other magicians goes against magical law, describes the disorientation she felt in the seconds before Laurel was going to deliver a fatal blow. It all paints a picture of a confused girl who didn't want to witness any unnecessary killing. No one could take her words and prove without a shadow of a doubt that she was in league with Nigel and Ori.

Pallavit nods along as Jaleesa speaks, a satisfied smile tugging her mother's lips upward the entire time.

When Jaleesa's interrogation is over, she gets up and says the truest words she's spoken all day. "Thank you for showing me how important it is to fight for what's right."

Pallavit's smile couldn't reach any further if she tried. Alister looks at her with pride, the only time Jaleesa can ever remember him looking at her without disdain.

But when she's out of the room, the other magicians in the entry hall too lost to their own conversations and conviction to take notice of her, Jaleesa whispers softly to herself, "This is such bullshit."

She believes it so strongly that her magic reacts, flinging her from the marble floor up, up, up, past dozens of levels until she's back in the library. Only this time, she's not among the tone tomes. Now, she's staring at row after row of nymph texts, nestled inside hollowed-out trees.

Alister is the prime suspect, after all.

This is where she should have started her search.

Jaleesa plucks a book from the nearest trunk.

"Time to see what mischief a nymph can get up to."

CHAPTER
NINE

The next four days go by slower than molasses. It figures that the minute we make a decision about the Resistance, half its members are called away for questioning. Yamato, Kenneth, and Jameson promised us they had spells in place so their minds couldn't be peeled back like onions to expose the Resistance layers. They left Ori, Bex, and me inside Jameson's heart home until they could come back.

Magic is out of the question since we don't want to inadvertently destroy Jameson's transitory locale by testing the limits of our connection. Ori thought it'd be okay to practice, but I couldn't take the added guilt if our power got out of hand. I can't call Jaleesa, either, for fear that she's being hovered over by senior Guild members. I've practically gouged tracks into the hardwood floors from pacing while imagining what she may have learned, especially if any of that info has to do with Meema's involvement in the Culling.

Bex and I try to keep each other occupied, but we just end up obsessing over when her dads might get back. All that's done is make us both more worried, so Bex has retreated to her room to blare music from her record player while I scuff my boots nervously and eat nonstop from Jameson's ever-refilling fridge.

"I swear I'll turn you into a pig myself if you make one more ham sandwich," Ori says as I shut the fridge for the seven thousandth time. "The smell of deli meat and mustard is going to make me throw up."

"What?" I say, spreading a giant dollop of the yellow goop onto a waiting slice of bread. "I eat when I'm nervous."

"You're kidding," Ori deadpans.

"What else am I supposed to do? If Kenneth, Yamato, or Jameson slip, we're toast. *Ooh!*" I hold up the piece of white bread not yet piled with ham. "Maybe I should toast this. Mix it up."

"Incorrigible."

I plop the untoasted slice on my sandwich and take a massive bite. "You should have one of these, by the way. You've hardly had a bite to eat the last four days."

Ori shrugs. "I *can't* eat when I'm nervous."

I swallow. "What about when you're not nervous? What's your favorite food?"

Ori doesn't even think about it. "Hands down, my Italian grandma's lasagna. Recipe passed down through five generations."

The way he lights up at the thought of his grandma's cooking makes me feel like I've been doused with cold water. I'm glad he's happy, I really am. And I hope to get to experience that lasagna for myself someday. But he'll never get to experience Meema's world-famous barbecue or sweet tea or banana pudding. There's so much he's missed out on. So much I'll never get to have again. She loved making sure everyone was well-fed and felt welcomed with her offers of a heaping plate. She was so good.

Was she? Maybe it was all a ruse so no one would ever suspect her of being behind the Culling.

I've got to distract myself before I sink down into yet another Meema-centered rabbit hole. "You know, with the intensity of the Culling and all that—"

Ori snorts at the understatement.

"—we've never gotten to ask those run-of-the-mill, getting-to-know-you questions that most couples cover on the first date."

Ori stares at me, his expression unreadable for a solid thirty seconds. Then that telltale smirk creeps across his face and he pats the stool next to him. "Get over here, cowboy."

And so we spend the next few days finally getting to know each other. Favorite animal, favorite color, favorite movie. For Ori, it's sharks, black, and *Trolls*. The first two aren't surprising. He's got just about as much bite as a great white, so that feels on brand. And I've only ever seen him in black pants, black or white tees, and gray cardigans. Color isn't really his thing.

Which is why *Trolls* totally throws me off.

"Your favorite color is black, but your favorite movie follows the most flamboyant animated characters out there?"

Ori shrugs. "I mean, my favorite singer is Taylor Swift. Are you really that surprised?"

"I still can't wrap my head around why you like her so much."

"If you say one thing against Miss Swift, I'll—"

"Whoa there, Sprite Boy." I wrap an arm around his shoulders and pull him close. "Taylor's great. But her bubbly personality isn't very *you*. No offense."

"So you're saying I'm an asshole?"

"No. Just dark and broody. Which, coincidentally, has become exactly my type."

"I had you hooked from the moment we met." It's a statement, not a question, and it makes every part of me light up like a Christmas tree. I push my lips against his, letting the warmth of this silly conversation flow through us.

I quickly discover my favorite stories come from Ori's memories of family. He reminisces about crowding into the kitchen with his sister, practicing their magical carving while their grandmother worked her own kind of magic with food. Ori may not let many people in, but it's clear his family means the world to him. It makes me wonder what stories he'll tell about us someday. If we can get through this without being stripped of our powers, or worse, killed. But those worries get pushed aside the more we share with each other, the agonizing days of waiting turning into an opportunity to get to know each other as soulmates.

Which is why it's so disorienting when I discover a picture of Jameson and my dad on the fireplace mantel in the library. It's the eighth day since we arrived here, and I haven't noticed it in all the time I've spent in the house, too caught up in Ori to notice anything else. They're young, probably midtwenties, Jameson pulling Dad into his side, stupid grins breaking their faces. They look like total bros, but it's almost . . . sweet. A word I never thought I'd associate with Dad.

The timing is too coincidental, like looking at this picture summoned him to me, because when I pick up the frame, the front door bursts open and footsteps echo through the foyer. It isn't long until Jameson strides into the library, stopping when he sees what I'm holding.

"You're back."

Jameson nods. "Indeed." He motions to the frame. "I see you found my favorite photograph."

"It's not like it was hidden," I say, defensive. "It was on the mantel for all to see."

"It was. It's a reminder of why I joined the Resistance."

"You two were friends?"

"Mmm. But that word doesn't quite seem to encompass the bond we truly had."

I don't know what to say. What kind of person can get close to a guy who would emotionally abuse his own son?

"He wasn't always like this, you know," Jameson nearly whispers. He looks . . . hurt. In pain. "And I'm sorry to say that I had something to do with the man he became."

I didn't think before that I'd ever care to know what made Dad the way he is. What does it matter when you wreak so much havoc on your family? The end result is the same. Even still, I ask, "What happened?"

"I can show you." Jameson saunters over to one of the bookshelves and plucks a leather-bound book. "I crafted all these myself, immortalizing our history as the Resistance so that if any of us dies, our mission lives on." Of course he would. It's not uncommon for a magician's skills in the ordinary world to mirror their preferred abilities in the magical one.

Jameson has been hard at work putting those skills to use. There are hundreds of books lining the shelves, every last one the exact same size, shape, and color. They're all black with gold numbers on the bottom of the binding. The one in Jameson's hand has *2005-3* written on it, the only indication of its difference from the other texts around us. Jameson didn't even have to look for it, just knew where it was like he's been waiting for this moment for a long time.

"Here is where your story and involvement in this organization began." He grabs the top corner of the cover, on the cusp of flipping it open. "Are you ready?"

Something in his voice makes me stop. I thought I'd be getting answers, but he sounds like there's something he's about to tell me that I won't like. That might hurt.

But that's all my life has been lately. Pain. Will a little more really make that much of a difference?

So I nod.

Jameson opens the cover, the crackle of old leather filling my ears, before everything blurs in a swath of color.

CHAPTER
TEN

When everything comes back into focus, it's night. Not in the in-between space of the Resistance headquarters, but out in a field. I can tell by the smell, by the occasional squawk of a grackle, and by the never-ending chirp of cicadas that we're in Texas. With a jolt, I realize we're even closer to home. Dad's ancient yellow pickup—his junker from the '70s he called Old Yeller—is just a few yards away, and there's movement in the truck bed.

"You recognize the truck," Jameson says, making me jump. He's come along for whatever this vision is, just like the one back in the Guild, where Meema and Jameson showed me Great-Grandpa Barrett's story. I give Jameson a look like What is this? *Jameson motions for us to move forward. After a couple steps, I hear voices. Dad's first.*

"It's the competition where I lost my power," he says. As I get closer I can see he's under a blanket with my mom. Kyle. It's the first time I've ever seen her living and breathing. Well, moving *at least, since I guess we're inside a story. But I've seen her picture before, her wild auburn*

hair, the playful tilt in her mouth that's surprisingly like Ori's. Dad absentmindedly plays with her fingers while they both stare into the stars. "The Culling. I was supposed to kill a Depraved on my own. I was so close, too, but at the last second it got the better of me. Had its rotten hands around my neck. My vision spotted and black crept in at the edges. Just when I thought it was going to be the end, Ma stepped in and finished it."

"Of course she did," Kyle says in a husky voice. "You're her son."

"But not Pa's apparently."

Kyle's lips clamp into a thin line. I guess Dad's told her about his own father abandoning him already.

"Fuck 'im," Kyle drawls.

Dad laughs, and it's so real that my breath catches. I've never heard him like this before. Even though he's talking about his dad leaving and his magic being stripped away, he sounds carefree. He flings his arms out and around Kyle, drawing her in for a long kiss.

I shuffle my boots awkwardly, but they don't even make a mark in the dirt. We're not here, but we are, right in the middle of my parents' story.

When Dad pulls away, he looks up at the sky again. "All our power came from the stars. There have got to be others out there."

"Aliens?" Kyle asks it without a hint of disbelief. I guess if she's accepted that magic is real, it isn't that big of a stretch to think aliens exist, too.

Dad shrugs. "Some might call them that, but I think they're more like ancestors. Ancestors to the magical races, at least. And I just keep wondering if they're watching all this happen now. If they're watching the Guild strip magicians of their power. And if they are, why don't they step in and help?"

"There's no way to stop it?" Kyle asks.

Dad shakes his head. "Not without magical imbalance. And this year's Culling is about to start. I just keep thinking of those kids who aren't going to make it. Most of them won't. There will be hundreds of devastated souls in just a few weeks' time, their whole world crashing around them."

This Reggie is nothing like the one I know. He sounds genuinely concerned for someone other than himself. This is the son Meema always knew she had, the son she never gave up trying to bring back after Kyle left him. It's disorienting to want to root for this couple in front of me, knowing how they both turn out.

Kyle moves her hands around her stomach. "So Nigel's going to be born with magic, and the Guild could take it away from him just like that?" *Her stomach isn't even swollen yet, but I guess I'm in there, waiting to become the Horde-awakening awkward cowboy I am today.*

"Mmm." Dad sits up. "I wish there was a way we could escape all this. But Ma wouldn't rest until she found us. She's going to be on us like fleas on a dog. She'll want to try again. She'll want to raise him to bring pride to the Barrett name. Since I couldn't do it."

"That's bullshit." Kyle pulls Dad in for another kiss. "You're perfect, Reggie."

Dad puts his hand on Kyle's belly. "Let's just hope this kid's got what it takes. I don't know what Ma will do if she's the last Barrett in the Guild."

My blood runs cold. Even Dad doubted her. Even he thought she had the capacity to be evil if she was distraught enough.

Kyle slowly gets to her knees, looking Dad dead in the eye. "Maybe he'll be the most powerful Barrett ever seen. Maybe he won't. Maybe he'll never make it into the Guild. But who gives a shit? No matter where Nigel goes, he'll have us. I doubt there's a magic stronger than that."

Dad pulls Kyle in again and the scene blurs, Jameson and me standing together in the swirl of colors. *I should be thinking about how weird it is to see my parents so young. I should be feeling that awkwardness at knowing they were probably about to get down to doing what they did that made Kyle pregnant in the first place, and no kid should ever be faced with that.*

But instead, I can't stop playing Kyle's words over and over in my head. "No matter where Nigel goes, he'll have us."

What a crock of shit. I didn't have her from the day I was born.

"What changed?" *I ask, a lump building in my throat that has no right to be there.* "Why didn't she stay?"

Jameson says calmly, "From the moment she knew she was pregnant, she has always had and still does have your best interests at heart."

I scoff, sounding an awful lot like Ori. "That's fresh."

Jameson holds out a long-fingered hand. "Patience. The story continues." *He turns to me as the colors around us begin to stabilize.* "Your father and I remained friends even after he was expelled from the Guild. We shared the same hopes that someday there could be a way for former magicians to be able to remain in the Guild, for humans and magicians to work together and stop the Depraved from ever being created. He, Kyle, and I were the founding members of the Resistance. We called ourselves that even though by revolutionary standards our methods were fairly quiet. One magician and two humans doing research, slowly but surely, trying to find evidence of magical and human cooperation. I'd bring back ideas to the Guild in an attempt to convince them that we should work with humankind so that they didn't create Depraved in the first place, but the excuse was always the same: If we told them what we could do, humans would only use us for our powers. But when I voiced my theories, a small, steady trickle of magicians came to be allies. Kenneth and Yamato, a couple dozen others."

"It was *this* moment, *just before you were born, that changed everything.*" *He cocks a wary eyebrow.* "But how, I'm not quite sure."

The colors around us finally solidify. Kyle and Dad hike through the forest, Kyle's belly noticeably swollen.

"A last trip before you were born," *Jameson explains.* "They loved to explore the outdoors together."

They gently hold hands as they walk between the trees, but Kyle's hand flies to her mouth as they enter a meadow.

"Reggie, look!" Kyle's alarmed shout echoes through the space, but louder still is the panicked cry of a unicorn in the middle of the long grass, trying but failing to get away. Their right front leg sits at an angle, their creamy hide reddish-brown with blood as it drips off the hoof they tenderly hold in the air. Their golden horn is just a metallic nub, the top half held between their teeth. Their eyes are wide, their breaths quick and heavy.

"They're hurt," Dad says, and Kyle sprints to the unicorn's side faster than a woman as pregnant as she is should be able to.

The unicorn tries to scurry away, but they trip and fall, the top half of the horn tumbling from their mouth.

"It's okay," Kyle coos. "You're all right." She places a hand on the unicorn's heaving side, and their breathing instantly slows. It's as if she's the one who's magic.

"Kyle worked at a stable all her life," Jameson says. "The universe knew what it was doing leading her to this unicorn's path."

Kyle doesn't hesitate, shuffling to the creature's broken leg. She holds it gently, cooing again as the unicorn whimpers at her touch. "It's not a compound fracture, thank god." She looks up at Dad. "Find me a sturdy stick, would you?" She rips the bandana from around her head and starts tearing it into strips.

Dad hurries away and is back in a flash, a bough as thick as his wrist in his hands. He flings his backpack over his shoulder, grabs a pocketknife, and hacks at the stick until it's the right length for a brace. "It's strange," he says as he hands the bough over. "A unicorn should be able to heal themselves. They're some of the most magical creatures on the planet. But I guess with their horn broken, their magic is gone."

Dad plops down onto the grass to place his own soothing hand on the unicorn's side. "Just like me, huh, buddy?"

JASON JUNE

"I wish we had some magic right about now, because this part's going to hurt," Kyle says, gently patting the unicorn's head. "But it'll be over fast." She meets Dad's eyes. "How about a distraction?"

Dad doesn't even hesitate. He scoots next to the unicorn's face, sitting by their side, talking the whole time. He launches into their story, explaining what they're doing in the mountains, talking about me baking away in Kyle's womb, telling the unicorn how his own magic was sapped and how he wants a different future for me. It's only been about a minute, but his deep gravelly voice seems to put the unicorn into a lull.

Then he says the magic words.

"You'll get used to not having your power. I've had to, and I think I turned out all right. But I got to be honest with ya. There are times when I wish my power didn't have to be taken. If only it wasn't for magical imbalance."

Crack!

Kyle's focus is dead set on the unicorn's leg, making sure she places it right as she tightens the strips of fabric around the bough. She doesn't notice the unicorn's head snap to the side. Doesn't see how their attention goes from their injury to Dad's face.

Magical imbalance?

The unicorn doesn't say the question out loud, exactly, but it's easily heard, the words reverberating in their minds.

Dad scowls. "Yeah. You know how if too much magic is allowed to gather, its energy destroys every living thing in its path."

The unicorn huffs. Magic doesn't get imbalanced. Magic is pure. Magic is good. Magic *is* life. It could never destroy.

Dad and Kyle stare at each other for seconds that I'm sure for them feel like hours. I know what it's like to have everything you've believed shattered in only a moment. I glance up to Jameson to see the same shocked look on his face as he relearns this news. What a strange coincidence that my story in the Resistance begins at nearly the same time my parents discovered the truth. It's almost like . . . destiny. Like I was meant to stop the Culling.

Kyle reaches for Dad to pull her up. "Reggie," *she starts.* "That means the Culling—"

"Is a lie," *Dad breathes. His head whips back to the unicorn.* "You're sure?"

Before the unicorn has a chance to answer, flashes of gold, silver, and bronze light up the sky, even though it's broad daylight. In the blink of an eye, a herd of hundreds of unicorns surrounds them, neighing and braying and foaming at the mouth. Horns lower and steady millimeters from Kyle's and Dad's chests. One false move and my parents will be skewered through.

AWAY!

The voices of the entire herd swarm their minds, making even me clutch at my head.

Then, one quiet, gentle voice.

Wait.

The injured unicorn hobbles to their feet. Seeing their companion's leg, a black-and-white unicorn's silver horn flares, and the break is healed. The brace Kyle crafted falls from their leg, and Kyle stares on in awe at the feat of magic.

They helped me.

The herd backs off, only a couple feet, some still poised to strike, until the newly healed unicorn steps in between their herdmates and my parents.

And they need help.

The scene blurs again, too soon for my liking.

"Wait!" *I say, turning to Jameson, but he places a calming hand on my shoulder.*

"It's coming back to me now, immersed in the memory like this," *he explains.* "This is where the herd explained that everything we knew about magical imbalance was a lie. It was the moment we realized that* *someone had set up the Culling for terrible reasons. Well, the moment your parents realized it. They told me immediately, but of course I forgot the fact minutes later, just like I'll forget in the moments after we leave these memories.*

"But we quickly set a plan to get more answers." His face darkens. "Unfortunately, it required more sacrifice than any of us could have anticipated."

A new scene materializes. We're in a hospital now. Dad hovers over Kyle where she lies with a few tubes stuck to her. She cradles a baby in her arms.

Me.

For the briefest moment, the three of us look like the picture-perfect family. A single happy tear slips down Dad's cheek as Kyle kisses my head, already covered with a bushel of brown hair.

The door creaks open and Jameson walks inside. Even in his midtwenties he has an air of mysterious confidence.

"It's time," he says simply.

Immediately, surprisingly, Kyle bursts into tears.

"I guess this is goodbye," she chokes out.

"For n-now," Dad says, his voice breaking. He clears his throat. "Only for now. Nigel and I will be okay. We'll always wait for you."

"Where is she going?" I ask.

"She had a mission," Jameson says. "The most important of the Resistance yet. Unicorns are known for being reclusive, hidden away from humans for sins of our past. Yet the herd member she helped that day bonded with your mother and father. The unicorn told an Ancestral acquaintance of your parents' misconceptions and encouraged us to end the Culling. That Ancestral requested one of the humans within our ranks join them so the magical being could share information they thought would be useful in our efforts. Your mother and father were the only two humans we had."

That fire of anger ignites in my belly again. "Ancestrals haven't been heard from in hundreds of years, and the first thing they do is ask a parent to abandon their newborn child?"

Jameson shakes his head sadly. "It wasn't that simple. Your father and mother wanted to go together. They even wanted to take you. Their whole allegiance to the Resistance was to create a better future for you. But they both couldn't just leave, and they certainly couldn't take you. With your grandmother one of the most important Guild members alive—"

My heart clenches so hard I gasp. "Don't you dare blame Meema for this."

Jameson gives me an apologetic smile. "There's no blame given. Her devotion to you was unmatched. And because of that, she insisted on having a hand in raising you. Your parents knew if they both left with you, Adela wouldn't rest until she found you. She'd do the same looking for Reggie if he suddenly disappeared. So that left your mother. And with your father always under Adela's eye, it presented too many opportunities for her to discover his work with the Resistance. At first, your father wanted to tell her of our existence, but her desperation to restore the Barrett name made them question whether she would help us in our missions or destroy us before we could change the Guild."

Relief floods through me that I'm not out of line for suspecting Meema of being a part of the Culling lie. Then I instantly feel guilty for wanting others to doubt her. I have to find definitive proof of whether or not she was behind this, because I know one thing for sure: If she wasn't, she doesn't deserve any of us shitting all over her memory.

"Your mother agreed to leave," Jameson continues, "to meet the Ancestral and hear what they had to say. And your father agreed to stay at the Barrett ranch with you and Adela.

"But to ensure your grandmother never learned the real reason Kyle left, there was one more important step we had to take."

Jameson motions toward his phantom self.

"We have to move now," memory-Jameson says. "Before Adela comes back."

Kyle nods and promptly removes the sensors attached to her. The heart rate monitor tones a solitary note, signaling a death. My heart aches as I realize that it is one, in a sense. The death of the life we could have had.

Dad holds me in his arms, so gentle. Kyle rushes to his side and gives him one last kiss. "We'll see each other again," she says.

"I know it," Dad agrees.

Kyle turns to Jameson. "Do it."

Jameson's hands are already glowing gold, and in one quick wave his magic pours out of them and covers Kyle. She glows brilliantly for a single second before disappearing entirely.

"Go," Jameson commands. The door to the room opens seemingly on its own, then shuts.

"She's gone," Dad says, his eyes lingering on the door, the harsh fluorescent lights reflecting in his tears. Memory-me squirms in his arms, and that seems to snap Dad back to his mission. He blinks, meets Jameson's gaze, and says, "My turn."

"I'll be there for you," Jameson says. "When you deal with your new reality."

Dad smiles weakly. "I know."

Jameson takes a deep breath, gathering elven power in his pointer finger. The power trickles out of his skin, twisting into the shape of a key. Jameson presses it gently against Dad's temple, just over his left eye. Even though Dad saw it coming, even though Jameson's touch is clearly feather-soft, Dad flinches.

"It's all right," Jameson says with the same love and tenderness he showed me when we arrived at his heart home.

But Dad doesn't seem to hear him. His eyes lose focus; his mouth drops open.

"What's happening to him?" I ask.

"Your dad knew Adela would be suspicious of Kyle's sudden disappearance. She always had a way of finding out if her son was lying."

I think of how many times she gave me that stern look as a kid or threatened to use the Weight of Truth spell on me. She rarely had to go as far as using magic to get me to be honest.

"The only way to be sure she couldn't find out the real reason Kyle left and discover the Resistance was to wipe your father's memory. He forgot we ever created the group, and I implanted a memory of a massive fight in which Kyle declared she never wanted to be a parent and that your father had ruined her life."

Memory-Jameson turns the key and pulls it from Dad's skull. The elf lowers his shirt collar and places the key there, where a thin tendril wraps around his neck, making it a necklace hidden beneath the folds of fabric. Dad comes to, sucking in a breath. His head whips to the empty hospital bed, then back to Jameson.

"She's gone," he whispers. "Kyle left us."

Memory-Jameson swallows. "She did."

Dad's eyes wander down to me, sleeping softly in his arms, my tiny fists clenched tight even in my sleep.

The hospital door opens and suddenly Meema's there, in her usual denim-on-denim getup, her golden longhorn belt buckle shining brightly from her waist. My throat tightens seeing her so full of life, already smiling at me like she's known me for years.

"There's my grandso—" Her energy drops when she sees Dad's face. "Reggie?" She notices the empty bed, then glances around the room in confusion. "Where's Kyle?"

Dad doesn't say a word. He just steps toward Meema, passes memory-me to her, and walks out the door. My tiny little eyes are open now, watching Dad's retreating back. It was the first of hundreds, maybe thousands, of times I saw him walk away from me.

It all started on day one.

CHAPTER
ELEVEN

THE MEMORIES FADE AND WE'RE BACK IN THE LIBRARY. I FEEL NUMB, so many thoughts swirling through my head that I can't even register my boots back on solid ground. My parents were as shaped by the terrible forces of our magical world as I was. Even still, that doesn't change the outcome of how they treated me. My mom abandoned me physically, and my dad did the same, but emotionally. Just because they struggled, does that mean I have to forgive them?

Can I even forgive them?

But as the seconds tick on, I know it's not comfort I need right now. I need answers.

"What happened to Dad's plan to raise me? *Meema* did that. All he did was—" My brain floods with memories—Dad yelling at me the day I gained my magic, him laughing horribly any time one of my spells went haywire. And then—the hospital room. He held me lovingly in his arms, like a real dad should.

Why did he never do that again?

"What happened to him?" I croak.

"None of us anticipated just how broken your father would become, thinking Kyle left him," Jameson says.

My derisive laughter echoes through the library. "Oh, you couldn't *anticipate* it, huh? Okay then, you're off the hook."

"We were young and stupid," Jameson says flatly. "We wrongly assumed the love he felt for you would be enough to keep him afloat. But instead he rejected you. I think he saw you as a reminder of the woman who broke his heart. I tried so many times to reach him under all that anger, but nothing worked."

"*You* told him you'd help him through it." I can feel my anger building, pushing me to lash out.

"I promise you I did everything I could short of revealing what transpired. It would have threatened our entire mission." Finally, emotion reaches his voice. Regret, I think.

"Well, you didn't try hard enough, apparently," I say. A brief moment of hurt flashes across his face, and it feels good. "You let him succumb to his heartache and left me to deal with the damage he'd cause. Left me without a mother *and* a father."

Magicians are always so full of themselves. Unbelievable.

"What happened to my m—to Kyle?" I ask.

"Your mother came back once, six months after her initial departure," Jameson says.

"Why didn't she stay?" I ask, pain like a whole new knife blooming in my back at the realization that she left me not once, but twice.

"Her new Ancestral ally was a part of a resistance of their own. The majority of our magical ancestors don't want to interact with human- or magiciankind, but this one promised they could show her ways to change everything. She left, thinking she'd be back in another six months, but—" He shrugs, frowning. "—she was never heard from again."

I know I should feel bad for her, but I honestly don't have the capacity for that right now. I'm the one who had to deal with the monsters dad created, who had to find some way to go on each and every day living with the consequences of their decisions. And my heart is full worrying about Meema and whether or not her legacy is going to be that of a woman hellbent on power or one who truly did lead her life in service of others. Maybe that makes *me* the heartless one, not able to feel bad for Kyle even knowing she went missing while working for the Resistance. Regardless, it's where I'm at.

"I should tell you, I'm restoring your father's memories," Jameson says. "Have been, and will continue to do so, bit by bit. He'd like to speak with you. To apologize."

"Right," I say. "As if that will make up for everything."

"You have no obligation to forgive him."

"I know." It comes out more like a bark than a reply.

Truthfully, I might never be ready to face Dad again.

Two more days go by before Kenneth and Yamato reappear. Two days in which I keep from Ori everything Jameson shared with me about my parents. It's too soon. I need to process Jameson turning what I thought I knew about them upside down. Every time I think I need to talk it out with Ori, something snaps my mouth shut.

Luckily, seeing Bex's dads standing in the foyer with grins on their faces is the perfect distraction to get my mind off all my family issues.

"All right, let's get this party started!" Yamato is way more chipper than I feel.

"Maybe tone it down a little, babe," Kenneth says, giving him a gentle pat on the back. It strikes me how much more understated he is than his husband. To look at Yamato's ripped pants, ear studs, and eyeliner, then Kenneth's simple beige turtleneck, you'd think their paths would never cross. Unless Kenneth secretly likes mosh pits or Yamato goes to . . . I don't know, HR conventions?

But you could say the same about Ori and me, I guess. I'm flannel and muddy boots; Ori's skinny jeans and baggy cardigans. I guess it goes to show that all that really matters is how we connect.

Bex squeals from the second floor. "Dads! You're back!" She hops over the railing, shifts into a finch, then dives in front of her fathers before shifting back to get wrapped up in a hug. "Took you long enough."

Relief is written all over Bex's face. With Jameson coming home a couple days ago, she's had nothing to do but worry about when— or even if—her dads would come back. She stuck to her room all this time, while I've had Ori—and Jameson's revelations—to keep me occupied. With a pang, it hits me that I never once checked on her.

Some friend you are.

"Oh, I'm sorry," Yamato says, "did we not go through *five* senior members' questioning quickly enough for you?"

Bex cringes. "Five?"

Kenneth nods. "All together. They pulled out the big guns for us. Because of *you*, you little spitfire." He tugs his daughter into his side.

"I'd do more than spit fire if they hurt you."

"We're okay," Yamato says. "I was able to shift my thoughts. All they know is that as your father, I'm concerned that you backed out on the Guild."

"You can shape-shift *your thoughts*?" Ori asks.

Yamato's smirk could rival Ori's. "And my husband's. Thanks to our connection. What, you boys can't do that yet?"

Ori just rolls his eyes.

"We've got more than two decades on you," Kenneth says,

elbowing Yamato. "But your training starts today. Yamato and I were talking about the best place to start, and we decided you need a space of your own to practice in." Ori and I lock eyes. That's what we were hoping for, and it's a relief for something to go according to plan for once. "So we're going to guide you through creating your *own* heart home. It'd be tough for most magicians your age, but with your soulmate boost that had the power to wake up the Horde, I think we can walk you through it."

My stomach rolls at the mention of our unrestrained power, but Kenneth barrels on. "Your heart home will be the perfect place for you to hide if you're ever found by the Guild. Plus, you'll be able to explore your connection without impacting the rest of the world, so it'll be the safest place to contain your magic should any of your spells go awry."

"Not that anything will," Yamato adds.

"We can't promise that, Yamato."

Yamato shrugs and speaks out of the side of his mouth. "I'm *setting intention.*" He says it like he's reading from a self-help book.

"And I'm trying to give *realistic expectations,*" Kenneth replies.

Bex sidles up between Ori and me. "They've been on a relationship therapy kick lately, if you can't tell."

That makes Bex's dads both blush. "Sorry to make it so obvious," Kenneth says. They share a quick kiss before Yamato hollers, "Okay, let's get this show on the road."

He flips around and flings open the front door of the Resistance, that sourceless magical sunlight swirling beyond.

Footsteps echo through the foyer as Jameson joins us from the library.

"Where've you been?" Ori asks.

"Crafting a new book to add to our collective history," Jameson explains. "One that details the Guild questioning."

THE MAGIC YOU MAKE

"All right, then," I say, taking a deep breath and nodding toward the door. "Let's do this thing."

"We can't just hop through the portal," Jameson says. "Only because there isn't anywhere to go *to*. We first need to create your heart home. The name, however, makes it sound easier than it really is. People so often fool themselves about what's truly in their hearts. Look at humans. The vast majority think of themselves as the good guys, yet still they have the capacity to make monsters."

"Is this your version of a pep talk?" Ori asks, grimacing. "Because if you want to make me doubt myself before going into this thing, your plan is working."

Yamato laughs. "Where's Adela when you need her, right? If there was one thing she was good at, it was pep talks."

It feels like the air is sucked right out of the room.

"DAD!" Bex shouts.

How dare he talk about her like that? Like she's just off on a trip instead of murdered in cold blood.

"Oh my god, Nigel, I'm so sorry!" he says, fidgeting with his rings nervously. "I didn't mean anything by it. If anything, I was—"

"Don't dig it deeper," Kenneth says, and Yamato slams his lips shut.

Ori puts his hand in my back pocket and tugs me close. "You okay?"

"It's fine," I say, the words dead even to me.

Not as dead as Meema. Dead because of you.

No. Focus. Spells of the heart.

"Let's continue," I say, and thankfully Jameson dives into it even though everyone else is still looking at me like I might break down at any second.

"The beginning of this spell is the easy part," Jameson explains. "Not so different from elven concentration methods, actually. You need to have clear intention about what you want to do. Where you want to go. An environment that makes you feel completely safe. It can be inspired by a real place or somewhere you've never set foot before. Either way, it must feel like a place where you can be your truest self."

I don't need much. All I need is a place where I can ride and a farm with enough hay to feed horses for a lifetime.

"Envisioning that place tends to be the easiest part. Next, you have to conjure a complete picture of your heart that will be housed in this safe place. The good, the bad, all of it. Picture the person you are today, your strengths and your weaknesses, your successes *and* your faults. Then imagine the person you want to be, paired with that space you envisioned where you'd feel safe to make that transformation. Your heart will *become* that place."

Ori shakes his head. "But how do we make it real? How does it become somewhere we can be?"

"It's sort of like the opposite of a summoning spell," Kenneth says. "At least, that's what it felt like for me. Instead of bringing something to me on the wind, I had to sort of blow that wind out, from within here." Kenneth holds his hand over his chest. "Moving my heart to a physical space."

"Normally, this sort of spell would take years for someone to master," Jameson says. "Some never *can* land on a mental image that truly encompasses the ins and outs of their soul. But having a soulmate, someone connected to your heart who can feel your emotions, helps move the process along. With what we've seen you do, I'm sure you can handle it."

What he's seen us do. Like unleash the Horde? Though we also stopped the Knife, in ways my great-grandpa Barrett never could have. Who's to say we can't do this? And I have been reading up on elven breathing and meditation for over a decade. Thanks, Meema, for the homework, I guess.

"Craft the vision of your heart *together*," Kenneth says. "A vision that makes space for both of you. It's all about communication. You've each got to know what the other is feeling the entire time. I don't just mean tugging on your connection for phantom sensations of your partner's emotions. I mean you've got to be open and honest, at all times, *especially* when it's hardest. Share when you're frustrated with the other, when you're worried or nervous, when you're downright angry with them. If you keep those feelings bottled up, they'll corrupt the connection, weakening your magic. That goes for casting any spells together, not just this heart home."

"Consider the cracks in your relationship the weak points for all your magic to leak out," Yamato says.

"Right." Kenneth jumps back in. "Your connection needs to be as strong as possible to make this space."

Worms wiggle their way through my gut. I'm already keeping secrets from Ori. I haven't told him that I'm in contact with Jaleesa, or that I'm pretty sure I'm hearing the Knife's voice in my head. Just thinking about it makes the claw in my pocket flare with heat, and it takes everything in me not to jump.

"I don't think Ori has a hard time being honest," I say, trying to keep the attention off me.

"But you could work on not being so silent all the time."

He's just returning a gentle ribbing, but his words hit a sore spot. I *am* the one to keep my feelings more to myself, or to work them out inside first before saying things. And ever since Ori brought me back, I'm feeling my emotions stronger than ever. Does that mean I'm going to have to constantly be giving him a play-by-play of my guilt directly as I'm feeling it? That feels less like open communication and more like never getting any privacy. Like I'm a prized pig constantly getting sized up at the county fair.

"So." Bex looks between us eagerly. "Have at it!"

"Um . . ." Sweat beads on my upper lip. This tender moment with my soulmate seems so intimate. It feels *weird* that everyone is watching.

"We just do this right here?" I ask.

Kenneth nods. "I know it's not ideal. But we can just—" He twirls his finger in the air, indicating for everyone to turn around. They follow suit, but this isn't exactly the privacy I imagined.

I let out a breath. "So . . ."

But Ori's already on it, digging through his backpack until he pulls out Woody and Buzz Lightyear figurines from *Toy Story.*

"The cowboy I get, but do you think of yourself as a space hero?"

"Ha-ha," Ori deadpans. "It's all I could come up with in a pinch."

Ori coats the toys in his pink magic, handing me Buzz while he holds Woody. "You're a piece of my heart," he says, uncharacteristically bashful. His pale cheeks get splotchy with his blush, and it may be the sweetest thing I've ever seen in my entire life. "So I think it makes sense if I hold you and you hold me."

"That's great thinking, Ori," Kenneth encourages, and both he and Bex are peeking behind their backs with puppy-dog eyes. I guess mushiness runs in the family. "That will help a lot. And the easiest way to trigger your connection, as you've already seen, is through touch."

Ori places a hand on my shoulder. My fingers pulse bright gold as pleasant tingles gallop full force through my stomach.

"Good," Kenneth says. "In time, we will teach you how to trigger that reaction without physical touch."

Ori looks at me with his perfect smirk and whispers, "But I signed up for the connection *with* my hands all over you."

Those tingles are at full-on stampede levels now.

"What was that?" Kenneth asks.

"Nothing," Ori says, winking at me.

"I'm sure," Yamato says, and I have a sinking suspicion he knows exactly what Ori said. He's turned back around, any semblance of privacy out the door. "Anyway, the biggest hurdle for us at first was to get over the engrained instinct to preserve magical energy." Yamato puffs his chest proudly. "So far, Kenneth and I have yet to run out."

"Humble," Ori says.

"That's right," Yamato says. "We're two queer Japanese American men, bouncing between a human world that tries to tear us down for who we are and who we love and a magical world full of monsters that try to kill us. So yeah, I'm going to boast about the powers that have kept me going all these years."

Ori smirks harder, impressed by the clapback. "Good point."

"As I was saying," Yamato continues, "you've got to fight that inkling to preserve your power. You've got an unending well that will flow between the two of you, and you can tap into it as often as you want."

"That goes back to creating your heart home," Jameson says. "You need to believe your magic can stretch further and perform greater feats than it ever has before. So give it a try." He motions for us to get on with it, like it's as simple as that.

That's the annoying thing about new spells. Every magician has to come up with the way to make their magic do what they want it to on their own, through intent, focus, and confidence. Imitation of others' spellcraft can be successful, although with this spell so focused on who we are, that's not going to work.

But with Ori's palm on my shoulder, I do feel boosted. My hands glow gold, his pink, just like the effigies we hold. We're always strongest when we blend our powers, so it makes the most sense for me to cast a spell on his bewitched effigies.

"What if I create a Magic Magnet?" I suggest. It's the natural counterpart of a summoning spell. Summoning spells call an item from a known location to a magician; the Magic Magnet pulls *you*. "It sort of creates this tug in you toward whatever it is you need most, even when you're not sure what it is." Whenever I had questions about elven magic but didn't know which book in Meema's library might have answers, she'd bark, *"Quit your bellyaching. Just cast your Magic Magnet, darlin'."*

What if any of those books showed her how to cast a spell against the entire Guild? What if she was feeding Alister the tools to use against magicians all this time?

Shut up, shut up, SHUT UP!

My hands clench into fists, I grind my teeth. Now is *not* the time to let this demonic asshole take control of my thoughts.

"Nigel?"

Ori squeezes my shoulder, the electricity of his touch enough to make my fingers uncurl.

"Sorry," I say, taking a shaky breath. "Just nervous. Like I was saying, for the magnet, I could cast the spell, and we'll picture this home of ours. Our heart home. I know it doesn't technically exist yet, but—"

Ori smiles, his confidence in me passing through our connection. "I get it. When we dream it together, our hearts will lead us to it."

The spell is easy, and I've done it countless times, always taking inspiration from my magical tool of choice, my lasso. To keep it simple, I'd craft a tiny string and create a mini-lasso to loop around my finger, fueling it with intent to pull me toward my heart's desire. So now, I pull my magic into two tiny strings, looping them at the ends and tying them around the wrists of our effigies. When my magic touches them, my gold and Ori's pink power flare bright before shifting into the shining abalone color of us.

"Now," I say, locking eyes with Ori. "Think of home. *Our* home. The perfect place for you and me. Picture what that could be."

Ori swallows, his Adam's apple bobbing. I know he thinks this moment is just as tender as I do. More intimate than anything we've done yet. He places his hand in mine and laces our fingers together. As one, we close our eyes, and my thoughts fill with dreams of what our life could be: the two of us together, somewhere with lots of land—enough outdoor space for me to raise animals, enough indoor space for him to keep his collection of toys. This feels so right. This feels so *us*.

Warmth builds, my magic pumping with each beat of my heart. I can feel my thoughts of this place coalescing, until a pressure builds underneath my skin. It doesn't hurt, exactly, but it's a wanting, a hunger, a need to get out. A need to spread this feeling of love.

But the millisecond before a brilliant abalone beam of light bursts from my chest, doubt crashes through my mind like a bull let out of its pen. I hear the echoes of the Horde chanting "Heal. Awake," see Meema preparing to use the claw just before Alister stabs her, feel the flare of anger burning inside me as Guild members chase after us on Mount Rainier, feel the despair as I watch Cullingmates sapped of their power and Meema watching on as if nothing is wrong.

Nothing will ever be right again.

I feel such a certainty of despair at the exact moment my power cascades out of me. My eyes snap open, watching that beam of abalone light join with another coming straight out of Ori's chest. Swirling together, our power shoots for the portal. To where, exactly? We can't know.

But Ori's ready to find out.

"Come on," he says, pulling me behind him, his stride so sure where mine is wobbly. "Let's go home."

CHAPTER
TWELVE

WHEN ORI'S SNEAKERS HIT SOLID GROUND, HE FINDS HIMSELF standing in the middle of a meadow. A gentle breeze blows through tall grass. Purple, yellow, red, and blue flowers create bursts of color all the way up to a copse of tall pine trees a hundred yards away. The trunks stretch into the sky, blocking the view beyond, but Ori suspects that the magical border marking the limits of their heart home isn't too far past the tree line. Movement in the shadows catches his eye: a doe and her baby grazing, completely undisturbed by the arrival of Ori and his . . . boyfriend? Does he call him that now? They haven't really had that talk yet, but it might bring down some of the pressure of calling Nigel his soulmate.

It's not quite been two weeks since he truly met Nigel (that time as toddlers doesn't count), and he still wouldn't quite call what he feels for the cowboy "love." But Ori can't deny he feels more connected to Nigel than he has to anyone before. Maybe the L-word isn't too far off. Either way, this place was created through the magic of their hearts, and it's . . . perfect.

Ori smiles softly, hoping this peaceful entry is a sign of the positive change they're going to bring to their worlds, both ordinary and magical.

"Whooee," Nigel breathes. It sends tingles through Ori's stomach. He loves it when Nigel acts so stereotypically Southern. Not that he'd go on about that, in case Nigel got a big head, but still. The elf's wide eyes are trained in the direction opposite Ori's, and they swim with tears. Ori follows his gaze to a tiny log cabin with a thin trail of smoke curling from the chimney. He squeezes Nigel's—his *boyfriend's*—hand, motioning toward the house. "Let's go see."

Nigel only nods, and Ori can feel something nagging at him. He tries to lean in to their connection for some clarity on what's overwhelming his soulmate. But the further he leans in, the more he's kept out, a boundary blocking Nigel's heart. Ori figures it's best not to press. Nigel might just need some space. Even soulmates deserve that kind of autonomy. Maybe Nigel has doubts. After everything they've been through, Ori wouldn't blame Nigel if he's waiting for the other shoe to drop. Well, boot.

The long grass swishes against his side as Ori pulls Nigel behind him. It tickles, and that makes him laugh, which feels so good compared to constant uncertainty. Nigel eventually follows suit. Every step makes the sprite feel more and more at ease, his steps getting lighter and faster, eager to see the heart home of their creation.

Their footsteps clunk against the pinewood cabin porch as they race to the front door. Nigel pushes and it swings forward effortlessly, like it's been waiting to welcome them home.

"We made this?" Nigel asks, his throat clogged with emotion.

Ori smirks. "We did."

It's not huge. A single open space with pinewood floors. Directly ahead is the kitchen—just a sink and a camping stove, really—behind which sits a large window that looks out on the sunny meadow. The window panes are cracked open to let that gentle breeze pass through.

To the left is a king-size bed, made up with gray sheets and a red flannel duvet, all tucked in cozily and framed by a wooden headboard made of interlocking branches. Along the right wall—flanking the gently crackling fireplace in the center—are empty shelves, waiting to be filled with Ori's effigies. He catches the glint of a blade and a small block of silvery-pink sprite wood, ready and waiting in case he wants to make one from scratch.

"This is ours," Ori says. He feels it in his bones, a pleasant buzzing that grounds him. He belongs here.

"It's perfect," Nigel says.

Ori nods. "It is."

As if compelled by a Magic Magnet, the boys turn to each other at the same time, their lips meeting. Both drop the effigies they'd been clutching this entire time, neither caring about the loud clunk the toys make as they clatter against the floor.

Ori doesn't know how much time passes, or whose breath is whose, or whether he puts his tongue against Nigel's or vice versa, or whether any of it even matters. This place is *theirs*. Forever. They can use it to grow their connection until the day they die.

Which better not be soon. They already got too close to death. Ori still isn't really sure how he brought Nigel back. Any tales his mom told him of magicians resurrecting dead loved ones always ended up as horror stories, the formerly dead just a husk of the person they once were. But Nigel says he doesn't feel all that different. Ori's so relieved he pushes harder into the kiss, grateful to feel Nigel here, warm and whole.

Footsteps make the two of them pull apart. Jameson, Kenneth, Yamato, and Bex have arrived.

"Way to ruin a nice moment," Ori quips.

"We wanted to give you your first moments here alone," Kenneth says sincerely. "But we had to make sure everything went smoothly and that you could find your way back."

Bex looks around in awe. "This space is adorable. True love can really make some gorgeous property."

There's the L-word, dropped before he's ready. He glances at Nigel, whose face blares with a blush. Best to just move on like *love* wasn't mentioned.

"Yeah, it'd be hard to beat this place," Ori says.

Yamato looks skeptical. "I don't know. At least my heart home has a bathroom. What are you supposed to do—go in the woods? You made a home where you have to wipe with leaves?"

"Okay," Nigel says. "Could we not talk about wiping right now?"

"Agreed," Jameson says. "Nigel, your heart home is breathtaking." He takes in the cabin, his eyes lingering on the view out of the window. "Your grandmother would be proud. I can practically hear Adela saying you're a testament to Barrett power."

Ori feels Nigel's shift in mood like a slap to the face. He doesn't even have time to breathe his soulmate's name before glass shatters as the window is blasted apart by sickly green magic. *Depraved* magic. The monster responsible cackles in the meadow. Its mottled, rotting skin is out of place within the beautiful landscape they created; the grass around its cracked and bloody feet has turned dead and gray.

Ori turns to Nigel, whose eyes are wide in fear. "How— How is a Depraved here?" Nigel's hand hovers over his pocket, the one where he keeps the claw. His face is twisted in pain, his fingers twitching like he's debating tearing the old relic from his jeans.

The Knife. Maybe it's affecting Nigel more than he let on.

Bex shifts into her black-coated unicorn form. "Kick ass first, ask questions later." She gallops out the cabin door, her dads and Jameson following right behind.

Nigel's mouth opens and closes like a fish. He's shocked. Too shocked. Nothing like the Nigel Ori saw in the Culling. That Nigel would see a threat and rush into battle with a lasso around his arm and a cheesy shout of *Yup.*

"Come on," Ori says, grabbing Nigel's forearm and tugging him toward the door.

"It's in us," Nigel says. "Our hearts made this."

Ori snaps back, sucker punched by the elf's words. "Nigel. That's not it."

"How else could we do what we did?" Nigel asks, lips trembling. "How else did we wake the Horde? How else could we set off a chain of events that got so many people killed?"

Bile rises in Ori's throat. Maybe Nigel's right. Their magic *has* created monsters. Within the Guild was one thing, but here? Inside this place made from what's in their hearts?

RAAAAAAAAAWR!

An angry bellow snaps both of them back to the moment. Through the blasted window, Ori sees Yamato—in the shape of an unnaturally giant grizzly—try to tear the Depraved apart with his massive claws. Every swipe of his paw moves through the monster as though there's nothing there. But there has to be, because the streak of green lightning that pours from the Depraved's bloody fingers definitely singes Yamato's fur. The goblin roars again as the smell of burning flesh coats the air.

"Great-Grandpa Barrett. Even he can't stop what's inside of me." Nigel stares, wide-eyed, lost to his despair.

It's no use trying to tug him into the fray. Nigel will just get himself killed. "Snap out of it, cowboy," Ori calls as he sprints to the door. "That's not your grandpa."

Nigel makes no indication that he's registered Ori's words. He just stares as the Depraved moves in for another attack.

Ori races out and around the cabin to Kenneth's side. Bright white power lights up the air nymph's hands, and with a snap of his fingers the formerly clear blue sky is covered in ominous gray clouds. The meadow goes dark as night, and rain lashes them from above. Ori's cardigan whips fiercely in the building wind as lightning cracks directly over their heads, the bolts of electricity headed straight for the Depraved.

But Kenneth's magic has no more effect on the monster than Yamato's claws. The lightning barrels straight through its middle, but the monster just tilts its head back and releases a high-pitched, maniacal cackle loud enough to be heard even over the thunder.

"You cannot kill me. Not without killing yourself!" the monster bellows, its hate-filled eyes glaring past Ori, focusing through the destroyed window on Nigel. "You'll never be rid of me!"

Then, inexplicably, the Depraved reaches out a decaying hand and grabs the lightning. *Holds it in place.* The monster takes a deep breath and then, with a fierce exhale, sends its own power racing back up the lightning bolt. Rotten-green light arcs across the sky, saturating the gray clouds until they're all glowing the same ghastly color. Everyone and everything is tinged by the hue.

Kenneth's magic sputters out, the nymph staring in shock as his wind quits on a dime. Everything is silent. No birds chirping, no swish of the gently swaying grass. Then—

BOOM!

Columns of green light catapult into the ground, sending dirt and grass flying. One strikes right beside Bex and sends her tumbling tail over hooves until she shifts into a hawk, taking flight to dodge new streaks of light. Jameson grabs Ori's wrist and screams, "BLINK!"

Ori doesn't need telling twice. But first—

He blinks back into the cabin, right next to Nigel, who still hasn't budged beyond his lips trembling as he mumbles to himself.

"Nigel," Ori says, wrapping his hand around the elf's arm. There's no telltale buzzing when their skin makes contact. Nigel doesn't seem to register Ori at all.

Kenneth, Yamato, and Bex burst into the cabin just as a streak of the Depraved's power blasts through the roof, decimating the bed. The trio huddles against the opposite wall.

"We have to go," Kenneth shouts as he touches his husband's shoulder and triggers a portal with a quick whistle. "If we're in your heart home when it's destroyed, we're all dead."

Now it's Ori's turn to freeze. It seems unreal that this beautiful home they created is crashing down around them, their field and forest devoured by green flames.

"Ori," Jameson urges. "Go!"

The sprite lets the magician pull them along. With a grunt and a tug, Nigel stumbles into Ori—and together they trip through the portal and away from the short-lived paradise of their hearts.

CHAPTER
THIRTEEN

Bᴇx's ᴄʀʏ ᴏꜰ ʀᴇʟɪᴇꜰ ᴇᴄʜᴏᴇs ᴛʜʀᴏᴜɢʜ ᴛʜᴇ ᴇɴᴛʀʏᴡᴀʏ ᴀs ᴏᴜʀ
ꜰᴇᴇᴛ slam on the creaky floorboards of Jameson's heart home.
I know I should feel relieved, too. But I can't stop thinking about
the Depraved in a place built on our connection. How could such
hate exist there? With magic in our blood, we shouldn't even be
able to make Depraved in the first place. If our magic is taken from
us, then yeah, it can happen, but . . . Depraved creation is a human
thing to do. Like Dad. God, am I taking after him all these years
later?

But no. I'm worse than Dad, aren't I? He didn't have a Depraved
inside of him. Not like I do.

That has to be it. A Depraved was in our heart home because
somehow, deep inside of me, the fucking Knife is not just in
my mind.

It's in my heart.

"What just happened?" Bex asks. "*How* did that happen? A heart home isn't even really a place. The Depraved shouldn't be able to get in." Everyone turns to me with questioning looks.

"I don't know!" I snap, resentment making my heart race, making my palms sweat as I curl my hands into fists. "Maybe it's a soulmate thing." I glare right at Bex. "You wouldn't understand."

Her nostrils flare as her mouth forms a thin line, but I have bigger things to worry about.

You cannot kill me. Not without killing yourself! You'll never be rid of me!

It's what the Depraved said. No, it's what *the Knife* said—I know it in my heart. Clearly its energy, its spirit, or whatever the fuck that was, is strong enough to make an actual appearance. At least in a world created by what's inside me.

The claw in my pocket flares with heat. The heat of vengeance, of burning anger, of smoldering hate. I feel it all, emotions that aren't mine but somehow perfectly register.

I'm going to be sick.

I race for the second-floor bathroom, my boots heavy on the stairs.

"Nigel!" Ori calls. "Wait."

"No!" is all I'm able to muster before I slam the door behind me and thrust my head in the toilet. Everything in my stomach pours out.

You can't just blame this on the Knife. Your actions killed dozens of magicians long before Ori brought you back. This is you.

It's true. Kenneth, Yamato, Jameson, Bex, the entire Resistance, took us in, invited Ori and me to help them make change through our connection, and that's never going to happen. I'm not good enough for that.

I'm evil.

Jameson said it himself. You're really living up to the Barrett name.

Because that's the only way it'd be so easy to become a tool for the Depraved, isn't it? Monsters feed other monsters. It's why demons and Depraved are attracted to one another. The Knife couldn't live within me if something monstrous wasn't already inside of me. In my blood.

Dad is a monster, literally creating a Depraved with his hatred for me. Mom's a monster, abandoning her newborn son. My grandfather was a monster, turning his back on Dad when he failed the Culling.

That just leaves Meema. The more time I have to think about it, the more likely it seems that she did have something to do with the Culling.

I pick my head up as a major light bulb goes off.

No. A bell.

Jaleesa's been searching for clues. I need to know what she's found out about the Culling, even though dread threatens to make me throw up again if she's found any evidence linking Meema to the unnecessary violation of thousands of magicians.

My body reacts before I even know what I'm doing. My hands glow gold and I let my power pool into the cracks between the door and the wall, filling it so that no sound can get in or out. I don't need anyone overhearing me. I reach into my pocket, where Jaleesa's fae bell has been waiting all this time.

The little fae bell glows faintly purple in my palm. It's barely bigger than a bracelet charm, looking too much like the bell in the Taco Bell logo. The thought makes me laugh, loud, and it's like a pressure valve releases, allowing me to let go of some of my anxiety.

I can fix this. I can get things back on track.

Latching onto that bit of confidence, I ring the bell. The sound is quiet, gentle, a soft tap on a glass. A purple drop of fae magic beads on the bottom of the bell's tiny ringer, growing bigger until it drops into the white hexagon tiles of the floor. The tiles ripple out, like a drop in a pond, making me jump back. But the ground stays solid, my boots firmly on the ground. Even still, a figure pushes up from the ripples.

"Jaleesa."

She's standing in front of me, but she's hazy. Like one of those social media filters where it seems like she's filmed on an old-school camcorder. Still, it's so much more than the first time we spoke when she was just a voice in my head.

"Somebody's magic is getting stronger," I say. It's only been ten days since we last spoke, and her skills are already demonstrably better. I can't help the flare of jealousy that she's having these successes when my magic almost killed every person I care about.

Jaleesa doesn't gloat, just gives a tight-lipped smile. "Thanks. I've been practicing. Trying to perfect the spells that could help us out with—" She stops, her forehead furrowing. "Whatever it is we're doing."

"Have you found any leads on a Guild-wide spell yet?" I ask hurriedly, not willing to waste time explaining *again* that the Culling isn't needed.

Jaleesa shakes her head. "Not really. I've found out lots of ways magicians could cast against groups of people, but nothing specific about spells that have been cast recently. I need to find someone involved. I need to get into Alister's office, but it'd be so obvious if I just asked to visit. You only go to the Baumbachs' when the Baumbachs invite you."

"How did your questioning go? Do they suspect anything?"

"No. Alister made sure they didn't pry too deep." She grimaces. "Mom too. I can't tell if she's working with him on this mystery spell. She's closer with him now than ever before."

Of course the questioning was manipulated. I'd like to begrudge Pallavit and Alister for pretending everything's fair and transparent in the Guild, but their corruption actually helped me out for once. I wouldn't get anywhere on trying to end the Culling if Jaleesa was imprisoned for sparing my life back in the claw cavern.

"It's only been a week and a half and I'm losing hope of ever getting anything done," I say. "Ori and I, we're tainted." No. That's not right. "*I'm* tainted. And no good can come from my magic anymore."

"Nigel?" Jaleesa looks genuinely concerned, so different from how she looked at me as one of my most vocal competitors during the Culling.

The shame burns deep in my gut, sweat breaking out on my forehead, my cheeks flushing. I think back to our log cabin, our heart home, crashing down around us, decimated by the evil that lives within me. Even if Ori and I are fated to be soulmates, our connection isn't strong enough to cure me of this. If everyone in my family has only ever looked after themselves at the expense of others, I may be just as fated for destruction.

It's in my blood.

That's when a memory hits me in the head as hard as a *rampaging bull.*

I barged into Meema's study so many times, catching her journaling. I asked her what she wrote about once, and she said, *"When your thoughts won't stop stamping around like a rampaging bull, sometimes you just got to get 'em out."*

I never thought I'd open that journal. Meema's secrets were hers to keep. But now she's gone, and Jaleesa and I aren't any closer to answers. Meema's words could show me if she really was a monster, keeping the Culling going when it was never needed. Or maybe her writing will clear her name and show we aren't so monstrous after all.

"I need to get to the ranch."

CHAPTER
FOURTEEN

Bex can't sleep. She can't stop replaying what Nigel said. How it slipped off his tongue with such heartless indifference. *"Maybe it's a soulmate thing. You wouldn't understand."*

Usually sifting through her record collection helps calm her thoughts, but no matter how high she turns the volume on her headphones, neither Stevie Nicks nor Joan Jett nor Yoko Ono can drown out Nigel's voice in her head.

It figures. The entire Culling and every day since have been all about him. Him and his connection to Ori. Sure, she'd signed up to help the boys discover what it's all about. She recognized so much in them from what her dads told her of their own power. She really thought teaching Nigel and Ori to lean in to love could help end the ruthlessness within the Guild. But now? Nigel is just as ruthless as any other magician.

As if it's *her* fault she hasn't met her soulmate. Nigel struck *gold* finding his soulmate in the very first days he spent with other magicians. He has no idea how *rare* this is: Her dads haven't encountered another pair of fated magicians in all their time together. Before Nigel and Ori, Yamato and Kenneth only knew they weren't the lone soulmates ever to have existed thanks to a scant few texts with passing mentions of love magic.

And for all that the Resistance preaches about love, the *second* she brought another matched couple into their lives, her own *parents* brushed her to the side and focused all their energy on the boys. As if *she* hasn't committed her whole life to the Resistance cause. As if her help means nothing, even though prior to the boys' arrival it had been *Bex* who could remember the Culling wasn't necessary, and no one else.

They haven't even offered to help her create her own heart home. Why is that?

It only takes a moment for her doubts to fill in the blank.

Because they don't think you're strong enough. Because Nigel and Ori might be able to save the world, and all you can do is shift into a pretty little unicorn.

"Aargh!" She bolts up, throwing her door open—to go where, exactly, she doesn't know. As her feet carry her down the stairs, her fingers shift to claws that leave gouge marks in the wallpaper.

Bex instantly feels guilty. It's not fair to take her anger out on Jameson's heart home. The elf is just as hopelessly single as she is.

"Wait a minute." Bex's words fill the silence as a realization hits her.

She isn't the only one without a soulmate.

She flies—literally, shifting into a canary to zip to where she knows she'll find the trusty elf mentor: his library. Sure enough, he sits on a tufted sofa, flipping through one of his spelled histories of the Resistance. Bex shifts into human form in an excited silver burst.

"Bex," Jameson says, not even glancing up at her sudden appearance. "You're up late."

"Couldn't sleep," she says. She's startled to realize she's out of breath, even though she only flew through a room and a half.

Jameson turns a page and asks, "What can I help you with?"

"I—" But Bex stops short, her spirits popped like that time she missed out on a limited-edition Griff vinyl. How do you bring up your lifelong singledom without sounding like a hopeless loser?

"Can I venture a guess?" Jameson softly shuts his book and turns to Bex with kind eyes. "I'd imagine you're still thinking about what Nigel said this afternoon. I believe it was about you not understanding what it's like to have a soulmate."

Bex sighs. "What are you, a mind reader?"

Jameson shakes his head. "You were visibly upset."

"That's even worse."

"You don't need to be ashamed of your feelings. I'd have a hard time not taking that personally myself."

Bex realizes she's hungry for his next answer—hungrier than she's been for anything else in her life. "How did you do it? How did you find your place in a Resistance that seems to prioritize the couples over everyone else?"

Jameson motions to the sofa across from him, and Bex practically leaps on top of it.

"We didn't start this way," Jameson says. "This Resistance began with me and Nigel's father, Reggie. Two best friends, devastated when one of us couldn't continue on in the magical world. Our goal from the start was to see how magicless members could remain in the Guild, even before we discovered the Culling isn't necessary at all."

Bex's heart skips a beat. "You remember?"

"Sadly, no." Jameson holds up the book in his lap. "But you've caught me in the middle of a refresher. Our little stitched reminders lead me to this story every time I stay here. Funny, I remember picking this book up—hundreds of times after all these years—but never what's inside."

"I really wish you did. I'm a broken record around you guys."

Jameson smiles. "I'd say that means you're already on the right track."

"Look, I know I can transform into a parrot, but I'm not just going to squawk that one fact back to all of you until we reach our goal."

"Well, then." Jameson lifts a steaming mug of tea from the coffee table between them and takes a sip. "You've got to find your strengths, then think about how those unique characteristics can serve the overall mission. Look around you." Bex takes in the thousands of books lining the shelves. "I use my way with stories to fill this library with information that could be helpful. When we first discovered the Culling was unnecessary, I recorded it in these books page by page with the help of Reggie and Kyle, Nigel's mother. What are your strengths, Bex?"

Her mind goes blank. "I don't know."

"You have plenty," Jameson says. "Once you see in yourself what I see, your role will be clear."

A floorboard creaks behind Bex. She turns to find Nigel hovering in the space between the drawing room and library.

Great. Not only is Nigel the last person she wants to be around right now, but he's overheard her talking about how insignificant she feels in the shadow of his *soulmate* connection.

"I guess that's my cue," Bex mutters.

"You don't have to go," Nigel says. "I didn't mean to interrupt."

"Then what did you come here for?" she snaps.

"I just had some questions for Jameson." Nigel looks at his boots. Does he ever take them off? It's like he's paid for the cowboy aesthetic. "I need to get to the ranch."

"Sounds to me like you *did* mean to interrupt, then." Bex stands and shoulders her way past Nigel, avoiding his eyes. For a split second she wonders if she's being too harsh but thinks better of it.

Nigel clearly isn't concerned about her place in the Resistance. So she's going to figure that out on her own.

CHAPTER
FIFTEEN

Laurel's hands *still* won't stop shaking. She's tried brewing calming teas from spelled plants, but none have helped. Nothing can soothe her churning stomach; it goes way beyond butterflies, more like a swarm of locusts gnawing at her insides. It only gets worse each time she thinks of the Guild members lost during the Culling. She'd met so many of them as guests at her family estate, but none of them will visit again.

A hole has been left in their wake. As she walks into the training grounds forest, Laurel silently vows to fill that hole. She'll be strong enough for a dozen Guild members. And she'll do it on her own—she'll prove she doesn't need to be like Nigel and Ori to unlock her potential. She and Jaleesa *do* have their own special bond, but there's no way they can walk the same path as the boys. She can't. She can't cause any more damage, can't become any more of an embarrass-ment to her father, can't become a monster.

Her shaky wrist starts to warm. Along with all the other

apprentices who succeeded in the Culling, Laurel had the five-pointed star of the Guild spelled onto her skin when she was inducted. A warmth spreads through her body from the tattoo on her wrist to her heart, letting her know that someone is in danger.

The call fills her with so much pride for the Guild. It's just what she needs to chase the faces of the dead from her mind. How could an organization that helps people ever be bad? How could any of her actions be bad, if she feels this empathy for a human in need who she's never even met?

As the warmth fades, it's replaced by an urgent tug toward Dispatch. She swings up from the training grounds to the tenth floor, slower than usual. Until recently she could ascend four, five, six levels with one vine. Only now, she doesn't trust herself. She takes it floor by floor, sweaty with exertion by the time she gets to Dispatch. Exhausted. Not a good sign when she's supposed to head into a mission.

The tug from her Guild mark leads her to the nymph-enchanted fountain that will display her assignment, but she stops short when she sees the magician waiting there.

Lyra. Ori's mom. How the sprite made it out of questioning is beyond Laurel's comprehension. It's so clear that she must be helping her son somehow, even if her memories didn't reveal any interactions with Ori since the Culling. She's one of the last people Laurel wants to work with, but the Guild forbids reassignments. One, because it wastes valuable time; two, because petty squabbles mean nothing when lives are on the line. Regardless of what the Guild says, Laurel knows she should be on the lookout for suspicious behavior with Lyra.

"Laurel," Lyra says in disinterested acknowledgment. The sprite gives a gentle nod of her head toward the fountain. It shows a Depraved attacking a girl who looks an awful lot like Jaleesa: South Asian, around their age, with the same high cheekbones and button nose. The girl's long black hair flies behind her as she runs from the monster in a panic. Laurel's chest tightens, her lungs unable to get enough air. Is this some cruel joke from the Guild? Some test of her will? If it's a test, Laurel knows already that she's failed, because the scene before her sends her heart into overdrive.

"Let's go!" she shouts. She sprints to the banister, ready to fling herself over the edge, but just before she jumps an arm appears around her waist.

"Let me," Lyra says. Her tone is even and confident, but something squirms inside Laurel. She feels *seen*. She's sure Lyra can tell how tired she is—and her father always warned Laurel never to let anyone see her falter.

Laurel doesn't have time to worry about it, because one moment her feet are on the marble of the tenth floor and the next they're firmly on the entry hall platform. Lyra pulls a small wooden figure out of her pocket and coats it in pink magic. With a blink-blurred hand movement, she says, "Take us," and a portal opens.

A pang strikes Laurel's heart at the sight of the portal—conjured without beautiful lyrics like those Jaleesa would sing. She misses that. She misses the dynamic she and her girlfriend used to have. But if she can show Jaleesa how she truly does care about others, how she entered the Guild to save lives, Laurel thinks she might be able to connect with the fae again.

And so, Laurel dives through the magical doorway. Normally, the purple swirl of a portal comforts her, fills her with energy, makes her ready for battle. This time, as she and Lyra are transported to their rescue mission, Laurel's heart hammers in her chest. Worry consumes her. Every second their journey takes is one second less to save Jaleesa. *No.* The victim.

The moment her shoes hit sidewalk, she takes off running. It's midday in whatever part of America they're in, nearly identical houses bordering a park that this Jaleesa look-alike was probably taking a jog through. A jog that turned into a run for her life as a Depraved set its sickly green eyes on her and now tries to kill her. It cackles with glee every time the girl shrieks, soaking in her fear. Feeding off it.

That's the thing about human hate and the deathly magic it creates. It doesn't need big flashy scenery. More often than not, it occurs in a dull place just like this. Somewhere in this suburban neighborhood, someone or—more likely—multiple people let their anger fester, let it pollute their home and swell into a living, breathing thing.

"Jaleesa!" Laurel's cry pierces the air.

Lyra blinks beside her. "Laurel," she says, clipped. "Get it together. That's not Jaleesa."

The sprite disappears and reappears a millisecond later, blinking in between the Depraved and the runner. With the Depraved distracted, Jaleesa's near-twin runs without looking back, racing out of the park. The tightness in Laurel's chest eases. This is what the Guild is all about. Saving people.

It's time she get in on the action.

Lyra, glowing effigy in hand, freezes the monster in place. It still has use of its mouth, its grating voice chanting curses that call bugs up from the grass. Ants, spiders, beetles, roaches swarm toward Lyra, their movement so fast and fierce that Laurel's ears flood with the menacing clicks of their tiny legs and pincers.

Lyra blinks again, trying to shake off the insects climbing up her body. But every time her feet hit the ground, more latch onto her. From her tight-lipped grimace, Laurel knows they're biting, scratching, clawing into the sprite's skin.

With the Depraved's back to her, Laurel realizes this is her time to strike. She calls her power to her hands, relishing the beautiful, plant-inspired green of life that lights her fingers—so different from the sickly, rotting green of death and the Depraved. But still her hands shake.

"Don't. Show. Weakness," Laurel whispers.

She summons a bamboo spear from the ground, it launches through the grass, and—*YES!*—she catches it. She takes a deep breath. If she can just kill this monster, she can prove to herself and every magician out there that she's meant to be in the Guild. That she only did what she had to in order to preserve the organization and protect humans from the evils they create.

Planting her feet, Laurel hoists the spear over her shoulder, aims, and throws.

Only, her hands shake with nerves she can't control. Her spear flies crooked, sailing right over the Depraved's head . . .

And impaling Lyra straight through her chest. The projectile knocks Lyra back until the bamboo tip embeds in the grass behind her.

Bile burns Laurel's throat. She can't have another life on her hands.

The Depraved takes advantage of the moment, sending its cursed insects to swarm the sprite's body where she's pinned to the ground, screaming through the pain. The monster looms over her, taking deep breaths of Lyra's fear in what are surely her last moments.

But with a quick burst of green magic, Laurel makes the grass beneath the monster's feet grow so suddenly that the Depraved stumbles. With another blast of power, the grass pushes the monster forward, hard and fast, to impale it right through the neck on the same spear holding Lyra in place. The monster crumbles to bones; the bugs disintegrate with their master. Rotted remains and insect husks rain down on Lyra's still-struggling body.

"Lyra!" Laurel runs over to the woman, whose breathing now comes in ragged, gurgling gasps. Blood dribbles down her chin. Laurel doesn't need a spell to know Lyra is on the brink of death.

She snaps her fingers, and with a green blaze of light, thick tendrils of ivy burst from the ground. They wrap around Lyra's limbs and lift her up, bamboo spear and all. Laurel presses a thumb to her

Guild mark. It activates the fae enchantment that lets her summon a portal to the organization.

"GUILD! NOW!" she barks, and a purple portal springs to life.

One more snap and Laurel's ivy throws Lyra through the magic door, Laurel racing right behind. *Please, please, please let her be alive.* Portal magic is healing, but it can't bring anyone back from the dead. Laurel exhales a hurricane-force sigh as Lyra's nicks and cuts from the demonic insects seal shut one by one. The spear pops out of Lyra's chest and is lost to the ethereal void as her skin starts to knit back together.

The portal moves fast, though, and before the healing magic can finish its work, Lyra lands on the entry platform in a crumpled heap. Blood still trickles from the wound, and Laurel wonders how much Lyra's already lost. Even one more drop could be too much.

Laurel tries to conjure any number of the healing plants she's been trained to craft all her life. But she's tapped out. Too much magic used in too little time. Not to mention the nerves and doubt and guilt seeping through her body make it difficult to pull on reserves she knows should be in there.

"We need a healer!" Laurel shouts, and to the Guild's credit, at least a dozen magicians from the floors above spring into action. A sprite blinks to their side, grabbing Lyra's arm and popping them both away. Laurel sees them reappear on the fifth floor, entering a medical bay.

She'll be all right. That's what Laurel tells herself. If she's wrong, that's another number to add to her body count.

"What happened?" Laurel doesn't realize she's been staring at the blood-marred floor until her father's perfectly polished shoes enter her line of sight.

The events of the last fifteen minutes flash through her mind in a second. She knows how her father will react if she tells him she accidentally maimed her mission partner. She's vowed to be as strong as a dozen Guild members; she can't stand to think of herself as a *threat* to other magicians.

Alister can't know. She can't disappoint him yet again. She can't lose control of her future.

"She tried to blink to Ori." The lie falls out of Laurel's mouth before she's even thought it through. "She asked the Depraved to tell her where they are, Ori and Nigel—and the monster knew." The lies continue to fly from her lips as if she truly believes them.

Yes, this is the right track. Lyra has to have been scheming.

"It was giving her coordinates, and she was going to kill me so I couldn't follow. But I got her first."

Alister's face is blank. "And if she says differently when questioned?" he asks.

"Then *you* do the questioning." Laurel knows her father will realize she's lying. But she has a feeling that it won't matter. That she might actually be giving him a tool he needed all along. "We both know there are spells that can be used to alter memories," she says. "Or the playback recorded in Dispatch. If Lyra's thoughts show anything different from what I've said, if the fountains betray me, we can safely assume she's changed them. *She's* the liar."

Alister's lips finally curl into a smile. "That's my girl." He extends a hand, offering to help her up. It catches Laurel so off guard that tears well in her eyes. Her dad hasn't acted like this since that day in the forest, so many years ago, when he told her how strong she'd have to be to lead.

Laurel places her hand in her father's, and he lifts her from the floor, wrapping her up in his sturdy, unshakeable arms.

"That's my girl," he says again, patting her head softly. Then he pulls away and bellows, "There's a traitor in our midst! Lyra Olson tried to help the boys!"

CHAPTER
SIXTEEN

IT TOOK AN EXCRUCIATING FORTY HOURS BEFORE JAMESON SAID THE coast was clear to head to the ranch, but finally, *finally*, my cowboy boots hit the dry ground, dirt billowing up around my legs. Bex's combat boots are next, followed by Ori's sneakers. I'm staring at their feet because I can't bring myself to look up. I'm back home, back in the place where Meema raised me. But when I look around, it will be obvious that nothing is the same. Meema won't be here. She'll never be here. I don't know that this place will ever feel like home again.

"Hey," Ori says, making his way to my side. "It's okay."

"No, it's not," I say, too harsh. "Not without her."

"I—" Ori stops himself. He's been getting the brunt of my brooding the past couple days. He used to be the grumpy in our grumpy-sunshine relationship, but now it's clearly me. Anger and resentment burn heavy in my gut all the time now. I think it has everything to do with that Knife-fused effigy sitting in my pocket. Heat flares beneath the denim. That's been happening more and more, each time I think about the claw. Like it's taunting me. It does the same whenever I question Meema's motives. If I can just get the answers in her journal, answers that hopefully clear her name . . .

Or they'll simply prove you're all monsters.

I finally look up, trying to distract myself from the grating voice in my head. The property takes my breath away. The sights and smells are familiar, yet not. I've spent thousands of days on this plot of land, but I feel like I've never stepped foot here before. A quick flare of hurt burns when I turn my attention to the limestone house: Black mold is already creeping across the stone, and the rain-streaked windows would make Meema's skin crawl. It's like all the mess Meema magicked away was just waiting for her to die. Without her, it's taken over.

The barn isn't any better. Paint already flakes off the wood and the doors hang off their hinges, allowing the livestock to roam at will. Horses, cows, and sheep are scattered throughout the property, from the grassy pastures close by down to the forested hills in the distance.

All Meema's work—gone to hell. What's left of her here? Who remembers her, if even the ranch has forgotten? Have any of Meema's clients come by, wondering what happened to her and the hay, dairy, and eggs she used to provide? She worked her whole life to make this farm a paradise for our family, and now it's rotting before my eyes. All because of the Horde.

All because of you.

"Nigel." Bex waves slightly to grab my attention. "We should get moving."

"Right." I pick up the pace, keeping my eyes straight ahead and focused only on the front door. If I look around too much, if I notice too many other details of things gone wrong, I won't make it. At the front door, the golden longhorn knocker stares down at me, and all I can think about is Meema riding triumphantly on her golden bull.

Magic pools in my hand. When I touch the door, it swings wide open. I brace myself, half expecting to see Dad there, as always, to tell me how badly I've fucked everything up.

And he wouldn't be wrong, would he? He always knew I'd be a piss-poor magician. Meema's death is proof that he's right.

Guilt swirls in my belly. The great room is full of memories, too. Meema making biscuits and gravy in the kitchen or dancing in the living room to her Dolly Parton records. I need to move fast before I'm paralyzed by despair.

I take a step, moving past a log pillar in the foyer just in time to see Jameson and Dad rise from the leather sofa with soft smiles on their faces. Jameson said he's been preparing Dad for my arrival, but they look like two old friends just shooting the shit. Guess they've been having a ball over here while I carry the weight of the world on my shoulders. White-hot heat starts in my toes and rushes up to my face, my cheeks blazing, pinpricks of sweat dappling the skin under my eyes.

I stomp over to the couches to chew Dad out, but he speaks first.

"Nigel," he says in his gravelly voice. "I'm so happy to see you."

That stops me dead in my tracks. He's never said those words in his life. "Y-you are?" My voice is high-pitched, childlike. I've become a scared little boy wishing his dad would just love him.

Pathetic.

Dad nods. "Yeah, son. Wanted you to see that I actually figured out how to mop." He nods around the room, and for the first time I notice that while the outside of the house is a mess, the *inside* is perfectly clean. "Now, I'm still trying my hand at taming the Texas elements, and so far Mother Nature's winning. But I'll keep at it. Best part is, haven't seen a demon or Depraved on this ranch for over a week. And look." He plucks the collar of his flannel. "No stains. Not bad for your old man, huh?"

It's true. He's clean shaven, the bags under his eyes are nearly gone, and there's not a beer can in sight.

Even still, that white-hot rage comes roiling back twice as strong. My hands clench into fists, tingling with angry magic.

But Ori's scoff steadies my nerves. "Are you serious?" he snaps. "You've been the world's shittiest father for eighteen years, and the first thing you do when you have half a brain again is ask your son— who you've tormented his whole life—to be proud of you because you can *mop*? Do you hear yourself?" He hooks a hand around my waist as if to say *I've got you.*

Dad tracks the movement, and I wonder if he notices the way I let my weight rest on Ori, how I literally lean on him when times are tough. A second passes, then Dad crosses his arms over his chest. "So after all we've been through, you still can't speak for yourself." He nods at Ori. "You're gonna let him do it? I thought you were more man than that."

Bex sucks in a breath while Jameson says warningly, "Reggie."

But you know what? Dad's right. I don't need Ori or Jameson or Bex to stick up for me.

So I let him have it.

"Oh, I can speak plenty well for myself." I shrug Ori off and stride forward until I'm right in Dad's face. "You were a terrible father. You never once encouraged me, you never once taught me a life lesson, you never once asked me what kind of man I wanted to be. And apparently you're fine with that, because I'm not *man enough* for you now. Well, you know what? I'm glad! Because every single atom of my being is hellbent on never becoming a monster like you. So if I'm not the type of person *you* want me to be, I've got to be doing something right."

Despite my big speech, shame flares through me. Every single word that flies from my mouth, every fleck of spit that lands on Dad's smirking face, makes me sound more and more like a kid with his feelings hurt. A roar escapes my throat in my body's desperate attempt to let loose this rage.

The Dad I know would laugh. He'd tell me to quit acting like a baby. But instead he puts his hands on my shoulders and says, "That's right, son. I've been a shit pa. I deserve to hear it."

It only makes me madder. That's not even an apology!

Gold magic bursts into my hands, and Jameson turns his warning tone on me. "Nigel. We have so few people on our side already. Scream at him all you want, but we're not casting against each other."

I throw up my hands. "But we're letting people excuse their eighteen years of terrible parenting because, *whoops*, I forgot the plans I made in an effort to take down the Culling because magical imbalance isn't a thing?! What about emotional imbalance? What about me?"

Jameson's brow furrows. "Magical imbalance isn't a—"

"NO! GO BACK TO YOUR LIBRARY! YOU LITERALLY WROTE THE BOOK ON IT!"

"Nigel," Ori says.

"No, Ori. Not you too. Just give me some space!"

I stomp out of the room without looking back. I know I shouldn't take this out on Jameson or Ori. Neither of them deserves it. I know we're all just pawns in the Guild's game. Or, not even the Guild, but however many magicians have teamed up with Alister to put us in this shitstorm. But it feels so good to yell. It feels so good to get angry. All this time I've tried to be the perfect little grandson, an obedient magician, but after everything I've been through, I think I've earned the right to really go off on somebody.

All the anger leaves my mind when I find myself down the hall, standing in front of Meema's bedroom door. She never did like me coming in here without her, and somehow the fear of disappointing my grandma still lives on even if she doesn't. I always thought that as a busy magician and rancher she just needed a truly private place to call her own. Now I can't help but wonder if she was keeping secrets from me. Did she know more about the Culling than she let on? If I go in that room, I might not like what I find.

I hate myself for doubting her. But if I don't go in, I'll never get the answers I need. The answers my heart craves more than anything. I'll never know if she was in on it, or if she ever documented anything about a Guild-wide spell.

So I turn the knob and enter.

Her room is bright and cheery as always, with cowhide-patterned curtains pulled back to let sunlight pour in. But despite the place being so full of her cowgirl aesthetic, I can feel her absence. A thin layer of dust mars her nightstand. Her pillows aren't as expertly fluffed as she'd like them. A pen sits at a slant on her writing desk instead of in her University of Texas mug. The spells she cast to keep her room *just so* have faded now. Now that she's gone. The ache in my heart is so strong I actually clutch my chest.

"Wow," Bex says to my right, surprising me. "That's a lot of boots."

I turn to where Bex is standing in the open doorway of Meema's walk-in closet. Normally, it would have stretched farther than it should have, based on the footprint of the house, some spell that let her store pair after pair of cowgirl boots along the wall. But with her gone, the walls are back to normal, the boots that were once lined up perfectly in rows on the extended shelves now strewn haphazardly across the floor. They're made of every leather, both animal and magical, in every color. On the opposite wall are jeans and hats crammed together when before they were perfectly spaced. In the center of the closet sits an island, wooden and bordered with twisting ropes, dozens of drawers that were once loaded with more belt buckles than they should be able to carry now bulging open as the extra accessories push out.

"You've been kind of an ass lately," Bex says, curt and to the point. "Not kind of. A total ass. But I'm sorry you're going through this. I'm sorry she died." She shakes her head. "I'm sorry she *was killed.*"

Bex is right. I have been terrible to her. Two seconds ago, I would have lashed out at her for calling me an ass. But now, surrounded by the items that brought my grandma to life when she has no more life to live, I don't have it in me.

"Bex. I'm really sorry about everything lately. How *I've* been lately. I—" I stop, about to let loose all my secrets—namely, the Knife fused within me—but I promised Ori I'd keep that to myself for now. So instead, I just stand there like a real jerk, not voicing the apology she deserves.

Like she should, Bex stands there expectantly, waiting for any words from me that actually mean something. When they don't come, she rolls her eyes, sighing. "That's not enough, Nigel. You're going to have to do better than that. I'll give you the benefit of the doubt, *for now*, seeing as how you're facing your grandma's stuff for the first time since she died." Bex motions toward the wall of hats. "She sure had her own style, didn't she? Dad always appreciated that about her."

I go over to the nearest pair of boots, one of the many she had in her favorite texture: kraken-hide. "She made these herself. Meema would spend her free time crafting spells that could re-create the leather from any animal. She couldn't hurt a hair on their heads—unless they were trying to kill her first."

Bex smiles softly. "She truly was iconic."

"She was."

We stand there in silence, me taking in the details of Meema, before Bex finally says, "I didn't mean to interrupt your alone time. I know you said you needed space. But after your little outburst back there, Jameson thought I was the safest person to come tell you that we need to go soon. The longer we stay here, the more likely something could happen to alert the Guild to our presence."

With that, she turns on her heel and leaves.

Time to get what I came here for.

I head straight for Meema's writing desk and open the lone drawer. Inside is a worn leather diary, bound shut with a strap of the same material that wraps around the horns of a little brass longhorn on the cover.

I know I should follow Bex right now and wait to read this back at the Resistance, but my fingers move on their own. I unwind the leather strap, lift the corner of the diary. Just as I'm about to open it, my heart clenches. I'm about to break Meema's trust. I'm about to read her secrets.

And once you find out she's as terrible as you think, there will be no more denying what runs through your veins.

"STOP!"

I can't let this go on any longer. I flip open the journal. The pages curl naturally, almost as if Meema reread the same page over and over, the binding always open to an entry in late June almost thirty years ago.

I can't believe I have to write this. Reggie's magic was taken. A lifetime of training for the Culling, and I've failed him. He was so close, excelling in the first two challenges. But then he nearly died in the third. I had to step in and

stop the monster that was going to rip him from me. I knew
even as I saved him that I was dooming him. That he'd be the
first Barrett since the founding of the Guild to fail its tests.

Every motherly instinct in me wanted to protect him
from losing his power. But I know better than anybody the
ramifications of letting him keep his magic. The Culling must
continue.

Her entry brings more questions than answers. What ramifications is she talking about? Does she mean the Guild lie, the belief
that if apprentices weren't Culled, magic would kill us all? Or does
she mean the ramifications if Dad got to keep his power and nothing
happened, exposing the ruse she worked so hard to keep alive?

I feel a hunger to know more that spurs me on to turn page
after page. I craft a magic set of glasses with the intention to
speed-read, and the words fly together in a completely compre-
hensible blur. There are entries of her missions, of magicians she
can't stand (plenty featuring Alister), of her detailing our successes
as she trains me in elven ways. And every year around the Culling,
she relives Dad's failure, reiterates her regrets, but always finishes the
entries with *The Culling must continue.*

I flip all the way to the very last entry, desperate to find any
proof that she hasn't been in on the conspiracy. But all I find is this:

Nigel's made a mess of things, teaming up with that
Olson boy. And somehow they've awakened the Horde. Had
to show Nigel his great-grandpa Barrett's crowning
achievement so he could retrieve the claw. I wanted to show
him that moment to teach him his lineage and demonstrate
all that Barretts can do, not to show him the one tool that
could help clean up the mess he damn well made himself.

It seems that's not the only mess Guild members are making. After showing Nigel the claw's history in the Relic Hall, I went to the Cornucopia pedestal. For the briefest second, I considered if we should use it to fight the Knife. Magical magnification of our powers could come in handy, after all. But when I picked up the envelope waiting there, it was a fake. Nothing written inside. Somebody has the real envelope, and if they went so far as to put a decoy there, knowing no one in their right mind would look for a cursed, forbidden weapon . . . I bet that means they have the Cornucopia, too. Did Nigel use it? Is that how his powers got so out of hand?

I hate myself for even doubting him, and I certainly can't tell anyone now in case it puts even more suspicion on that boy's shoulders. Not to mention, the Culling must continue. But as soon as it's over, I'm going to find who took the Cornucopia.

My heart jumps into my throat. I have no idea what the Cornucopia is, but I can tell from Meema's frantic scribbling that it's bad. Especially if it's so powerful that she thinks I used it to wake up the Horde. My first order of business once I'm out of here will be looking into just what Meema is talking about.

Yet the jury's out on whether or not your grandma was behind the Culling. She could still be a monster. Most likely is. And everything you've done that's shocked her is because of her.

The claw in my pocket flares, the heat so strong I'm certain it will burn through the denim and melt my skin. "GOD DAMMIT!" I grab the claw and fling it across the room. My chest rises with heaving breaths. "I'm tired of this shit. I'm tired of it!"

I need the claw away from me. It's got to be what's fueling the

Knife's voice in my head, always flaring to life whenever I hear that grating rasp. What better place to leave it than the sanctuary of the only woman who ever looked after me?

I hustle back to Meema's closet, tucking the claw inside one of her hundreds of boots. There'd be no reason for anyone to look inside it. And if there's any ounce of Meema left in this room, I know she'll protect me and make sure the wrong hands don't get ahold of this effigy.

I feel back in my pocket just to make sure it's good and gone, no traces of the Knife's heartstone left behind to haunt me. Nothing there. Nothing, except Jaleesa's fae bell.

I ring it, and her figure materializes in a heartbeat, her spell stronger again.

"You rang?" she says, cracking a smile at her own joke.

"I can't talk long," I say. "I need you to look for something called the Cornucopia. Got it?"

"Any clues you can give me? What it does? What it looks like?"

"I have no idea."

Jaleesa sighs. "Great. I'll search for it. Listen, there's something else you should know. Ori's mom has been imprisoned. The Guild thinks she's been working behind the scenes with him."

"Bullshit!" I growl. "Ori hasn't seen her since Mount Rainier."

"That's what I thought," Jaleesa says, deflating. "Laurel insists it's the truth."

"Who would have thought *Laurel* would turn out to be a liar?" My words drip with sarcasm. "Like father, like daughter."

Jaleesa opens her mouth to speak, but a piercing screech cuts her off.

We'd recognize that sound anywhere.

"Depraved!"

CHAPTER
SEVENTEEN

I pocket Jaleesa's fae bell and sprint out of Meema's room as fast as my boots will carry me. The great room is empty, but flashes of sickly green power shine through the window, followed by the pink, gold, and silver of Ori, Jameson, and Bex already in the fray. I can't have them die when I was the one who asked to come here. I spell the front door open so hard it flies from its hinges.

The Depraved lets out another grating screech, the sound immediately met by a trio of roars. Three demons circle around the paddock: a fox, a coyote, and a goat. Sensing the threat, the horses nearby book it into the barn.

"We've got to move fast!" Jameson says. "Every second these monsters are here increases the likelihood the Guild will see us in Dispatch."

Fuck.

Pounding footsteps come from around the house, and there's

Dad wielding a pitchfork. As if that will do any good. "I thought you said the Depraved haven't shown up in over a week!"

"I wasn't lyin'!" he growls as he skids to a stop next to Jameson. "Go!"

"We aren't leaving you here to die, Reggie." The elf pulls a golden arrow from the quill he's magicked on his back. He sends it straight into the leg of the Depraved, but it doesn't stop the monster from surging forward.

With a faint glow of silver, Bex shifts into a unicorn, her black hide glistening in the sun. She turns to me with flared nostrils. "Nigel? What's going on with you? You smell different."

"We're about to be torn to shreds by monsters and you want to tell him he's not using enough deodorant?" Ori barks. "We can talk about this later!"

Bex huffs, then rears on her hind legs with a whinny and gallops past the Depraved to face the fox demon head-on. Her shining horn pierces it straight through its open maw, cutting off its bark. Its rotten yellow teeth gnash at her horn—bone scrabbling against the pristine silver—before the monster goes limp. With a toss of her head, Bex sends the monster's body flying and neighs victoriously.

Meanwhile, the coyote demon has set its stare on Ori and me. Ori blinks us backward, then yanks his bag from his shoulder. He grabs a dog plushie with long, fluffy ears and bathes it in pink power.

Ori wags the effigy back and forth. "Brought you a little chew toy."

The coyote demon's putrid sheen mixes with pink light as the effigy works its magic. The monster howls, hungry for Ori's fear. But Ori rips a long ear off the stuffed animal, and the coyote demon's ear rips from its skull, green sludge oozing from the wound. It lets out an anguished yelp and locks its eyes on my soulmate, ready to kill.

I spring into action, bringing golden power to my hands and stretching it out into a long tendril followed by sixteen short ones. My hands pull and shape until a glowing muck rake rests in my grip.

Ori's eyes flick to the rake, even as he twists and tears his effigy. "I think we're a bit too busy to get started on pooper-scooper duty, cowboy."

I shake my head. "Nah, it's time to get rid of the shit."

With a dramatic swing, I arc the rake overhead and bring it down, swiping the effigy from Ori's grip. Just as my rake pierces Ori's effigy, our magics combine into the abalone color of us. Putrid gore leaks from the coyote demon's newest wounds, and warmth cascades through me at a spell well performed with my soulmate. But I don't have long to celebrate. With the coyote demon down, I have the perfect view to see the Depraved closing in on Dad.

Green power builds in its claw-like fingers, ready to burn Dad to ash. But a purple light over Dad's shoulder distracts the monster as a portal opens. Ten magicians pour out of it, many that I don't know. The familiar faces make my stomach drop. Alister and Laurel are in the lead, but Pallavit and Jaleesa bring up the rear. Seeing the fae makes my spirits lift a little; I don't know where her mom's allegiance lies, but Jaleesa might be able to help.

Alister gets right to work. He thrusts a glowing green hand forward and—*fwip, fwip, fwip!*—three thorns, each a yard long, fly from the ground. Even knowing Alister is leading the charge for my capture, a lifetime of being taught the Guild fights monsters makes me naively assume they're meant for the Depraved. It catches me entirely by surprise when all three projectiles lodge themselves in my torso. Heat sears through my body as they pierce my stomach, dripping red blood. Ori stands beside me in shock.

My mouth drops into a surprised O, gurgling breaths barely making it through my parted lips.

"You got him!" Laurel shouts, gleeful. "You did it!"

Her voice snaps me back to reality, and pain takes over every atom of my being. I can feel each individual beat of my heart, feel the strained effort of the muscle trying to regain normal blood flow.

"NIGEL!" Ori screams. He grabs my shoulders and blinks us away from the newcomers. A flare of abalone—completely pure, untainted—flares down my body, forcing the thorns out. I drop to the ground along with them.

From the dirt I watch as Bex, Jameson, and Dad put up a fight, buying us time. But ten against three can't buy much.

"I've got you." Ori hustles to touch the exposed skin of my belly, and I can feel him pouring his heart and soul through our connection, his caring for me, his desperate need to never see me die again. He's lost all color in his face, his eyes wide with panic, with *hurt*, even though I'm the one who's been impaled. I wonder if this is what he looked like after I used the claw, when he first thought there was no way to bring me back.

Ori's fingers graze the three round holes that have gored me open.

"I can practically see through your stomach." He gags.

"D-don't go soft on me now," I say.

"You're getting—" *Heave.* "Better."

He's right. The pain subsides as our contact makes my body stitch itself back together.

"Thanks for the assist," I say, my voice shaky with nerves. Yet again, Ori's pulled me back from the brink of death.

Because of them. Because of the Guild.

I need to make them pay for ever making Ori feel like this. For making him fear my death *twice*.

You know how to stop them. Get rid of them. All of them.

That overwhelming fury, that need for revenge, rushes through me as strong and hot as it did when we escaped Mount Rainier, just before we blinked away with our lives.

I move without thinking, coating my boots in gold, spelling them with speed, then hurl myself back into the fray.

"Howdy, y'all." A maniacal laugh escapes my throat, and pure glee tingles through my veins at the thought of making Alister pay. *"What a pleasant surprise!"* I whip out my hands and send tendrils of gold lightning zapping toward each of the newcomers. It's a good ol'-fashioned offensive spell, nothing fancy, just magic meant to destroy. I don't think it's my imagination that there's the slightest hint of green among the gold. It barely registers that I should be worried about that—right now, I don't care.

Just like that, half the Guild members are down without a fight, their unmoving bodies crumpled in the dirt. Alister escapes in the nick of time by spelling a Venus flytrap to swallow him. My bolts of lightning fail to penetrate the thick, meaty flesh of the plant. Laurel ducks and rolls, but my magic catches one of her long braids and sets her hair on fire. A sprite grabs hold of Jaleesa and Pallavit and blinks all three out of the way.

I look around for my next target, and my eyes land on that damned goat demon. It lets out a surprisingly normal *Baaaaa* as we lock eyes, its horizontal pupils wobbling. Everything goes hazy. I can't discern the shapes in front of me, can't tell who's a friend, who's a foe, or whether Alister's out of his stupid plant to deal a death blow while I struggle. The more I try to clear my head—shaking it, rubbing a magic hankie over my eyes—the dizzier I get, and as my vertigo increases, I fall to the dirt.

I barely register a subtle shake in the ground before a blurry mass lands in front of me. It thrashes and with a garbled *BAAA,* everything becomes clear. Bex is there, in unicorn form, standing over the demon she kicked so hard its neck snapped.

THE MAGIC YOU MAKE

"God, I hate goat demons," Bex says. "Their messed-up pupils give me the creeps!"

Ori laughs, but he's cut off by the Depraved, which shrieks with glee as it strangles Laurel and lifts her high. She struggles feebly, her legs flopping, her face turning purple the tighter it squeezes.

I take a quick inventory. The sprite who helped Pallavit and Jaleesa is down for the count. Alister, the coward, is still shielded inside his Venus flytrap. When Jaleesa's and Pallavit's throats glow purple with power, the Depraved laughs even louder.

"One drop of magic and I'll kill her," it says in a twisted singsong.

My own smile matches the monster's.

That's one less magician to worry about.

"We should go now," I whisper to Ori. "Get out while they're distracted."

I expect Ori to nod, to grab my hand and blink us out of here. But he scowls, sympathy coating his expression as he watches Laurel on the brink of death.

Jameson, however, moves with confidence. While the Depraved eyes the fae, the elf sends gold magic to his hands. He takes a deep breath, holds one golden hand before his face, parallel to the ground, and blows. Magic billows from his palm like a powder, but the Depraved whips around just in time to use Laurel's body as a shield. As the magic coats her, her skin begins to bubble, melting from Jameson's curse. If she had any breath at all I'm sure she'd scream, but all that comes out are strangled gasps.

Jameson staggers backward. "Laurel!" He stumbles in his rush to heal her, his ankle twisting beneath him. The Depraved moves fast, tossing Laurel to the side and sending a bolt of electric power straight toward Jameson. There's no way he'll be able to block the evil magic, not while he tries and fails to gain his footing.

"AAAAAAAAAARGH!"

Two twisted yells join together at once. There's the Depraved, high-pitched and vengeful, celebrating its anticipated victory. But the second scream is Dad's. With a bellow of pure conviction, he leaps forward and blocks Jameson with his body in the millisecond before the Depraved's power would kill the elf.

"STOP!" I've never heard this amount of desperation in Dad's voice, never this love or determination.

A wave of red light washes over the entire scene. At first, I think it's a shower of blood—Dad can't have survived that power. But though the red *is* coming from Dad, it's not a gruesome end. It's a glow from within him. A bright, shimmering, crimson light blossoms out from his chest, right over his heart. The Depraved's evil magic is absorbed by that red light and made obsolete. "You *won't* kill my friend," Dad says. His voice is deep and husky, as usual, completely unpained. "You won't."

The red light bursts outward, so bright that I have to shield my eyes. I wait until the red recedes to a dull pink behind my eyelids before I peek them open. "What in tarnation?"

Meema always said it when she was truly surprised. It's popped out of me now because I have no idea what I'm seeing. A new figure has joined our group, one with ruby-red skin—if you can call it skin; it's more like a bejeweled coating—that glistens in the sun. They stand equal height to Dad, assuming a protective stance directly in front of him.

"Ori," I breathe. "What is that?"

He shakes his head in confusion while the Depraved blares green with another attack, aimed straight for the newcomer. At once, Jameson, Bex, Ori, and I flare with defensive power. But this red-jeweled creature doesn't need us. They don't balk at the stream of evil magic. The sickly green power flows harmlessly into their body, and their smile grows wider with every particle of the Depraved's magic they soak up.

All I can do is stare. The figure looks almost human: two arms, two legs, even wispy, hairlike tendrils of red moving in the breeze. And their *smile*. Not one of malice-filled triumph like the grin of the Depraved. This smile looks confident, peaceful—like the creature knows everything is going to be okay.

The bejeweled being keeps pressing forward, step after step, absorbing the power still pouring from the Depraved. The monster roars in frustration as it puts everything into its power, its rotten green nostrils flaring. But this strange being never stops. When they're directly in front of the Depraved, the monster lets loose a scream that puts all others to shame, but the red being doesn't flinch. In fact, they glow brighter.

All that power that's been absorbed by the being flows through their body and down their arms. The magic creates a kaleidoscope of sparkles along the creature's jeweled skin. When they're only inches away from the Depraved, the being throws their arms wide and wraps them around the monster. They're literally hugging the Depraved. The monster's green magic goes out in a blink, and with another squeeze, the Depraved simply disappears.

Gone, just like that.

Gone, with an embrace.

"Whatever it is your dad created," Ori says, his eyes wide with shock. "It destroyed the Depraved with *a hug*."

The glistening red creature looks over their shoulder, nodding once when they lock their ruby eyes on Dad. Then they flick their gaze to me and give me the softest, most tender smile. Somehow it reminds me of Meema, of the look she'd give me when she was truly proud of the work I'd done on the ranch and the way my magic was developing. Sometimes I'd catch her just looking at me like that for no reason at all.

I have to blink away tears.

Then, as quickly as they appeared, the being shines bright red once more, their brilliant light mixing with the rays of the sun, and they're gone.

Dad meets my eyes. "You okay, kid?"

I'm reeling, to be honest. I've experienced too many emotions since we arrived on the ranch. All I can do is shrug. "What was that?"

He shakes his head. "No idea."

Thank god for Dad.

That's something I never thought I'd find myself thinking. But whatever Dad did to create that being, he saved Jameson. I can't stop staring at him, and it hits me that for the first time in my life, my mind is not bombarded with phantom echoes of all the disgusting things he's said to me. I don't worry about him putting me down. I don't worry about him saying I'll never live up to the family name.

But my relief is short-lived. My own internal monologue clamors for attention, and it's more than happy to tell me all those things. I let my need for revenge get away from me again. I felt that hate surge in my soul, felt it control my magic all on its own. That green hue mixed with my power.

The Knife, manipulating me.

The ground feels wobbly beneath my feet. But it's not an enemy this time. At least, not one I can see. The sinking realization that the Knife really has some control over me and my power makes my head spin.

"Nigel?" Dad's voice is tinged with concern. Before I can respond, a few small dots of green magic float right under Dad's nose. Unaware, he inhales them, and his eyes roll back into his head. He collapses to the ground.

Slow claps fill the silence.

Alister.

Little bits of that enchanted pollen cling to his fingers.

"Sorry to interrupt such a *heartwarming* moment," he says, looking between me and my dad, whose chest is thankfully moving. He's asleep, not dead. "That was quite the spectacle."

"God, could you just give it a rest already?" Ori snips. "Focus on the important things, like, I don't know, how some mystical creature just destroyed a Depraved like it was nothing?"

"We'll figure all that out," Alister says. "While you two are locked up." He snaps his fingers. "Better yet, while you're *all* locked up." He turns to Jameson, who's joined Pallavit hovering over an unconscious Laurel, casting countercurses. The pockmarks up and down Laurel's arms, legs, and face are healing over. "Don't think that helping my daughter will get you out of this, Jameson. Working with these two. Really? I should have assumed when you jumped at the chance to watch over the Barrett property."

Jameson doesn't look up from his spellwork. "Do what you must, Ali."

"Come on." Ori grabs my hand. "Alister loves to hear himself speak. It's the perfect time to get out of here."

I can feel his intent to blink. His eyes drift shut, his long lashes fluttering as he envisions where he wants to go.

I know we'll blink any second.

Any second now.

I'm sure of it.

Or not.

Ori peeks an eye open. "Why aren't we moving?" He squeezes his eyes shut again, his whole face smooshed with concentration. Still nothing. He throws his hands in exasperation. "What the hell?"

This is not good.

The world's worst derisive laughter pierces my eardrums. Alister cackles, relishing the moment while we look at each other in confusion.

"Something stopping you?" Alister mocks. "Oh, right. That would be my colleague."

Alister nods to Pallavit, a lump of silvery sprite wood in her hands, in the shape of a human, glowing purple. Using fae magic to create an effigy. I've never seen anything like it.

"We had to retrieve that little relic from the vault," Alister says. "An ancient artifact, from a bygone war between sprites and fae. The fae were brilliant, really. Enchanting the sprites' own wood to use against them and block all blinking. It's something I say in DC all the time. Why choose progress for progress's sake when tradition has already given us everything we need?" The smile drops from his face in a heartbeat. "The jig is up, boys. You're coming with me."

The nymph snaps at Jaleesa, whose neck glows purple. She gives me an apologetic glance that lasts only a millisecond before clearing her throat to sing.

"The boys are captured.
Time to rebuild.
In the hallowed halls
Of the Magicians' Guild."

A portal opens beside her. Alister flicks his fingers and grass blooms in the dirt at our feet. It undulates like waves to push us straight toward the magical doorway. Dad's sleeping form rolls through the portal, and I'm surprised by my urge to run after him. To protect him and whatever the being was that came out of him. Jameson, too, looks pained to see him taken.

Next through the portal is Laurel, unconscious, then the six magicians who collapsed during our fight. My heart constricts then, remembering how my magic got away from me, wondering if they're just knocked out, or dead. More casualties to my power.

Jaleesa follows them of her own accord, catching my eye one more time before she's gone. Alister and Pallavit remain as Alister's roiling grass shoves the four of us Resistance members closer. If we go through that portal to the Guild, there's no way we're getting out again alive. The murderous glare in Alister's eyes proves it. We know about the Culling, and he can't let us out of his clutches again, even after stripping our powers.

Bex shifts into a hawk and takes off, but a vine from Alister's fist snatches her back. It's incredible, the power he has, a practiced magician with years of experience. But we've got one on our side, too, and Jameson's fist lights up gold before he shoves it into the earth, shattering the ground. Grass and dirt fly in all directions, knocking everyone off their feet, forcing Alister to break his hold on Bex and stopping his spell from pulling us through the portal.

Jameson moves fast. With a quick motion of his hand, he opens his own portal. The door to his heart home. "Boys! Bex! Now!"

Bex dives through the portal. But Alister and Pallavit are back on their feet, pulsing with power. They're not going to let us go that easy.

Ori turns to me. "This is your ranch. Any big ideas, cowboy?"

He's right. This *is* my ranch. And whenever I need to get somewhere quick, there's one way to do it.

Ride.

I snatch Ori's wrist in my right hand and let magic pool in my left. "Make an effigy of a horse," I say.

Ori doesn't hesitate, and the toy he grabs reminds me so much of the figure he used that first day we met, when we tamed Frosty together. Warmth blooms in my gut despite the urgency of the moment. That day led us here, brought us to our soulmates. We can do this. We've gotten rid of bigger villains than Alister.

Have you?

That warmth in my gut turns just as quickly to cold, wriggling worms, but if I focus on the Knife, Ori and I are both dead. I stick my middle finger and thumb into my mouth and let loose the loudest whistle of my life, thinking of every last animal on this ranch and urging them all to my side, *now.*

The effigy in Ori's hand, glowing our abalone color, smacks straight into my chest and drops to the dirt. I barely feel the impact because at the same moment, the ground starts to shake as every last animal on the property barrels toward us. Horses, pigs, goats. Dust clouds in the distance signal the movement of hundreds of cows answering my call from the farthest pastures.

Alister and Pallavit hold steady, and it isn't until the horses—the fastest of the bunch—are upon them that I realize my spell has done more than create a sense of urgency in the animals. Their eyes are bulging, they're frothing at the mouth, and when they catch sight of our attackers, they bite and thrash, aiming to kill.

I've turned them feral.

I look down to the shining effigy at my feet. A slight green tinge creeps up the plastic figurine's tail. Just like the green that tainted my magic earlier.

Who's the villain now?

Alister and Pallavit are more than distracted by the animals. They're fighting for their lives.

"NIGEL! ORI! RUN!" Jameson's magicked voice rises over the chaos. With a tug on my arm, Ori leads us sprinting through Jameson's portal, away from capture, away from danger.

Yet I feel anything but successful. We may have escaped the Guild again, but with the Knife corrupting my power, will we ever truly be safe?

CHAPTER
EIGHTEEN

As soon as we arrive inside Jameson's heart home, Kenneth and Yamato rush over from the dining room, where an entire turkey dinner has been laid out.

Ori scowls at the food. "We were almost captured, and you were here whipping up mashed potatoes and gravy?"

"What?" Kenneth says. "I cook when I'm nervous." And I'm a nervous eater, so we're perfectly paired. I'm leading the group to the table when Yamato asks, "What happened?"

"I've been made," Jameson says simply as he takes his seat. "Ten Guild members saw me defend the boys. It won't be long before I'm called in."

"Forced in," Yamato corrects.

Jameson nods.

"Can they do that?" I ask. "Why don't you just stay here?"

I punctuate my question with a massive bite of turkey.

Bex pulls out a chair with more force than necessary. "How you can eat at a time like this is beyond me." She says it harshly—back to the Bex who's pissed at me now that I'm not faced with Meema mementos.

"When you enter the Guild, they take a bit of your essence, a bit of your power," Jameson says. "It's for moments exactly like this one. They can use that bit of my magic to call me to them. They only use it in dire circumstances, when they think members are going rogue and need to be intercepted. It's a wonder they didn't do it the second we stepped through that portal just now." Jameson's eyes wander as he thinks. "Alister must be up to something."

Ori grunts. "Bet those assholes wish they'd inducted us. Then they'd be able to call us right back."

"Be grateful they can't," Yamato snips. "You'd be dead if they could."

"Yeah, I get that," Ori snaps back. "Or did you think I forgot that every last Guild magician wants to see me murdered?"

Bex's face flashes to a wolf's to snarl at Ori before shifting back. "Could you quit barking at my dad? We have more important things to tell them."

"The only one barking is y—"

A gust of wind flies from Kenneth's white-glowing hands, carrying Ori's words away. A pleased smile on his face, Kenneth says, "Go ahead, honey."

Bex launches into it, describing the red being that burst from Dad's chest, detailing how they destroyed the Depraved in seconds. "They were the most beautiful creature I've ever seen. Shining red, but not like blood. Red like warmth and safety. Red like love." She's silent for a moment, an awed expression on her face, until she slams her fist on the table. "I knew it all along. The solution has always been love."

Yamato and Kenneth beam at their daughter.

My skin itches with impatience. They're acting like we've found all the answers when there are still more questions than anything else.

"Does anybody know what that even *was?*" I ask. "Not to rain on this parade, but—" I wiggle my fingers in front of me, miming a storm. *"Whoosh."*

"I've never heard of anything like this," Yamato says with a look at his husband, who shakes his head. "What about you, Jameson?"

"Never," he says, looking almost pleased with today's developments despite shit hitting the fan. "But it's meaningful that it was Reggie who summoned them. If there's another kind of magic that humans can create, and that magic can counteract their Depraved creations . . ." He unfolds his napkin, his eyes catching on a familiar slogan stitched there, before draping it across his lap. "The Culling is a lie?" He looks up just as Ori, Bex, and I all say *"Book 2005-3!"* with equal amounts of frustration.

Ori is first to recover, bumping his knee against mine. "I'm just shocked something that felt so good could come out of your dad. A guy who's a total monster couldn't do that, right?"

"Reggie's not a monster," Jameson says. "He sacrificed a lot for our mission." He holds up his napkin, slogan faced out. "To end the Culling, apparently. And now he's being held by the Guild."

I poke at the potatoes on my plate, each jab of my fork stronger than the last as they keep talking.

"To ask the obvious question," Yamato says. "How long before Reggie rats us out?"

Jab, jab.

Jameson shakes his head. "He wouldn't do that."

Sure, let's just ignore that Reggie *was the most emotionally abusive parent you could imagine. Oh, he's a such a good person, and* I'm *overreacting!*

"Come on, Jameson." Yamato looks at the elf in disbelief. "You know how easy it will be for the Guild to crack into his restored memories without any magic to ward them off. It's why you wiped his mind to begin with, so Adela couldn't do it."

Jab, jab, jab.

Right, Meema *was the problem all along.*

What do they know about changing the Guild? I can change it. I should let the Guild catch me, and I'll make them pay. One by one, starting with Alister.

"All I'm saying is, he wouldn't do it willingly. Reggie is—"

I stab my fork down so hard it splits my plate in two, grinding metal tines into the table while gravy spills into my lap. The hot liquid startles me, and I push backward, my chair scraping against the floor.

Everyone stares with open mouths.

Everyone except Bex, who looks just about as angry as I feel.

"What the fuck is wrong with you?" Bex spits at me. "Let me guess, you're having a tantrum because, for *once*, our conversation isn't centered on you. Ever since you got here, it's been *all about you*! We went to the ranch because *you* asked us, too, and now look where that's gotten us. Jameson's going to be taken, your dad's memories are going to be combed over until they discover the Resistance and that we're all a part of it, and now you're having a hissy fit? Because your dad did something right for once? Grow up! *My* family is in danger, something I've been trying to prevent my entire life, and it's *because of you*!"

Who the fuck does she think she is?

Bex treating me like a piece of cow shit these days—always giving me distrusting looks—is really starting to get on my nerves.

"What I don't understand," I say, darkly, quietly, "is why anyone would listen to *you*?"

Bex quirks an eyebrow, unimpressed. "What's that supposed to mean?"

THE MAGIC YOU MAKE

"It means all you've done this entire time is shape-shift into silly animals, while I literally sacrificed myself to bring down monsters." I get louder with every word. "It means *you're* not the one the Guild is after—"

"You can shut the fuck right up," Yamato growls. "You don't just abandon the Guild mid-Culling without becoming a target."

My eyes flash to Bex's dads. Their stress is *nothing* compared to what I'm going through.

"Sure," I say, mocking. "I bet they want to get Bex, too, when all is said and done. But who is it that's really on top of their hit list?"

Kenneth scowls while Yamato looks like he wants to shift right now and beat me to a pulp. Even still, he doesn't say anything.

"That's what I thought," I snap. "It's Ori and me who are in the deep shit. Yet if I acknowledge that, I'm somehow being *selfish*."

"You're not selfish, you're a narcissist! You can't admit that you keep fucking everything up!" Bex is screaming now. Her cheeks are red, and her hands keep shifting between tiger paws with claws ready to slash and gorilla fists too big for her body. "Do you think I want it this way? Do you think I asked for any of this? That I want to be in hiding, worrying that my dads will be found out any minute now? *I'm not the reason we were caught.*"

Oh, so that's how she wants to play. "You're just jealous that the only people who are key to changing the Guild are Ori and me."

Bex scoffs, her face twisted with derision. "Yep. That's it, Nigel." She's not yelling anymore. Her hands are perfectly still. Yet her words still pack a punch. "You think you're this big-hearted cowboy, but you're just like all those other self-centered white boys who make every story about them."

Her face falls then, shaking her head as she keeps going, but it's more like she's talking to herself than me.

"I am *so . . . tired . . .* of chasing after magicians who are too up their own asses to care. I'm sick of being pushed to the side."

Ori leans forward. "Bex, I promise that's not—"

Bex throws her hand up to stop him. "I really don't need promises right now, Ori. Not from you." She locks eyes with me. "And absolutely not from *you.*"

Kenneth moves to stand but freezes when Bex shoots to her feet first.

"No, Pop," she says. Kenneth looks like he's been slapped. "You and Dad aren't any better. All you two talk about is changing the Guild. It's always about what we can do for everyone else, and not once have you asked what I need. What I want. I'm *done* taking on other people's burdens. You can deal with this shit by yourselves. Good fucking luck."

She marches to the front door and throws it open. She transforms her head into a lion's and roars, the bellow triggering the portal. With a silver flash she's back to herself, weight heavy on her shoulders.

Part of me knows that Bex's anger *is* my fault. I put her dads in danger, and I didn't even think of that.

No matter what you do, you bring everyone else down with you. You've put everyone you love in danger.

But I see such an easy out of the heaping pile of guilt waiting for me down that road. A way to shift the blame. So I rush to get in the last word. "Not all of us have the option of running from our problems."

Bex looks over her shoulder, her face blank. "No. You just cause them."

And with that, she vanishes.

"Don't you talk to her like that," Yamato spits. "Ever."

I can't stop the wave of pleasure washing over me, sloughing aside the painful truth of Bex's words. It's like my body needs this. Needs to think someone *else* is to blame.

"Don't take it out on *me* that *you've* failed to recognize what your daughter actually needs." I feel a twisted spark of joy watching him recoil.

"Nigel," Jameson says, low, steady. "Watch yourself."

Ori grips my arm, tight.

"Nigel, you're not yourself," he whispers. His already pale fingers go bone white as he squeezes my bicep. And though his touch is intense, I don't feel sparks.

Is this how it will be forever now? The Knife inside of me, cutting off our connection? Tainting our beautiful magic with its rotten power? Those flashes of green I know I saw on the ranch haunt me, and I still hear those Depraved's words in our heart home.

Ori puts every ounce of muscle into pulling me out of the dining room and up to the second floor. Without a word, he leads me across the landing and climbs the attic stairs. When the door slams behind us, he finally lets go, flinging my arm away in disgust.

We stand there, staring at each other, both of us seething. I'm so mad at myself, so mad at Ori, the Culling, the Guild, Meema, *everything*. My life is nothing like it should be.

"Aren't you supposed to be on my side?" I ask. "Aren't you supposed to be my *soulmate*?" I spit the word out, making a mockery of it.

Like he's making a mockery of me.

Ori doesn't respond. He crosses his arms and turns his back to me. For a moment, I feel victorious.

He can't even defend himself when I point out he's a backstabbing, weak fake.

"You're not yourself," Ori whispers again. "You're acting this way because of *it*."

A hot burst of anger flares through my body. It starts in my toes, a tingle running the length of my legs, then my torso. My breath comes shorter, my heart rate gallops.

He put that thing in me. Now he wants to act like *I'm the monster?* Ori made me what I am!

But then, so strong it takes my breath away entirely, a vise grip crushes my heart. I fall to all fours, my right hand racing up to slam against my chest. I'd fling the organ out of my body if I could; it hurts that much. My vision goes black at the edges.

And just like that, it's over. My body registers the sensations, but my mind knows now that they're not real. Physically, at least. This is emotional pain. *Ori's* emotional pain. I'm feeling it through our connection—which is coming back, somehow. It's overwhelming, the depth of his sadness and confusion and anger. The anger he feels at *himself.*

Ori falls to his knees, taking my face in his hands.

"I'm so sorry," he whispers. "I'm so, so sorry. I should have found another way. There had to have been another way to bring you back."

My body sags with relief that I can feel him again. His thumbs stroke away the tears that I didn't know were falling freely down my face. He's worried, anxious, not just because I've become someone neither of us recognizes, but because he blames *himself* for my transformation.

"We should tell them," Ori says. "Tomorrow. Tell them everything about the Knife. Our power's not the same anymore. *You're* not the same anymore. Because of me."

I swallow, nod. I feel it, too. It's only going to get worse with time. Maybe Jameson and the rest of the Resistance will have some idea how to get the Knife out of me. Maybe I'll end up dead if they try. But that's got to be better than letting the Knife get stronger within me. It's got to be better than letting it use me.

And if we tell them now, Ori might never have to know the things I hear it say. Never have to know the extent of the evil in me.

"I didn't even give you a ch-choice." Ori's voice catches, and I know he's holding back tears of his own. He doesn't think it's fair to be upset when I'm the one who's morphing into a beast. "I just . . . brought you back. Without thinking. Without knowing what it would do to you."

"It's not your fault," I breathe. "It's not your fault."

Ori shakes his head, just slightly, not believing it. Then he pulls me in, and when our lips meet, I hope he can feel that I don't blame him for this. Not really, not in my heart of hearts.

I sense in my soul how intense Ori's emotions are right now, and maybe that chased the Knife away, like that creature Dad created decimated the Depraved. I'm so grateful to Ori. I'm so thankful to have him. Whatever magic brought us together, he's changed my life.

I kiss him, basking in the connection that feels even more precious to me now. Who can say how long this moment will last, how long I'll be free of the guilt and anger that's been festering inside of me since I came back to life.

Ori kisses me deeper, his long fingers reaching for the buttons of my flannel, flicking them back in quick succession until my torso is bare. He pulls off my shirt, flinging it behind me. Then he throws his arms around my neck, and in one quick motion I get to my feet, his legs wrapped around my waist. In three steps I'm over the bed, lowering Ori onto the mattress, our mouths locked together the entire time. Ori pulls away for one second so he can rip his shirt off, too, then pulls me down on top of him, our beating hearts pounding against each other's chests, finding that perfect rhythm, in sync. The tension leaves my body and I lean in to him, grinding my hips against his. I know he can feel how eager I am, through the layers of denim, through the connection between our souls.

I look into his eyes, long, deep, and Ori knows what I'm asking. He nods, telling me yes, telling me it's time we make magic, the kind only our bodies can make.

My heart soars. After days and days of guilt and sadness and regret like a never-ending fire in my gut, being lit up inside by something different—something *good*—practically bowls me over.

Who knows when the Knife will be back. For now, I need to savor the things *Ori* makes me feel. And as we explore each other's bodies, taking our connection to places it's never been before, I know he truly is my soulmate.

CHAPTER
NINETEEN

THE HARD HATE IN LAUREL'S HEART IS STRONGER NOW THAT THE Knife is dead than it was when the Horde and their Depraved master were on a rampage. She had such a pure purpose then: to defeat those monsters, to prove to her father she and Jaleesa were stronger together than apart. Now, she just wants to see Nigel and Ori brought to justice by any means necessary. Along with any magician who's helping them get away with it.

Phantom pinpricks run up her arm as she thinks about Jameson and the curse he unleashed on her. She felt her skin bubble and slide, literally melting off. He acted like it was an accident, the curse meant for that Depraved, but was it? Even if it was, the end result is the same. Jameson is so hellbent on helping the boys that he doesn't care who he hurts to protect them.

Laurel stares out the massive windows of the log house of her family's Wyoming estate, into the expansive forest, dark this late in the night. Her blank expression reflects back at her in the glass, reminding her of the haunted faces of Guild magicians who lost loved ones during the Culling.

Laurel sighs. She'll never forget the ones they lost. Many would come here to Wyoming, talking Guild business with her father or meandering through the acres and acres of forest to use their nymph gifts. Laurel's personal favorite was shaping the branches, boughs, and trunks of their pine trees, far surpassing a tree house and creating an entire tree village she could run and swing and play through with the kids of her dad's colleagues. Even at eighteen years old, it was hard for her to find something more thrilling than leaping from their tallest trees and landing with her nymph friends in the nets of vines she'd make on the spot.

Many of those friends' parents are now dead. A couple of those friends are, too. Speared through by the sharp bones of the Horde or swept up in the Knife's massive fist to have their hearts sucked out of their chests. Laurel's still beats, but it's filled with guilt. Guilt that she's alive, that she never even fought in that epic battle. Guilt that she will walk through those trees again, when so many who have visited before never will.

Laurel's body aches to return to the forest, to lean into its thrills and wash away the memories of all that's happened with a surge of adrenaline. She'd climb to the tallest boughs, make them grow even higher, then let gravity take her, using her power to create pillowy flowers to land in or vines to catch her at the very last second. If her powers aren't up to the task, maybe she doesn't belong in the Guild after all. Maybe she's meant to be with those people they lost, the people whose lives she had a hand in ending.

Laurel balls her hand into a fist, pounds it against her thigh. Whether she's felt guilty or afraid or angry or sad, one emotion has been a constant alongside the others: hatred. Hatred for Nigel. Hatred for Ori. An intense anger that they would put her in this spot to begin with, that they would put the entire Guild through this. Their power was so strong that something had to be done about them. All her actions were justified.

The front door bursts open, and the familiar sound of her father's boots stomping against the stone of the foyer snaps her to attention. More footsteps follow, and Laurel's heart skips when the only person who could even slightly settle her nerves walks into the house: Jaleesa. Along with Jaleesa's mom, who uses a steady hum to keep Nigel's dad afloat, his legs, arms, and mouth bound by vines.

Alister doesn't even acknowledge his daughter as he whips a commanding finger toward the leather sofa next to her.

"Place him on the couch," he barks. Pallavit lets out one sharp, shrill note, and Reggie is there in a flash of purple.

Still, Alister doesn't look at his daughter as he marches into the living room, pale eyes zeroed in on Reggie with a ferocity Laurel rarely sees. Her father has always been a politician: cool, confident, aloof—level-headed, even in times of crisis, always ready to debate his point. But now, his hands shake, his eyes are bloodshot. He'd never be seen this way in public.

"What was it?" Alister asks. "That thing that came out of you."

The vine covering Reggie's lips slithers away—and the man actually *smiles*. He laughs, the sound throaty and low. "Are you k-kidding m-me?" Reggie coughs through his words. He probably hasn't spoken since he was captured. He clears his throat, swallows a bit to coat his mouth. "You know as well as I do that my magic was taken from me. You were there—you and your father, rubbing it in Ma's face. So how the *fuck* should I know what that was?"

Alister makes a slicing motion with his hand and an inch-long thorn embeds itself in Reggie's cheek. He grunts in pain.

Jaleesa cringes, and Laurel is at her girlfriend's side in an instant. Her instinct is always to protect the fae. Through everything.

"It's okay," Laurel whispers. "Just a little coaxing to get him to tell the truth."

Jaleesa nods, once, her lips pressed tight.

Alister locks eyes with Pallavit. "Do it."

Pallavit steps forward, her throat glowing purple. She puts her middle fingers on either side of Reggie's head, letting out shrill staccato notes. Reggie looks her directly in the eye as tendrils of purple magic crawl into his ears, invading his brain. His eyelids flutter briefly, the only sign in his stubborn glare that the magic is working.

Pallavit's notes cut off suddenly. "He's telling the truth," she says. "He doesn't know what that was. If we take him back to the Guild, we could—"

"NO!" Alister roars. "Do you realize what you're suggesting? We welcomed his *son* into the Guild with open arms and look what happened! The Horde awakened. The Guild in pieces that we had to clean up. Lives *lost*, Pallavit. Who knows what devastation that boy's *father* could cause if we bring him into our headquarters. What if that *thing* shows back up and trains its power on our own? Do you want to have more lives on our hands?"

The fae shakes her head. "Of course not."

Alister grins coolly, always winning his debates. He then whips his head back in Reggie's direction, ambushing him with questions. "Where is your son? Who else is in league with you? Are you trying to take down the Guild?"

Blood trickles down Reggie's face from the thorn still lodged in his cheek. Red slithers into the crook at the corner of his mouth, and his tongue darts out to catch it.

"Thirsty, Reggie?" Alister asks. "We could give you something to ease the pain. I always want my guests to be *comfortable*. I seem to remember you have an affinity for beer. More than one of our members have seen you positively *soaked* in it through the years."

Sweat beads along Reggie's brow. "Appreciate the hospitality, Ali." He swallows, his lips quivering for the first time. "But I'm off the stuff."

"Shame," Alister says. Another whip of his hands and a dozen thorns pierce Nigel's father in his thighs, his arms, his chest. Reggie shouts this time, and Jaleesa squeezes Laurel's hands.

"It's all right," the nymph coos again. "Everything will be fine."

"Any answers coming to mind, Reginald?" Alister asks, his voice tinged with a sort of glee that makes Laurel's heart pound. They could get answers. They could end this.

But still, Nigel's father doesn't talk.

"So be it."

Alister snaps his fingers and steps back, looking at Pallavit expectantly.

"Don't snap at me," she says, arms crossed. "I'm not at your beck and call."

Alister rolls his eyes. "Really, Pallavit, is that your biggest concern?"

Pallavit sighs and fills the space Alister left for her. She sings those staccato notes shriller, sharper than before. Her purple magic flies into Reggie's ears, the power snaking deeper and deeper with each note. His feet twitch this time, his arms convulse, until his whole body writhes like his soul is trying to escape from the prison of his bones.

Then Reggie screams.

Laurel looks on, her heart pounding faster, faster, faster, her eyes getting wider with anticipation. Will they finally learn the truth?

"You're hurting me." Jaleesa snatches her fingers from Laurel's grip and massages them.

"Sorry," Laurel says, and while she means it, she can't stop staring at Reggie.

"It's fine," Jaleesa mutters, barely audible over Reggie's screams. "I just— I need a minute. I'll be right back."

Laurel doesn't register the absence of her girlfriend's warmth.

Not even her own mother looks her way as Jaleesa hurries down the Baumbachs' halls. Reggie's cries of pain follow her, though, and she knows it will be a long time before they stop echoing in her mind. If they ever stop at all. Fae aren't known for forgetting sounds, especially ones as tortured as this.

How could she have been so naive? She's been trained in magic all her life, but never once has she considered the tactics Guild members might use to extract information from supposed enemies.

If there's anything good to be salvaged from this terrible day, it's that she finally has a moment to look closer into Alister. With the Baumbachs distracted, she can search for clues about Guild-wide spells and the Cornucopia like Nigel asked. She can't remember why he wanted her to look into these things, exactly, but he insisted the information could help change the Guild. And if there's anything she's learned in her short time in the organization, it's that the Guild needs changing. If she hadn't thought so before tonight, the scene she just witnessed would have done the trick. If she'd stayed in that room another second, she'd have been sick.

The twisted enjoyment on Laurel's face was the final straw. How could Jaleesa have been so wrong about her girlfriend? She had been sure that the girl she fell in love with wanted to make the world a better place. Yes, Laurel was hypercompetitive, but all magicians are. Jaleesa never thought she could be so . . . perverse.

And her own mother was going along with it! Isn't that the

cherry on top of it all. These people she thought she could trust just tortured a human like it was nothing. Laurel would argue it's for the greater good, but is it? Or is it payback? Payback for the boys being more powerful than her. Payback for one-upping Alister's family. Payback for the devastation Nigel and Ori caused in the Culling.

All this flies through Jaleesa's mind as she hurries to Alister's office. She's lost count of how many times she's visited Laurel's house from childhood until today. For Guild celebrations, for casual hangouts, for massive sleepovers where they'd play magical versions of tag with a few friends. It was during Laurel's fourteenth birthday party here that Jaleesa realized the thrill of being chased by Laurel was about something bigger. So Jaleesa knows every nook and cranny of the house. And she knows Alister's office is the place she's most likely to find answers to Nigel's questions.

When she reaches the pinewood door, Jaleesa looks over her shoulder. The coast is clear, so she grasps the wooden knob decorated with intricate carvings of crawling ivy. Laurel once told her that the wood was enchanted so that no one could open any of the doors unless they had the heart of a Baumbach.

"Try it," Laurel had urged that day, motioning to the door that led to her bedroom.

"What?" Jaleesa had looked at her girlfriend skeptically. *"But I'm not a Baumbach."*

She remembers how Laurel had smirked. *"I didn't say you have to be a Baumbach. That's just the* literal *interpretation of the spell."* She'd reached forward then and grabbed Jaleesa's hand, bringing the fae's fingers up to her lips and kissing them so softly. Jaleesa's heart had fluttered with emotion as Laurel placed Jaleesa's palm over her chest. *"But you have my heart,"* Laurel had whispered.

She'd then placed the fae's hand back on the knob, and the door swung open easily. They'd collapsed on Laurel's bed as they had so many times before, kissing this time, sharing their deepest secrets and desires.

"I don't even think Dad knows about that little loophole to the spell," Laurel had said, her eyes darkening. *"Because he doesn't know how to love."*

Ever since, Jaleesa had felt closer to Laurel than to any other person. That is, until the very last day of their Culling.

Just as it had that time before, the door opens smoothly when Jaleesa turns the doorknob, this time to Alister's office. A pang hits her chest as she realizes this means she still has Laurel's heart. Especially when the fae isn't sure how much of her own heart she'll ever give to the nymph again.

Jaleesa tenses, wondering if some sort of secondary alarm has been triggered. She glances back down the hallway, but the only sounds coming from the living room are those of Reggie's agony. Of course Alister didn't add any extra precautions. Nobody is quick enough to outsmart a Baumbach.

Jaleesa steps inside and shuts the door quietly behind her. The office is all dark wooden walls and paneling. A mahogany desk sits in front of a wall of shelves loaded with pictures of Alister. Alister with his conservative colleagues, Alister on the steps of the Capitol Building, Alister with the host of some conspiracy theory cable news show, Alister holding up a copy of his best-selling book on how to raise a "traditional" family. Looking at these photos, you'd never know Alister even has a family. Every last picture features only *one* Baumbach, and it's not Laurel. And it certainly isn't his wife, Jane, who prefers socializing in Aspen over spending time with her husband and daughter.

"It's all bullshit," Jaleesa says.

She blows a raspberry at Alister's smug faces before clearing her throat, her skin igniting with purple power.

"Cornucopia's the word
I'm searching for here.
If you feel it inside,
bring it near."

Her magic billows out from her neck, washing the room in a lavender haze. This summoning spell is one of Jaleesa's favorites. Her power soaks into the books lining the opposite wall, slides into the drawers of Alister's desk, seeps into the floorboards looking for hidden nooks. If any item has the word *Cornucopia* in it or on it, the magic will bring said item to her.

Jaleesa holds her hands out expectantly. But as the haze begins to fade, Jaleesa realizes she's come up empty.

"Dammit."

Jaleesa sighs, collapsing against the wall in defeat. When her back hits it, she feels something move behind her, a knot in the wood clicking into place. Too fast for Jaleesa to comprehend, the wall slides away and she falls down a set of stone stairs.

She tumbles head over heels, her thoughts as jumbled as her spill. She's sure she's seconds away from cracking her skull against the last step. At best, she'll be concussed. At worst, she'll crack her neck.

"Wait!" The word flies out of her, a bright flash of magic bursting from her lips. She freezes in midair, upside down, her long hair piled up on the rock step beneath her. With a tug, her power lifts her right side up, the blood rushing back out of her head, and sets her gently down on her feet. She fumbles for the wall to steady herself, only to find it's moist and moldy.

Jaleesa snaps her hand back. Slimy stone is the last thing she'd expect anywhere within the pristine wooden architecture of the Baumbach mansion. Magic flares in her throat, the hairs on her arms stand on end. *Nothing* about this place feels right. What *is* this place?

The pounding of her heart fills her ears as her eyes adjust to the darkness. She can feel the ceiling over her head, low, within reach. She hunches on instinct, as if the house might collapse and crush her at any minute.

"Breathe, Jaleesa," she whispers. Everything in her begs to turn back, but she must be close to answers. Nothing screams secrets like a hidden passageway.

Taking a deep breath, she gingerly places her fingers on the grotesque wall and feels her way along the stone. She places one foot in front of the other, step-by-step, until she hears a sort of rhythm in the way her heartbeat mingles with her breath and the soft smoosh of her shoes in the damp earth. She follows the rhythm—the music of life—tension easing from her shoulders with each foot forward. Until finally, she sees a light.

It's soft, gentle, maybe a hundred feet in the distance. It's just a pinprick at first, only a portion of what truly lies beyond. It's green— not the rotten, decaying green of the Depraved, but the green of growth, of plants, of life. The color reminds Jaleesa of the Laurel she once knew, the one who would lead her through the Baumbach forest and make flowers bloom with the flick of a finger.

And so, reminded of that light that once filled her girlfriend, Jaleesa marches forward. She breaks into a jog, that pinprick of nymph magic growing until Jaleesa finds herself at the entrance to a cavern. No—the entrance to a forest, in the most unlikely of places.

Here, in the dank, dripping dark, where the warmth of sunlight has never been felt, there are dozens of trees. The leaves covering their branches emit that green glow of nymph magic. She eagerly descends another set of stone steps to inspect these marvels. Her feet hit the earth, softer even then it was on the pathway here, slowing her.

As she makes her way through the muck to the nearest trunk, her nostrils flare with an acrid smell. Burnt rubber, something totally unnatural, something that shouldn't be coming from a tree. She coughs and covers her nose. Two yards from the nearest plant, she's close enough to see that the wood is a dark gray, flakes of ash sloughing off it and littering the gnarled roots below. Dark sap oozes through crevices in the bark, slowly dripping down the length of the trunk, as if the tree is bleeding.

Jaleesa doesn't know what to make of the grotesque appearance of the trees' trunks paired with the ethereal glow of their leaves. She steps under the nearest branch and examines the leaves hanging just inches above her head. Their veins stand out stark in their glow, twisting and turning to form intricate patterns.

Jaleesa's heart skips a beat. She squints.

Those aren't patterns.

They're names.

Familiar ones.

Her Cullingmates.

Her fingers fly fast through the leaves, uncovering name after name spelled out by those intricate veins—all of those who were inducted into the Guild with her not even two weeks ago. She doesn't know what this forest is, but rotting and hidden in the darkness like this, what could it be but something sinister? The once-enchanting veins now look like snakes, poisoning all those who worked so hard to become members, to dedicate their magic to a life of service.

Then she gasps.

Jaleesa Devi.

She knew, deep down, that her name would be here. If all her other Cullingmates' names were, why not hers?

Not all, as it were. One name seems to be missing. She rushes to the next nearest branch, where even more names are etched inside leaves, this time of Guild members a year older. She runs to the next tree, scans those branches, its leaves filled with names of magicians who are older still.

Back to the first branch, she double, triple checks.

She's sure of it.

Laurel's name is missing.

She sings a summoning spell again, but just like with the Cornucopia, nothing with Laurel's name turns up.

Jaleesa trudges back through the ominous forest, her feet weighed down by more than just the mucky earth. She runs down the muggy pathway until she spots the glow of Alister's office in the distance. Jaleesa's heart pounds. Will someone be waiting for her there? What if Laurel finally realized she's been gone so long? What if Alister has caught her snooping?

But fear can't crowd out the question that looms largest in her mind:

What were *those trees?*

Soon she's up the stairs and out of the pathway, squinting in the bright light of Alister's office. Her eyes throb, but a pressure eases off her chest, knowing the chilling timber is behind her. The secret wall panel slides back into place with a heavy *thunk*. She braces herself for voices, for punishment for seeking out a place that was clearly meant to remain a secret.

No voices come.

Just laughter, from the living room.

Laughter that should be familiar. Laughter that used to mingle with her own and float among the trees surrounding this house.

But this laughter is twisted, like the veins on the leaf that spelled out her name. It's the twisted laughter of her girlfriend, mixing with Alister's, then mingling with grunts of pain.

Jaleesa dashes out of the office, firmly shutting the door behind her. She takes a second to splash water on her face in the powder room just down the hall, but her face won't cool and her stomach won't settle. The cackling she hears shouldn't be able to come from Laurel's lips.

Jaleesa looks at her phone. She's only been gone for twelve minutes, but it feels like a lifetime. Nigel said to look for a spell that's been cast on the entire Guild—and almost the entire Guild was named on those leaves. That has to mean something.

Jaleesa clears her throat, takes a deep breath, then reenters the living room. The sight of a bloodied and unconscious Reggie almost makes her vomit. She catches eyes with her mom and is relieved to see that Pallavit, at least, is clammy, running her hand along her smooth scalp like she always does when she's nervous.

Alister, however, seems ready to celebrate. He grabs a decanter of whiskey out of a bar in the corner. Laurel races to Jaleesa, and the fae tenses, anticipating questions, but Laurel hardly seems to have noticed her absence.

"We got them!" Laurel crows. "Reggie's mind cracked in *minutes*. Humans are so weak!" She snorts, then pulls Jaleesa close, something she never does in front of her father. Alister clears his throat with disapproval, but Laurel doesn't seem to hear it. "There's a resistance, and they're all in it. Nigel, Ori, Bex, her dads, Jameson. This is it. We'll take them all down!"

Laurel collapses on the couch in a fit of laughter. All Jaleesa wants to do is run.

She might have discovered that strange forest, but the pit in her stomach tells her it's too little, too late.

CHAPTER
TWENTY

THE BEST THING ABOUT BEING A UNICORN IS THAT THEY TRAVEL *FAST*. Bex feels power in her hooves with every step. She's crossed at least three states now, just running. The wind through her mane, the smell of grass as it's churned up by her hooves, the dew that coats her eyelashes as she takes in the sunrise. It's magic.

When it's finally time for a break, Bex shifts back to her human form and meanders through a meadow. Galloping across state lines is catching up with her. Until her magic recharges enough to hold her unicorn shape again, she'll have to hoof it—*not* literally, this time—in her black combat boots through a lush mountaintop forest not far outside Boulder, Colorado.

Bex isn't sure why she ended up here, exactly. As soon as she burst out of Jameson's heart home, she shifted and took off. She dashed across Missouri and Kansas, chewing on Nigel's words, wondering if she matters to the Resistance at all. Jameson had told her to do some soul-searching to find her place, but no matter how far her mind wandered as she lost herself in the rhythm of her hoofsteps, she always came up empty. So she kept running, following the tug in her heart, pulling her west, until finally, *finally*, she knew she could stop.

She walks aimlessly, soaking up the sun, until she feels a new sensation: a sort of buzzing through her skin, setting every atom of her being to vibrate. Maybe this is some instinct warning her of a demon or Depraved nearby. Her skin glows a faint silver as she prepares to shift and defend herself.

But wait. The vibration isn't unsettling. It's like a faint tickle, one that makes her laugh, loudly. It's nice to release the pressure of these last couple weeks.

It isn't until she plops onto the grass, lying on her back, that she finally catches her breath. This place feels good. This place feels right.

She looks at the mountains and jolts up, ramrod straight.

It feels different here because it *is* different. It stretches farther than before. Much farther. More of a plain than a meadow really, low hills stretching for miles, covered in grasses ranging in color from deepest green to gentlest blue to subtlest yellow. Streams run through them, pristine and crystal clear, filling the air with a soothing gurgle. Blinking light draws Bex's attention. Where rocky mountains once stood, giant, jagged crags of gold, silver, and bronze now tower overhead. Their metallic peaks reflect the sun like beacons.

This isn't Colorado anymore.

This is paradise.

A dust cloud billows at the base of those metallic mountains, building quickly. Soon the sound of hundreds of hooves reaches her, mingled with nickers and whinnies and neighs. Flashes of light in those same metallic hues dot the air as the sun reflects off the horns of the herd that's gaining on her.

The herd of unicorns.

Bex knows how fast they can move, so it's no surprise when they're on her in two seconds flat. *Literally* on her. Unicorns push and nip at each other to get as close as possible, nuzzling Bex with their downy muzzles. This close, Bex can see the individual curves in their spiral horns; the glittering sheens of gold, silver, and bronze; the varying shades of their black, white, cream, brown, or spotted hides. Her skin buzzes with that happy electricity as the unicorns press against her.

"Hello," she says through a laugh. "Where did you come from?"

She hears a voice without hearing it at all. *Hundreds* of voices: masculine, feminine, and everything in between or outside that spectrum, both high-pitched and low, coming from everywhere and nowhere at once. A massive herd-voice that resonates inside her.

Home. We are home. We brought you here.

"That would explain the tug," Bex says, pressing her fingers to the center of her chest. "But why me?"

You're the only one who can be trusted. The only one who wants real change.

The words reverberate through her, the unicorns' insistence making her skin itch.

You want to change humankind. The Guild. Everything.

"So you know about that, huh?"

Bex clamps her hands over her ears as the herd erupts with noise. Huffs, whinnies, brays. Their frenzy echoes across the plain, echoing off the mountaintops. Bex shields her eyes as their horns flash with emotion.

When they finally settle down, Bex says, "I'll take that as a yes."

We have much to tell you. Too much has happened that has forced us here.

Bex plops back onto the grass, tucking her legs beneath her. "I've got time."

The herd takes a collective breath, then launches into their story.

"Nigel!"

My eyes flutter open slowly.

"Mmm?"

I look down at Ori, but he's asleep. His head rests gently on my chest, rising and falling with each of my breaths, and he's snoring softly. Oh, I can't wait to use that against him. Snarky, confident, unbreakable Ori is a *snorer*.

"*Nigel!*" It's Bex. From the rise in volume and the creaking floorboards, I'm guessing she's headed up here. Sure enough, her stomps shake the stairs to the attic and she flings our bedroom door open.

"NIGEL!" I've never seen her this angry before, even when she left, and she was pissed then.

"Whassat?" Ori picks up his head, eyes half closed, trying to prop himself on my chest before falling back to the sheets. "What time is it?"

"It's four in the afternoon!" Bex screams, whipping an accusatory finger at me. "*And* you're possessed by the Knife! Because Ori brought you back from the dead using its heartstone!"

That wakes Ori right up, hurt flashing in his eyes. "You told her without me?"

"No!" Anger swells up inside of me to match Bex's. My skin gets hot, and I jump out of bed to meet Bex head-on. My heart beats so hard I think my chest might burst. My hands light up gold and—

"Whoa there, cowboy!" Bex says, her cheeks flushing pink as

she deflates so quickly it's disorienting. "At least put some pants on before we have it out."

I look down, and there goes all my emotion, too. I'm standing in red flannel boxers, one barely closed button and a thin layer of fabric away from Bex knowing *all* my secrets.

My face flares with the heat of a thousand fire ants. "I'll meet you downstairs."

But Ori has other plans. He coats his pink magic on an action figure of a Speedo-clad wrestler and slips a pair of doll pants over its legs. My jeans fly from the floor and slam into my chest—knocking me back onto the bed—before slithering up my legs, the button clasping and the zipper sliding up in one quick move.

"I'll miss the view, but I think now we can talk." There's Ori's smirk.

Bex grabs my shirt from the foot of the bed and hurls it at me. "Do you have any idea what danger you've put us in?"

"I was going to tell you," I say, quietly, darkly, getting to my feet.

"When?" she insists.

"Today, all right?!"

She looks at Ori, who nods. "We really were about to tell everyone."

"Oh, don't think that gives you some kind of pass. You've been here for two weeks!"

"And nobody got killed!" I yell.

"YET! I knew something was wrong with you! I could smell it in your magic every time I shifted to a unicorn. You know who else could sense it? Demons and Depraved! *You're* why they keep show-ing up. You put us all in danger! The Knife is in you, and it will take complete control of your power!"

Ori gets out of bed—somehow fully clothed, so *he's* spared the embarrassment—and gets in between us, hands extended like that's enough to physically stop us from lunging for the other's throat.

I will fling him aside like one of his dolls and rip her to shreds when I have control!

Magic flares in my hands, gold tinged with green.

This is bad. So bad. I smack a glowing hand against my skull, trying to knock the thoughts free.

Bex falters. "Nigel?"

"You're right. It's getting worse." I slouch down on the bed in defeat. "More violent. It's tainting my power. I'm afraid . . . it's going to make me do something I can't take back."

The mattress creaks as Ori sits beside me and laces his fingers through mine. "I won't let it take you, cowboy."

Bex doesn't look convinced. "Good luck with that. They told me a lot of things that might help the Resistance, but they have no idea how to get it out of you."

"Who's they?" Ori asks.

"The unicorns."

Ori scoffs. "You get how ridiculous that sounds, right? No one has seen a unicorn in centuries."

But that's not true, is it? A unicorn had answers for my parents once, not so long ago.

"What did they tell you?" I ask.

Ori looks at me like I've lost my mind.

"They talked to my mom and dad," I say. "Jameson showed me in one of his books."

Bex barrels on despite Ori's look of betrayal. "They were able to explain what we saw on the ranch," she says.

I perk up. "And?"

"That being your dad created is called a Beloved," Bex explains.

"They're created from a bond that can only be formed between a human and a magician. They're the antithesis of the Depraved, basically: magical entities triggered by selfless acts of love by humans for magicians. Your dad did that when he took the Depraved's blast to protect Jameson, knowing it could kill him."

Ori scowls. "Your dad loves Jameson?"

He never once thought to protect me.

1 scoff. "I guess. Jameson said they've been best friends since before their own Culling."

Bex nods. "Apparently, all kinds of love count: romantic, familial, platonic. Love is love. It's not always this"—she waves her hand at the two of us—"happily ever after bullshit."

Ori laughs. "You sure sound like a true romantic."

"So what if I'm not?" Bex snaps. "Is it so hard to believe my entire life doesn't revolve around finding a partner? But my power isn't as strong as yours, or my dads', and the only explanation anyone can give for that is being single. It's fucked up!" She shifts her foot to an elephant's and literally stomps through the floorboards. "But the unicorns summoned *me. I'm* the one who knows what the Beloved are. I'm the one who can start this new phase of the Resistance. Completely single, yet totally whole Bex. Got it?"

Her chest heaves while Ori and I sit, silent. Ori's expression is blank—until he laughs, hard. "You tell 'em, girl."

The defiant furrows in Bex's forehead disappear and she lets out a tentative laugh. "Thanks. For the support."

"Sorry things have been so focused on us," Ori says. "But you get that we didn't ask for this, right?"

"I know," Bex says. "But one day I was working alongside my dads, and the next I was pushed to the background. It sucks."

Ori nods. "I get that." He looks at me and widens his eyes the slightest bit, clearly nudging me to agree.

"Yeah. For sure," I say, not even convincing myself.

Bex breezes past me. "But that's what makes it so great that your dad created the Beloved. It's proof that other kinds of love are just as important."

"Right." I scoff. "Because my dad is such a *loving* guy. It's got to be a fluke."

"Why haven't we ever heard of this power, though?" Ori asks.

"Think about it: Magicians stay separated from humans," Bex says. "Even when we marry or befriend humans, they don't tend to be around when we're in life-threatening situations on behalf of the Guild."

"But if the unicorns know about it, it must have happened before," Ori says.

Bex nods, and a swell of jealousy makes my breath come in short, rapid spurts. The herd truly did give her all their information on this connection.

"Back in the time of the Ancestrals, a goblin and a human fell in love," Bex says. "They saw Beloved born of that relationship. But when colonizers came to North America and the Depraved numbers skyrocketed, the Ancestrals ruled the creation of Beloved an outlier. They determined that humans were inherently cruel and born to focus on the negative, so Beloved would never come to outnumber the Depraved. They gave up."

"Can't say I blame them," Ori says. "Humans suck. Magicians too." He pauses. "Well, I guess not *all* humans. My dad's pretty amazing, and he's a human."

"Right!" Bex says. "And now that we know about Beloved, magical and human separation needs to end. That's got to be the next goal of the Resistance: to reveal the existence of magic to humankind. Specifically, to show them the types of magic they make with their emotions—the good *and* the bad—in the hopes that they'll focus more on the good. We all saw what happened when that Depraved went head-to-head with the Beloved."

"This could be it," Ori says, the words coming out so fast they nearly jumble together. "If we can figure out how to end whatever spell is wiping Guild members' memories, stop the Culling, and reveal to humans that they're *needed* to destroy Depraved—"

"We could change the Guild once and for all," Bex finishes.

Ori shakes my shoulder. "I know this is a shock, cowboy, but come on. This is great news!"

I stare back at him blankly. This news should make me want to celebrate. But Bex is talking about my dad like he's ushering in an entirely new era for humanity and magickind. He's been nothing but a monster to me and now I'm supposed to embrace him? Not to mention I've got a literal monster inside of me, and Bex came blaring in here like that's *my fault*. I didn't ask for this! I would have just sacrificed myself and let the Knife die with me, but Ori had to bring me back. I could have died a hero! Instead, I've got to sit around and wait for the Knife to strike, wait for it to use me to become the monster that everyone fears. It's so fucking ironic, isn't it? My dad will be the savior and I'll be the villain, just like the Guild suspected all along.

My breathing gets shorter, shallower, but I know if I voice any of it, I'll lose control. So instead I just say, "Yeah. I'm fine. Just . . . taking it all in. It's a lot."

"Well, hold on," Bex says. "There's one other thing."

"What now?" I grunt.

"You ever heard of something called the Horn of Plenty?" Bex asks. "Sometimes people call it the Cornucopia."

It's like someone jabbed a cattle prod into my legs. I stand straight up. "Yes! Meema wrote about it. In her journal. She said it was missing. What is it?"

Bex's eyes darken. "So, the whole reason unicorns very rarely reveal themselves to us? A couple centuries ago, a corrupt magician killed one of the creatures and sawed off their horn. He created the Horn of Plenty by cursing the magic within. Unicorns have the ability to nullify evil magic, but the Cornucopia does the opposite: It *magnifies* the power of whomever the bearer targets when they blow it. And when it magnifies that person's power, it warps it, too. Turns it destructive. The Guild captured the magician and hid the Horn away, but they couldn't destroy it. Apparently, to be destroyed it has to be blown by the last person affected by its curse, but with the spirit of true forgiveness in their heart. I guess no one's been able to do that so far.

"Since the day the Horn was locked up, unicorns have only interacted with magicians a handful of times, and only when they're certain that magician's intentions are pure." She blushes. "For whatever reason, they chose me."

The unicorns spoke to my parents that day after their kindness when helping a herdmember. But now the herd has chosen to speak with Bex, out of the blue. The anger in my belly only worsens, sweat beads under my eyes as heat flushes from my head to my toes.

"Why contact you at all?" I spit. "Why was it so important that *you* know about this Horn of Plenty thing, and not us who have literally put our lives on the line to change the Guild? That's not *pure enough* for the herd?"

Bex puts her finger right in my face. "Because you're like this, dumbass. Because you can't control yourself and the unicorns don't know what you're capable of, not with *it* inside of you. Their magic can weaken power with evil intention, but even they aren't convinced they'll be able to nullify the Knife now that it's using a magician as a vessel. Long story short: They don't trust you, and they only confide in people they trust, especially considering someone's used it.

The Cornucopia. The herd can hear it, no matter where it's blown. A cruel joke by that fucker who made the Horn to begin with."

Ori's up now, too, anxiously pacing beside the bed. "Wait. When? When was it blown?"

"Two weeks ago, and they used it twice," Bex says. "During—"

"The Culling," Ori breathes. "During our Culling." He turns to me. "What if *we* were the intended target? What if they warped our power, magnified it, on purpose? With our magic already stronger thanks to our connection, that magnification could be devastating. *That's* why our power woke the Horde."

I can feel the weight on his shoulders ease with the hope that all that destruction—all those deaths—might not have been our fault.

"That's exactly what I thought," Bex says. "It would make sense. The effects last for one spell, so if they blew it at just the right time . . ."

"They're the monsters," Ori says. "Not us."

He flashes me a true smile—no smirk, no cockiness, just pure joy—and it takes my breath away. I want to kiss him right this very second. I want to throw him on the bed and celebrate that we might not have to live life always wondering when we'll hurt someone next.

But you still can't be trusted. Not with what's inside you. Not with this destructive power waiting to be let loose. Ori might not be a monster, but you are.

That fucking voice! Is this what our life together will be like? No reason to run, but stuck with a monster in my soul that I can't possibly escape?

"The Cornucopia used to be in the Guild's relic hall," Bex says. "We need to tell my dads to investigate. Where are they?"

I shake my head. "I'm not sure."

"They were here when I left," Bex insists, "but they're gone now. Pop didn't tell you where they were going?"

I look at Ori, who shrugs. "We've been passed out all day."

Bex's eyes flash with worry as she races for the door. "How could you sleep until four p.m.?!"

Bex shifts into a hawk and zips down the stairs, Ori and I following after and reaching the second-floor landing just in time to see her fly into her dads' room.

"FUCK!" she screams.

We race in behind her and find Bex panting next to one of Yamato's dress forms. Pinned to the center of its chest is a piece of paper with three words scribbled on it, slanted as if the writer was being pulled back while they tried to finish the note.

THEY HAVE US.

CHAPTER
TWENTY-ONE

"Tribunal!" The call echoes throughout the Guild, repeated again and again while magicians of every type spell their way to the fifteenth floor. Jaleesa hums a single note, one that makes her float. Her flight is shaky thanks to her rattled nerves. She tried to call Nigel last night, to update him on what happened to his father and the discovery of the twisted forest beneath Alister's office. But he never answered.

The names Jameson, Yamato, and Kenneth are on everyone's lips. Right after gulping down whiskey at his estate, Alister returned here to spread the news of the men's betrayal. Every last magician knows why they've been called, all arriving in person and gossiping as they make their way to the tribunal.

"A resistance! Working to take down the Guild!"

"I never would have suspected Jameson."

"Or the Sasakis! If we can't trust our own, who can we trust?"

Jaleesa stumbles when her feet clunk on the marble floor; she's distracted imagining what those voices would say if anyone realized she's in contact with Nigel. That she trusts him. That she, Jaleesa Devi, knows something is wrong with the Guild—she just can't quite remember what.

She's lost to her thoughts until Laurel grabs her hand and pulls her into the seat beside her. The nymph is practically buzzing. Her eyes are wide and slightly bloodshot, flicking to the open seats of the tribunal room as if she can will everyone to arrive and the trial to begin. Her nails are bitten to the quick, something Jaleesa hasn't seen in years.

A pang of deep longing hits Jaleesa, right in the center of her heart. She misses her girlfriend—the one she'd tell every secret to, share every first with, the magician whose determination and conviction to uphold the Guild's legacy truly inspired her. There was a time when Jaleesa thought Laurel made her both a better person and a better magician. But this nymph is so different from the girl she once knew. Hungry for revenge, performing all kinds of mental gymnastics to convince herself it's okay to harm the people she perceives as monsters. Staring at Laurel, Jaleesa knows the chasm between them is so wide now they may never be able to close the distance.

Laurel meets the fae's eyes, her smile ravenous, oblivious to Jaleesa's sense of loss. "It's happening!" she whispers, and turns her gaze to the center of the hall, where four empty chairs appear on the marble floor. A mass of twenty people blink onto the stage. Jameson, Kenneth, Yamato, and Reggie are circled by four magicians each, the Guild not taking any chances that the men will get away. They double down on security with magic ropes that shackle the captives' wrists as they're shoved into the vacant chairs. Alister prowls before the scene, cool triumph tilting his lips up. Not a smile exactly. More like a predator licking its lips before devouring its prey.

"The men before you are traitors."

Alister doesn't yell it, doesn't have the unbridled disgust in his voice Jaleesa would have suspected. He simply states an irrefutable fact, one that snaps everyone to attention.

The nymph moves behind Reggie's chair, placing his hands on the former magician's shoulders. "This man's memories revealed all. He's part of an organization that calls itself the Resistance. In addition to Reginald Barrett, their numbers include at least these three magicians who sit beside him. They wish to stop the Culling."

The Guild erupts.

"That would end everything!"

"Everyone would die!"

"What about balance? The world can't handle that much magic!"

Jaleesa watches as Alister smiles softly, taking in every word like a fae soaking up sound. He lets the anger swell, not moving until the crowd quiets on its own. The mood in the room has changed; the crowd's energy pulses with the desire to stop the Resistance, with anticipation to hear Alister's plan.

"Even more concerning, this man—" Alister increases the pressure on Reggie's shoulders. Jaleesa knows his hands sit right on top of puncture wounds from the night before, covered now by Reggie's soiled button-up. The man's jaw clenches and a vein in his forehead bulges. "*This* man created an entirely unknown magical being. Many of you saw it yourselves from Dispatch." Alister lets go of Reggie to circle around in front of the chained prisoners, pacing in front of all the assembled magicians. "This creature came from the Barrett bloodline, the very bloodline that brought death to our organization mere weeks ago. It would be ludicrous for us to assume the being we saw is benevolent. We must take action now, before this new monster can gain power. Why, it might one day become as mighty as the Knife. How can we say we truly serve humankind if we allow that to happen?"

The room is silent, rapt with attention.

"We cannot let him fool us. We all know what we *think* we saw—this creature defeating a Depraved—but hear me when I say: If it came from a Barrett, we have every reason to believe it's a weapon that can be harnessed against us. I propose we imprison Reginald Barrett until we can determine the threat his powers pose and swiftly remove them."

Nervous rustling ripples through the crowd, the punishment of having powers removed never taken lightly. But as Jaleesa scans the anxious faces, there are more nods of assent than calls for restraint.

"Good." Alister tilts his head to the side, assuming a sympathetic look as he turns to the three stoic magicians bound in front of him. He steps between Yamato and Kenneth, then faces the crowd once more. "A parent's greatest instinct is fierce loyalty to their child." Somehow he's able to say this without once glancing Laurel's way. Jaleesa's gaze flicks to the nymph, catching the want that flashes in her eyes for just a second. It breaks Jaleesa's heart, knowing Laurel will never get it.

Jaleesa searches the room for her mom and finds Pallavit already looking directly at her. A swell of warmth fills her chest. They're not perfect—her dad travels all the time for work, but he floods her phone with texts and makes as many family meals as possible before he has to jet off again. Her mom has certainly let her down recently, but she's taught Jaleesa all she knows about faecraft, like how to harmonize together to create even stronger spells, or to adjust volume or timbre to fine-tune her power. Jaleesa knows her parents love her.

But would that love be able to stand up to the truth? What would Pallavit do if she knew Jaleesa was in contact with Nigel? *Helping* him, even.

Maybe she'd end up on that dais, chained just like the Resistance.

"It's that loyalty that's turned you against us." Sympathy coats Alister's words to the Sasakis. "We know your only desire was to protect Bex." And then it's gone, back to the cool, calculated, assertive nymph Jaleesa's always known. "They fooled us once before, clearly altering their memories to resist our questioning. They should be imprisoned and we should use every power at our disposal until we get honest answers. Even if their minds break."

A few grumblings echo through the crowd. These men were once trusted magicians. Even now, even though Jaleesa can tell the Guild is certain Alister tells the truth, they hesitate. They've known Jameson, Kenneth, and Yamato for decades. She wouldn't be so quick to condemn her friends, either.

"I know it's an extreme measure. But what does this moment in our history call for, if not extreme measures? We must do whatever it takes to prevent another massacre like the one we just experienced."

The hall quiets instantly. Jaleesa knows Alister has them. Which is why no one bats an eye when Alister adds, "In an abundance of caution, I propose we temporarily hold *any* of those among us who are known to be close confidants of Jameson Adebisi or Kenneth and Yamato Sasaki. It stands to reason that they could be involved in this 'Resistance.'"

The seven or eight members Alister's referencing scoff, but no one comes to their defense. Guilty until proven innocent.

Alister nods, satisfied. "When we have all proven ourselves loyal to the Guild, when we have all the answers we can magic out of these betrayers, I call on all of you to join forces with me and stomp out this resistance. Our work will only be done when we get the locations of Nigel Barrett and Orion Olson from the recesses of these traitors' minds and end them. We won't stop until we can assure ourselves that we did everything in our power to prevent *true monsters* from raining terror on this world!"

The crowd goes wild, Laurel's cheers ringing loudest of all. Jaleesa's heart clenches, pity and dread warring inside her. Because even if her girlfriend has never felt undying loyalty from her father, Jaleesa knows Laurel will do everything she can to earn it.

"I call for a vote," Alister bellows over the fervor. "To approve the measures I've suggested. To approve a new age of unity and devotion to the Guild. To approve taking down anyone who will destroy the safety we've worked for centuries to uphold!"

Alister motions toward Pallavit. It pains Jaleesa to know her mom is as swayed by Alister's words as everyone else. With a simple sung note from Pallavit, the scales of justice materialize, yea and nay curling out under each side.

"All in favor of these plans . . ." Alister yells. "Plans to move the Guild forward, to cast out the bad weeds, to create a new era of magical security and prosperity, vote now!"

Bright balls of light in every color of magic soar across the room. It's clear where this is headed. Not a single bright orb sits on the opposing side, not even from the members being accused by association. It would only make them look guilty. Jaleesa wishes she could be that vote, wishes she could explain how Nigel and Ori want nothing but a peaceful world. She knows in her gut that everything Alister declares is wrong, that the boys' power could be *all of theirs* if they'd only give them a chance to explain. To demonstrate. But if she said all that, she'd be shackled like the others.

So for now, she just stares at the bright ball of purple light she sent soaring into the air as it lands among all the others. A single vote that may have linked her to the wrong side of history.

"We have to do something!" Bex says.

"Like what?" Ori asks. "There's three of us, thousands of them. And they all want us dead!"

They turn to me like I'll have all the answers. "I'm just as in the dark as you."

"Maybe I could go back to the unicorns."

"Why not?" I snap. "They sure do love to info dump all over you."

I know it's not fair. I know the unicorns are wary of me because of the Knife. I'm wary of myself! But still, it hurts. And I'd be lying if I said it didn't feel good to spread some of that hurt around.

"Nigel," Ori says warningly. "Don't."

"What?" I say. "I'm not wrong."

"No, you're not." Bex steps right up in my face. "Not wrong at all. Why would they want to work with someone who, when his closest friend realizes her parents were taken by murderous magicians, decides to get jealous about *magic horsies*! But being self-centered is kind of a Barrett thing, isn't it? Your own grandma was such a showboating narcissist that her own son didn't trust her! Why else would they keep her out of the Resistance? She probably knew all about the Culling!"

My hands blaze gold. Nobody talks about Meema like that.

"You think *I'm* the jealous one? *You're* jealous that Ori and I have a connection. You feel left out, like a stupid kid on the playground!"

Bex laughs. "Oh yeah. I'm *so* jealous of the super-secret special powers you haven't even been able to use! You've been hiding here like cowards while my dads put their lives on the line for the Resistance. For *you*!"

My magic fizzles out. My body goes cold.

She's right. I've let her dads, Jameson, all the members of the Resistance that I don't even know face the Guild and risk discovery.

And the day has finally come. They've been caught.

It should be me standing before the tribunal.

It's not too late. I can go to the Guild. I can search for the Cornucopia.

I can set them free.

I step back. One, two, three times. Getting surer of my decision with each clunk of my boots against the hardwood.

"Where are you going?" Ori quirks a suspicious eyebrow.

"You're right, Bex," I say, the vitriol gone from my voice. "I've let everyone else do my dirty work. But we started this mess. Well—that group of asshole magicians started this mess when they decided to fuck everything up with the Culling." I look at Ori with a sad smile. "But we definitely made mistakes. Like bringing the Knife back, for one. It's time to start fixing that. It's time to start fixing the Guild."

GO THERE NOW.

I walk out the bedroom door and down the stairs to the foyer, reaching into my pocket to find the fae bell nestled there. The tiny tinkling noise it makes sounds much louder in the silent, near-empty house.

Jaleesa materializes instantly, her image snaking up from the floorboards.

"Nigel!" Jaleesa says, panting. "Where have you been? I've been trying to tell you—"

"You're working with *her*?" I can't deny the hurt in Ori's voice. I turn to see him glaring at me from the second-floor landing, Bex standing with crossed arms just behind him.

What was it that Bex's dads once said? Secrets corrupt our connection. I should have told him about this all along. "She can be trusted, Ori. She's been helping me the whole time."

"The *whole time*? I thought—"

"Enough!" I've never heard Jaleesa this upset before. "They

have your dads and Jameson locked up in the Guild prisons with Ori's mom."

Ori sucks in a breath. "My mom? What do they want with her?"

Jaleesa turns to me. "You didn't tell him?"

"You knew?!" Ori sounds like he's been punched in the gut.

"I truly meant to tell you," I say. "It just got lost in all of this."

Ori's hands clench into fists. "My mom being imprisoned *got lost?*"

"I'm sorry, Ori. I really am. But it doesn't matter now. Not when I can go in and rescue them all."

"Don't be stupid," Bex says. "They'll capture you on the spot."

"They'll kill you, Nigel." Ori's words are soft. I can hear the rage quivering underneath them, but still he's thinking only of keeping me safe.

Which is why I have to keep *him* safe.

I have to get inside the Guild.

"I've got a trick up my sleeve," I say, giving Ori one last long look. I know he's hurt by my secrets, but if I tell him what I'm thinking now, he'll never let me go.

The Knife is inside me. I'll never get the monster out. But maybe, before I lose control entirely, I can use this monster within me to create enough of a distraction for our dads, Jameson, and Lyra to escape. I can rescue all the people who put their lives on the line for me.

Then I'll let the Guild take my life. Because there's no other way to get rid of the Knife. I know that now, for sure.

I turn to Jaleesa. "Can you take me there? To the Guild?"

Jaleesa nods. "Okay." She sings a quick rhyme, one that makes the front door open and the portal swirl beyond. Jaleesa motions toward it, and I know it will take me to the Guild.

"NIGEL!" I feel Ori's pain through our connection. The abandonment a sharp knife in his back. "Wait!"

I have to get inside the Guild.

I bolt through the door and slam it closed behind me.

Ori feels like he's been punched in the gut. Like he ate too much queso the night before and now his stomach roars awake to announce that was a terrible decision. Only this time, it's worse.

Because Nigel jumping into the Guild alone is *definitely* the world's worst decision.

He looks to Bex, shaking his head in disbelief.

"He left," Ori mumbles. "He left."

Then the disbelief is pushed aside by a wave of indignation. "He's walking into a death trap! He's going to get himself *killed* and leave me behind after everything! After I brought him back!"

Ori sways, emotional whiplash making him woozy. Nigel's only this desperate *because* Ori brought the elf back by fusing him with the Knife. He's felt those moments the Depraved monstrosity burrows into Nigel's power and taints it. It adds to the guilt that's already there from their Culling, from waking up the Horde. Neither of them can forget that if they had never combined their magics in the first place, all those people would still be alive. While the Cornucopia may be to blame, nothing is certain yet, and Ori knows Nigel can't stand the thought of losing control of his power again, even if it is because of the Knife.

That's when it clicks.

Nigel's plan forms in his mind, not through their connection, but because Ori knows that stupid sunshine elf so well. Nigel's going to the Guild because he *wants* to be caught. Ori knows it with a bone-deep certainty. Nigel will go into those marble halls and cow-boy out, rescuing the Resistance. Then he'll *let* the Guild take him. They both know Alister will kill Nigel. And Nigel knows that if he dies, the Knife goes with him, along with any threat that the monster could use his power. Ori will have to feel that loss again, with no way to save him this time.

"You asshole!" Ori screams, blinking down to the foyer, to the spot where his stupid soulmate disappeared with Jaleesa. There's no trace of the fae's spell left behind, no way to follow. "I can't believe you did this!" He blinks again, this time to the front door, and flings it open with so much force it bangs against the wall.

Jaleesa's spell has faded. When Ori stares at the swirling mass of light beyond, he contemplates throwing himself through it, materi-alizing in the real world and luring the Guild to him, just so he can get inside those marble halls and give Nigel a piece of his mind. How could Nigel make this decision, one that affects both of them, and give Ori no say whatsoever?

But then, that's not so different from what Ori did, is it?

"I didn't give him a say, either," he whispers. "Before I made the Knife a part of him."

He steps backward, numbly. As his feet shuffle against the wood floor, he hears a faint ringing. He looks down to find a small pur-ple bell against his sneaker. The spell Nigel used to go behind his back and communicate with Jaleesa. Jealousy and hurt flare in Ori's gut, but he bends down and snags the bell, pocketing it. He doubts Jaleesa would pick up if he rang, too determined to help Nigel with his plan.

He's all out of ideas.

He crumples to the floor, right there in the foyer.

"I don't know what to do," he says flatly.

"I meant what I said," Bex replies, taking slow steps down

the stairs. "We could go to the unicorn herd. See if they have any ideas."

"They can't get the Knife out of him. You said it yourself." Tears prick Ori's eyes. It's his fault they're in this situation.

Bex shakes her head. "No, they can't."

"But you think your horny pals can help us get him out of the Guild?"

"Maybe. It's the only shot we've got."

"You'd do that, even if he has the world's worst demon stuck inside him?"

Bex chews her bottom lip before saying, "He's been a colossal dick, but I would."

That's what makes Bex the best of them, Ori realizes. She knows when to step up. All this time, Ori has wanted nothing more than to go into hiding, to live life with Nigel and forget about the world, while Bex is actively trying to make a difference not just for herself, but for every magician and human out there.

Maybe it's time he does the same.

"Let's go. That elf isn't going to save himself. And maybe we can convince those horsies to help us take down the Guild while we're at it."

CHAPTER
TWENTY-TWO

My heart pounds in anticipation as the portal pulls us forward.

Almost there!

I know this is the Knife's voice, but its excitement mingles with my own thoughts and sense memories. The portal just *feels* right. I'm reminded of how I felt less than a month ago, heading to the Guild for the first time: hopeful for what's to come. I know without a shadow of a doubt that I'm supposed to get inside the Guild. That I'm supposed to change things. *I* will shape the future, and there's nothing the Guild can do to stop me. I coat my body with golden magic and cast an invisibility spell when I feel that pull recede, ready to get my plan started.

But when my feet hit the gold-streaked marble, that feeling of conviction and hope fizzles. We're not in the entry hall like we're supposed to be. I expected to make my way to the prisons, free the Resistance, then let the Guild end me and the Knife within.

Instead, we're higher up on an unfamiliar floor I was never

brought to during the Culling. It's stark, smooth marble as far as the eye can see. It's shockingly bright, too, making me squint. To my left, I can just make out a strange shimmer in the air, the open space of the Guild tower just past it. Magicians don't traverse the floors, no flurry of activity with members going from the entry hall to the library, medical bays, or training facilities. Their absence puts all my senses on high alert.

"Where are we?" I ask, wiping my invisibility spell clean. I step up to the shimmering layer near the banisters and gently place my hand against it. A ripple of gold flares out from my hand, like a stone dropped into a pond. Elf magic.

"It's the twenty-third floor," Jaleesa explains, rolling her eyes before getting one tiny jab in. "Of course you weren't paying attention during our tower tour in the Culling. This is the space we use to create and experiment with new spells. That wall makes it so that if there's any unexpected results from the magic, the wayward power can't . . ." Realization dawns on her face. "Can't get out."

The floor explodes. As I fall to my butt and Jaleesa is knocked off her feet, I'm immediately filled with visions of the last time I watched the Guild's halls crumble. Horde skeletons burst free from the spells Ori and I cast then. That was what really started this chain of events. That is what made me complicit in so many deaths. And whoever's come to get us is purposely re-creating that scene, trying to mock me.

They cannot get the upper hand. They have to bend to **your** *will, not the other way around!*

Anger rises in my belly, knocking aside the guilt with the red-hot bubbling of indignation that burns from my feet to my face. Its trajectory parallels that of the gargoyle, a shape-shifted goblin, who's used the magical monster's ability to eat stone and rampage through to our floor. Following right behind him are half a dozen magicians, glowing purple with a fae levitating spell. A spell from Pallavit. She looks at her daughter with disbelief and concern, while the rest all look smug. The one with the shittiest of shit-eating grins on his face is none other than Alister Baumbach. Laurel steps out from behind him with a matching expression as she takes me in from head to boots.

"Of course it's you," I say.

"Oh, Nigel!" Alister says with sarcastic surprise. "I didn't see you there. How good of you to join us."

"But how did you bring us here?" Jaleesa asks. "How did you know we were coming?"

Alister sneers before turning to Laurel. "How you put up with this girl's insufferable nagging is beyond me." Back to Jaleesa, he says, "That's the thing with teens, isn't it? Always thinking they have everything figured out, able to best stronger, smarter, more cunning adults who've been dealing with brats like you for decades. I knew Nigel would do something like this. I set the trap that his precious Resistance was in trouble, knowing he couldn't live with himself if they were harmed while he sat back. So predictable." He stalks toward Jaleesa, step by slow step. "But I think the bigger question is what you were doing with the Guild's number one enemy?"

Alister turns his condescension on Pallavit. "Were you in on it, too, Devi?" he says. "Tricking me all along?"

Pallavit shakes her head fervently, eyeing Jaleesa like she's never truly seen her before. "Jaleesa? What have you done?"

"Is that really all it takes, Mom?" The betrayal is evident in Jaleesa's tone, but blaring even louder is the anger in her voice. "For one asshole to tell you I can't be trusted, and you just go along with it? Something kept telling me I couldn't depend on you, despite everything you've done for me. I was right, wasn't I? When it comes down to it, you'll choose being unquestionably loyal over loving your own daughter."

Pallavit staggers back while Alister cackles at Jaleesa. "Oh, how *noble.*" He whips his glare on Laurel. "I told you she'd only bring you down. But you're just like every other desperate teenager, aren't you? My own daughter, shortsighted. Hormonal. *Stupid.* You're such a disappointment, Laurel."

Laurel doesn't say a word. Tears well in her eyes, her cheeks flush red, my formerly fierce nemesis turned into a defenseless little girl. It almost makes me feel sorry for her, but I can't take my focus off her dad. Alister turns to me with hunger, his teeth flashing in the light.

He has no idea what he's in for.

I take stock of the magicians before me. Alister and Laurel, Pallavit, a sprite, a goblin, and an elf. An enemy of every ability to take down. I plant my boots shoulder-width apart, gold lighting up my fingers. "I'm not going down without a fight." That magic in my skin takes on a slight green glow.

"Suit yourself." Alister's hands glow green with his own power.

This is always what you wanted. To fight back. To cause chaos. To make them **pay.**

The hairs on my arms stand on end, my body pumping with adrenaline. Something's about to happen, and not a moment too soon.

They have no idea what lies inside of you. They have no idea **they've** *walked into* **your** *trap.*

Sickly green power flares over my gold magic, the blaze of light making everyone move at once. Alister summons lavender blossoms and grinds them between his palms. He takes a deep breath and blows the pulverized petals my direction just as I send a bolt of power for him, a ball of energy meant to destroy. It's the first time I've ever spelled with the intent to end a magician's life.

I should be terrified. I should wish I could take it back.

But it feels *so good.*

"This isn't the way.
Will versus will.
We won't make allies
by aiming to kill."

An arrow of purple fae magic meets my power head-on as Jaleesa's spell takes effect. My magic makes hers sizzle up, but her arrow was just enough to knock my stream of energy off course. The way is clear for Alister's petalled breeze to blow over me. My eyes droop, the anger in my belly swept away by a wave of exhaustion.

He thinks it will be that easy?

The indignation is enough to give me a tiny jolt, just enough energy to craft the one thing I know always gets things moving.

A cattle prod.

My tainted gold magic forms into the long-pronged rod, and I jam it against my thigh. White-hot electricity shocks me awake as my veins pulse with pain.

Alister's sprite ally soaks the effigy in her hands in pink power. My body seizes and I fall ramrod rigid to the marble floor. My nose slams against the rock and bright white explodes behind my eyes. Warm, hot blood pours down my face, oozing over the stone. My stomach swims with nausea.

Seriously? The Knife's voice is filled with derision. **You're going to let the sight of your own blood get in the way? You're weak. GET UP!**

My feet twitch, just the tiniest bit. I'm still bound by the sprite's effigy, but the nausea drifts away.

GET UP!

Magic builds in my fingers.

GET UP, YOU PATHETIC EXCUSE FOR A MAGICIAN!

Gold power pours from my fingers, flecks of rotten green

dotted along it, until it coalesces into the last shape any of us expected, myself included: a carton of eggs.

Alister howls. "What are you going to do? *Scramble* us?"

Heat flares in my heart. Magic is all about intent. My rage at Alister making a mockery of me fuels my curse. The golden lid of the carton blows open as all eighteen eggs explode. A brood of four-foot-tall roosters cluck ominously, their eyes directed at my enemies.

"Now!" I yell, and they descend on the magicians, golden talons outstretched, beaks pecking at every inch of skin they can get their feathers on. One plucks the effigy from the sprite's hands milliseconds before she blinks out of harm's way. The rooster jerks its head back and swallows the effigy in one, two, three gulps.

I did not see *that* coming.

My body slides across the floor, heading straight for the rooster that ate my wooden copy. The rules of sprite magic dictate whatever happens to an effigy happens to its real-life counterpart. But as my back collides with the rooster's golden-green scaly feet, the power soaks back into my body. My muscles unclench and I spring to my feet, just in time for Pallavit to sing a long low note that knocks me right back down. Pinpricks like my legs have fallen asleep travel up and down my calves. Every time I put weight on them, my legs fall out from under me.

From the floor, I see the goblin member dive over the railing, shifting into a bat as six of my roosters chase after her. But they disintegrate as they hit that shimmering wall of elf power preventing any magic from escaping. Only four are left on the floor, nearly a dozen others destroyed while I was struggling with Pallavit's curse. Alister dispatches them effortlessly while Laurel watches through glassy eyes. Pallavit keeps me pinned, while the sprite gets working on another effigy. Jaleesa is nowhere to be seen—probably hightailed it out of here like the coward she is.

But I'm no coward. My legs might be jelly, but I've still got my hands. I send magic to my fingers—

But . . . wait.

My magic comes in a slow, unusable trickle.

Weak! You're impossibly weak!

Alister and his gang watch me struggle, with wicked smiles. Their hands still blaze with plenty of power. Maybe Alister was right. They're all practiced magicians, while I'm just a hotheaded teenage nobody.

Looks like I'm busted.

"Well, well, well. Not nearly as strong as you once were, are you?" Alister gets down in my face, his breath hot and muggy. "What happened? All dried up? No *soulmate* to boost your power?"

He spits the word like it disgusts him. Like *Ori and I* disgust him. Just like his daughter always did. His daughter, who—even after the way he's treated her—is lapping at his feet like a desperate puppy.

"Just think, Dad," she says, her voice quavering. "After we take Nigel's power, we'll be able to pick Ori off without breaking a sweat."

Alister looks like a kid in a candy store. "Indeed."

"We need to act fast," Pallavit says. The purple glowing from her neck flickers as she nervously clears her throat. "While we have him."

"Before they can kill more of us," the sprite agrees. "Like they killed my husband. They're the reason so many of us lost those we love."

My nostrils flare with haughty pride, an indignant laugh barking from my throat. "Come on. Who are you kidding? You didn't love your husband. You didn't *love* anybody. If you had, you'd have been able to stop us from the jump. But no, you're nothing but pathetic, selfish magicians. Their deaths are on *your* hands. Ori's sister is dead because of the Culling." My fingers curl into fists when I lock eyes with Alister. "Meema is dead because of *you.*"

"Oh, please," Alister drawls. "You don't think I've been told I have *deaths on my hands* before? The voting public is just as prone to hyperbole as you young magicians."

"You're going to stand here and tell me you didn't kill Adela Barrett?" I grind my teeth so hard I think they might crack.

"Adela's death was a tragedy to us all. Killed by the Horde. Don't place that blame on me." His voice is strong, confident, no trace of the lie whatsoever. "*My* magic has never led to the deaths of hundreds. Yet you and your little boyfriend can't say the same, can you?"

A flap of wings signals the goblin member's return, and with their pack complete once more, Alister and his gang surround me.

"The monsters die here," Alister says.

That was always the end goal, but it can't happen until every other plan I've laid is complete. If Alister acts first, I won't rescue anyone from the Resistance so they can usher in a new Guild that ends the Culling and embraces the Beloved.

I'll never free Lyra. What if she's next?

I have to do this last thing for Ori, before the Guild destroys his family. Before I let the Guild take me.

I have to act now. I may be drained of my power, but I know what's deep inside me waiting to be unleashed. The unicorns said there was nothing I could do to get the Knife out of me, after all.

It's time to use it.

I shut my eyes and let go of every last wall I've tried to put up between me and the Knife. I focus on the ball of rage that's been growing inside me since the Culling. I concentrate on my fury that the Baumbach ancestors and their cronies perverted the mission of the Guild. I relive, again and again, Alister murdering the only person who ever loved me.

My eyes snap open, but my body is frozen. Not from fear, but because it can't comprehend anything except for the furious rage coursing through my blood. My heart races, sweat beads on my forehead and upper lip, my breathing increases. With one fell swoop I feel the Knife push away everything that makes me *me*: my compassion, my loyalty, my desire to do what's right. All that's left is hate. Pure, unadulterated hate.

I'll kill any person who gets in my way. Human, magician, nemesis, soulmate. It doesn't matter. I'll split them open and eat out their heart.

I've never felt a conviction like this before, and it's not even my own.

I *am* the Knife.

Things are going to get very, very bad.

And that's *exactly* what I want.

"I'll kill you," I say, the voice that drips from my lips the one I've been hearing in my head. It's my voice but tinged with something sinister.

Alister laughs, cruel and cutting. "I'd like to see you try."

All six of these magicians look at me with hunger in their eyes. Eager to get rid of me. It feels so familiar.

My vision swims, Alister's smug face replaced by . . . Alister. Again. Only this time we're not in gold-streaked marble halls. We're on a mountaintop—Mount Rainier, to be exact. The nymph whips me with vine after vine, he teams up with others like him to summon magic thorns the size of semitrucks that pierce my toes.

Only, I'm different. I'm not fighting on the snowy rock, slinging my golden lasso as I battle the Horde. I'm a thousand feet high, my limbs bloated skyscrapers, my fingernails cracked and bloody.

This isn't my memory. It's the Knife's.

The Knife felt so powerful on that mountaintop. The monster had been asleep for hundreds of years and had finally, *finally*, been awakened. Ready to claim this country.

If not for the stupid gnats at its feet.

A vine lashing around my wrist brings me back to the Guild. Thorns pierce my skin in quick succession, traveling up my arm and around my torso. I hardly flinch with each new wound, barely register the blood trickling down my arms, my chest, soaking through the fabric of my flannel and jeans. Acid-green energy blazes across my body, burning away Alister's vines, sealing up the bloody wounds left behind.

A guttural, triumphant roar bursts from my throat. It's unlike any noise I've ever made before: grotesque, murderous, monstrous.

"You cannot defeat me! I AM THE KNIFE!"

Sick pleasure courses through my veins. I'd like to say that my last thought before giving in is of my friends in the Resistance. I'd like to say I hope they get away in the havoc I know I'm about to cause.

But I don't think of them for a single second.

All I can think of—all that consumes the Knife—is revenge.

CHAPTER
TWENTY-THREE

THE LAST WAY ORI HAD ANTICIPATED DYING IN THE PAST COUPLE weeks was by getting skewered at the hands—hooves?—of a dozen unicorn horns. But the moment he and Bex walked through the unseen barrier into the unicorns' meadow, the beasts swarmed him, their metallic horns blazing with light as they shouldered their way in between him and Bex and bore down on him. One member of the herd pierces Ori's bag of would-be effigies and trots off, surrounding themself with other unicorns who bare their teeth in warning. Ori knows if he blinks to try to get it back, those unicorns are definitely going to make sure that he pops right on top of one of their horns.

Bex, meanwhile, is met with happy nickers and nuzzling. Ori hates asking for help, but if he's to walk out of this alive, he's going to need it.

"Uh—"

The unicorns go wild, pawing at the ground, neighing wildly. He's surprised none of them are foaming at the mouth.

"A LITTLE HELP!" Ori shouts.

Bex looks at Ori, wedged in between so many horns, and she actually has the audacity to laugh. *Crack up* would be more accurate, bending over double.

"So that's a no, then," Ori snaps.

"H-he's all right," Bex says as she tries to catch her breath. "H-he's a f-f-friend."

He's connected to the Knife.

Ori jumps at the voice—audible but not. It's all around him and nowhere, in his mind but outside of it.

Bex shakes her head. "No, that's Nigel, remember?"

But he's Nigel's soulmate. Connected in heart and magic. He cannot be trusted to make the right choice.

"Choice?" Ori asks. "What choice?"

He's met with silence, but Bex gasps. "You can't be serious," she whispers, but in this quiet, it seems more like a yell. Her eyes flick to Ori's with sympathy. "There has to be another way."

There isn't.

Ori has never heard a more resounding finality than in the herd's voice. It makes Ori's stomach fall, or fly skyward, he can't quite tell. All Ori knows is he wants to throw up. He knows he's not going to like whatever it is the unicorns just told Bex. But even still, he has to know.

"What is it?"

"They've been trying to come up with a way to get the Knife out of Nigel," Bex says. "They think the only thing that will ensure the Knife doesn't use Nigel's body for terror is . . ." Her eyes glisten with tears.

"To kill him." Ori finishes the sentence for her, and Bex's shoulders sag with relief. Probably didn't want to voice it herself. But she nods, and all feeling leaves Ori's body.

"That's the only thing they can come up with?" Ori asks, only to be met by a herd-wide indignant huff.

Sometimes one must be sacrificed for the good of many.

"That sure rolled off your tongue easily," Ori says. "Or, whatever the hell you're speaking with! Is that how you excuse yourselves hiding here while the rest of the world deals with demons and Depraved?"

It is not our responsibility to take on the burdens humans have brought upon themselves.

"That's convenient," Ori snips.

The herd loses it again, whinnying and bearing down on Ori. He doesn't even flinch this time. They can get as pissed as they want, it has nothing on the anger he feels at seeing yet another group of magical beings excuse themselves from stepping in to help when they should.

It is not convenient, it is survival! One of your kind killed a herd member for the Cornucopia, and it's humans' unbridled negativity that costs lives, creates monsters. It is not our duty to make you see that.

Suddenly, a pressure like a fist squeezes Ori's heart, sending him to his knees. "AH!" He so rarely lets himself cry out in pain, but this unrelenting grip is the most unbearable agony he's ever experienced. Even though they are dimensions apart, Ori knows this feeling comes from his connection with Nigel. It's the pain of his heart being corrupted, through and through.

The Knife has control. And every single atom of Ori's being knows the pain is worse for Nigel.

He's got to make his soulmate's hurt end.

Because he's the reason Nigel feels it in the first place.

The realization makes his heart thump heavy in his chest, even after the pain fades, even as the herd parts to let Bex run to his side.

"Ori!" she says. "What happened?"

The unicorns answer for him.

The Knife has him now.

"And you're going to do nothing to help?" Ori asks again.

He's met with silence.

Ori shoves through the herd until he reaches the cream-colored unicorn who stole his bag. "I'll take that, thank you. Once again, it looks like I'm going to have to do everything myself."

He reaches into his pocket and pulls out the tiny purple bell. He saw it as a symbol of his soulmate's betrayal, but maybe it's really his last hope. Maybe Nigel knew the only person who would be willing to help was their least likely ally.

"What are you doing?" Bex asks.

"You can sit around playing My Little Pony as much as you want," Ori says. "But they're never going to get off their stubborn asses and help. And if they won't, I know someone who will."

With that, he rings the bell.

Laurel doesn't hesitate to chase after her girlfriend, jumping through the hole that goblin-turned-gargoyle ate through the marble. She knew Jaleesa was up to something the second she left the fight, taking advantage of everyone's focus on Nigel to escape unnoticed. But that is the thing about her girlfriend: Laurel could never take her focus off her. She loves her. Jaleesa is her sun, and despite everything they've gone through these past weeks, despite the growing distance between them, she still would do anything to bridge the gap so they can continue on as they always have.

Laurel bounces harmlessly off two toadstools she grows from the hard floor as Jaleesa's throat glows purple, ready to spell herself from this level. They're in the armory, full of crystal cases that hold all sorts of enchanted tools for battle. But Jaleesa has her eyes over the banister, about to take flight. Where the fae plans on going, Laurel doesn't know, but she's positive it would be against the Guild's wishes. Laurel's already done so much to protect Jaleesa from falling under their suspicion, and she'll go to the ends of the earth to make sure they both get out of this weird transition phase unscathed.

"Jaleesa! Wait!"

It's a relief to watch her turn, to know that somewhere inside of her, Jaleesa still cares for Laurel and hasn't completely left her yet.

"You were right," Laurel says, letting her guard down, soaking her words with pure desperation. "Just . . . please. Don't leave me." Begging has always been beneath the Baumbachs. If her father could hear her now, he'd be livid. He'd use it as yet another example of why she and Jaleesa shouldn't be together. If anybody makes his daughter *plead*, then they must bleed. The thought brings a small, sad smile to Laurel's lips. Her girlfriend's rhyming does rub off on her at the most unexpected moments. *That* is the sign she's going to go with. The sign that points to just how compatible she and Jaleesa really are. Love doesn't have to be in big grand gestures. It can be in the small things, too.

"I went too far," Laurel says, her voice shaking as she finally admits it out loud. "I see that now. So much has happened that I'll never be able to take back. But it will be over soon. All we have to do is let Dad do his thing. Give him five minutes. That's it. Five minutes and everything will go back to what it once was. We'll go back to *us*. If you get in Dad's way, he'll take you out, Jaleesa. I'd never be able to live with myself if you were hurt because of all this. Just let him have this one. Then the future is ours."

Jaleesa's eyes glisten. Laurel wants nothing more than to wipe her tears away. But Jaleesa has to understand the heartache will end if they let Alister take out the boys. She knows her father will stop at nothing to get rid of the people in his way. Including his daughter and her girlfriend. If she can just let her dad do what needs to be done, everything will end.

"I don't think it is," Jaleesa whispers. "We can never go back to how things were, Laurel. There's something happening between Nigel and Ori, and now Nigel's dad and Jameson, but instead of letting them show us that, you'd let your dad kill them?"

Laurel doesn't feel angry. She doesn't feel betrayed. She just feels sad. So sad that after being on the same page for so long, they can't seem to see eye to eye on anything much since that day they went to retrieve the claw. Since the day she went too far and fucked everything up. One mistake and it made Jaleesa doubt that everything Laurel has ever done has been for them.

"You saw with your own eyes what they can do," Jaleesa continues, her voice clear and confident now. "I know you've felt a tug with me, too, pulling on our magic, making it more. We haven't been able to tap into it like them, not yet, but I'm certain we can." She sighs. "At least, I was once. I'm not so certain anymore."

Laurel tugs on one of her unkempt braids, nervous to finally reveal the truth. But she knows she has to now. She did it for her father, and even still, he calls her a disappointment. Her loyalty to him didn't go both ways. And now it's destroyed her relationship.

"I have to show you something." Laurel's voice is low, ominous. Because she knows once she shows Jaleesa the truth, there will be no more denying what a monster she's become.

Laurel hustles past rows of crystal weapons, past sprite blades and shape-shifting goblin swords and fae maces that hunt their targets with a simply sung note. She goes to the very last case, tucked away in the back, and releases the latch her father had unlocked. With a snap of her fingers, a blossom of fairy wing grows in her palm. Not literal fairy wings, but the magical plant, one with pollen that reveals hidden things. She crushes the light blue petals in her fist, then blows the detritus into the case. It coats the fantastical swords lying there, though nothing happens to them, as they're already visible. But along the side, the pollen gathers in an oddly twisted shape. In the blink of an eye, the Horn of Plenty appears.

Laurel grabs it, feeling its weight against her heart. When she first used it, she felt the weight of her purpose. Now, she feels a pressure from something more. The pressure of guilt, of doubt, the force growing by the minute as she relives her father calling her a disappointment again and again. She will never be good enough. Nothing she can do will ever win his love.

She takes a steadying breath. If she doesn't tell Jaleesa now, she'll lose her nerve.

As Laurel makes her way back to Jaleesa, the fae looks at her in a way she never has before. In the past couple weeks, Jaleesa's been confused, anxious, unsure of her girlfriend. But now, a whole new emotion is written plainly on Jaleesa's face.

Fear.

"Laurel." Jaleesa's voice quavers. "What have you done?"

The question stabs a knife straight through Laurel's stomach. It's a knife of accusation that Laurel knows she deserves.

"Answer me," Jaleesa says, her chest heaving. "That's the Cornucopia, isn't it?"

So she's heard of the weapon before.

Laurel nods. "I blew this." She holds out the Horn. It catches the light, the slick black of the Horn somehow seeming wet, somehow looking like it oozes even though it's dry as a bone in her hand. "Against Nigel. I thought—" Laurel stops, gutted by what she has to admit. How could she have been so stupid? How could she have ever thought this was the solution? "I thought it would clear the way for us to be the best of our Culling class. Nigel and Ori were too strong, and I knew that would stop Dad from ever seeing what we could be. He was so upset, constantly hounding me, said I was embarrassing the Baumbach name. But he found the Horn for me."

She recounts her dad taking her to the twenty-fifth floor, enlisting his friends, who followed the directions to find it. So many of them were tired of Adela's smug ways. They wanted to see her taken down a peg if the last in her line failed to make it through the Culling. They convinced Laurel they were all experienced enough to magic away any negative effects of the Cornucopia's curse.

When it was clear Laurel was not going to be the best in her class, Alister offered to blow the Horn. But Laurel wanted to do it, to prove her loyalty to her father. During the second task she saw her chance to strike. She'd just completed the challenge, Bex wailing on and on about extra victims she could have saved. While senior members were busy consoling the goblin, Laurel saw the boys in their own medical bay struggling to cure their victims. But she wouldn't underestimate them. She saw in the first task how strong the boys' power could be and knew when they set their minds to it, they could easily succeed. She had to act fast before they cast whatever spell would get them through to the final task.

Everyone was too caught up in the challenge to watch her, so Laurel snuck back to her bed—her perfectly woven cocoon in the trees of the nymph dorm—and blew the Horn, thinking only of Nigel. Thinking of his downfall. Thinking of her and Jaleesa rising to the top, of her father finally accepting them and letting them be together.

"It worked," Laurel says. "Their magic went wrong. Their magic magnified."

"And they woke the Horde." Jaleesa's voice is soaked with horror, her eyes wide as she backs toward the balcony railing. "*You* woke the Horde."

Laurel moans, hearing the truth come out of her girlfriend's mouth. It physically pains her, makes her clutch her stomach as her muscles constrict. "I know! I tried to convince myself it was them all along. If someone used the Horn against me, my magnified powers wouldn't pose such a threat. If my power's a ten, when squared, it's only a hundred. They *start* at a hundred. I thought they were inherently *too* powerful. That they could be used against the entire Guild, and had to be stopped by whatever means necessary."

Jaleesa reaches the banister, using it to hold herself up. "It was all you. *You* blew the Horn of Plenty. *You* were the one who warped their power. You did this. All those deaths." Jaleesa's voice trembles. She places a hand over her mouth like she might throw up. "They're your fault. Not Nigel's. Not Ori's. Yours."

If Laurel thought her girlfriend's words stabbed her before, it has nothing on the pain she feels now. She feels gutted. Her legs give out, but the shock of her knees hitting the unforgiving marble barely registers over the torture of hearing Jaleesa—*her* Jaleesa—confirm that she's the monster.

"I know," Laurel whispers. "I know."

She can't bring herself to look Jaleesa in the eye. A lifetime of staring at the floor is all she deserves.

"You cannot defeat me! I AM THE KNIFE!" Nigel's twisted voice echoes from the floor above.

It makes Laurel look up just in time to see a figure careen past the balcony railing in the open air of the tower. Laurel would recognize that auburn hair anywhere, that expertly styled beard.

"Dad!"

Laurel stumbles to her feet in a panic. She's too disoriented to walk, to run. Magic flows to her fingers and she flicks vines from her wrist that wrap around the railing. She pulls herself to the banister beside a shocked Jaleesa, and they both look down just as her father slams onto the entry platform.

"DAD!" Her scream echoes through the tower, but there's no one around to hear it. They're all gathered in the prisons floors below, pressing Nigel's father for more information about the creature he made. Even if her father hadn't told her years ago, Laurel would have known the Guild line about "everything being in the open" was a lie. There are chambers so deep into the marble that no sound can get out. Chambers where the Resistance prisoners are being held now, where spells are being used to cram hundreds of magicians inside so they can break the supposed traitors. The cruel irony is that their absence means there is no one around to see Alister fall. No one around to use their magic to catch him.

A flash of light out of the corner of her eye grabs Laurel's attention. She looks up to find Nigel atop a magically conjured horse that looks more monster than equine. They both crackle with grotesque green power as they launch themselves up to the topmost floor, leaving a path of destroyed marble in their wake.

Depraved magic. Nigel isn't himself anymore. He called himself the Knife. She has no idea how or why. And her father— Is he—

"We have to go to him." Jaleesa looks over the banister, down to Alister's unmoving body. Laurel feels a pang of love; Jaleesa's beautiful heart always did value life above all else. Even the lives of the people who've wronged her. "Maybe he's all right."

"Or maybe he's dead." Laurel's blood runs cold with the thought. All this led to her father's undoing. It's all her fault, blowing that horn that led everyone here, to this moment.

A faint jingle floats across the air, followed by a familiar snarky voice.

"I hear you have a Knife problem."

Laurel turns and there, right behind Jaleesa, is a faint, sparkling version of the last person she'd ever expect to offer help.

"Let me in, would you?"

Ori.

Jaleesa doesn't hesitate. She grabs Laurel's hand and spells them to the first floor, where she opens a portal and pulls Ori into the Guild.

CHAPTER
TWENTY-FOUR

THE ENERGY WITHIN ME BUILDS UNTIL IT HAS NOWHERE ELSE TO GO but out. A wave of mottled green-gold power bursts from my chest, sending my enemies flying. The elf and the sprite smash their heads against the hard marble, Pallavit and the goblin falling through the hole in the floor, and Alister's unconscious form flies through the golden power-stopping barrier and over the banister. The spell stops magic, but does nothing against Guild members.

I walk through the barrier to see Alister unmoving on the floor hundreds of feet below. Never in my life did I imagine I'd kill a human or a magician with my own hands. But any guilt I should feel about it is pushed aside by utter glee: the Knife's. I can feel the monster like a living thing inside me, puppeting my limbs. I can't move a muscle, can't even twitch a finger.

Your body's mine now, Nigel. I'll use it to kill. I'll use it to feed on fear and hate. And when all this is done, I will find your soulmate and eat his heart.

Part of me wants to throw up, but it's tiny, insignificant compared to the ravenous hunger rampaging through my gut. It's a want, a *need*, an all-consuming desire to kill.

I should have possessed a magician from the start. I was foolish when I possessed that giant, thinking brute strength was all that mattered. You and that sprite almost got the better of me. Your connection was strong enough to keep my crown from returning to my head, making me vulnerable to attack, your love *weakening the magic that kept it with me. But your shortsighted little boyfriend made it all too easy for me. You have so much anger, Nigel, so much hate. And now, your body, your power is mine. The Guild will be* mine. *The* world *will be mine!*

The Knife's hunger is so strong I double over. That's the entire drive for the Depraved. Fear and hate to feed on. There can never be enough. And the Knife knows there's one tool it needs to make sure it gets a supply of both to last an eternity.

Power builds in my hands, but what has always come so naturally to me now feels like a complete violation. I don't get the swell of pride or accomplishment in my chest as my magic does its work. I want to vomit, while the Knife wants to celebrate. My previously gold power isn't just tinged with the sickly green of the Depraved anymore. It's completely consumed by it.

The Knife combs through my memories, a worm wiggling its way through my thoughts. Something slick and slimy rubs against my soul as it searches for ways it can use my power. When the Knife finds what it wants, it presses my green-glowing middle finger and thumb to my lips and blows. A summoning spell. A trickle of warm blood slides out of my ear with the shriek of the whistle.

As the note rings, green magic pools outward and coalesces into a shining, maniacal horse. It thrashes, spittle-like energy flying from its mouth, its eyes rolling and wild. It's the evil twin of Frosty, and the Knife laps up every last drop of anger I feel toward it for making a mockery of my friend.

The beast lunges when I get closer, baring its teeth before sinking them into my forearm.

"That's it," the Knife coos in that voice that's mine but not. *"Drink."*

I know what an insatiable craving the thirst for blood can be.

The horse drinks until it calms, the Knife pouring its cruel purpose into me, pumping it through my veins so that this creature recognizes the life force and will of its master.

When the beast has had its fill, I jump an inhuman height to hop on its back. It bucks, trying to throw me off, but my body knows what to do and the Knife takes advantage. I expertly maneuver with each frenzied movement until Dead Mr. Ed knows there's no way to get rid of me.

"'Yup!" It's the first time I've shouted it in weeks, the first time I've been able to ride, and it's completely ruined by the Knife. I urge the beast forward and expect the Knife to lead us to the floor below. To the armory where crystal cases hold all sorts of deadly weapons from every magical race.

But with a squeeze of my knees on either side of the beast's heaving flank, we jump over the banister and into the open air of the Guild tower. Jagged streaks of lightning crack from the creature's hooves, blowing apart the marble walls on impact and giving us a boost as we climb higher and higher, headed for one floor in particular.

The twenty-fifth. Where magical relics are etched into pedestals, the instructions to locate them tucked on top.

The last time I was here, Meema revealed the location of the claw and showed me Great-Grandpa Barrett's memory of defeating the Knife.

Defeated? I'm not the one who's possessed!

Floating in the center of the tower, I scan the pedestals. The monster inside me only has eyes for one.

The Cornucopia. The Horn of Plenty.

The Knife forces another recent memory to the surface of my mind: of Bex describing the cursed unicorn horn, explaining that one blow will magnify a magician's power. That it will turn their power destructive.

Just what I need to get my revenge.

It knows the relic could be missing as that journal entry from Meema flits through my brain. But magicians are foolish, and whoever took it had to leave a clue behind.

The beast's hooves land on the marble floor with a crash, cracks branching out from its feet. I swing off its back in one graceful movement. *"Good boy."* I snap my fingers and the horse fizzes out in a final pulse of green light. *"I'll have use for you soon."*

My boots echo across the hall as I march past the pedestals and their unassuming plaques. A burst of anger makes my nostrils flare as I pass the etching of the claw.

They flaunt their success as if they killed me. But here I am, walking through their halls, even after they took my former body from me.

"I cannot be killed!" My fist launches forward, glowing with green magic. The claw's pedestal disintegrates into dust.

I march down the line, staring at the etchings on each pedestal. A fae ring, another elven crown, a legendary sprite switchblade.

I stop in front of the eighth pedestal. But, unlike all the others, this one holds no envelope, as expected. I lean in, inspect the cold rock, look for anything that could tell the Knife where to go next.

Nothing.

The pedestal is totally empty.

"AAAAAAH!"

Power catapults from my fists, pulverizing the Cornucopia's former marker.

I'm so **tired** *of magicians.*

"ENOUGH!"

The scream echoes from floors below. Despite the distance, I feel the slight tug of fae magic trying to snap me to attention.

What are the little gnats up to now?

My feet fly to the banister. Laurel, Jaleesa, and Ori glare up at me from the very first floor.

And the nymph has exactly what I've been looking for.

Magicians truly *are* ***foolish. The Cornucopia is mine!***

CHAPTER
TWENTY-FIVE

As Laurel stares down at her father's unmoving form, Ori resists the impulse to make magic pool in his hands and grab a toy. The nymph has been his enemy all this time, having an effigy to defend himself would be smart. But no. Now is not the time to fight.

What he would have given to have another magician's help when Cassie was about to die. This is his chance to make sure another magician doesn't die needlessly. Not even a magician who has spent every day of the past couple weeks trying to end *Ori's* life. An eye for an eye and all that. Despite everything, Ori wouldn't be able to live with himself if he let Alister perish.

"Come on," Ori says, holding his hands out for the girls to take. "We can blink."

Jaleesa doesn't hesitate. Laurel, however, stares at Ori's out-stretched fingers, a battle clearly raging in her mind.

"The longer we wait, the less likely we'll be able to help your dad," Ori snaps.

That gets the nymph to place her hand in his, and in a heartbeat, they're on the first floor. Laurel drops to her knees next to her father's still form and turns his body over.

Alister moans. His face is bloody, his nose clearly broken, but he's alive, for now. The sight of the bright red blood makes Ori think of Nigel before, when blood made him so nauseous he could pass out. Would it affect him now? Would he actually *enjoy* the sight of it, now that the Knife is in him?

"DAD!" Laurel's scream snaps Ori back to reality. She wraps her father up in a hug, blood smearing her shirt. "You're alive. You're alive." Tears pour down her face, dotting her father's cheeks as they fall.

"Get yourself . . . together . . . Laurel." His words are pained, soft but heartless as ever.

Laurel nods, obedient. "Right." She clears her throat. "Sorry."

Alister's breathing is ragged. Several of his bones are clearly broken, and the damage likely goes deeper, after a fall like that. By the way he's wheezing, a rib could have punctured his lung. They have to act now.

Laurel turns to Jaleesa, eyes hopeful. "Heal him, would you? This is more than I can do with herbs. But you can sing him to health."

Jaleesa moves quickly.

"All of us injured.
*   The pain is real.*
*   Tables are turning.*
*   It's time to heal."*

"Jaleesa." Laurel's tears flow again, her entire body shaking. "Thank you."

Ori squints at Jaleesa, trying to make sense of her song. Maybe Nigel was right, and she does want the Guild to change.

Ori hears the crunch of bone as Alister's nose straightens out, the pops as who knows what critical internal injuries heal. And somehow Jaleesa's song works emotionally, too. Ori feels bolstered, his heart beats faster, more confidently. The tables *are* turning.

When Jaleesa's spell is finished, Alister appears to be asleep.

"Thank you," Laurel sobs. "Thank you."

"I didn't do it for you," Jaleesa says bluntly. "I can't stoop as low as you and your dad. I can't become a monster, too."

Laurel wipes her nose, nodding.

"What's that?" Ori's attention has fallen to the Horn of Plenty, glistening black on the floor beside Laurel. But he knows. It seems familiar, after Bex's descriptions.

Jaleesa and Laurel share a look. "You better tell him," Jaleesa says.

Laurel hesitates. But then her whole body sags, like she's had the weight of the world on her shoulders and can't hold it up anymore.

"It was all me," she breathes. She looks away from Ori to meet Jaleesa's eyes. "You were right. If I had never done what I did, the Horde would never have been awakened. None of those people would have died. I wouldn't have become—" She picks at her shirt, at her unkempt braids, rubs her bloodshot eyes. "This monster. The first time I think someone threatens my place at the top and I unleash an army of dead soldiers on them. Meanwhile, my dad has been *horrible* to you, and still you jumped to save him. You're so good, Jaleesa. You're meant for the Guild. I shouldn't be here."

"Laurel," Ori snaps. "Now is not the time to indulge in a pity party. What *exactly* did you do?"

"I blew this," Laurel says, holding the Cornucopia, looking at it like it disgusts her. She recounts everything about her actions in the Culling. How her dad retrieved this cursed relic, how she used it against Nigel, how *she* warped their connection and made it evil and powerful enough to wake the Horde.

Laurel finishes speaking, and Ori feels weightless. He looks down and is surprised to see his feet are firmly on the floor. He didn't want to get his hopes up too high when this possibility was floated before. But now, he could actually have a future where he doesn't wake up and go to sleep feeling like a monster each and every day.

"You're saying none of those deaths are our fault," Ori says, breathless. "This isn't on us."

"No. It isn't," Laurel says, her voice thick with guilt. With the guilt she *should* feel, yet somehow placed on his and Nigel's shoulders all this time, siccing the wrath of the entire Guild on them in the process.

"We can just *be* magicians," Ori whispers. He laughs with pure glee as the fantasy of living a normal life with Nigel comes galloping back. He laughs even harder as he realizes he's thinking in horse metaphors now; Nigel's rubbing off on him. But this is what he's wanted all along, isn't it? To lean on and love someone else, instead of holing up inside himself and avoiding any connection that could hurt him like it hurt when Cassie was killed.

Cassie.

He can practically see her smiling face. She would be so proud of him for not running from the guilt, for trying to find a way to make it right. She would be so relieved that he's free of the burden of dozens of magicians' deaths.

And then, he cries. Gut-wrenching sobs escape his lungs as the grief and guilt leave his heart. He isn't letting Cassie down, his mom doesn't have to worry about him anymore, he'll be able to see his dad again.

He'll have a *life* again.

That is, only if they can get the truth out. Only if he can get the Guild to see Alister was behind framing the boys and perpetuating the Culling.

But then it hits him like an arrow straight through the heart. Nigel might not get the same luxury. What Nigel does as the Knife could change everything. Nigel won't get to have any life at all, unless Ori can bring his soulmate back.

In order to do that he's got to get to Nigel. Nigel needs to know none of this is their fault. Nigel needs to know that if he fights the Knife within him, he could still avoid having a single death on his hands.

Ori turns back to the girls. Laurel's face is soaked with tears as she looks between Ori and Jaleesa expectantly, as if waiting for them to lash out at her for what she did. But that can wait.

"Listen," Ori says, "we can save the guilt trip for later. I have a confession of my own." He takes a fortifying breath. "I brought Nigel back to life by fusing him with the Knife." He cringes at the rhyme. "What I'm trying to say is, he would have died when he smashed the claw against the heartstone in the Knife's crown. But I couldn't live with that. So I created an effigy of him, and I used a piece of the heartstone to pump life into him. I just wanted to bring *him* back. But it brought the Knife back, too." He's knocked off-balance as doubt rushes through his body. He may not have caused all the damage that led here, but he still has some share of the blame in what could come.

"AAAAAAH!"

The scream from the very top floor makes the three of them jump.

It's Nigel's voice, but not. Ori knows through their connection that Nigel is more frustrated than he's ever been. *The Knife* is more frustrated. All because it can't find the Cornucopia.

"Speak of the Depraved," Ori mumbles.

"I blew it twice," Laurel says, sharp and fast, like the words need to get out now before she buries them deep inside.

"When was the second time?" Jaleesa demands.

"During that final challenge. We weren't on the mountaintop, but I watched you, Ori. I needed to know how everything turned out, so I used Seer Sap to show me your location and I watched every move you made. I didn't want you to bring Nigel back. He was gone, and I needed him to stay gone, so when you were so determined to resurrect him, I blew the horn again, wanting whatever bit of magic was left in Nigel to warp and refuse your connection. I just wanted him to stay dead. Everything did end up warped. Just not in a way either of us anticipated."

Ori had only ever felt this all-encompassing fire of revenge for the Depraved. Ever since that day he saw one take his sister, he knew he would do anything to stop each and every monster until the day he died. But now, he feels that bubbling of his blood for another person. Usually, his instincts would make his magic flare up, ready to curse his enemy. But this time, his whole body reacts. His muscles tense and spring so he can lunge at Laurel, his hands out like claws ready to strangle her.

To Laurel's credit, she doesn't resist. Ori even thinks she extends her neck a little bit to give him a better shot at getting a good grip.

"ENOUGH!"

But Jaleesa has other plans. Her shout makes Ori stop in midair, places him back on his feet, and snaps his outstretched hands to his sides.

"We've got bigger priorities." She looks up to the ceiling, where Nigel gallops down the tower on a grotesque green horse. Frosty's evil twin.

Ori can feel the Knife's determination. It's hellbent on grabbing the Cornucopia.

"We've got to get rid of that thing," Ori says, pointing to the twisted horn. "Or else the Knife is going to use it."

Ori can only imagine how awful that will be.

First step: Destroy the Horn.

Second: Knock the Knife out of his soulmate.

Third: Save the Resistance and get out of here.

Should be easy, right?

If only. But a long-shot plan quickly forms in Ori's mind.

Time to get his cowboy back.

CHAPTER
TWENTY-SIX

"WELL, LOOK WHO IT IS," ORI SAYS CALMLY, LIKE A DEMONIC HORSE carrying his possessed soulmate isn't barreling toward him. "Howdy, cowboy."

I want to cheer that Ori is so defiant, ready to save me. I'm shocked that he's here with Laurel; Jaleesa, I could have predicted. Yet the emotions inside me are swept aside by the Knife's overriding urge to bash their faces against the hard marble walls.

I'll wipe the smug little grins right off these brats' faces.

"Give it here." I beckon with my fingers, palm up, then swing down from my beastly sidekick before it disappears with a crackle. *"There's no use resisting me."*

"Somebody's cocky," Ori says. "But I know it's not you, Nigel. You're too kind, too loving, to ever talk like that. I know you're in there. You need to fight."

A sudden flare of warmth in my heart makes the room go fuzzy.

It's not anger or lust for revenge. It's the warmth of Ori, of our connection, of that *spark* lighting me up from the inside. Instinctually, I move my hand to my chest.

Wait a minute.

I move my hand to my chest! *I* did that. I controlled my body.

Not so fast.

A tug in my mind makes my vision blurry and my hand whips back down to my side.

You are* mine*!

"Oh, please." I laugh, my voice still saturated with the Knife's bloodlust. *"You think one cowboy can defeat* me*? I've murdered thousands of magicians in my lifetimes, ones much more experienced than you."* My arms blaze with power, gold mixed with green. *"Give me the Horn now and I'll let you walk away."*

"So you can kill us with it later?" Jaleesa says. "I don't think so."

"Nigel," Ori says. "I need *you* to use the Cornucopia. Not the Knife. Remember what Bex told us? If you blow it in the spirit of true forgiveness, it will be destroyed. The Knife won't be able to use it."

My fingers curl into fists as the Knife's indignation burns through me. The monster knows that Ori's right. This plan could work.

"And then I'll get you back, cowboy." Ori's smiling now, coming closer, not afraid of the Knife in the slightest. His confidence unnerves the Depraved within me; no one approaches it without a trace of fear in their heart.

"I've got good news," Ori continues, his voice soft, meant only for me. "We were right. That horn?" He points to the spiral of bone in Laurel's hand. *"It's* the reason our magic got so out of hand. It wasn't because of us."

A new flare of heat ignites in my heart, responding to Ori's words, at odds with everything the Knife stands for.

The flare of hope.

"Our connection could never have made that happen." Ori keeps stepping forward until there's barely any space between us. "Laurel blew it against you. *That's* the reason our power was out of control. She's the reason the Horde woke up. Not us." He reaches forward and grabs my hands.

The Knife wants to lash out. It wants my power to surge through my skin and into his body, frying Ori to a burnt black corpse.

But the power never comes.

"Our love would never lead to something like that." Ori leans forward and kisses me. The Knife wishes it could suck my soulmate's heart out through his throat, but it can't overcome the soul-boosting, love-filling emotion Ori puts behind his parted lips. Nothing can overpower that passion and true feeling.

The Knife is frozen, unsure how to combat such genuine emotion. Ori kisses me deeper, lets his tongue lightly pad against mine. It's a kiss so full of true love, there's no hope for the Knife. My vision wavers, my feet give out from under me, and it's only due to Ori holding me up that I don't fall to the floor.

I gasp, hacking coughs making my whole body convulse. I feel like I've been underwater this entire time, holding my breath for hours, impossibly long, and this is the first breath of air bringing me back to life.

I'm in control again.

I'm me, and I cling to Ori's cardigan like he's a lifeboat keeping me afloat.

"It's okay, Nigel," he says, patting my back, holding me up even though I'm so much bigger than he is. "It's okay."

When I finally catch my breath, I gain my footing, look down, and meet Ori's eyes. There's that perfect smug smirk.

"Welcome back," he breathes.

It's so Ori, so self-assured and sexy as hell. It brings me back to our connection, the power we have that never led to bloodshed and misery. That responsibility doesn't belong to us. I'm filled with so much relief that I lift Ori off his feet—literally—and bring my mouth to his again. I kiss him harder, deeper, more lovingly than I ever have before.

Ori puts his hands on my face, keeping our kiss for a few more seconds—or minutes or hours, who knows. When he pulls away, he says, "All this time with you gone, with that *thing* in you, it made me realize what a gift you are."

"Who knew getting possessed by a Depraved titan would be so romantic?"

Ori laughs. "Shut up, cowboy."

"You weren't supposed to do that," I say, regret tinging this intimate moment. "I'm supposed to save our parents, get them out of here, then have the Guild take me prisoner, and . . ." I can't say it. I knew coming in here was a death wish. I can't let the Knife live on. "I've got to get it out of me," I whisper. "They'll take care of it."

"Yeah, about that." Ori smacks my chest, hard. "We've got to talk about you making these decisions by yourself. And *keeping things from me.* You knew my mom was here all along? We're going to free all of them, and *then* we're getting you out of here. I'm not letting you get yourself killed. Not when I've got a second chance with you."

Laurel holds the spiral horn out to me, desperation in her eyes like she doesn't trust herself with it. "If you destroy it, we can make sure this never gets into the wrong hands again."

"Meaning yours?" Jaleesa says, her words cold as ice.

Laurel chews her bottom lip, before nodding.

"The Cornucopia," I say. I'd pictured it as the beautiful,

glistening horn Bex has when she shifts into a unicorn, not the twisted bone it truly is. Wherever she is now, she really has done so much for us, and all I've done is make things worse for her. Her parents are trapped, just because they were helping me. The least I can do is end this once and for all.

My eyes zero in on the Cornucopia. "So all I've got to do is blow that? As the last person cursed by it?"

"But you have to do it with true forgiveness in your heart for the person who cursed you," Ori adds. He waves his hand toward Laurel. "Which means coming to terms with this bitch."

Laurel sneers. "This bitch?"

"What would you like me to call you?" Ori asks. "*Delusional asshole who was so hellbent on pleasing Daddy that she let dozens of magicians die* seems a little long, don't you think?"

Laurel doesn't have anything to say at that.

"Not to put pressure on you," Jaleesa says, looking up to the floors above. "But we have to move fast. Who knows when the Guild will be done questioning your parents." She nudges Alister, unmoving on the floor, who I've just noticed for the first time. "Or when he'll wake up." She turns to Laurel. "I think in order for Nigel to truly forgive you, he has to know everything you've done. Tell us about the forest under your house. What is it?"

"It's how they're doing it," Laurel says. "How they're making everyone believe the Culling is needed."

Jaleesa sucks in a breath. "Wait. Are you saying the Culling isn't—"

But Laurel carries on. "The trees are poisoned with a nymph curse. When your name is written on one of their leaves, the memories of whatever the caster wants you to forget completely rot. My family's been keeping the forest alive for generations, with the help of others, so the magic never drains. And I, um, I want you to know . . ."

She picks her head up, looking me in the eye. When our gazes lock, that flare of anger bubbles in my gut again. I grip Ori's arm so tight I'd leave bruises if it wasn't for our connection. "Your grandma knew nothing about what Dad was up to. She wasn't part of the deception. Her name was written there, in the leaves. She didn't know about the Culling. She wanted the Guild to be as honorable as it could possibly be."

I feel a temporary moment of relief, looking to Ori to make sure I heard right. He nods, smiles even, and at least one thing in my world is righted again. I would never have been able to reconcile the Meema that I knew with one who was so selfish she'd keep a tradition going just to hoard power.

Laurel doesn't give me a moment to process. She barrels on and adds, "Adela truly was a good person. I know she'd want us to move forward." She holds out the Cornucopia again, the Horn resting on her palm for me to take. "She'd want you to forgive me."

Her words give me whiplash. It's wild how quickly one person can go from saying all the right things, to saying the literal worst thing you could ever want to hear. Anger rises in me, a stampede of those demonic bucking broncos unleashed in my soul.

Who the fuck does Laurel think she is to tell me what Meema would want? She never even spoke to her. She never came to the ranch to see how powerful she was. She didn't sit next to her for hours on end, learning her secrets to spells well-cast. But now that she's the one who pushed the first domino toward her death, Laurel thinks she's an expert in my grandmother?

A small part of my brain registers that those thoughts are mine, but warped. Altered again by the gravelly hatred of the Knife. But altered or not, there's so much truth in them. Any sense in my brain is knocked aside by physical sensation cascading through my body, starting with a tingle in my hands that has nothing to do with touching Ori. It's that feeling of my limbs going to sleep, pinpricks stabbing along my skin. My breathing comes in short, ragged spurts; my heart rams against my ribs like it's trying with every fiber of muscle to burst from my chest. Heat flushes my face; my teeth grind. Rage builds and builds, an avalanche sweeping away every last ounce of control I have left. I can feel the Knife within me again, can feel it feasting on the hate I have for Laurel, getting stronger. But I can't stop it. I can't stop the need to make Laurel pay.

"M-must you tell them everything, Laurel?" Alister coughs from the ground as he comes to. "Even more reason we'll have to kill them now."

"No." Laurel's voice quavers. "This has to end."

Alister shows no remorse. "Not until they're gone. Jaleesa too. Your blithering has sentenced her to death."

Laurel stares at her dad, her face hardening. Even as my rage grows, I can see that something in her shifts.

"How could you, Dad?" she whispers. "You know how much she means to me."

"Which I've tried to dissuade you from all along," Alister wheezes. "No witnesses. Better safe than sor—"

Laurel's foot barrels down fast, without warning, landing on Alister's head with a crack. He's knocked out cold.

Or better yet, dead. And Laurel should be next. For daring to speak about the woman she murdered.

"You didn't know her at all." My words are the quiet before a tsunami. "Don't you ever speak about Meema again. You killed her."

"Nigel." Ori's tone is full of warning. He knows something's wrong.

"NO!" I scream. "She needs to pay." I turn on Laurel, stalking toward her with each word. "You're a murderer. You killed her. *YOU KILLED THEM ALL!*"

My body ignites, lit from within by ghastly green power.

The Knife is back.

And this time, it won't lose control.

CHAPTER
TWENTY-SEVEN

ORI WATCHES IN HORROR AS NIGEL'S BODY GLOWS THAT green-tinged gold. One second Nigel was back—his soft, sunshine cowboy—the next he's a monster again. Even without the green magic cloaking his soulmate's body, Ori knows the Knife is in control by his eyes. Rage shines in them, a need to kill.

This all registers in the infinitesimal moment before the Knife's destructive power bursts from Nigel's skin. It collides with the sprite, the nymph, and the fae, knocking them off their feet. Ori's body burns with the intensity of the Knife's anger and hate. The Cornucopia falls from Laurel's hand, and with a quick, whistled summoning spell, the Horn of Plenty flies into Nigel's waiting palm.

He laughs, deep and hoarse, a demonic cackle more suited for the Knife's former rotted vessel, not his soulmate's beautiful body.

"It's just too easy," Nigel says through that skin-crawling laughter. *"What delicious emotions you young people have. So quick*

to anger." He twirls toward Laurel, whose eyes are unfocused, a concussion likely after the blow of Nigel's power. *"I have to thank you. You chose exactly the wrong words to get Nigel to your side. Claiming to know his grandmother like that. The hate that seethed through him."* He takes a deep breath, licks his lips, like the Knife can still taste the rage in Nigel's blood. *"It was just the thing I needed to regain control."*

Ori props himself up on his elbows, fighting the pain from the burns left in the wake of Nigel's blast. "Nigel!" He blinks to his soulmate's side before the possessed cowboy can react, gripping Nigel's wrist with unnatural strength. A toy in his hand glows pink, its plastic fingers lit brightest of all, the source of Ori's enhanced strength. "Come back."

Ori focuses with all his might, a bead of sweat dripping down his forehead. He pours all his intent into their connection, every ounce of love he has for Nigel. He thinks of everything he adores about him: Nigel's kind heart; his yearning for family, found or otherwise; his belief in the true good of people. Ori remembers every special moment they spent together, defeating evil when their magics combined, that feeling of solidarity when they vowed to take on the Knife together, how he'd never felt more connected to another person than when they shared their bodies in ways neither of them ever had before.

"Oh, Ori." That's Nigel. His normal voice, full of softness and strength, sincerity and self-doubt. Ori leans in, his mouth quirking up in a smirk.

But with his lips centimeters from Nigel's face, the elf breaks into a wicked grin. *"Psych."*

Power cascades down Nigel's arm and up Ori's, the sprite's plastic effigy melting as the Knife's corruption coats it. Ori's grip loosens and Nigel slams his hand around Ori's neck to lift him high. Their touch does nothing to boost Ori's power now—the Knife is rotting their connection like it's rotted Nigel's soul.

"Nigel," Ori chokes, his feet dangling in the open air, kicking, struggling. He's too desperate for air to blink. "Nigel, come back."

The cold smile on his soulmate's face makes Ori more afraid than he's ever been in his life, more afraid than when he was facing down the Knife on Mount Rainier.

"You wish it was that easy," Nigel says. *"Goodbye, Ori."* Power surges through Nigel's muscles, hurling Ori into the hard marble wall. The sprite crumples to the ground, unmoving.

"You've got to fight back," Jaleesa says. "Nigel, this isn't you!"

"What is it with you children?" Nigel sneers. *"The magician you are trying to dial cannot be reached! Nigel is gone forever!"* The possessed elf snaps his fingers and that crackling, demented horse appears out of thin air. *"Although he does know some useful tricks!"* Nigel jumps an unnaturally high distance and lands on the beast's back.

"'Yup!" The horse charges Jaleesa, dead set on destroying her, yet she refuses to give the Knife her fear to feed on. But at the last second, Nigel veers toward Laurel instead. The beast opens its fanged mouth and green power pours from its gaping maw. It collides with Laurel, slamming her against the wall. She crumples to the floor next to Ori and doesn't get up.

Nigel grins wickedly, turning slowly until his frenzied eyes lock on the fae. *"You can go now,"* he says. *"Tell everyone that I'm back. Tell them to fear me. To run. Because if you stay, you'll wish that I'd killed you."*

Jaleesa swallows, her eyes darting between Nigel and Laurel to the Horn in the possessed elf's grasp.

"Don't even try it." He waves the Cornucopia back and forth. *"This is mine. If you come for it, it'll be the last thing you do."*

Jaleesa knows he means it. She walks slowly with hands up to Laurel. She leans over and tries to pick the girl up, but the dead weight of her unconscious body is too much. So she summons magic, the tiniest amount, to cast the easiest spell in her arsenal.

Calling her mother. A single note that, when sung, would call them to each other in times of extreme need. It doesn't even take a second.

She feels a tug in her heart and knows that her mom has heard. Pallavit is on the way. They may have had a hard time connecting these past couple weeks, but nothing would ever keep her from answering Jaleesa's call.

"Uh-uh-uh." Nigel wags a glowing finger, making Jaleesa's body whip toward him. *"No magic, princess. Why don't I just help you?"* He snaps his fingers and Jaleesa rises in the air. *"Have a nice flight."*

He flicks his wrist, and Jaleesa's body explodes with pain as it connects with the wall and she lands beside Ori and Laurel.

"Three magicians down."

The Knife's voice drips with pleasure, but I feel nothing. My rage at Laurel was so strong, even stronger than my love for Ori. Maybe it burned away my capacity to feel anything at all. I should definitely feel something as I look at Ori's unmoving form, his limbs splayed like a discarded rag doll.

But I don't. I feel nothing. I *am* nothing—and that's the opportunity the Knife needs to fill the silence inside of me.

Pity I had to hurt him. Ori has been so helpful, after all. He gave me you. Your body. Your power!

It's time to use it.

My chest swells with the Knife's pride as I take a deep breath and bring the Cornucopia to my lips. It's freezing, the kiss of death, of a corpse long gone cold.

The Knife loves it.

"NIGEL! DON'T!"

The familiar voice makes me stop, the Knife having to fight down the desperate child within me wanting to please.

Dad, shackled six floors above, leans over the balcony. His face twists in horror, mirroring the expressions of Yamato, Kenneth, and Jameson chained with him. Pallavit stands beside them, her eyes searching until they land on her daughter.

I register dozens, hundreds, maybe even thousands of flares of light as the rest of the Guild joins and realizes what's happening.

They're too late!

With thoughts of my power becoming warped, twisted, as destructive as possible, the Knife takes a deep breath and blows.

The sound is low and deep, the roars of long forgotten monsters crawling their way from the depths of hell. The sound is frantic, frenzied, a stampede of demonic beasts ready to wreak their destruction on the planet. The sound is pain and suffering, screams of tortured victims begging for mercy.

It makes my skin crawl. It makes the Knife's heart—or whatever rotted body part makes the monster tick—soar.

I feel the curse take hold as the last of the Cornucopia's note echoes around the Guild. A clammy hand grasps my elven power deep inside of me. It worms its way into my magic, even deeper than the Knife, corrupting it, rotting it.

I've got you now.

The Knife whispers it in my head. Not a triumphant yell, but a quiet certainty that nothing will derail its plan.

I've got all of you.

The echoes of the Cornucopia's call reverberate against the marble for only a heartbeat more. The hall is eerily silent for one, two, three seconds before a cacophony of footsteps echoes from floors above. Bursts of light soon follow with the sounds of wings flapping, sprites blinking, vines snapping as magicians prepare to fight. Curses and spells already barrel toward me, spells that my monstrous companion dodges effortlessly, dancing on its hooves.

"If only it were that easy," the Knife says, my thighs squeezing on either side of the demonic horse. *"'Yup!'"*

The horse springs from the floor, thousands of eyes following our rocketing trajectory. There's a ripple in the air as they all tense, readying themselves to defend the Guild.

"Nothing will stop me."

The Knife says it for its own ears only, savoring this moment. It's been waiting nearly four hundred years for this; it wasn't sure this day would ever come.

With a piercing whinny, we dive headfirst, plummeting back toward the entry hall. Beams of power chase after us, goblins shapeshifted to dragons and phoenixes and birds of prey following. None are fast enough to stop us, not with the destructive power of the Cornucopia fueling my magic.

We're nearly to the first floor, traveling faster than the quickest sprite can blink. But I see everything crystal clear, this hyper speed the perfect tempo for the Knife's plan. I watch as its beast balances out, its hooves now pointed toward the floor, ready to land. I feel the way its body absorbs the impact as we crash into the marble with incredible force.

Cracks zigzag across the floor and up the Guild walls. The stone crumbles, balconies buckle, jagged gashes rise level after level until they reach the ceiling. They converge right in the center of the Guild symbol, that five-pointed star that once gave me hope, and I watch as each of those points crashes down.

"RETREAT!"

Pallavit's magically amplified voice rings through the Guild before she flies to the floor, headed for her daughter. She revives Jaleesa with a spell, Laurel and Ori next.

Awake for their torture.

Once more, I bring the Horn to my lips and blow.

As the monstrous call rings through the halls, Guild members flee, opening portals and leaving as quickly as they can. I spot Alister, that coward, disappear in a flash. Others hesitate, like Pallavit, who pulls her daughter to her, ready to protect her at any cost.

Good. I need the bravest among them to stay.

Memories flash through my mind of years cursed asleep inside that volcano. Locked in the depths, where lava oozed over the Knife day after day, burning it even in its slumber. I can hear phantom echoes of magicians' spells penetrating the Knife's dreams, imprisoning it in sleep, in pain, even as the magic crown that kept it immortal healed its wounds—a never-ending cycle of misery. It raged against the cursed sleep, trying to wake itself, to no avail. It was torture. Pure mental and physical torture.

Until that day the Horde poured into the mountain, their hate a lava of its own. They swarmed the magicians defending the Knife's hulking body, killed them all, and pooled the little magic they had to wake the Knife. Finally.

I'll pay the Guild back tenfold for what they did to me. A fate of hell, of anguish, for all eternity. Sleep would be a mercy. These magicians and their precious headquarters and all their magical relics must be gone, forever vanished so they can never rebuild.

They must feel the torture I did for so many centuries—knowing they'll never return to the life they once lived, the glory and power they once felt.

With a snap of my fingers, the Guild stops crumbling. The hunks of marble littering the floor—from the tiniest pebbles to boulders as big as houses—pop back into place.

The assembled magicians hesitate, unsure what to make of me cleaning up my own mess.

"You don't honestly think I'd let you suffer in squalor, do you?"

I'll send the Guild far, far away. Those trapped inside will be filled with paranoia, claustrophobia. Their never-ending fear will fuel my curse and keep the Guild undiscoverable for the rest of time.

I hop down and land on my feet gracefully. With my summoning spell in my fingers, I whistle, a piercing screech that makes all those assembled smack their hands to their ears. When they pull their hands away, their skin will be coated in blood.

As the whistle rings out, my demonic horse multiplies until there's no room left to stand, every square inch of the entry hall covered by a grotesque new herd. They stamp and bray, eager to fulfill their master's ghastly desires. I hate seeing my way with horses used for such monstrous ends, and that hatred only further fuels the Knife's magic.

The Depraved raises my hand high, glowing with magic. *"'YUP!"*

I slap my hand on the hide of the nearest beast, and it rears up on its hind legs. All around me, the hundreds of horse duplicates do the same. As one, their hooves slam onto the marble, and they charge straight for the walls. Beast after beast disappears into the stone, until the entire Guild is no longer glaring white and gold but shining with sickly green power.

The floor shakes, the shake of anticipation, of energy waiting to be released. The Knife gleefully fills my mind with visions of what its curse will do: Within seconds, the Guild will be off, flying through the unknown, through the ether of its in-between space, never to be found again. It will never rest in one spot long enough for the magicians who escaped to reenter or for those trapped inside to leave, fueled for eternity by this wicked herd.

"Enjoy the trip!" the Knife calls, then snaps once more, activating a shining portal as I laugh maniacally. *"Farewell. Forever."*

CHAPTER
TWENTY-EIGHT

JALEESA'S EYES FLUTTER OPEN, ONLY TO WINCE BACK SHUT THANKS TO the throbbing pain in her skull and the acid-green light shining from the center of the entry hall.

"Nigel," she says, only to be met by her mom shushing her. Pallavit's throat glows bright purple and she lets out a long, clear note. The throbbing lessens as the seconds tick by, precious seconds Jaleesa needs to rescue the only people who might be able to help.

"We have to get out of here," Jaleesa says, pushing her mother's worried hands off her to cast the unconscious nymph at her side awake.

"Need to escape.

Lots to undo.

We can't turn the tide,

If you don't come to."

Laurel's eyes drift open, and Jaleesa unceremoniously hauls her to her feet.

"Wh-what's going on?" the nymph asks groggily.

"No time." Jaleesa snaps her fingers and points at Ori. "I need you to heal him," she tells her mother. "I don't have the strength to bring Ori to. And we need the Resistance."

Pallavit shakes her head. "Jaleesa, what are you saying? They've been working with Nigel this whole time and—" She blanches as she looks to the elf cackling atop the entry platform. "They'll destroy the Guild."

"They don't want to destroy it, they want to change it," Jaleesa snaps. "For the better. That's why we all need to go together before Nigel takes us out."

A deafening whinny makes Jaleesa's head throb again, and she turns to see twisted, monstrous horses made of magic pour out of Nigel by the hundreds. "Get us out of here. Take us home."

Pallavit hesitates again, but there's no time.

"Trust me," Jaleesa pleads.

Pallavit's eyes bounce back and forth between her daughter's.

"Argh!" Jaleesa cries. She leans Laurel against her mom and drops to her knees, trying futilely to summon her power.

"H-heal now—"

The crack in her voice is enough to get her mother to move.

"Let me."

With a quick note, Pallavit opens a portal by her side. She thrusts her hand into the shimmering purple light, rummages around, and pulls. In quick succession, Kenneth, Yamato, Jameson, and Reggie all tumble through, still in their shackles. With a hum, purple bands snap over their mouths, preventing them from speaking.

Two short bursts from Pallavit, and Laurel and Ori float; another high-pitched croon and a new portal has opened. With two gentle shoves, the nymph and sprite disappear through the glowing door. Pallavit grabs the shackles keeping the Resistance chained, then twines her fingers with her daughter's. "Let's get out of here."

Jaleesa steps through. But she turns back, just for a moment, in time to see Nigel walk into a portal of his own. The Guild blurs, and she knows it isn't because of the spell tugging on her. But then she's pulled away by the fae magic, dread for everyone still inside those marble halls wriggling inside her.

The dread stays with her through the whirlwind of her mother's magic, fighting against the emotionally healing power of the portal. A brief feeling of relief sweeps through her when her feet hit the hardwood floor of their New York townhouse, where the soothing sounds of the city stream through a cracked open window. But that relief evaporates as the gravity of their situation hits her.

And she's not the only one.

"We have to get to him now," Ori insists. "I know where he's going. I could feel it. The Barrett ranch." He turns to Pallavit. "The claw is there and the Knife wants it. Open another portal."

His chest heaves with anticipation, his eyes practically bugging out of his skull the longer Pallavit takes to move.

Ori taps his neck. "Is this thing on? We've got to go *now*. I'm the only one who can stop him." He motions to the adults roped together. "Let them out of those chains already! And where's my mom?" He rounds on Jaleesa in accusation, and her stomach flares with guilt. There was so much happening, too little time.

Pallavit doesn't acknowledge the sprite's questions. She walks calmly to their lilac sofa, taking her time to find an elegant, seated position, not making eye contact with any of the assembled magicians. Finally, she looks up at her daughter, a small smile on her face. "Don't just stand there. We aren't going anywhere until someone tells me what's going on." She gestures to the chained Resistance. "And it's not going to be these known traitors. *You* better fill me in." When nobody moves, Pallavit's throat flares purple. *"Sit."*

Magic tugs each of them onto various furniture scattered throughout the room, Jaleesa by her mother's side, Ori on an ottoman, Laurel in a rocking chair, and the four Resistance members crammed onto a settee, their mouths still sealed. "Much better," Pallavit says. "Jaleesa, you are the love of my life, but if you tell me you're in league with these boys, I'm not above recommending you for a tribunal myself. You know I adore magic and everything it can do—but if you're using yours to destroy alongside Nigel and Ori, I won't hesitate to have it taken from you."

A stab of betrayal slices through Jaleesa's back straight to her heart. "You know me better than that, Mom. You know I would never use these gifts for evil." She steps beside the sprite, her head held high. "And neither would Ori or Nigel."

"Jaleesa, I've seen with my own eyes what they can do. We all just watched Nigel use the *Depraved's* power!"

"It was an accident!" Ori blurts. "After he sacrificed himself to *kill* the Knife, I brought him back. I thought a piece of the heartstone could just work as a heart and not . . . you know . . . a bloodthirsty monster's soul." He shrugs. "My bad."

Pallavit blanches. "Your *bad*? You're telling me Nigel is possessed by the Knife and he just cursed the Guild with who knows what, and all you can say is *my bad*?"

"Oh, is it time for critiques?" Ori snaps. "Because I've got all kinds of feedback on how the Guild has handled things."

Jaleesa knows they're wasting time when there's one person in this room who could clear everything up. She shoots her girlfriend a glare that could cut glass. She doesn't even know why she still thinks of Laurel as her girlfriend after everything that's gone down. She doesn't love her like she once did, doesn't even recognize her. But as Laurel meets her eyes, the determination there *is* recognizable. Jaleesa saw it so many times as they strolled these city streets together or prowled through Laurel's property, talking about all the good they'd do once they joined the Guild together. How many monsters they'd kill on the spot, fantasizing about their heroics long before Laurel became the monster that needed to be stopped. The nymph nods, a nod of acknowledgment that she finally knows it's her time to step up, to be the person she promised she'd always be on their walks. After all Laurel's done, Jaleesa finally thinks there may be some clarity in Laurel's heart and mind, showing her how to get back on track.

"They're not the evil ones, Mrs. Devi," Laurel says with a sigh. "I am."

Pallavit's jaw drops further and further the longer Laurel talks. Each new revelation—that the Cornucopia's been used, that enough people are working with Alister to keep this covered up, that a spell has been cast to wipe the memories of Guild members—seems to hit the fae harder than the last. Jaleesa is with Laurel right up until she reveals that the Culling is a hoax. She plops next to Ori on the ottoman. It feels like there's been an earthquake.

"Wait. What?" Jaleesa says at the same time her mother does. They lock eyes, Pallavit's hand covering her mouth.

"But that would mean," Pallavit says, "we've sapped the souls of thousands of magicians for nothing. Cursed them to a life without magic. That's torture."

"Bingo," Ori says, jerking a thumb at Laurel. "And it's all thanks to this one and her family."

Laurel may seem to be on the path to making it right, but Jaleesa can't help the burning desire to punish the nymph.

"You're going to forget that last bit about the Culling," Laurel says. "Because of the spell. But I promise, when we get everything back on track, if we can get the Knife out of Nigel, I'll burn the rotten forest to the ground myself."

"How do I know this isn't all a lie?" Pallavit asks. "Children always act like they know better, thinking they've got the world figured out when they only just became adults a few short months ago. This could be a trick to get what you want."

Jaleesa gets up from her seat and kneels down at her mother's feet. "Mom, you know me. You raised me. That same fascination with magic and all the good it can do that flows through you runs through my veins, too."

Pallavit stares into her daughter's eyes, her lips pursed.

"You can cast any truth spell on me to make sure I'm not lying," Laurel adds.

Pallavit waves her off. "Just like lie detectors, truth spells can be fooled."

Jaleesa racks her brain for a way to ease her mom's fears. How do you convince someone that everything they've held true, everyone they've trusted, needs to be reexamined?

But that's the problem, isn't it? Jaleesa realizes that all this time she's been so concerned about saying the right thing that she never really said the truth.

"Mom, I know exactly what you're going through right now. It took me a while to even entertain the idea that the Guild might need to be changed. *Not* destroyed, if that's what you're worried about. But changed. The Guild can be a force for good, but we've *got* to be sure we don't unquestioningly follow those who speak the loudest. I mean, we know better than anyone that just because someone can shout, it doesn't make their magic stronger or their purpose truer.

"But I saw with my own eyes the beauty of the bond between Nigel and Ori. I saw it heal, I could *feel* its goodness. I felt how it was built on love, and it reminded me of your love for magic. It reminded me how you always believed magic could make the impossible possible, and how you've never wavered in your belief that one day we'll defeat evil with our powers. Nigel and Ori can do that, if we work with them and let them lean in to their connection. And there's someone in my life who I know I could share this kind of power with. Someone who's been in my life since day one."

Laurel scoots to the edge of her chair, her eyes full of hope.

"Who is it?" Pallavit whispers.

"You, Mom. If the magic Nigel and Ori have is fueled by love and connection, *why* aren't we seeing it between a parent and their kid? I think I know. We're partly to blame. The kids, I mean. *I'm* partly to blame.

"So I'm here at your feet, Mom, to tell you I'm sorry. I've been closing myself off, these past couple years, to prove to you that I can bear the burden of the Guild's expectations and the responsibilities of being a magician. I didn't want to seem weak or overwhelmed or worried that I actually *couldn't* be the best. But I don't think that was fair to you. I didn't let you in to see my worries and doubts and fears. I didn't let you in to see the whole *me*. I don't think any young magician does, for fear of not living up to an impossible standard. But if we don't let people see all of us, including what we worry might be our ugly sides, how can a connection truly be built, even between a parent and their child?

"I never let you share, either. I put you on this pedestal, thinking you'd always had it figured out. I didn't once ask if you ever felt the same things I did when you were in the Culling. All so I could be *strong*. Really the greatest strength would have been asking for help when I needed it."

Jaleesa thinks of all the times she felt disdain from Alister for falling in love with his daughter, thinks of all the times she let that hurt and brutal sting fester inside of her, because romance felt so trivial compared to the mission of the Guild. Maybe she was wrong.

Maybe those moments weren't trivial but necessary to build a bond with her mom and the magicians around her.

"And I've needed it, Mom. I've needed it so badly. But I've been too afraid to ask for help. That's going to stop today." Jaleesa holds her hand palm up, an offering of her heart. An offering of her vulnerability. "Will you help me?"

Tears fall silently down Pallavit's cheeks as she says, "Of course, beta. Of course."

She grabs Jaleesa's hand and wraps it behind her, pulling her in for the most important embrace of their lives. The relief and love that wash over Jaleesa are so strong, she's almost certain it's the result of a spell. But no. Neither of their throats glow purple with fae song. This is a different kind of magic. One only she and her mother could create.

"We don't have much time," Pallavit says, as if she wasn't the one who forced them all to stay and chat first. She gets to her feet, marches over to Jameson, and rips off the magic band sealing his lips shut.

"Do you have anything else to add?" Pallavit asks.

Jameson meets Jaleesa's eyes, shaking his head softly. "You learn as a writer that there's such a thing as overediting. That, Jaleesa, was perfect."

CHAPTER
TWENTY-NINE

THE KNIFE WISHES IT COULD STAY TO WITNESS THEIR REACTIONS. The terror the Guild magicians will feel when it sinks in that they'll never go home would be so filling.

But there's no time for the Knife to feast. The magicians who made it out are still in the back of its mind, *our* mind, as we whip through the hurricane-like frenzy of the Knife's portal. The monster has to find them, stop them once and for all. Then the world will be the Knife's for the taking.

But first, to ensure that I truly am unstoppable.

An image of the claw fills my mind, gray and scratched, the heartstone red and shining in its center. I watch as the Knife replays the memory of me shoving it inside a boot, and I feel its determination to get the claw back.

It's the Knife's weak point. If the claw, the effigy that brought us back, is destroyed we'll both be killed with it.

Seeing Meema's room again, even in memory, sends a pang

through my heart. I miss the days when my biggest worry was whether or not I would make it into the Guild. When all I wanted was to use my magic to fight for good. I miss the ranch and the peace I used to feel there.

The second I think it, I know it was a mistake. The Knife latches onto the hope the ranch used to give me and pores through my memories, finding all the good ones. The memories of Meema teaching me to ride a horse, spellcraft in the barn, watching my grandma bond with animals and pass that talent down to me.

My stomach fills with dread as I sense the Knife's intention.

I'm going to force you to watch while your home burns to the ground at your own hand. Hate for me will fill your heart, and I'm going to lap up each burning ember of it. Combined with your power, you will give me more strength than any magician has ever had before.

I want nothing more than to be able to dig my heels in, to spell my boots so that when we land, the Knife can't use my body to decimate my home. But hopes and dreams are nothing compared to the Knife's lust for revenge. The only way to stop it is to get rid of the vessel it will use for its destruction. I have to remember why I went to the Guild in the first place, despite Ori's insistence that we can find another way.

I have to die.

I've never felt so sad to see the ranch. Even though last time I could see the signs of Meema's magic fading—grime growing in the nooks and crannies of the limestone that would make her skin crawl—at least the buildings still stood. At least there was a possibility that Ori and I could turn this back into a home, recast her spells, settle in with the animals, and pick up our family business. But the Knife aims to end all that.

I take a step forward. The crunch of my boots in the rocky soil is too loud. For a giant's step? No. But in this body? Someone's here with us.

I turn, a cool smile spreading up my cheeks as I spot my soulmate's silhouette, backlit by the orange light of the sunset.

"Fancy seeing you here, Orion."

His full name feels so weird on my lips, the lips that want nothing more than to smash against his, grateful that he's still alive. Saying his name with such animosity feels wrong, too, the hairs on my arms standing on end, that is until the Knife notices the effigy in Ori's hands. A Mr. Potato Head, glowing pink.

"I'm sorry, Nigel." Ori's eyes fill with sympathy as my hands fly for the Cornucopia in my back pocket. "But the Knife can fuck right off." With a flick of his fingers, he pops the tiny white arms off the plastic potato, and my shoulders wrench from their sockets.

The Knife cries out in agony. I've never wanted to be in pain more—for every blow Ori deals me, it means we're winning. I can sense within the Knife that healing spells are not in its wheelhouse. Health and vibrant life are not the realm of these monsters who want nothing more than death and decay.

So Ori's just got to kick my ass.

"I'll get you back," Ori says to me, not the Knife, before shouting, "It's done!"

Magicians appear, surrounding me. Kenneth, Yamato, Jameson, Jaleesa, Laurel, and Pallavit. But the Knife doesn't care about any of them. It wants to be sure Dad didn't come, too. It doesn't know exactly what he can do but is sure if he made a Beloved once, he can do it again.

My stomach sinks. Dad's not here.

"Please don't hurt me." The Knife makes me sound completely wrecked, no trace of its gravel in my voice. Tears well in my eyes, my nose clogs. *"I don't know what's going on. Get it out of me."*

"Can it, Knifgel," Ori says. "The *real* Nigel is never that pathetic."

"It was worth a shot." My tears dry up as if they were never there.

Suddenly, the air shimmers as all around me sunlight prisms. Intense rays of light, as if refracted through a magnifying glass, splinter in every direction. The Knife whips my hand up to cover my face.

It's a trap. A spell from the air nymph.

Kenneth. My memories are giving the Knife all the clues it needs to anticipate the Resistance. Even though I can't see a thing, the Knife is ready for whoever will strike next. So when I feel a presence land behind me, the Knife throws my body back, my muscles fueled by its power. I land on top of Ori, and the blaring sunlight disappears in time for me to see his head smack against a rock. My heart races with the Knife's victory and my despair, but we're both wrong. Ori's eyes snap open and my shoulders pop back into place.

Your connection has its advantages.

Our contact. A jolt runs up my spine as my power recharges, power the Knife is eager to use. For the first time since I met him, I don't want Ori to touch me.

"Thanks for the boost," I say, getting to my feet, taking stock of the magicians around me. It's just Ori, Laurel, and Jaleesa. The Resistance members are gone.

Suspicion floods the Knife. Ori knows how the Depraved titan was brought back, and it wouldn't be a stretch to imagine the sprite told his allies. If they know about the effigy that gave the monster life, the Resistance will safely assume it can give him death.

They're after the claw.

Power surges in my boots, ready to run, only to be pulled back with a violent tug. *"AGH!"*

A vine constricts around my throat, making me cough and hack like a cat with a hairball, struggling for breath. I have barely enough mobility to twist and find Laurel controlling the plants, just as her dad appears behind her. Anger flares through the Knife, and it burns the vines to ash.

My chest heaves as I take in the half a dozen newcomers. Alister brought reinforcements.

"Oh, Alister," I say. *"How nice of you to join us."*

The nymph waves his hand dismissively. "A seed of magic I planted in my daughter's heart the day she was born," he says. "To find her, wherever she may be. Convenient that it led me straight to you." He turns his glare on his daughter. "And to realizing she's working with the very people who are trying to destroy the Guild."

Laurel can't meet her father's eyes.

With no mind for his daughter, Alister shoves her away and the Knife eats up Laurel's sense of betrayal. Meanwhile Alister's elf friend glows gold, blowing a force field bubble that surrounds the Guild newcomers. The bubble levitates and heads toward me, bringing the magicians closer by the second. The Knife unleashes spell after spell, but it's not enough. The force field is fortified with the purpose of these experienced magicians, and that's something to contend with.

But they're not the ones with the Horn.

I reach for it in my back pocket but I'm stopped by a hand lacing through mine, so softly, so tenderly. Ori's blinked behind me, and I can feel his love. He's trying to get me to remember what it's like to be *us*. But instead, his touch just magnifies my power again, the perfect opportunity for the Knife to strike.

"Oh, how sweet," I purr, before flexing my bicep and, with a rush of tainted magic, flinging my soulmate a hundred yards away. As Ori rockets toward the side of the barn, Jaleesa sings a song at breakneck speed.

"Fly through the air.
   Racing fast.
     Nothing will hurt you.
      Wrapped in this cast."

A glowing purple body cast envelops Ori, seconds before he slams into the side of the barn. He's up in a flash, then in a blink he's back by my side. He struggles to grab my arm in his stiff cast, but he doesn't need dexterity when he has bulk. Just as I'm bringing the Cornucopia to my lips, he blinks again, directly in front of my face. The mouthpiece of the Horn knocks him square in the back.

Magic fuels my hands on hateful instinct. But Ori's prepared this time. He registers the green light of my power and blinks out of harm's way just before a stream of evil magic bursts from my body. I whip the Horn to my mouth but—

Dammit!

Ori's blinked again. The Horn bounces off the top of his head.

"Let it go, Nigel!" Ori yells. "Make it drop the Horn."

"How sweet of you to include him," I say. **"I'm in control now, Ori. Your precious** soulmate **is gone."**

A shadow passes over us, and a familiar note makes the hairs on my arms stand on end. It's Alister and his friends, hovering over us in their protective elf bubble. The fae song makes my blood run cold as the Knife combs my memories to identify it. It's the note used in the spell to strip a magician of their power.

Somewhere outside the Knife's control, I register that this could be it: a way to defeat the Depraved inside of me, without dying along with the monster. If the Guild takes my power, the Knife won't be able to use it. For a moment, I feel like we've won.

But closer to the surface, overpowering my hope, is the Knife's anger and hatred for the Guild.

"ENOUGH!" I roar, a wall of power cascading out of me. It knocks Ori over and shatters Jaleesa's protective spell, but the golden bubble of the Guild posse wavers for only a moment before surging forward again.

If the sprite won't let me blow the Horn, I'll just have to kill him.

I'm not stupid enough to think the Knife is bluffing. The way to trap Ori comes quickly to the Depraved. While the Guild members hover closer, the Knife takes a deep breath, making sure to make eye contact with Ori. We can see the determination in his eyes, and we both know he's going to blink.

My heart, my mind, my soul scream for Ori to stop, begging him not to fall for it. But Ori can't hear the signals I struggle to send through our connection. I hate the wicked smile that spreads across my face, the glee of betrayal that will be the last thing Ori ever sees.

Because at the last second—right before Ori materializes in front of me to knock the Horn off course—I snap my hand back. I whip it to my side, switch my grip so the glistening sharp point faces out, and stab it forward just as Ori reappears.

The Horn of Plenty slides smoothly into his stomach. I feel it pierce skin and slice organs, the wet, mushy thickness giving way to the twisted bone. Careful not to touch Ori and trigger our healing connection, I shove the unicorn horn as far in as it will go. I hear muscles and tendons give way, the sounds of Ori's life force slipping.

I feel Ori try to blink, but his strength is waning. He grits his teeth—bloody now thanks to the carnage inside his beautiful body—and tries to muster the power it will take to move. But he can't.

Easy.

The Knife yanks the Cornucopia out of Ori's belly, triumphant. I'm numb when it brings the Horn to my lips, ready to make its victory complete.

But the ground falls out from under me before I can blow. I look

THE MAGIC YOU MAKE

to the sky, expecting the Guild members above to be casting against me, but they've paused. A knee digs in my back, pain shooting up my spine. My power reacts, radiating out from my body to incinerate whoever it is that tries to stop me. But the pressure doesn't budge. A hand shoves my face to the side, my cheek scraping into hard rock and dirt.

From this position, I can see all the magicians who have gathered to bring about my downfall. The members of the Resistance are back, alongside Jaleesa and Laurel. Ori twitches on the ground.

So who is it that's holding me down?

"No, Nigel."

I recognize that voice. The Knife turns my head just so in order to confirm my suspicions.

Dad. His arms and scraggly bearded face are covered in burns from the magic that pours out of me, but he resists. He fights on.

"I know this isn't you," he says, his skin flaring red, welting, as my power tries to melt him. He nods toward Ori. "We can't let him die. You're a better man than I ever was, Nigel. I don't want the person you've become to crumble if you get out of this and he's gone."

Keeping his weight firmly on my back, Dad leans forward and grabs Ori's foot. He heaves Ori's unconscious body closer. Then he lifts my right hand, slides Ori's jean leg up just a few inches, and wraps my fingers around my soulmate's exposed skin.

He's trying to heal him, unaware that the Knife has the power to block our soulmate connection. Even still, and despite everything we've been through—despite how much I hated Dad growing up, how much I wished he'd just act like a real father—I couldn't be more grateful to him now.

I won't let a father's **love** *be my downfall.*

"NO!" I yell, the Knife's timbre shaking the ground, and I send another burst of magic down my arm. It's infused with the intent to torture, and I cover Dad's hand with it.

267

"AAAAAAAH!" Dad screams louder than I thought humanly possible.

"You will not defeat me." The Knife summons every ounce of power I have left, pouring all its rage into it. The Depraved gathers years of my anger to add to its power, bubbling every memory of Dad's mistreatment up to the surface. I hate myself for how easily the Knife found those, I hate myself for never truly letting go of my anger, I hate the Knife for using my entirely justified emotions against me. The rotten golden-green flares brighter; Dad's hand turns bloody and raw. I see muscle and sinew there as his skin burns away.

But still, he hangs on.

"This isn't you, Nigel," he says through gritted teeth. "You wouldn't want Ori to die. You wouldn't want this monster to control you. We've got to stop this." He looks me in the eye, and somehow I know he sees through the monster making me rage to the son waiting to be brought back. "Together."

A flare of red light shoots from his chest, blowing us apart. The Knife tries to get me to my feet, but it's losing control. There's too much hope in my heart.

Hope for my father.

You cannot defeat me.

Hope for my soulmate.

Your body is mine!

Hope for my world.

I'll be in your soul, pulling on your hate forever!

I'm regaining control.

That red light pouring from Dad finally coalesces into a beautiful being, giving me the final push I need to take my body back. Standing tall above Dad—one hand radiating their warm power over me, the other casting protective magic over my father and Ori—is a Beloved.

CHAPTER
THIRTY

"DAD?"

It's the first thing that pops out of my mouth when I have control again. The realization that Dad could make a Beloved out of his feelings for me—the son he tortured his whole life—is so shocking after all this time that I can't quite believe it's real.

But from the ruby-red prisms of light shining brightly in front of me, I know it is. Dad's Beloved towers over him, red beams overpowering the pinpricks of stars above. The being extends a ruby arm to place a hand on my father's shoulder. Dad stares up at the magical being with awe, occasionally glancing down at his own chest like he's surprised this came out of him, too. As the Beloved touches him, the raw wounds all over his body heal. His hands, arms, and face were bloodred, but now skin knits itself back together. Before long, the Beloved removes their hand, Dad's body good as new.

"It feels so . . . wonderful," Dad says, turning to me. "Being able to cast magic. I didn't let myself hope that this could happen again after the first time, but . . ." His thoughts trail off as his hand floats to his heart. "I thought I'd never feel like this, after they took my power." He glances begrudgingly at the Guild members, who no longer hover in their golden bubble but stare in fascination at the creature Dad made.

"It's called a Beloved," Ori says. He rises from the ground, dusting off his hands and jeans. Meanwhile, I sag with so much relief that I almost fall to the dirt.

He's alive. His shirt is stained with blood, making me woozy, but he's alive.

"They appear when a human performs a true act of love for a magician. Something about that connection creates a magic that's even more powerful than the Depraved." He looks at me with that perfect smirk. "Even stronger than the Knife, apparently."

"Whooee," Dad says, smiling, his hand still placed over his heart.

This version of Dad is so disorienting, the ground feels wobbly beneath me. It's not that I don't want him like this. I'm just so used to seeing him drunk, yelling, and belligerent. But now, he's created something built from his love *for me*. I don't know what to make of it. After all we've been through, I don't know if I could say that I love him, too.

Dad looks up at his Beloved, who nods as if encouraging him to go on. My father takes a breath and says, "I'm sorry, Nigel. Really, I am. I've had some time to talk with Jameson, and I know you didn't deserve the way I treated you. You didn't ask to be born a magician, and I never should have resented you for your power. And now you're stronger than I ever knew, all because you're connected to this boy." He motions toward Ori, who gives me a weak smile. "But I shouldn't be surprised. I know from all the times I watched you train out on this farm with your grandma that you *are* the strongest of your generation. Whatever is inside of you, trying to corrupt that? I know you can get it out. I'm sure of it."

All those walls I put up after a lifetime of feeling his hate and resentment come crumbling down. Maybe tipped over by the Beloved. I feel so bolstered by Dad's words that I'm certain my magic could light up all of Austin.

Dad looks back to his Beloved, who gives a final nod before dissipating, their work apparently done. They're so unlike the Depraved, who only feel satisfied when they've destroyed as much as possible. This Beloved didn't need to perform spells, didn't need to fight to be effective. They just gave Dad the strength to say what was in his heart, and that's a magic I didn't even realize had power until I felt it myself. It certainly was strong enough to knock the Knife loose, at least for now.

"But if there's some reason you can't do it on your own, I think there's one person who can help get rid of that varmint," Dad says, motioning for Ori to step closer.

"Nigel." Ori's voice is soft, unsure, not the confident sprite I'm used to. He's tentative. I can tell he doesn't want to set me off. But I feel our connection growing stronger already, those phantom pulses of his emotion rushing back. He doesn't know how close he can get, wary of triggering the Knife.

"Come here." I scoop him into a hug, holding him as close as I can, feeling as *me*—with my soulmate pressed against my chest—as I have since Ori first brought me back. I feel my flannel dampen, and I pull back, gently holding Ori's face. He's crying. "Ori, I'm so sorry. I'm so, so sorry."

Words alone won't ever be enough to show him how truly awful I feel for everything that's happened. So I bring my lips to his and try to soak our connection with every positive feeling I have for him:

trust, belonging, comfort, and most importantly, love. I feel it from him, too—mixed with the taste of salt from his tears, of dirt flaking off my face from when Dad shoved it into the ground, of the metallic remnant of blood after I stabbed my soulmate.

"I'm so, so sorry," I say again, into his lips.

"It's all right." Ori tips his head, just slightly, resting his forehead against my chin. "It wasn't you. It was the Knife."

Movement out of the corner of my eye snaps me to. It's Alister, stepping forward, his cronies just behind him. While they still look a bit dazed by Dad's creation, Alister is clearly ready to pounce.

"This has been my point all along," he says, ignoring me, Ori, and the rest of the Resistance, focusing instead on the allies he brought with him. "The Knife is in him. Ready your spells. We can't let the boy walk out of here alive."

Alister's gang steps forward, no longer fazed. I have half a mind to let them have me so they can do away with the Knife. But that flare of hope ignites in my chest again at the possibility there could be a way out of this without dying. Pallavit seems to think so too as, with a sharp note, the fae stops the Guild members in their tracks.

"Alister," Pallavit says coldly. "Did you tell all your friends here that *your daughter* cursed their connection with the Cornucopia? The boys' power never would have been able to wake the Horde if not for her."

I hope for any sign of surprise from Alister's allies. But of course, it doesn't come. They already know. And none of them seems upset about it.

"Gasp!" Alister says in mock surprise. "Don't act so high and mighty, Pallavit. Who among us wouldn't use desperate measures to help their family? Besides, the Cornucopia would never have had such a strong effect if the boys' power wasn't warped to begin with."

"It's not warped," Kenneth says, taking his husband's hand. "It's a bond all of us could have. One of extreme emotional connection between magicians. One of love. Something I doubt any of you have ever experienced. Tell me I'm wrong. Do you have true friendship with one another? Have any of you never doubted the ambitions or intentions of your fellow magician?"

No one speaks up.

"You saw yourselves what love can do," Jameson insists. "With the Beloved. Perhaps, rather than take Nigel and Ori's powers, we give them a chance to lead by example. To lead through connection, rather than competition."

"I'm in," Pallavit says. She looks between Ori and me to add, "I'm sorry I doubted you." She hooks her thumb toward Alister. "I let *him* get into my head."

"You should have doubt!" the nymph yells. "The Knife still lives! It is our duty to stop it!"

"*You* need to stop!" Pallavit's voice doesn't need a spell to command everyone's attention. "We've seen a new kind of magic with our own eyes today. The Beloved made the Knife retreat within Nigel. It must be good. I want to learn how we can control that. I want to hear how the boys make their power so strong in the spells they cast. I want to learn how to re-create their bond, so that we all can have it." Jaleesa puffs her chest with pride as her mom continues. "I've had about enough of your rants, Alister. Worst of all, I let you have them. Even when it affected my daughter. But no one needs your opinions. And that's coming from *me*, a fae who loves to hear herself talk, so you *know* it's bad."

Jaleesa laughs and lunges into her mom's arms. Laurel's eyes drift from Jaleesa and her mom to the cold gap between her and her father.

"But none of you care about that, do you?" Ori says to Alister and his cronies. His tone makes it clear he thinks they're the scum of the earth, and he's not wrong. "You don't want more people to have power. Especially not humans. You all know the Culling is fake.

Why would you let humans make Beloved when you don't even let magicians keep their magic, right?"

Shock ripples through the magicians in the Resistance. "What are you talking about?" Pallavit asks, whipping around to face Alister. "What is he talking about?"

God, it's going to be great when we don't have to keep having this revelation.

Alister waves her away. "Oh, come on, Pallavit. So there's no such thing as magical imbalance." He shrugs. "Who cares? Think of the competition if *everyone* could keep their powers. Think how many magicians would just take their abilities for granted. It *is* about balance: We protect the world from the Depraved, and we reap the rewards we deserve for that service."

"And what makes you think you get to call the shots?" Yamato growls. He's got that same determined and defiant look Bex always gets.

"He's right." Jaleesa speaks up, her voice strong. "This needs to be aired out in front of the Guild, so *all* magicians can decide how we move forward together. We got here thanks to your secrets." Pallavit beams with pride, Alister's friends look unmoved, and Alister himself just rolls his eyes.

"How would we even get started?" Laurel asks. "I've tried calling a portal to go back, but I can't find the Guild."

Alister's allies look worried at that, and a few mutter incantations meant to trigger their own portals. None of them work.

"Where did you send it?" Laurel asks.

I open my mouth to speak, but dread seeps into my gut. "I don't know." I can feel the Knife's twisted glee, wherever it is inside me. "It sent it into limbo. Forever galloping through the magical plane it exists in. You won't be able to find it. No one will."

I practically hear the Depraved's evil laugh in my head.

"You could try using this." Kenneth's hands glow white with

power, then a wisp of wind twists around the Cornucopia in my back pocket and carries it to his hands. He holds the Horn of Plenty high, its slick sides catching the moonlight. "We should destroy it."

Jameson nods. "That might work. Theoretically. When the source of any magic is destroyed, the spells or curses that have been cast from it wear off. With the Horn destroyed, the curse should go along with it."

"So I'd have to blow it?" I ask. "And forgive *the Knife*?" The Depraved last used the Cornucopia against *me*, warping my magic to send the Guild far away. I look to Ori in disbelief. Having empathy for the monster inside me is a tall order.

The longer I consider it, the more a thought nags at me, buzzes in my skull, dying to get out. It's not the Knife this time.

It's my doubt.

"It would have to be forgiveness for so much more than just the Knife," I say. "I'd have to forgive all the actions—all the hate—that created the Knife and Depravedkind to begin with. And the Guild's a part of that, isn't it? Thanks to the pressures this organization puts on us, that our families put on us, that have led magicians, since the very first time Ancestrals gave us their skills, to hoard power. It's made us dead set on proving that we're better and stronger and more *worthy*. Even more so than our fellow magicians, people we should see as collaborators in the fight against evil. And for what? Money? Influence? Is it worth it? Who does any magician even enjoy sharing all that privilege with?

"If I blow that horn, I'll have to forgive every last magician. The ones who started the Culling, the ones who kept it going, the ones who—even if it's no fault of their own—never did a thing to stop it, allowing monsters to be made from those who we cast aside. Monsters like the Knife, who never would have been here if it wasn't for the actions of others. Of us."

Most stare back at me with defeated looks, but Jaleesa steps forward, determined.

"I think that's what makes us human," Jaleesa says. "We may be magical and have always considered ourselves superior because we can change our surroundings with a spell. But we still have hearts, and hearts carry hurt. What makes us think we're so special that we wouldn't have to deal with past damage just like everybody else? Everyone has to try to move forward from the hurts of the past to make the future better. And we can never move forward if we fester on how we were wronged. There has to come a point where we acknowledge the shit of the past, but decide we aren't going to let it continue anymore, and actively do better. Maybe this is that point."

She seems so confident, but I've never been more unsure. The Guild has done so much shit, and Bex's words about how true forgiveness is such a rare characteristic won't stop echoing in my head. I'm not even sure *Bex* has it in her to forgive me—or that I deserve it. But I solidly won't deserve it if I don't try this. It would say so much about me if I didn't take this opportunity to destroy the Horn when I had the chance. If this works, I'll owe Bex the biggest apology of my life. Even if it doesn't work, I'll still owe her that.

"All right then." I place my middle finger and thumb in a circle and bring them to my lips. With my skin glowing gold, I blow. The Horn leaves Kenneth's grasp, flying straight for me. I stretch my hand out to catch it. Everything could change in a matter of seconds.

A vine shoots up from the dirt at Kenneth's feet, snatching the Cornucopia and flinging it to Alister.

In one fluid movement, he catches it and blows.

An evil laugh that could rival the Knife's mingles with the melancholy sound of the Horn.

"I'm afraid there's been a change of plans."

CHAPTER
THIRTY-ONE

BEX CAN'T STOP RIPPING GRASS NERVOUSLY. SHE SITS IN THE middle of the starlit plain, staring at the unicorn herd while they go about business as usual: chewing wildflowers, galloping wildly while their manes whip majestically behind them, zapping butterflies with their magic to change their color or turn them into birds or have them make fart noises.

For the purest magical beings on the planet, unicorns have an unfortunate affinity for fart noises.

It only annoys Bex further, and the last thing she thought she'd be feeling for the unicorns was annoyance. As soon as Ori left, she tried to switch tactics. If they wouldn't help with the Knife, maybe they'd help her rescue her dads. They talked for hours, but nothing. Bex knows she can't leave empty-handed. *She* doesn't have super-powered soulmate strength—as the boys and her dads constantly remind her—so if she's going to be able to do anything, she'll need an advantage, something no one saw coming.

Like a unicorn herd, for example.

But no matter what she's said, she can't convince them.

WHOOOOOoooooooooom.

Bex can't help her full-body shiver at the sound, if you can even call it a sound. It is but isn't there, an awful lot like the way the unicorns communicate. She feels the low, tinny, ominous ring of danger to come.

Of danger that already *is*. Because it's the second time she's felt it, a buzzing in her bones that clearly signals something is *wrong*. The first was roughly an hour ago, but the unicorns act like everything is just fine, even though she knows good and well they can hear this, too.

"What is that?" Bex asks.

She glances at the nearest unicorn. Their bronze hide shimmers in the starlight, and only the tiniest flick of their ears indicates they heard her. They go right back to zapping another butterfly with their magic so it farts.

"Grow up!" Bex snaps, and the bronze unicorn gives her some serious side-eye.

But Bex isn't going to let this unicorn off the hook. She marches right on up to them.

"What's going on?" she asks. "Something's happening, and it's not good. I can sense it."

The unicorn turns so their ample backside is right in her face. The herd may have taken to her, but that doesn't mean she gets to call all the shots.

"Hey!" She jabs a finger into their left hindquarter, which of course makes them kick back. Bex just manages to avoid the careening hoof by shifting into a hummingbird. She buzzes into the unicorn's face. "I know you can hear me." She shifts back, planting her feet firmly in front of the creature. "I know you can feel it."

The unicorn finally acknowledges her. A series of images and an innate knowledge flow through Bex, a faint glisten in the unicorn's horn the lone sign that they're communicating.

The Horn has been blown.

As soon as the unicorn names it, the herd goes wild: stamping, braying, baring their teeth. Their maelstrom of emotion stampedes through her mind and heart. Many were alive when a member of the herd had their horn ripped from their head. It was the day the Cornucopia was created.

Bex's instinct is to leave. Right now. Her magic flares subconsciously, making her shift into her own unicorn form. The last time the Horn was used, the Horde was awakened. Whatever fresh hell the relic has unleashed can't be good. Maybe *now* the herd will see how important it is that they step in.

"We need to go," Bex insists. "We have to help."

As one, the hundreds of unicorns turn their backs on Bex. It's horse butts as far as the eye can see. Their horns shimmer in quick succession, their message coming across loud and clear.

Why should we help those who would use our goodness against us? They'll just hunt and kill us for their own selfish needs.

Bex shifts back. "Not all magicians are like that," she says. "I mean, yeah, some definitely are. But most aren't."

The response comes quickly: *It's not worth the risk.*

"How can you say that?" Bex asks, and she realizes she's echoing Ori's defiant words. "Aren't you supposed to be the good guys? The pure ones? How can you be pure when you stand by while innocent people get hurt?"

Purity is not about self-sacrifice. You should question your assumptions. Why would keeping to ourselves and doing no evil not be considered pure?

Bex throws her hands in the air. "Because—" But she doesn't

have an answer. What is it about this idea of *pureness* that implies a responsibility to make *others* good? That's too much weight for anyone to carry.

And that's when it hits her: This is the weight she's carried her entire life. Her dads always wanted to do good, so they made it her responsibility to *make others* good, including her in the goals to change the Guild. She was handed the charge to make her peers see the power of connection when that responsibility is theirs and theirs alone. But she went along with it, feeding those expectations. Expectations also held by a human world full of stereotypes for women who look like her. Expectations that she be submissive, that she serve others at her own expense. Then there were the expectations of the magical world, where selfishness and hoarding power was something *others* had to fix and not the people doing the harm to begin with.

The unicorns are right. That bullshit has to stop now.

She's got to live for herself.

She sways, her legs ready to give out from under her, so she takes a deep breath and plops into the grass. She leans back, looking up at the sky, feeling the ground beneath her, letting this new conviction sink in.

"The cruel fucking irony of it all is if I'd just focused on myself all along, maybe I would have been the person to implement real change. Like, what if I'd dated humans in high school? Maybe my partner would have made a Beloved. Or if I hadn't been so focused on watching my dads learn about their connection, I might have met my own magical soulmate. In allowing everyone else to depend on me, I let all this power go."

She's been slighted by whoever made this *soulmate rule*. It's like she's being punished for not having wanted to be in a relationship yet. Why should her power suffer because of that? She shouldn't have to feel incomplete without a partner, but here she is, having her lack of romance shoved down her throat.

"So what does life look like going forward?" She props herself on her elbows, and not a single unicorn looks her way. "Guess it's up to me."

She knows she can't stay here forever. She couldn't live with herself knowing her dads were in danger and she did nothing to help. And she doesn't want to let Nigel and Ori suffer, either, if she's honest. She did create a real friendship with them, despite how self-centered they've been lately. But would rushing to their aid make her a pushover or a girl fighting for the people she cares about? Would she be making herself a side character or the main character of her own story?

Could both things be true at once?

The worst option of all, she realizes, would be to simply let life happen to her. To do *nothing*. She's got only one thing to say to *that* idea:

"Fuck that."

The bronze unicorn finally acknowledges her, turning with a mischievous twinkle in their eye.

Bex rises to her feet. She has to find the words to convince this herd that they have to do something. That they, too, can't just hide here as the world passes them by.

"That's it," Bex whispers, before she approaches the bronze one, whose playfulness turns to suspicion. "You're letting *your world* pass you by." She gestures to the plain, the metallic mountains in the distance. "I don't mean this one you hide out in. You *left* the world that was meant for you. Our world.

"I kind of did that, too. I left the wider world to humans, hoping if I made the magical world a better place, it would somehow negate the evils all around me. But it's not just the humans' world, and it's not just the magicians' world—it's all of ours. Yours, mine, magicians', magical species', Ancestrals', humans', all of ours. Hiding away here doesn't make you smarter, or above it. It makes *hate* win. It makes the worst among any group win, when they shouldn't be the ones the rest of us are judged by anyway. It makes the Depraved win.

"You're inherently *good*, filled with magic that can combat hate. It's not even about doing good for others when they should be able to do good for themselves. It's about willfully giving away your home to monsters. Not even fighting for it. Who does that?"

Bex knows there will be no going back from what she's about to say, but she's done censoring herself for others' benefit. She's done being what other people—or unicorns—want her to be.

"Cowards, that's who. You're not protecting yourselves. You're giving up. Isn't it time to take your world back? This willful separation we've created between humans and magicians and unicorns and Ancestrals is what's made this the biggest shitstorm possible. I mean, if humans and magicians lived together, Beloved would have been discovered long before now. If Ancestrals hadn't ditched us after they gave magicians their gifts, maybe we could have truly found a way for everyone to develop their power together, in tandem, and defeated the demons and the Depraved we vowed to fight centuries ago.

"I know it's easy to believe that people won't change." The image of that Beloved popping out of Nigel's dad flashes through her mind. "But I've already seen a man who'd been so heartless create the most beautiful being born of love. There's good and bad in all of us, and when we let people lean in to the good, truly magical things can happen."

She sucks in a breath. *God, that was cheesy.*

"I mean, why else would there even be a type of magic created from the connection between humans and magicians if magickind, *all* of magickind, isn't supposed to be out there in the real world?

That's the kind of balance we should be focusing on: creating space for all of us in the one world we share, instead of magicking little corners for ourselves.

"We need to leave. We need to make this world ours, too. We need to help."

Bex's chest heaves as she ends her speech, doubt filling her now. The bronze unicorn still stares her down, and it isn't until she's taken a beat that she notices all the unicorns have finally turned to face her. She's looking at a sea full of their angry glares.

"So, yeah," Bex says, awkwardly scratching her elbow. "Um, thanks for listening."

She turns, shifting while she does, her hooves striking the dirt as she prepares to race back to her friends and family. What the hell she's going to do she doesn't know, but she knows without a shadow of a doubt she can't sit by while everyone else fights.

Bex rears back, ready to take off.

Wait.

CHAPTER
THIRTY-TWO

ORI'S AND MY HANDS BLAZE WITH POWER SIMULTANEOUSLY, LIGHTING up the night sky. However the Knife wormed its way into our connection, it's been pushed down so deep by the Beloved that it can't take control. Good thing, too, because if there's anybody who can stop this narcissistic nymph, it's Ori and me.

I grab his hands and our magics combine, creating that abalone color of us.

"God, I've missed this," I say.

"No time to get sappy, cowboy." But Ori smirks. I know he feels the same way.

We take a deep breath as one, and just when we're about to work our magics against Alister, Kenneth yells, "WAIT!"

I nearly fall over with the sudden change in plans. *"Wait?"*

"We don't know who he's cursed with the Horn," Kenneth explains. "Any magic cast could get wildly out of hand."

Alister laughs that outrageously obnoxious laugh again and says,

"Oh please. You don't think I'd waste the Horn on you, do you?" He holds the Cornucopia high above his head. "This is for *me*. I will be the greatest magician of all time. *I* will reform the Guild, stronger and more powerful than ever before."

His hands crackle with energy, his nymph-green power brighter and more sinister than usual, verging on that sickly Depraved green.

"God, he's so obsessed with himself." Ori grabs an effigy with his free hand and coats it in pink. "But he won't be able to beat us. Not now."

Alister snaps his fingers and in the blink of an eye the blades of grass at our feet grow to the size of swords—sharp as swords, too. One goes straight through my foot, others nicking and slicing me every way I move. A blade pierces Ori straight through the wrist.

"Fuck!" Ori drops his effigy, while blood pools around the wound.

Meanwhile on the ranch, Alister's spell has turned every last root or shrub into a weapon, threatening to skewer the Resistance members. A blaze of red light catapults by, colliding with Alister. His grass withers and dies while we watch a phoenix blast Alister with fire. It's Yamato, shape-shifted. His flames are fed by the supercharged wind of Kenneth's air nymph abilities. While the colors of Ori's and my magics combine to create a magnified spell, the physicality of their powers is what's most evident in their connection.

It's badass.

"We've got to move," I say. "Strike while the enemy's hot. Literally."

Ori rolls his eyes. "You are so cringe."

I give him a quick peck on the lips. "But you love it."

We jerk apart as a mournful sound echoes through the ranch.

The Horn.

Its sound is followed by a booming crash, and I whip around

just in time to see the barn crumble to pieces, knocked over by the world's biggest tumbleweed. The plant's at least thirty feet high and growing in size as we watch it crush everything in its path. The barn is gone, the stables are decimated, and the surviving livestock run wildly to get out of the way. The weed is headed straight for Yamato and Kenneth, Yamato's phoenix flame unable to set it alight. Yamato flaps to Kenneth and grabs him in his talons just before the weed would have crushed the nymph.

In a few more rolls the weed swallows up Alister, who cackles from its depths. "Got to run!" With unnatural speed, Alister's swirling plant behemoth carries him away.

"We have to stop him," Jameson says.

"Way to state the obvious," Ori shoots back.

While Alister may be gone, his allies remain and their hands ignite with magic. "You're not going anywhere," the elf member says.

Pallavit sings a shrill note, bowling all five of them over. Jaleesa laughs, but the victory is short-lived as the enemy magicians spring to their feet.

"Boys! Go with Kenneth and Yamato," Pallavit calls. "Use your connections to stop Alister." Another sung note and she and Jaleesa take defensive stances next to Jameson. "We'll keep these ones busy." Even Dad stands beside them, brandishing the claw like a weapon. It's only a few inches long, but it's clear Dad plans to cut anyone who takes a step toward me. He must have found the relic while we were distracted in the fight.

A twinge deep inside me makes me grit my teeth. The Knife wants that claw, but it's too weak to do anything about it. We have to move fast.

Ori, meanwhile, rolls his eyes. "They get that they're not the Avengers, right?"

We might be in a hurry, but I do love Ori's snark. If Ori's snarky, he's not worrying about what could go wrong, he's not thinking he doesn't know me anymore or of how things have changed. It's reassurance that he's his normal, confident, ready-to-take-on-the-world-and-everyone-in-it curmudgeonly self.

"I know, I'm pretty great," Ori says, feeling my emotions. "But we don't have time to bask in it."

"No, you do that enough for the both of us," I say with a smirk of my own. "Let's go."

I know just how to speed us up. Inspired by the ranch, this environment that's so much a part of me, I bring my thumb and middle finger to my lips. Thinking of Meema and all her badass cowgirl ways, I whistle. I pour as much power into it as I can muster, trying a spell I've yet to accomplish on my own. I feel my magic pool in my chest, the ball of energy getting tighter and tighter, becoming so hot it almost burns, until *finally*, a golden mustang erupts from my chest. It whinnies and paws at the earth, ready to ride. I know wherever she is, Meema's looking down on me from her magicked bull with pride. Frosty, too.

I leap up onto my horse's back and Ori blinks behind me. His pale fingers lock together around my waist, and the feeling of rightness that surges through me could power a ride to the moon and back. For now, we have to chase after the massive dust cloud billowing out from Alister's trail of terror. When all this is over, though, daily rides with my soulmate have to be a thing.

We gallop at a breakneck speed, Kenneth and Yamato soaring above, and keeping up thanks to the nymph's powers. With a start I realize we're in Austin proper, getting closer to the brightly lit skyline of downtown. A path of destruction the width of a football stadium marks Alister's route. The air gets thicker with dust and detritus the closer we get to Alister. I spell goggles and hankies to keep the crap out of our eyes and lungs. There's so much debris, it's like a protective force field around Alister; the thick weeds grab cars and trees and—holy shit, even people. I can see flailing limbs in Alister's creation, can hear their screams. He's truly so hellbent on maintaining control he'll take out innocent humans in the process. We can't aim any spells his way without risking those humans' lives.

"Blink," I say. "We're going to have to blink inside."

With each passing second, Alister causes more havoc. He flattens a Torchy's Tacos, then careens right over the Rudy's B-B-Q and gas station, explosions blasting in his wake. More screams fill the air, and sirens join the cacophony. Kenneth and Yamato fly back and forth, lifting humans out of the way to minimize casualties.

"Who's going to heal them all?" I ask. "Who's going to cover this up? With the Guild gone, can anyone fix this?"

Yet despite the danger, people swarm out of office buildings and churches, screech their cars to a halt to take a look at the action. It's this bizarre part of human nature. While folks in Alister's path literally run for their lives, others head as close to the danger as they can, recording it all with their phones. Alister either doesn't care or assumes he can use the Horn to wipe away everyone's memories of an American senator decimating one of the country's biggest cities.

AAAIIIIIEEEEEEEE!

Another fact of nature? That Depraved show up where there's despair. Demons, too. The cruel laughter and demonic shrieks of those monsters mingle with the chaos of human fear and suffering.

"Could we just *once* catch a break?" Ori cries.

Jameson floats beside us, hands fluttering over his cuts and bruises to heal them as he talks. "We stopped his allies," he says. "Those of us without a connection will fend off the monsters. See what you can do about Alister."

Then he's running at superhuman speed, just in time to save a baby before they're plucked out of a stroller by the talons of a possessed demon grackle. Jameson aims a spell at the bird, incinerating it in a puff of feathers and decayed flesh.

"I think it's time to do what we do best," Ori says. "What do you think, cowboy? Can we lasso him away? Use this supercharged soulmate connection and blink him out of town?"

Ori says it like it's so simple. Like the breeziest of spells can thwart a guy who's used an ancient relic to magnify his powers to catastrophic levels. But I don't have any better ideas, so it's the best shot we have. We've got to time this right that so Alister doesn't use the Horn against us, and I'll have to keep my anger in check to make sure I don't reawaken the Knife within me.

"Let's give it a try." Power builds in my hands, and with a gentle squeeze from Ori, my magic surges. A lasso appears around my arm just like that. Charged by my soulmate, charged with the knowledge that when we set our mind to something we *can* achieve it—and *without* casualties—I squeeze my thighs on either side of my magic steed. "'Yup!"

Swinging the lasso high above my head, tension eases from my shoulders. For the first time in weeks, I genuinely feel in my element. This *is* my purpose. Meema trained me my whole life to use magic to defeat enemies, and that's what I'm here to do.

"Alister! I'm going to hog-tie your ass!"

My voice rings down the decimated streets, magically magnified by my emotion.

"I just want you to know I'm rolling my eyes," Ori says, head propped on my shoulder.

"But you love it."

He squeezes me tighter. "But I love it."

As we gain on Alister, I can feel Ori rustling around in his bag behind me. Before long, he holds out a glowing pink ball of yarn.

"Unravel this, would you?" he asks, and I understand his plan immediately.

In no time, I've got magic in my palm and coat Ori's makeshift effigy. As my gold combines with his pink, that abalone sheen of our connection covers every inch of the yarn. Ori plucks the free end of it, the material unspooling in his hand. As the yarn slithers off of Ori's palm and falls to the ground below, a new sound joins the chaos left in Alister's wake.

Snapping.

A branch the size of a semitruck sticks out of the tumbleweed, and no matter how hard Alister's green magic fights back, the wood keeps tugging apart. But still it barrels on. We're cruising down Cesar Chavez Street now, parallel to Lady Bird Lake, which lines downtown Austin. Joggers jump into the water to avoid getting hit, and cars careen through the streets to race out of Alister's path. But as our magic takes hold and the tumbleweed's speed slows, more and more people are able to escape. His spherical "vehicle" is now jagged and wrong, too many humongous stakes of wood jutting out for a smooth roll.

This is our time to strike.

"'Yup!" I yell again, and we ride higher into the air. My horse gallops straight up until we're ten stories high, flush with the largest protrusion.

"Yah!" I let my lasso fly. Ori places a hand over my heart, giving my magic the boost it needs for the rope to land right where I intend. I cinch it quickly, the wood creaking under the force of my determination.

"All right, Sprite Boy. That's your cue. Where we blinking him to?"

"Nigel!" A gravelly voice from down below makes me lean over the side of my magical horse. Jameson's with Dad on the street, magnifying Dad's voice. "Assholes always need a trip to the trough!"

If I could see him clearly, I'm sure I'd see a knowing smile on Dad's face. It was the trick Meema used the day Dad went off on me because my magic had manifested. Getting dunked in water shocked him enough to snap him out of his Depraved-making hate.

But with an asshole as big as Alister, we're going to need one massive trough.

"The ocean," I say. "The *deep* ocean, where there's no plant life. Think we can blink to the middle of the Atlantic?"

"That's, like, thousands of miles from here," Ori says.

"So you're saying you can't do it?"

Ori jabs me hard in the ribs. "I did *not* say that, cowboy."

"All right, then, on the count of three. One." I can feel Ori's magic build. "Two." I can sense his thoughts homing in on the waves. Envisioning the water so our blink will be seamless. "Thr—"

WHOOOOOOOOOM.

The Cornucopia. Blown again by Alister inside his tumbleweed.

Cold dread seeps into my soul. The creeping nausea worms its way into our connection, that dread weighing me down, sitting right in the pit of my stomach.

It keeps me glued to my magical horse, while Ori blinks away.

But I stay right here. My horse and I hover in midair. Alone. Fearing what curse Alister's going to bring to life with the help of the Horn. *What if he used it on us?*

The branches in Alister's decimated vehicle twist and rise, carrying him slowly to my level. He stands there, completely at ease. He's already triumphant. He thinks he's won.

And I have a sinking feeling he may be right.

"Oh no," Alister mocks, "have we lost Ori?" He looks around, holding a hand over his brow as he scans exaggeratedly from left to right. "Ori? Ori?" When he laughs that terrible laugh, I wish his weeds would grow right down his throat. "Too bad. He won't be here to see the arrival of my friends."

"The Depraved are already here, asshole," I say, trying to sound more confident than I feel. I might be one of the few magicians strong enough to stand up against the Cornucopia, but that's only *with* my fated partner. Right now, I'm just a barely adult magician using a measly golden rope to face off against a magically magnified monster.

But you could be so much more.

My palms go slick with sweat at that grating voice in my head, quiet but present. A monster of my own inside me. But I'm not about to welcome it into the fray. Who knows what damage the Knife could do with half the city of Austin within its magic's reach.

"Nigel, I'm offended you'd suggest I'm in league with those things," Alister says, sounding genuinely slighted. "You've got to know by now that I truly wish all the Depraved dead. Which"—the offense is wiped away by that frenzied look I'd become so accustomed to seeing on Laurel—"includes you now, with that *thing* in you. Do you think the few magicians with me at your ranch were the only ones on my side?" He laughs. "You're so naive, Nigel. There are others, many others, who *you* locked away in the Guild. But using this"—he hoists the Horn—"I've found them. And when they arrive, we'll end you once and for all."

I should be focused on Alister, readying myself for what he's going to do next. But camera flashes in my peripheral vision pull my eyes away. Humans press their faces to glass in the skyscrapers to my left; cop cars and SWAT teams pull up below, guns raised; and news choppers descend on downtown to get a bird's-eye view of the action. Like our battle on Mount Rainier, thousands of humans are witnessing magic they never knew existed. Memories of the Knife were wiped from human consciousness, but maybe this time could be different. If I can stop Alister, if the Resistance can change the Guild, we could make sure this memory lives on. We could reveal the existence of magic—specifically, the magic humans make that can beat the Depraved.

I need humankind to know that I'm someone they can trust. That *magicians* are people they can trust. Which means I need to prove that Alister and his destruction are not the norm. I have to show them the Guild is not to be feared.

But the deep rumble reverberating through the city is trying to prove otherwise.

Alister looks expectantly at the shaking ground, at the source of that growl-like sound growing ever louder.

"Alister," I say, my voice soft. "What did you do?"

A block of marble bursts from the ground, brilliant white and streaked with gold, carried by gnarled beanstalks that have grown to epic proportions.

It's the Guild. The library. Bursting through the asphalt directly in front of the downtown branch of the Austin Public Library.

"How poetic!" Alister says, clapping his hands as bookshelves topple and ancient magical texts spill onto the pavement. The former twenty-fourth floor of the Guild now sprawls across Cesar Chavez Street. And rustling among the mayhem are magicians, some of those formerly trapped by the Knife's curse, finally free.

"Look! Allies!" Alister says. "Magicians I have saved. Magicians *I* brought back. Magicians who will realize you must be stopped so they can never be cursed again!"

Another rumble, this time from across the lake.

"Ah! More reinforcements!"

With an earth-shattering crash, beanstalks push the nymph hall right through the middle of Zilker Park. The former grassy field is now a mosaic of environments. A chunk of forest erupts with giant redwoods, a gushing stream pours into the lake, a mountain pushing up from the dirt spews lava, and clouds hover above it all. The perfect settings for each elemental nymph.

But this isn't the Guild; it's the middle of downtown Austin. As the magical building displaces the park, humans are pushed aside, thrown in the lake or directly in the path of lava, or pierced through by tree branches.

More rumbling, more moving of earth and asphalt, and four blocks over, the golden cavern of the elf dorm erupts from the ground, a new shining gold skyscraper joining the Austin skyline. Alister doesn't care what damage he causes. With the Horn of Plenty, the world is his board game and we're all just pieces he'll move around as he sees fit.

Everywhere I look, more levels and arms of the Guild arrive, pushed up by Alister's massive beanstalks. The newly freed magicians look as confused by the turn of events as the Austinites; they look around, dazed, unsure how they escaped the Knife's curse, confused as to why they're in the middle of a Texas town. But they snap out of it immediately when they notice the Depraved feeding on the chaos. These Guild members send whatever spells, curses, or elements they have at their disposal to fend off the monsters. I think I spot Lyra among them, blinking this way and that, and feel the briefest flare of relief that she's okay.

Even with the incoming magicians fighting the Depraved, it's clear that humanity thinks we're monsters, too. Watching the destruction Alister wreaks on their city, how can we expect them to ever trust us?

As the chaos continues, humans begin to fight back. Some try to run down magicians with their cars; others pull out guns—bullets and vehicles mixing with the bright bursts of power from magicians and Depraved alike.

A hand clenches my heart, so strong that I think it's real, that Alister might have sent a vine twisting into my insides. I reach down, but there's nothing there.

Hello again, Nigel.

The Knife.

I hear its laugh echo in my head, feel its determination to reawaken grow as mayhem erupts throughout the city. The monster may have been tamped down by the emotion in Dad's Beloved, been kept there by Ori's and my connection, but both are nowhere to be seen. I have no one whose love could weaken this monster inside of me.

Evil always prevails. Love can fight back, but it never lasts. Humans and magicians are just so prone to dwell on the negative. You insist otherwise, but you must relish it. The suffering. The pain. Why else would your hate and fear be so strong?

Who's really depraved? Me? I've always been honest about my intentions. Or is it you? Your entire kind? Insisting you serve others when you've always been in it for yourselves.

For the briefest moment, I wonder what would happen if I let the Knife in. Would I be strong enough to take on Alister alone, without my soulmate?

No. The monster would only take advantage of the chaos to kill as many magicians and humans as it can. It would only prove to the panicked people that they're right to be suspicious of us, that nothing about our magical world can coexist peacefully with theirs. I can't let the Knife take over.

"I have to thank you, Nigel," Alister says. "All this time I thought you were going to be my undoing. But the strongest unifier is a cause to fight against. Now, because of you, I'll be seen as the great defender, and no one will ever question the way we do things in the Guild again."

With a snap of his fingers and a burst of green light, a massive trumpet lily blooms in his hands. Pocketing the Cornucopia, he raises the plant to his lips and uses it as an impromptu megaphone to carry his voice throughout the city streets.

"Citizens of Austin." If Ori were here, I know he'd roll his eyes at Alister's cheesiness. But the humans who aren't actively being chased by demons or Depraved are captivated. "How jarring your introduction to magic has been. Monsters you hoped were only nightmares are real. Monsters, like this boy, whose actions have led to your suffering in this very moment." A branch of his tumbleweed catapults him to my side, close enough to grab my shirt in his fist, superhuman strength allowing him to lift me up and off my horse. "But this ends today. Magicians such as myself are equipped to destroy even the most barbaric of enemies."

"They'll never believe you," I say, sounding weak and pathetic even to me. "You can wipe these humans' memories, but magicians will remember. They saw you rampaging through the streets. They saw you blow the Horn."

But Alister's cool smile is unmoving as he releases the lily megaphone to flutter to the ground a hundred feet below. "Please, Nigel. Politics is all about PR. I don't think you understand how easy it will be to tell them that someone *else* caused all this damage. Someone who was already known for monstrous bouts of strength. Only those closest to me know how the Horn was retrieved. But everyone knows that you and Ori unleashed the Horde, who woke up the Knife. Which *possessed* the very boy in front of me. One simple suggestion will convince every magician that you found the Cornucopia, and *I* turned it against *you* to save us all. And, of course, they'll have seen me do this."

Alister snaps his fingers and his tumbleweed suddenly springs to life. Its branches twist and expand and shoot forward, piercing demons and Depraved every which way, growing through the streets at superspeed to catch any monsters trying to flee. Stab after stab after stab, the monsters crumble, and the looks of terror on human and magician faces alike turn to looks of awe. He's not just a senator anymore. He's a savior.

And I know that as Alister becomes their hero, I'm becoming their enemy.

He must be killed.

The Knife uses all its remaining strength to communicate the thought. I can't say I disagree.

My heart stops. When did I become this way? When did I go from trying to protect life at all costs to thinking that some people deserve to die?

As I take in the crowded streets from Alister's unrelenting grip, every face—Guild member and Texan—looks at me like I'm the monster.

Maybe they're not wrong. Because I don't think it's just the Knife convincing me Alister has to die. I think I truly feel it.

A shadow from above blocks out the moon as a new tumbleweed offshoot the size of a school bus rises over Alister's head. It may be thick, but it comes to a very sharp point. Alister hoists me to the side, and the plant hovers before me like a cobra waiting to strike.

The nymph grins. Have his teeth always been that fang-like, or does it only seem that way now that he's got me cornered?

"Time to defeat the worst monster of all."

With a burst of green, the plant strikes at an inescapable speed. I wish Ori were here now so I could blink. Wherever he is, I hope he's safe. I hope he knows through our connection that my last thought will be of him.

I don't flinch. I don't brace myself. I want to die facing Alister head-on, so at least he won't have the satisfaction of my fear. I know that's what he wants. Not all that different from the Depraved after all, is he?

When Alister's plant projectile is millimeters from me, I lock eyes with the nymph. I smile, refusing to cower. I brace myself for the pain, thinking of Meema, thinking of how I'll see her soon. But then . . . a second passes.

And another.

It should have happened by now.

An odd sensation envelops me. A sort of pitter-patter on my body, the occasional light poke sending tingles up my arm. Nothing painful, exactly. Just strange.

It's the tumbleweed shattering into millions of pieces. That pitter-patter feeling is the sensation of those wooden shards falling over and around me, cascading to the ground like so many toothpicks. Dozens of sprites blink in and out, their hands disappearing and reappearing as they use their carving skills to decimate Alister's tumbleweed. Hacking it to pieces. Slicing hardest of all, yelling taunts along the way, is Ori.

"Fixing this mess one little prick at a time," he yells. "And of course, I do mean you, Ali!"

Blinking next to his side with a burst of sawdust and a bark of laughter is Lyra, Ori's mom. "How one man gets such giant wood for himself is beyond me!"

Ori blanches. "Mom!"

"Oh please. Where do you think you get it from?" She blinks a few yards away and gets to work on the next section of Alister's tumbleweed with a group of sprites. The nymph drops me suddenly, but my fall is stopped by my magicked horse flickering to life beneath me, instinctually.

Ori blinks behind me, back in his position with his hands around my waist. My magic, my hope, my passion to win this battle—to change the Guild—reignites.

"One second longer and I would have been done for," I say.

Ori shrugs. "It's called perfect timing, cowboy."

"How did you—" I motion to the sprites, never slowing in their demolition of Alister's Cornucopia-enhanced vehicle.

"I was in the blink, and I could only think of Cassie—how in all my life, nothing ever went wrong when she was around. I thought of when things were simpler, with her and Mom and me making effigies together. I reappeared by Mom's side as she helped sprites who had just been freed from the Knife's curse. Together, we convinced them to help. Not that it was hard, with Ali so publicly having his way with this city. Fuck that guy."

Never a truer word. But Alister doesn't seem fazed by the sprites' work in the slightest. He watches them hack away with that shit-eating grin on his face and says, "Do you honestly think you're going to stop me?"

"Maybe they don't," a voice behind me calls. "But we do."

Nudging my horse to the side, my heart practically leaps out of my throat when I see the new arrival. "Bex!"

There she is, in unicorn form, galloping through the air, her horn shining silver with power. Whinnies echo all around as more and more unicorns appear behind her, stampeding through the streets, the air, the parks, carrying what injured humans they can to safety. Their horns blaze brighter than the lights from nearby skyscrapers, shining beacons of hope.

"She did it!" Ori calls. "She got those stubborn little assholes to budge!"

We might actually be able to do this. Unicorns weaken evil magic, after all, and Bex just brought us hundreds as reinforcements.

But Alister has other plans. He snaps his fingers again and

the limp beanstalks that brought the Guild to Austin spring to life. One sweeps him up to loom over his destruction, while the rest move like snakes, slithering across the cement and knocking down everything in their path. One swings wide and smashes into city hall, a group of unicorns galloping in just in time to save innocent bystanders.

The stalks converge, surrounding us, but Ori blinks us out of harm's way. With a whinny, Bex gallops right behind us, meeting us hoofstep for hoofstep in the sky before shifting back to her human form in a flash of silver light. I reach out and grab her hand, using her momentum to swing her up behind Ori as my magic steed grows larger to accommodate her.

"Thanks," she pants. "I can't hold that shape for long. Their power is just *so much*."

"Bex, you have all the power we could ever need," I say.

"I can't believe you got them to join us," Ori adds.

"They're in this now," Bex says. "*And* they're going to have some serious input on how magickind operates going forward." Her eyes linger on me warily, and I get a sinking feeling the unicorns have something to say about *me*. But she shakes her head and goes on. "They'll help us with Alister. As long as he has the Horn they might not be able to completely defeat his magic, but they can weaken it enough that we should be able to fight back."

As if on cue, the hundreds of unicorns swarming Austin's streets take to the air, charging for the nymph. He blows the Cornucopia, but its ominous drone is drowned out by the whinnies and huffs and nickers of the herd. It's an equine symphony I'm used to, one I didn't know how badly I've missed. I hear their annoyance, their determination to set things right, their sheer resolve not to let this guy ruin their fun. They remind me so much of Frosty, and I know if my ice horse were here, they'd join in on the catcalling—horsecalling, I guess—against Alister.

The nymph snaps his fingers to set his beanstalks' rampage on a new path. But they only shudder, wavering dozens of stories in the air. Poised to strike but unmoving. It gives the unicorns time to ascend farther, their horns glowing brighter and brighter. Dots of silver, gold, and bronze grow to spotlights, blazing so bright that I have to shield my eyes. I can feel their confidence, their *goodness*, radiating as brightly as their light.

"STOP!" Alister's voice booms as he snaps his fingers again. But this time, his beanstalks wither. They fall to the ground as beams of the unicorns' light strike them. By the time the plants collapse on the cement, they're merely the size of weeds.

The only stalk left is the one on which Alister stands. And without his monstrous vegetation blocking my line of sight, I can see Laurel using her vines to swing up skyscrapers, like some organic version of Spider-Man.

Power flares in my hands on instinct. Everything she's done these past couple weeks has been for her dad. I nudge my horse after her, trotting close enough so that I can act in case she turns against us.

But Alister doesn't notice. He's so focused on facing down the unicorns, blowing the Cornucopia to send twisted magic their way, but each new wave of plant life that violently bursts from the ground is destroyed by the power shining from the herd's horns. The ground is littered with plants of every color, confetti sprinkling down on the destruction below.

Finally, when Laurel has reached the height of her dad and his "showdown," she steadies herself behind him, balanced on a massive leaf of his beanstalk, and sends one last vine from her wrist. A vine headed straight for her father. It wraps around his arm, yanking it back, preventing him from using the Horn.

"Give it up, Dad!" Laurel shouts. The vine jerks again. "This isn't YOU!"

On her last word, a surge of green power travels down her vine. There is so much emotion in her eyes: rage, hurt, betrayal. It's fueling her magic. Her spelled vine yanks with every ounce of conviction left in her, prying the Cornucopia from her dad's grasp. It tumbles end over end, and Laurel uses her free hand to send a shoot of ivy at it, snatching it from midair. She swings the Horn up and away, making it arc toward Jaleesa, who stands a hundred feet below. As the Cornucopia soars, it glows bright purple, a sung spell making sure it heads straight for Jaleesa's hand.

This could be the moment when everything changes.

CHAPTER
THIRTY-THREE

Laurel's heart soars into her throat. *Come on, Jaleesa, catch it.*

But, of course, Laurel's father won't give up that easily. A Venus flytrap bursts out of the ground at Jaleesa's feet, mouth snapping at the fae. Jaleesa screams in surprise, her spell cut short, and jumps out of harm's way. The flytrap opens wide, humongous sharp protrusions gnashing like teeth when it swallows the Horn. As the plant gulps, the Horn rematerializes in Alister's hand.

"A summoning spell," Laurel breathes.

Alister works quickly now, dashing across his beanstalk in the last direction she ever would have anticipated. Toward her.

Could this be it? Could he be racing toward her to apologize, to atone for all he's done that's led him on this path?

But the closer he gets, the clearer the murderous rage purpling his face becomes. There will be no reconciliation.

"You ungrateful brat!" he shouts. "I gave you the world! I'm *giving* you the world! And you try to stop me?"

Laurel's never heard her father yell this loud in her life. He's always one to keep his composure. But now, spittle flies from his lips, his eyes nearly bulging out of his skull. Even still, Laurel doesn't falter. She stands tall, proud, not flinching once, even when that spittle lands on her cheek. Not flinching when her dad raises the Horn to his lips. She stares him down as the sad, low keen of the relic echoes around her.

She braces herself, expecting the ground to shake, expecting new destruction the unicorns will have to clean up. But nothing happens. Instead, Alister simply opens his palm, a tiny white flower blooming there, dotted with spots of red.

Laurel eyes the plant, relief slowly easing the tension in her shoulders, a warm smile lifting her lips. "Mountain laurel," she says. "My namesake. Dad." Hot tears fill her eyes as she looks up at him. Maybe she was wrong. Maybe that frenzy was to start a better future *now*. "I'm so sorry about everything that's happened." She steps forward, every bit a little kid in desperate need of a loving hug. But Alister's arms don't open as she gets closer. He just holds that flower between them, the tiniest barricade keeping her out.

"I named you after this plant," he says, barely more than a whisper. "Deceptively beautiful yet very deadly. You know its effects. Vomiting, drowsiness, even coma or death. A testament to how beauty and strength can go hand in hand." He gazes lovingly at the flower, looking at it the way she wishes he would look at her. But when her father looks up, all Laurel gets is a glare. "Yet you have been weak. *All your life*. You don't live up to your namesake. You don't live up to *my name*."

He curls his fingers oh so delicately around the flower, causing it to light up green. With a gentle blow, the glowing petals come apart and float over Laurel, rubbing against her arms, her face, anywhere there's exposed skin. At first, there's warmth, the spell mimicking that feeling she was hoping would come from her father's embrace. But then there's heat, searing, scalding, not just her skin, but deep down inside her, deep into a part that's never been touched before, deep into the source of her magic. She twitches and writhes, trying to shake the curse that's snaking inside her, her body seizing the longer his poison takes effect.

Alister watches on, eyes hungry. No whimper of pain, no cry of agony registers. Nothing brings to life the parental instinct Laurel's always wished was in there.

"This is what you get for going against me," he says calmly. "It pains me to say that you, Laurel, are one of those magicians not worthy of keeping their power."

She knows it should shock her to hear him say this, but it's what he's been saying all along, if not in so many words. So much pressure. So many disdainful looks. She never could have been enough for him, no matter how hard she tried.

As the petals continue to swirl around Laurel, green light pours out of her, straight into the mountain laurel, soaked up by the swirling plant.

She eventually becomes numb to the pain, to the horror of having her magic taken from her, drop by drop. She even laughs to herself, knowing that her father has still made her a part of history. Never before has one magician been able to take away another's power alone. Until now. Thanks to the curse her father cast on her with the help of the Cornucopia.

It's over nearly as quickly as it started. Laurel stands there, panting, a hand clutched over her heart. All that's left inside is a hollow emptiness.

Laurel stares at her father, open-mouthed. She squeezes her hand a few times, trying to make anything appear. But of course, she has nothing to cast.

"You took it," she says. It's barely a whisper, but everyone is silent somehow, humans and magicians watching with rapt attention, wondering what will go down next.

Voicing it makes something click inside her. Feeling rushes back, that stranglehold that's been latched on her heart for as long as she can remember finally loosening. Laurel sighs so hard she even sways a bit, before her lips quirk up in a smile. "Thank you."

"Wait, what?" Nigel's shocked words blurt from behind her, immediately met by a shushing from Bex.

"Shut up and listen!" the goblin hisses.

Laurel laughs, and it feels so good after all this time. She's never felt such a wave of relief before. Despite the pain, despite the stinging nettles clinging to her soul as her magic was taken. Now everything feels . . . different. Fine. *Right.* Like noticing that first bit of looseness in a knot she's been working to get undone—giving her just enough room to pull it apart until it's entirely, blissfully, unknotted.

That's how Laurel feels now: unknotted. Completely free. She's caused enough damage for a lifetime. For many, many lifetimes.

"I wasn't able to handle the pressures that came with my power," Laurel says, stepping closer to her dad with each word. "I wasn't able to handle the pressures *you* worked so hard to weigh me down with. Was there ever a day that I was enough for you? Even one moment when you thought, *If Laurel never lives up to the expectations I have of her, I can still love her?*"

Her father doesn't move. Well, perhaps the sneer on his face gets deeper, a feat Laurel didn't think possible. It's a wonder he's able to do it, and without a spell to boot.

"I didn't think so." Laurel doesn't say it with hurt. It's just a blatant statement of fact. She can't change the way her father feels any more than she can change the weather. "You've never been able to see past power and prestige. Past popularity. Past money. I wasn't either, thanks to you."

She peers down to the ground, so many stories below, where Jaleesa watches. Her throat glows lightly purple, and Laurel hopes the fae has cast a spell so she can hear every word.

"I had the best person I've ever met in my entire life by my side, accepting me for me, but I didn't see it. I couldn't give her everything she needed, because of *you*. That desperate need to make you happy led me to do the worst thing I could have possibly done.

"Dad, everything that happened during the Culling is because of *us*. Nigel and Ori aren't the ones who shouldn't have magic. Nor are all those magicians sapped of power because our family deemed them unworthy. *We* are the ones who don't deserve these gifts. We can't be trusted with them."

Her father clearly isn't affected by a single word she says. Instead, that sneer switches to a cocky smirk, not unlike Ori's. At least the sprite doesn't use his cockiness to destroy the world. He can be an arrogant prick, sure, but in the grand scheme of things, he could be a lot worse.

"Oh, is that so?" Alister asks, voice silky smooth. "You have no magic. You have no way to defeat me." He leans down until his eyes are level with hers. "So what are you going to do about it?"

"This." Laurel throws her arms wide and wraps her father in the tightest hug she can. Alister's mouth drops into a surprised O. Laurel knows how unfamiliar the kindness, this warmth, must be to him. He might have *preferred* it if she'd attacked him, flinging her fists with all the strength her puny human body could muster. But instead, she showed love. And love is unnerving.

"I forgive you, Dad," she says into his chest. "For everything. I know you act this way because it was instilled in you, too, for so long and so deeply that you genuinely think you're right. You don't see yourself as the bad guy. But you are, Dad. And me telling you this is an act of love. Doing this is an act of love."

Taking advantage of her father's stunned silence, Laurel moves quickly. Keeping one arm around Alister, Laurel snaps her other arm out to grab the Cornucopia. Laurel's conviction is one millisecond faster than her father's surprise. His fingers glow green as he begins crafting some plant to counter her, but he's too late. Because Laurel already has the Horn to her lips.

And she blows.

CHAPTER
THIRTY-FOUR

LAUREL BLOWS THE CORNUCOPIA, AND IT'S UNLIKE ANY SOUND TO come from the weapon yet. It's not dark and melancholic, it's high and hopeful, the timbre of an excited horse's whinny. Soon, actual whinnying follows as the unicorns buck and prance, taking to the air, to the streets, running with abandon, nuzzling one another as they celebrate. Their pure glee fills me with hope, makes me feel like I could float, makes me want to press my lips to Ori's and kiss him, for all that we've been through, for a future that we'll finally get to have together.

All thanks to the Horn of Plenty being blown with true forgiveness.

The Horn crumbles to ash in Laurel's fingers, drifting away on the wind. Rumbling noises begin again, the entirety of downtown Austin shaking as some new magic gets to work. I brace myself, worried that something has gone wrong. Maybe Laurel *didn't* blow the Horn with forgiveness but with vengeance. Maybe she's trying to finish what her dad started. But then the sections of the Guild that ripped the streets apart blink out of existence, the ground seals itself back together, asphalt and concrete and cement and skyscrapers healing, good as new. The restoration follows the path of the unicorns' celebration. Metallic magic pours from their horns as they gallop, Austin becoming whole again in their glee. I hope the same is happening to the humans who were hurt in all of this.

But our peace is short-lived.

While Alister may not be able to use the Cornucopia anymore and the damage he caused is being swept away, he's still a magician with decades of experience facing down a defenseless human.

"How could you?!" His body glows with power as he towers over his daughter. "You'd defy your own father?"

"I did this *because* you're my father. You've always instilled in me the need to be my best; now I'm doing the same for you. You're so much better than this monster you've become."

"I'll show you a monster!" Alister claps his glowing hands together.

Pollen bursts from his fingers, coating his daughter and burning her skin on contact. She screams in pain, writhes even more than when her magic was being taken from her. But still, she manages to eke out, "This isn't you, Dad. This isn't right."

Then, meeting her father's green power, a new light glows between them. A vibrant red. Not the red of hate or anger or blood, but the red of a brilliantly beating heart. The red of love.

A Beloved bursts from Laurel's chest, and in one wave of the being's hand, the pollen disappears. With another, Laurel's burns heal over, just like the city's pockmarks sealing shut.

She's human now, and this is the magic she makes.

"Look what she made," Bex says, awe filling her words. "It's an act of love to stand up to those you care for when you know they're wrong. It's an act of love to push back. She didn't run away, she didn't try to fight him, she just talked."

Laurel's Beloved scoops her up and carries her down to the ground, next to Jaleesa, before fading away. Jaleesa keeps her distance, but she seems to consider the nymph, like she actually knows her far better than she does the fatally cutthroat magician Laurel had become.

That leaves Alister alone, perched on the withering remains of his beanstalk, drooping slowly but surely toward the pavement. He looks so vulnerable, out in the open like that, and something within me stirs.

Something within me that wants to strike.

Who knows how many casualties were added today to the dozens that were racked up after he and Laurel released the Horde. Alister should pay for that. I'm surrounded by magicians who have seen him for who he is, seen the lengths he'll go to maintain his power. And by unicorns who know what a threat he is. If anything goes wrong, they can back me up.

I know what I have to do.

For Meema.

"Ori, take Bex and join the others." I nod toward the ground where Kenneth, Yamato, Jameson, Lyra, and Pallavit have joined Jaleesa and Laurel. Stumbling up after them, walking on his own two feet, is Dad. He made it out of the mayhem alive, even without magic to defend himself.

But there's one person here who won't be so lucky.

"Nigel," Ori says. His tone is dark, warning, and I know he feels my intent. "No."

"Ori, just GO!"

I don't care if he's my soulmate. This is *my* choice, and mine alone.

"Nigel." Ori blinks in front of me, landing so we're nearly nose to nose. His face is set in determination, stubborn, refusing to budge.

"Let the Guild take care of him," he insists. "It's something we should do as a group."

"Ori, don't fight me. Let me have this."

It's a stare down, and the longer we sit there, the more I can feel him probe our connection, trying to change my mind. But I can be just as stubborn as he is.

Ori tries to wiggle his way into my heart, trying to get me to change my mind. But this is for the greater good. One more monster has to be stopped. This will be the only death at my hands, and he will have it coming.

"Ori." I say it softer this time, sending a feeling of betrayal through our connection. It's manipulative, but this is the only way. "Please."

He gives me a half nod, reluctant. Then finally, with a blink, Ori and Bex join the others on the street.

I take the moment before Ori changes his mind. "'Yup!" I urge my magical horse forward, galloping straight for Alister.

That's it. Do it! DO IT!

I'd like to believe these thoughts are my own, but I know in my heart they're not. I know it's the Knife again, know that even in this moment of success it's found a way to tug on my hurt and pain and anger. I'm just as certain that once I kill Alister, a part of me will die, and the Knife will move in to fill the gaps. How long until it has full control again? How long until I'm gone entirely, no more chances to bring me back, to snap me back in my body before I do things that can't be reversed? Until my power is used to make the world a terrible place?

I urge my conjured companion on harder, even though I know I should stop. Revenge is all-consuming. I want it. I need it. *The Knife* needs it.

So it will happen.

Alister's skin glows green when he registers what's happening. But I'm faster. I'm alight with power, a speeding comet barreling over the Austin skyline to incinerate one person and one person only. No matter how practiced he is, Alister can't stop me. I'm going to collide with him in three, two—

WHAM!

The impact comes sooner than expected, the force of it so strong that I'm knocked off my horse. I free fall, spinning head over boots before—

Oof! Air whooshes out of me as I land on the back of a new equine. A unicorn. One with a blazing bronze horn who's giving me some serious side-eye. They shake their head ever so slightly.

No.

They're not going to let me kill Alister.

NO! The voice is mine now, only not. My hands light up with power while a fiery anger ignites in my belly.

No.

The unicorn again, calm where I am a storm of rage, confident while I'm vengeful, their horn glowing brighter than my hands. Brighter and brighter still, until my anger is pushed back. Until the *Knife* is pushed back. Until I can regain my thoughts, and relief makes my entire body sag. I started my whole journey with the Guild wanting to save lives and, thanks to this unicorn, I won't have a death on my hands.

"Thank you."

The unicorn tips their head, then trots to the ground as Alister's beanstalk finally wilts, the last bit of destroyed pavement sealing shut as it disappears. Alister falls to the asphalt unceremoniously, crawling to his feet, no doubt to make a run for it—but in a heartbeat, he's surrounded. All the members of the Resistance, the Guild magicians who witnessed the decimation, and even some of Alister's former allies shower the scene in every color of magic to stop him from leaving. Even Laurel and Dad widen their stances, using their bodies to make up for what they can't do with magic. How quickly Laurel's taking to her new life.

"What do you say?" Jameson asks the gathered magicians. "Should we call a tribunal?"

Yamato smirks. "Sounds like a plan to me."

Jaleesa clears her throat, her mom right beside her, and together they sing.

"Our work here is done.
Let's begin to rebuild.
Times are changing
For the world and the Guild."

Their spell triggers a glowing purple portal, a shining beacon ready to take us into the next chapter of magic and human relations.

Speaking of which . . .

"What about all of them?" I ask, motioning to the humans steadily making their way to the street or smooshing their noses against windows in nearby buildings. But they aren't looking at us anymore. They're looking through us, around us. With the Horn's devastating magic reversed, there's no more destruction for them to see. The Guild is whole again, safely tucked away in its own realm, and it's clear magicians are already at work shielding us from humanity.

I slide off the unicorn and they rejoin their herdmates. "Is that

it then?" I ask. "We just go back to wiping magic from human memory? Even now, after we've seen how they have the power to help end
the cycle of hatred and the Depraved?"

Ori laces his fingers through mine. "We'll have more to address
in this tribunal than whether or not Ali is a prick," Ori tells the magicians who continue to gather around us. "Which is a resounding yes,
obviously. It's time to consider when and how we move forward with
magical and human cooperation. When we tell them there's a magic
they make. Both good and bad. The Beloved and the Depraved."

Pallavit hums as she ponders. "I think you may be onto something," she says with a wink, then steps through the portal.

Ori and I watch as hundreds of magicians follow, eyes alight
while they recount what they just witnessed, mouths moving a mil-
lion miles a minute with ideas about what we should do going forward. Bex and her dads are wrapped up together in that familiar
group hug as they wait their turn, her face relaxed for the first time in
weeks, rather than twisted up in worry and frustration.

Frustration that I caused.

"Bex!" Her name bursts from my throat.

Her smile freezes, she meets my eyes, and that scowl comes
back. I know she's thinking about the way I've treated her ever since
the Culling. How awful I was to her. Her dads step aside, give her
some space, but Bex doesn't budge. And she shouldn't, really. This is
a step *I* need to take.

I let go of Ori and jog over to her. "I'm sorry," I say. "Sorry for
everything."

Bex quirks an eyebrow, crosses her arms. She tilts her head to the
side, but doesn't say anything.

"*Everything* is a cop-out, isn't it?" I mumble.

Bex gives one small nod.

"I'm sorry for being an absolute shit to you all this time, when you were just trying to help. I'm sorry I took that help for granted, and went out of my way to make you feel like your contributions were insignificant. We literally couldn't have done this without you. If you hadn't brought that herd, I don't know that Alister could have been stopped. He was so strong until you arrived and gave us the upper hand we needed. Upper *hoof*, maybe. Or horn?"

I laugh awkwardly, and Bex rolls her eyes.

"That was terrible, I know."

Bex nods again, but that's it. No smile. Not even a tiny quirk of her lips.

And that's okay.

"I don't expect you to forgive me right this minute," I say. "Take all the time you need. But I just wanted you to know that I'm sorry, *truly* sorry, and will do whatever it takes to earn your trust back."

"I second that."

I look over my shoulder to see Ori has stepped behind me. I didn't even feel him approach, not like I would have expected with our connection. But friends can be a type of soulmate, too, can't they? And I think right now, my connection with Bex—my apology to her—is the one that's most important.

"I'm sorry, too," Ori continues. "I should have said something. I should have called Nigel out when he snapped at you. I was an idiot for not realizing we were shutting you out. It won't happen again."

Bex scoffs. "I don't know, you two are pretty good at being idiots."

"Ain't that the truth," I say.

We stand there for a few quiet moments, the exiting magicians filling our silence with their celebration and relief. But things aren't settled yet. At least not for me. At least not until I can repair this with Bex.

"Thank you for that," she says. "I know we've all had the

weight of the world on our shoulders. And you were possessed by a monster."

I nod emphatically. "There is that."

Bex puts up a hand to stop me. "Not that it excuses what you did. But it does put things into some perspective. Even still, everything you said, everything you kept from me, the way you treated me, it all stung. I will forgive you. I think. I just need time."

"I'll be here waiting," I say. "And I'll do anything I can to show you I mean every word of this apology."

With that, Bex smiles. It's not the full bright smile that I was getting used to in the initial days of the Culling. But I hope one day I can get her to smile like that again. She turns around and joins the line to the portal, stepping through after a few short moments.

Ori and I are still waiting our turn when I hear sobbing behind me.

Jaleesa watches Laurel cry, does nothing to console her. The nymph doesn't deserve it.

"I'm so, so sorry," Laurel says, words warped by the lump in her throat. "I just wish we could go back to the way things were." She reaches for Jaleesa's hand, and the fae lets the nymph hold her limp fingers. But with each passing second, Laurel's fingers just feel like manic ivy, wanting to latch on and never let go, choking any sense of independence from the fae. She's had enough. Jaleesa pulls her hand back and crosses her arms with finality.

"We can never go back to the way things were," Jaleesa says. Her words aren't full of hate or anger. She's only speaking truth. "What you did, Laurel, was beyond what any reasonable person ever would have done. You deserved to have your magic taken away. Even if your dad hadn't done it, I would have voted with the rest of the Guild to remove your powers. Horrible things have happened that can't be reversed. Magicians *died* because of your actions. And I just—" Jaleesa's words trail away, the furrows in her forehead getting deeper as more and more memories of the good times they had together flash through her mind. But none of them, not even the brightest, the most loving, can push away all the nymph's choices since the Culling. "We won't be together, Laurel, but I appreciate what you did. Destroying the Cornucopia. It was the right thing to do. It doesn't erase everything else, but it's a start. I learned through all of this that I don't really know you. And maybe there are parts of myself I don't know either, if I was able to be with you all this time without recognizing what was inside your heart."

"It's not your fault, Ja—"

Jaleesa shakes her head, hard. "I know it's not. Everything you did is on you. But I need to find out what I want for *my* future. And you should want that, too. You have a lot to answer for."

With that, Jaleesa turns on her heel and walks through the portal, entering this next phase of life exactly how she wants to.

Alone.

I've never seen Laurel look so defeated. She watches her ex-girlfriend's retreating back until the fae disappears, the purple glow of portal magic reflecting in the nymph's tears. As soon as Jaleesa's gone, Laurel turns and meets my eyes. A small shrug makes it clear what's done is done. She won't go after her. At least for now. We're going to have to keep tabs on Laurel, just to make sure that monstrous part of her doesn't take hold again.

What happens to her next is hers to own. While I don't know

what the Guild plans to do, or what's in store for the Baumbach family, I do know that no matter what we decide in the coming hours, days, months of the Guild, Laurel deserves to be safe, just like everybody else. Even if it's within the Guild's prisons. Should Laurel feel guilty for what she's done? Yes. Should she be forced to deal with the aftermath? Absolutely. But leaving her alone to rot in a never-ending shame spiral wouldn't be right either. That's what led Dad to become the person he's been, carrying the kind of anger that generated so many Depraved. If we as magicians truly care about making the world a safer and better place, I think that starts with how we punish our own. Compassion and comeuppance don't have to be mutually exclusive. That compassion may not be as strong as love—something I don't think Laurel deserves from us—but I think it can be enough light to keep the monsters at bay.

Well, the ones out there at least, the ones made by humans every day.

There's one monster closer to home, though, that I'm even more worried about. And something Jaleesa said keeps echoing in my head.

We can never go back to the way things were.

That is the truest statement I've ever heard from a magician's mouth.

Things won't ever be the same now for the Guild, for humanity, or for me, not with the Knife burrowed in my soul.

But there's something I want to try to get it out. If this works, the life Ori and I thought we'd have together will be different, but at least it will exist.

Ori squeezes my hand, grabbing my attention. He nods toward the portal. "You ready?"

"Mm-hmm." I can't quite voice my thoughts just yet. I need to fully accept my plan before I speak it. For now, though, there's one major change in the Guild that requires Laurel's help, and that's the part of my plan I'm ready to tackle first.

"Come on, Laurel," I say, motioning for her to join us. "We need you for this next part."

She nods once, and with Ori's fingers tangled in mine, we step through the portal into our uncertain future.

CHAPTER
THIRTY-FIVE

ORI AND I ARE JOSTLED BACK AND FORTH IN THE GUILD'S FLURRY of action. Voices echo throughout the entry hall and bright bursts of color reflect off the untarnished walls. Not a hint remains that the organization was physically torn apart and, until just moments ago, scattered. In all the chatter, one word stands out, repeated by thousands of voices: *tribunal.* Whenever Alister's name is spoken alongside it, it's clear the group is turning against him, and quickly.

The biggest surprise of all is that nobody reacts to our appearance. The last time we were here, everyone saw us as criminals. Now, their eyes pass right over us.

Ori notices, too. "Would it kill anybody to offer a simple *I'm sorry? They* weren't the ones falsely accused of murdering dozens of magicians."

"That's never gonna happen, so you might as well give it a rest," I say, tugging him into my side. "And give me a kiss."

I press my lips to his, savoring this moment when everything seems to be getting back on track. I want to feel that connection, feel the way our powers buzz and combine, want to watch our hands light up our abalone light one last time. I lean my forehead against his, staring at our glowing fingers.

The light lasts for only a few seconds before Ori's worry seeps in. "Nigel? What's wrong?"

One tiny white lie for now, only until we get rid of the curse covering up the Culling.

"Just anxious to reveal the truth," I say, more breathless than I should be. "Which I think is going to have to happen before any tribunals take place. The Guild won't be able to comprehend all Alister's done until we wipe out that spell."

Laurel clears her throat, pulling our attention. The Resistance is already gathered behind her. I guess she's pushing the pace on making things right.

"Come on," she says. "I'll lead the way."

The steady *drip, drip, drip* of dank water falling from the low ceiling sets my already frayed nerves on edge. Just being on the Baumbachs' property is bad enough; the whole place creates a constant, unscratchable itch under my skin. Here, in this musty dark corridor, I can feel the evil intention behind Alister's spellwork burrowing into my soul, nestling against the monster that I know is already lurking inside of me.

Get moving.

A poke in the center of my back surprises me, making me yelp.

Scaredy-cat.

The voice is high and light, although stern. Not at all the grating sensation when the Knife speaks. It's Bex's bronze unicorn pal, acting as representative of their herd. They seemed suspicious of me at first, for good reason. But I guess the unicorns want to see for themselves what the Baumbachs and their allies have done all these centuries to warp the memories of magickind.

I quicken my pace and catch up to Ori and his mom, who march behind Laurel. The unicorn clops behind me, Bex and her dads just after, then Jaleesa and Pallavit followed by Jameson and Dad. Our new inner circle is finally able to be out in the open, thanks in large part to Laurel's admission that the Baumbachs have been altering the Guild's memories. Alister's being questioned as we speak, magicians working to identify who's been working with him to hoard power. When we finally get rid of this rotten forest that Laurel says is the source of the curse, they'll finally be able to fully comprehend how deep his betrayal goes.

"You weren't kidding." Ori's voice echoes down the corridor from where we stand at the top of a staircase, our bodies illuminated by a sickly green glow. "This forest really is rotten."

The cold cavern air makes me shiver. Or maybe it's the twisted, oozing trunks of the dozens of trees spread out below us. Their dry leaves wave eerily in some phantom breeze, crinkling in a way that makes me think of dead, flaking skin.

"Yep," Laurel breathes. "Behold the Baumbach family legacy."

I'm shoved aside as the unicorn shoulders past me, hoofing it down the stairs and baring their teeth at the nearest tree. They scrape their horn across it, leaving a bronze slash glowing across the dark gray bark. As we watch, the ooze covering the tree slowly seeps into the unicorn's magic, wiping away the bronze blaze.

"This magic has been reinforced by nymphs for generations," Laurel says. "By hundreds of us. Watered with our blood. My great-great-great-grandmother even discovered a way to capture bits of my family's magic after a relative dies, planting them at the base of these trees to feed the curse."

Ori's face looks like he just walked into a barn and smelled horse manure for the first time ever. "No wonder this place feels haunted."

Laurel stares into the trees as she continues. "You know, I've been wondering since Dad blew the Cornucopia on himself how the curse actually *warped* his magic. It magnified it, clearly, but did it warp it?" She scans the room, her eyes landing on every last trunk. "I don't think there's any way he could have become more warped. My entire family was warped, using our magic to take it from others. It's sick." She shakes her head, her hands balling into fists. "It's time to end it, once and for all."

Laurel heads down the rocky steps to the dirt below, all of us filing after her. The ground is mushy beneath my boots, and I can't help but imagine it opening up and swallowing me whole. I need to get out of here as soon as possible.

Laurel marches down the center pathway, trees looming ominously on either side of her. She stops in the middle of the cavern, where a path running right to left converges with the one we're on. She drops to her knees, then plunges her hands into the moist earth. She digs and digs, her panting breaths echoing, dark mounds of earth building on either side of her.

Nobody moves to help as Laurel grunts in frenzied determination. This is something she has to do on her own.

Minutes pass, sweat dripping down my neck in the muggy dank of the cavern. Tendrils of Laurel's long hair cling to her face when she finally turns back to us, a chest about a foot wide in her hands.

"This was our fail-safe, in case anyone found out about the forest," she explains. "A way to wipe it out before anyone saw it, eliminating all proof."

She flips the lid open, and a roiling red mass inside stirs to life. Thousands of tiny insects, clicking as they crawl over one another.

"Blood aphids," Jameson says. "Created by fire nymphs in a long-ago feud with the wood nymphs. When fed a drop of a wood nymph's blood, they'll feast on anything in their vicinity that was grown by that bloodline's power until there's nothing left."

Laurel nods. "They've been kept dormant after all this time. Waiting for this moment." She turns to the unicorn, who eyes the aphid chest warily. "May I?" Laurel asks, motioning toward their horn. "I need a drop of blood."

The bronze creature huffs as they think. I'd bet anything they're mulling over every last way this could go wrong. But finally, they nod.

She snaps her hand forward, like if she took her time she'd chicken out. Her palm lands dead center on the unicorn's horn, blood pooling there that turns my stomach.

"Thanks," Laurel grunts, then plunges her hand into the swarm of insects. The clicking increases as they cover her skin, desperate to feed.

It takes me a moment to feel the heat radiating out from Laurel. But in a burst of orange-red-yellow fire, it's impossible to ignore. Laurel's hands are covered in flames, her forehead beaded with sweat, her teeth gritted as the flame grows until—

FWOOOOOSH!

The fire soars from the box and covers the tree nearest her, setting the oozing bark aflame as thousands of tiny sparks—each little aphid alight with fire—crawl over the trunk and branches, incinerating leaves as they go.

Backlit by the growing blaze, I notice the letters in the veins of each leaf, watch as Cullingmates' names turn to ash. Jaleesa's goes up in smoke, and I turn to her to see if there's any indication she's changed. She rubs a hand through her hair, and the flames reflect in her eyes, but that's it.

"Get back!" Ori pulls me to him as the scorched husk of the nearest tree collapses, embers and ash flying into the air. Having devoured their first course, the aphids spring to the next tree they can reach in a buzzing wave of flame. The more they eat the faster they become, and it isn't long before every remaining tree is ablaze, the cavern glowing orange. A part of me wishes I could have seen Meema's leaf incinerate, seen that curse stricken from her soul. Wherever she is now, I hope she's watching, hope she's proud of me for bringing the truth to light.

As smoke builds, Pallavit sings a tune that keeps our lungs clear, allowing us to stay in the cave and watch until the end. It's over faster than I expected, the dozens of trees turned to piles of ash, not a single leaf left glowing with that green nymph magic.

"It's done," Bex says in a breath. "Dads." She turns to her fathers, her face set in conviction. "I have something to tell you. For the *final* time. The Culling isn't needed."

A collective gasp ripples through the Resistance. Their surprise is so genuine—their mouths dropped open and eyes wide—that it makes me laugh.

"What's so funny?" Lyra snaps. "This is serious. This—"

"We'll explain everything, Mom," Ori says as he looks at me with that smirk. "But this time it'll stick."

"It will," Laurel confirms, wiping her sweaty face with the hand that wasn't covered in aphids. That one is red and raw.

"Come on," Kenneth says, motioning toward her injured skin. "Let's get that looked at. And we can discuss what we'll do with this new bit of information about the Culling."

"Technically, it's not new," Bex says.

Yamato shuts her up with a glare. "You know what he means."

"WATCH OUT!"

THE MAGIC YOU MAKE

Bex's scream makes all of us duck just in time as a wave of orange flame shoots over our heads. It flies past, into the corridor that leads to the building above.

Laurel's the first to catch on. "The blood aphids will destroy anything in their vicinity that was created by Baumbach magic. The entire house is touched by it. We have to go!"

Magicians don't need telling twice. Bex and Yamato shift into a unicorn and falcon, respectively, while Kenneth follows just behind on a burst of air. Bex's unicorn pal ducks down and flips Laurel onto their back, taking off while Pallavit and Jaleesa sing their way out. Jameson spells his and Dad's shoes and they're gone in a blur of gold. Lyra and Ori nod at each other.

Ori takes my hand in his. "Time to giddyup, cowboy."

I feel a tug in the center of my gut before we blink away from the remains of that rotten forest and reappear just outside the house. Our motley crew is already gathered to watch the massive log mansion burn to the ground. The pops and cracks of wood swirl together with the roaring of the fire, and the orange of the flames blurs with the light blue of the sky as the sun begins to rise.

"Kind of pretty, ain't it?" Dad says in hushed awe.

I don't think I've ever heard him describe something as pretty. Going out of his way to shit all over something is more his speed. This new Dad is going to take some getting used to.

He catches my eye and winks. "But not as pretty as our ranch."

Our ranch. Yeah, that's *definitely* going to take some getting used to.

And I don't know that I'd call the ranch pretty, not without Meema's magic keeping it pristine. But maybe we'll be able to make the place shine again. I never imagined Dad and me working side by side to keep the Barrett barn up and running, but it doesn't seem so impossible now. Just two humans, working our asses off without magic. Just spit and elbow grease.

But, before we can get to that, there's one last thing I have to do to make our future safe. With the discovery of the Beloved, with the truth about the Culling finally revealed, magicians and humans alike will soon have more power than ever before to fight the evils of the world.

I've just got to ensure I'm not one of those evils.

I pull Ori into me, pressing his lips against mine. I feel that buzz of our power connecting, close my eyes and see that abalone color of us swirling together behind my eyelids. The perfect last bit of magic before I tell Ori the final step we need to take to build a new future. Ori's tongue lightly brushes against my own as he savors this moment, too. Before long, though, he feels how anxious I am.

"What's going on?" he asks with a scowl.

I tilt his chin up so I can look him square in the eyes. "Nothing. But you're not going to like what I have to say."

"I don't like what most people have to say. What else is new?"

I know he's trying to be his typical curmudgeonly self, but I feel his doubt. I pull him in for a hug, using the time to lock eyes with the members of the Resistance. I'll need them for this next step.

They gather around: Bex and her dads, Jameson and my dad, Pallavit, Jaleesa, Lyra, and Laurel. All eyes on me. I remember what it was like to be under the gazes of so many practiced and powerful magicians when I first started the Culling. It made Past-Nigel very nervous, but New-Nigel wants to get this show on the road.

"So," I say. "Alister's going to be punished, the Cornucopia is destroyed, and the Guild could get a much-needed refresh that's been centuries coming. A change that's been needed from our founding, actually. But there's still the question of what to do about me." I point to myself as if the group doesn't know who I'm talking about. My face flushes with heat. Why am I always such an idiot?

I look to Ori for a confidence boost, but his expression actually does the opposite. He's chewing his bottom lip and his cheeks are splotchy with pink. It's like he's trying to stop himself from crying. He might not know specifics, but he knows what I'm going to say. He knows that my plan will change everything from here on out.

"When Ori brought me back using the Knife's heartstone, it brought that Depraved along with it," I say. "It's inside me now. Sometimes my confidence or conviction or love weakens it." I motion to our new unicorn pal. "Other times some of y'all's magic keeps it at bay. But there are the times when it feeds on my anger and hurt. I'm not sorry for feeling what I feel—I think I have a right. But still, those natural emotions will always leave me vulnerable to the Knife making me snowball to an extremely unsafe place. There will always be a risk of the Knife tainting my magic and using it to destroy."

I take a deep, shaky breath. Time to dive in.

"That leads to how to stop it. Separating me from the claw would kill not just the Knife, but me too, since the heartstone brought me back after I died." Ori bites down on his lip even harder now. I may have been the one to die but watching it all was a trauma he won't ever forget. I pray to every cosmic being out there that this plan works, and he won't have to relive that all over again.

"I think there's another way," I continue. "The Knife wants my magic. It needs my power for its destruction. So what if we make sure it can never reach that power?" I don't look away from Ori as I voice exactly what it is I'm trying to say. "What if we take away my magic?"

"Nigel." Ori only whispers my name, but I feel a wave of

sadness hit me like a tsunami. I almost drown in it, but I can't let Ori's feelings pull me under. I have to stay strong. For us, for the Guild, for the world.

"What can the Knife do through me if I don't have any power? Even if it's still inside me, it's helpless without my magic. If it can still use my body somehow, you are all more than strong enough to stop it."

Confidence in my plan starts to swell through me, until a piercing hot poker stabs me in the heart. "Ah!" I fall to my knees, clutching my chest.

You're MINE!

"I'm not!" I say out loud, while the group looks at me in alarm. "Sorry," I mumble, catching my breath, trying to rub away the pain that lives up to my possessor's namesake. "The Knife doesn't like where this is going."

The flames flickering through the remnants of the Baumbach house reflect off the unicorn's bronze hide as they slowly walk over to me. They tilt their head down, their shining horn resting gently on my forehead. That stabbing pain subsides.

Hold on a little longer.

"Okay," I whisper.

"If the Knife doesn't like it, that's all the more reason to go through with this, I think," Dad says. He grips my shoulders, helping me to my feet. "This is very brave, kid. A sacrifice I'm not sure many would make. I know I wouldn't have been able to do it in my day."

I glance to Laurel, hanging on the outskirts of the group. Sometimes you just have to accept that what's done is done and move forward by doing what's right.

"I don't know that it's brave," I say. "I just think it's necessary."

"I'd be willing to perform the spell," Jameson says. "Now that we have your permission."

Bex looks like she's seen a ghost. "I can help, too," she says, her voice cracking. "This is above and beyond, Nigel. I'd be honored, if it's okay with you."

I nod. "I'd like that. I think it'll go better with friends, so, yeah." I'm fumbling my words. This is the right thing to do, but I still feel numb.

Pallavit takes the lead to organize the spell that will change my life forever. "Kenneth's our nymph, Bex the goblin, Jameson for elves."

Jaleesa bumps shoulders with Bex as she joins the growing circle. "Me for fae."

Pallavit smiles at her lovingly. "That's my girl. I'll guide you through the song." She turns back to me. "That just leaves—"

"A sprite," Ori says. Those two words finally unleash the dam of his emotion, tears rushing down his cheeks. He's more vulnerable than I've ever seen him, not even trying to keep up appearances. It's so unlike him.

"I wouldn't want anyone but you to do it." I can barely get the words past the lump burrowing into my throat. It's not sadness necessarily. Am I sad I won't be able to see how our powers could grow together? Absolutely. Am I going to mourn the visions I had of our future? Yes. But more than anything, the feeling coursing through me is gratitude that we have a future together at all, even if it looks a little different from what we first thought. *That's* what's choking me up.

Ori, however, isn't quite there yet.

"Nigel," he says again. "You can't ask me to do this."

I wipe his cheeks before linking our hands together, that electric buzz tingling through us. I have to believe that even without my magic, this feeling will never go away.

"If anyone is going to take my magic, I want it to be somebody who loves me. My power is the most tender part of me, Ori. It has to be you. You're my soulmate."

Ori is speechless, his least natural state. But I can feel all his emotions. His denial that there's no other way, his rage that he can't think of a better option, his pain when he accepts that this really is the best idea. It makes sense to drain the Knife of the power it would use against us, and he knows it.

"Besides," I say, "this doesn't mean we can't make magic. Beloved appear when humans perform acts of love for magicians, and there's no magician I love more than you. Because I love you, Ori. You stood by me when I was a literal monster. You knew I could be better, you wanted to make me better, and even when I didn't deserve it, you got me through this. If I didn't love you for that, I *would* be a monster. But the good news is, no matter what our future looks like now, you'll still have me. Your cowboy. The one who hopes to lasso your heart, even if I won't have a magical rope to do it with."

Ori scoffs, snot flecking his upper lip. Wiping it away, he says, "God, Nigel, you're so cringe."

"I promise that won't change even after the spell."

He lets me grab the edges of his cardigan and pull him into me. "Good," he breathes, then presses his lips against mine.

This isn't goodbye, but this kiss feels permanent. It closes this chapter, the one in which two rival magicians went in as competitors but came out as soulmates, even if they went through hell to do it.

"Okay," Ori says, a final tear sliding down his pale cheek. "I'm in."

Bex rushes forward and wraps us in a hug. She doesn't shift like she's done so many times before to squeeze tighter or keep out the rest of the world. This hug is all her, and I'm so grateful for her presence. She's as much a part of this moment as Ori and me. "Don't think this means you're not in the Guild anymore," she says. "You'll be as needed as any magician. The head human liaison."

Ori groans.

"Okay, yeah." Bex laughs through her tears. "The title needs some work. But you know what I mean."

I can't seem to find the right words to tell her how much that means to me.

When she releases us, Dad steps forward.

"I know I might be the last person you want to hear from right now . . ." Dad pauses like he expects me to lash out at him. But I don't. I can't just forget everything that's happened, but I am going to try to move forward with as much of an open heart as I can muster. The Knife is still in me, somewhere; I'm not giving it anything else to feed on.

"When this is over," Dad continues, "we'll have something in common. We'll both be human. I just want you to know that I meant what I said before: I hope you stay with me, if you want. While we rebuild."

He doesn't just mean rebuild the country or the ranch. He means rebuild our relationship. Or maybe *build* is a better word, since we never really had a relationship to begin with.

I know this is what Meema would have wanted. And the more I think about it, the more I realize it's what I want, too.

"Okay," I say. "I will."

Dad nods. It's not everything that needs to be said between us. It's not a tear-filled acceptance or apology or moment of gratitude, and I don't know if he wanted that. But at least it's a start.

"All right, then," I breathe, nodding to Ori.

He looks around, scowling, my most favorite Ori expression. "A little help over here? I don't know how this spell works. I'm not the one who's unnecessarily done this to thousands of promising young magicians." Leave it to Ori to give a dig at any chance he can get. But obviously, he's not wrong.

Jameson motions to Ori's trusty backpack. "Grab an effigy, Ori."

From there, the senior members guide Ori through the spell. He grabs an Indiana Jones figure and coats it pink, creating an effigy on which the others cast. As the group works, my magic rises to the surface. I glow gold, and when Ori looks at me with sadness and acceptance and pain and hope, that gold turns to our brilliant abalone. Kenneth uses his way with wind to hold me in place, gently but firmly, so I can't hurt myself as the magic twists out of me. Yamato coaches Bex through coating my effigy in a bit of her shape-shifting power, helping ease the pain as my body goes through the shift from magician to human. Pallavit demonstrates for Jaleesa how to sing a note in sync with Jameson's elf power, their combined spells tugging on my golden power to pull it up, up, up.

My body spasms, my muscles constrict. This *hurts*. But what hurts most of all is the burning inside me. Even with our unicorn pal's horn radiating goodness to keep it at bay, the Knife rages. It's too weak to speak, but even my conviction and my friends' pure purpose aren't enough to stop it from fuming, boiling, doing everything in its power to consume me with its anger.

But that's just the thing. The anger is only the Knife's, not mine. And when the last of my power lifts away and dissipates into the air, my relief knocks the Knife aside.

We did it.

The monster can't use me anymore.

A laugh of unbridled joy bursts from my mouth. "It worked! It wo—*AAAAAAAAAAAAAH!*"

My celebration is short-lived as anger floods through me. The surrounding magicians all glow bright with power, ready to fight the Knife. Ori, however, runs to me.

"Nigel!" He's flustered one second, regains his composure the next, that damn smirk creeping up his face. "Nigel. Come back. You have to come back. We've got years and years ahead of us, remember? You can't disappear on me just yet. You didn't even give me the chance to tell you I love you, too. You hear that, cowboy? I love you, and this sure as hell isn't going to be the last time you let me say it."

That's all it takes. I may no longer have power of my own, we may no longer be able to make our abalone light, but god dammit, we're still soulmates. And that lights up my soul. Cringey, I know, but what else is new?

I feel my love for Ori radiate outward, so strong that it pushes the rage from me. Pushes *the Knife* from me.

Literally.

My head slams back as mottled green sludge cascades from my throat.

"Oh shit!" Ori's eyes snap wide, but to his credit he doesn't jump back. "Full-on *Exorcist!*"

It's just like that day twelve years ago when I first saw one of these monsters form thanks to Dad's hatred. The thick green sludge pouring from my mouth gathers in midair, building and building until the torrent ends. The mass wriggles and pulls, coming together in a very familiar shape.

"A Depraved," I breathe. Then I bark out a laugh. "Just a run-of-the-mill Depraved!"

It whips its wicked head in my direction, eyes blazing that sickly green. ***"Run-of-the-mill Depraved? I AM THE KNIFE! I told you before you'd never get rid of me. I told you—"***

"SHUT UP!" A bright purple scythe whizzes through the air, slicing the Knife's head clean off at the neck. The monster crumples, its rotten skin disintegrating, leaving behind a pile of bones.

It's finished.

It's through.

Just like that.

I turn to find Jaleesa blushing, a surprised hand hovering over her mouth. "S-sorry," she mutters.

"*Sorry?*" I let go of Ori to lift Jaleesa in a bone-crushing hug. "Jaleesa, that was brilliant!"

I set her on her feet and that blush is replaced by complete confidence, as it should be. "That *was* pretty epic, wasn't it?"

"That's an understatement," Bex says, beaming at Jaleesa, who suddenly gets bashful again under her gaze.

"Brilliant, darling." Pallavit could not be happier. "I couldn't have done it better myself."

I think just an hour or so ago, in that moment when Jaleesa stood up for herself with Laurel, the fae grew stronger than ever before. If magic is fueled by emotion and intent, what better way to boost your power than finally sticking up for yourself? It looks like that strength was all Jaleesa needed to kick the Knife's malevolent, weak Depraved ass. Maybe in the long run we'll find out that self-love has power-enhancing effects just like soulmate love. Because, really, that's how it should be, right?

"Hey." Ori wiggles his way against my chest, placing his hand over my heart. "You okay?"

I don't even have to think about it. Not with the tingles that still flow through me with his touch. They might not light up my power anymore, and I have to admit the absence feels strange. But this electricity with Ori makes me realize I'm not missing anything. I just have a new reality to get used to. And Ori will be there the whole way through, whatever comes next.

"Just thinking about what it is you said back there." I give Ori a smirk that I know could best any of his own, not caring how many people there are to witness this. "Can you repeat that? I was dealing with the aftermath of possession and all that."

"Okay, here we go." Ori rolls his eyes. "You know my mom's watching, right?"

"Don't mind me," Lyra says, turning her back to us. "It's like I'm not even here."

I have a feeling Lyra and I are really going to get along. "See? Everything's fine." I put a hand up to my ear. "What were you saying?"

Ori takes the effigy of me, still glowing pink, and smacks his hand over my mouth. My lips seal shut.

"Finally," Ori says. "You just don't know when to shut up. Because if you kept blabbing, you never would have heard this." He leans in, his mouth just millimeters from mine. "I love you, cowboy," he whispers. With another smear of his thumb, my lips unseal in time for him to press his against my own.

I can't help the goofy grin that splits my face. There's no use hiding it. I've looked like an idiot, a monster, a cringey nerd the entire time I've known Ori, and that's not about to change now.

"I love you, too."

EPILOGUE

I't's wild how similar the halls of Congress look to the towering wings of the Guild. Sure, there's no marble streaked with gold elven spells—but maybe that will change in the coming years as magical and human cooperation increases. The way the Senate Chamber is arranged into a semicircle of desks even reminds me of the tribunal floor. But no matter how familiar the setting, my nerves make my stomach roil like snakes in a barrel.

The vice president motions us over. I still can't believe this is happening. I stand there, struck silly by the absurdity of it all, until Ori jams me hard in the ribs.

"Get moving, cowboy."

"Right." I clear my throat. "Coming!" *Jesus, Nigel.* Why do I always sound like a little kid when I'm nervous?

The vice president rises from her chair that presides over the chamber. "Thank you all for gathering today to discuss what has turned out to be a previously unimaginable future. I'd like to introduce you to three representatives of the Magicians' Guild, here to discuss human and magical relations. Before we begin, a thank-you to Senator Enrique Sapene, who has graciously stepped into the maelstrom left behind by Alister Baumbach and chaired the committee to create and maintain peaceful contact between our peoples. Through it all, Senator Sapene, the Magical Relations Committee, and members of the Magicians' Guild have made it very clear that while our abilities may be different, we are all, at our core, American. Now, without further ado, may I introduce Bex Sasaki, Orion Olson, and Nigel Barrett."

The room erupts in applause, my heart slams against my chest, and my ears roar. Man, there are a lot of eyes on us. A lot of *very important* eyes.

Yet, somehow, Bex handles it like she's been speaking in front of the most powerful people in America her entire life. Ori nominated her as spokesperson for the Guild in the Magical Relations Committee, seeing as how she's been preaching cooperation and leaning in to love all along. The Guild agreed, voting for her overwhelmingly. As she speaks, it's so clear she was the one and only person for the job.

"Thank you, senators, for seeing us today. My name is Bex Sasaki, and I'm a magician—goblin-descended, to be specific, able to shape-shift into any being at will." Rumblings echo through the chamber. It's going to take a long time for humans to get used to the existence of magic. It's only been a couple months since the Guild revealed the truth, after all. But once we stopped erasing the memories of humans who created the Depraved, it didn't take much convincing for the American government to reach out for help defeating the monsters they make. Other countries are starting to follow suit, too, magicians in their own Guild-like organizations helping ease their nations through the adjustment. Some of those organizations are pissed we took this leap without consulting them, but for now, we're moving forward with magic- and humankind working in tandem.

"But even with these abilities," Bex continues, "I'm just like you. That is to say, dedicated to service. Working tirelessly to bring peace and freedom for every one of us within this great country. But we do have one key difference between us. You have the ability to undermine that work, to tear apart all we have done on both sides to keep our nation moving forward."

The audience is dead silent now, Bex having their complete attention. She has this innate talent for telling people they're messing up without it coming across as an insult.

"You've been led to believe that humans are powerless," Bex says. "That unlike goblins, elves, fae, nymphs, and sprites—what we call Ancestrals, the species who gave magicians their magic—you don't have power of your own. But that's not true. Your emotions have power, not just to influence your thoughts and feelings, but to feed and create malevolent spirits known as the Depraved."

With a silver flash her body elongates, her skin rots, her eyes glow that brilliant green of dangerous power. The room gasps, a few senators even scream. Ori puts his hands up, trying to calm them.

"Please don't be alarmed," Ori says. "This Depraved is not real. This is only a demonstration of what can be created with your hatred and uncontrolled anger."

"That's right." Bex pops back to herself. "But you also have the key to controlling all that. To spreading love and kindness instead of chaos and division. While I demonstrate, I'm going to ask my friend Nigel here to explain because out of the three of us, he's the only one who can make them. He has that in common with all of you. *Humans* have the ability to create this being, while no magician can."

She transforms again, this time into a glowing red entity that will change the future. She motions for me to talk, but when I turn to the crowd, my mind goes blank. I clear my throat, take a breath—yet when I part my lips, nothing intelligible comes out. "Um . . . I, uh . . ."

All eyes are on me, everyone's attention zeroed in on my stuttering. I instinctively reach to my pocket, feel the lump of the claw there, still embedded with the heartstone, which is just a dull, scratched rock now that the Knife's gone. I've held on to it as a reminder of all we've been through, of how we've been to hell and back. If we can make it through that, I can make it through anything.

Except public speaking, apparently.

I look to Ori for help. He's got that come-on-already scowl, but with a bejeweled elbow from Bex, it turns to an only slightly encouraging smile. We all know that talking to crowds isn't really my strong suit. Bex thought this message would be most impactful from another human. Yet as I stand here with my mouth opening and closing like a freaking fish, I'm not so sure she was correct.

Come on now, Nigel, don't go getting all tongue-tied.

You'd think after being possessed by the Knife, I'd be used to voices in my head. But this one catches me completely by surprise.

It's Meema.

You can do it, darlin'.

It's not a spell. It's not a spirit resurrected from the dead. I think it's just my heart, finding the source of encouragement I need the most.

It starts slow as molasses, but eventually a smile spreads across my face.

There you go, sweetheart. Make me proud.

So I do.

"This is a Beloved. A being made of compassion and togetherness, of goodwill between humans and magicians. No magician or

Ancestral can create this. This is entirely a human ability. This is the magic *you* make, and it's the strongest magic there is."

I take another breath, feel my boots grounded beneath me, and glance at Ori. He doesn't look mortified anymore; his smile matches my own. I know he'll snark after the fact that what I'm about to say is cheesy, and he might be right. Okay, he *is* right. But, even still, it's the truth that will bring us together, human and magician. Whether or not we can ever win the battle against the literal and figurative monsters of the world, it's the strongest tool we've got.

"It's the magic of love."

ACKNOWLEDGMENTS

GOING INTO WRITING THIS, I THOUGHT I HAD SOME IDEA AS TO how hard it would be to write a fantasy sequel, but I truly had no idea whatsoever. *The Magic You Make* wouldn't be here without the massive spellwork of the following people. All the thanks I can muster to:

Rachel Stark! We did it, Rachel! Thank you for all the blood, sweat, and tears you poured into this alongside me.

Melissa de la Cruz! Mel, I can't even begin to express how much I look up to you and how honored I am that you asked me to be a part of the MDLC Studio family.

Brent Taylor! You are the most magical of magicians I have ever met. Thank you for always seeing what spells we can cast to keep this whole train moving! Mixed metaphors, I know, but you get me.

The whole Disney and Melissa de la Cruz Studio team! You make sure I use commas correctly, you market my books to the world, you send me around the country so I can talk about our gay elf cowboy.

All the hard work each and every one of you puts into these books means the world to me.

Thea Harvey and Marci Senders! You've done it again! This cover is everything, and I love how you bring my boys to life.

Stefanie! Thanks for giving my world another read and providing invaluable notes.

To the authors who went above and beyond to blurb *The Spells We Cast* and support my work: F. T. Lukens, Amparo Ortiz, C. S. Pacat, Adam Silvera, and Brian Zepka. Your kindness was just the magic I needed as a nervous author launching a fantasy novel for the first time.

Booksellers! Librarians! Teachers! I will say forever and ever that y'all are the reason we're here, as writers and readers, and your powers are legendary and so needed.

Readers! I hope after reading this (and even before reading this) you know how magical you truly are. Not just to me, although the joy you've brought me is so powerful it could cast any type of spell imaginable. But you're magical in the world at large, too. The energies you bring into every space are palpable. Choose to use that magic to bring people together, not push them apart. Choose to see each other as humans, not monsters. You get to shape this little ball of dirt and water we're all floating through space on, and I know when leading with love, you'll shape it for the better.

Jerry! Thank you for bringing magic into my life every single day. I love you.